Books by Morris West

Harlequin *
The Salamander *
Summer of the Red Wolf *
Scandal in the Assembly
The Heretic
The Tower of Babel
The Ambassador *
The Shoes of the Fisherman *
Daughter of Silence
The Devil's Advocate
Backlash
Children of the Shadows
The Navigator *

* Published by POCKET BOOKS

MORRIS WEST

The Navigator

A KANGAROO BOOK
PUBLISHED BY POCKET BOOKS NEW YORK

THE NAVIGATOR

POCKET BOOK edition published October, 1977

This POCKET BOOK edition includes every word contained in
the original, higher-priced edition. It is printed from brand-
new plates made from completely reset, clear, easy-to-read type.
POCKET BOOK editions are published by
POCKET BOOKS,
a Simon & Schuster Division of
GULF & WESTERN CORPORATION
1230 Avenue of the Americas,
New York, N.Y. 10020.
Trademarks registered in the United States
and other countries.

ISBN: 0-671-80986-5.
Library of Congress Catalog Card Number: 76-5504.
Illustrations by Terrence M. Fehr

Printed in the U.S.A.

Some island
With the sea's silence on it . . .
                    —ROBERT BROWNING,
                        Pippa Passes, Part II

. . . As it was in the beginning
Is now, and ever shall be
Through all ages of ages.
                    —Doxology

In 1882 Lloyd's agent at Rarotonga reported that
the Haymet Rocks were supposed to exist about 150
miles south-southwestward of Rarotonga. . . . This report however would seem to have originated in the
lost island of Tuanaki which appears to have existed
in this vicinity, but has now disappeared.

A depth of 68 fathoms was found in Lat. 24°07′ S.,
Long. 158°33′ W. by the *Fabert* when searching for
a low island, reported to exist in this vicinity, but of
which she saw nothing.

—*Pacific Islands Pilot,* Volume III, Ninth Edition,
1969, page 65, paragraphs 25 and 30

This book is for those of us,
Children still,
Who, even at the gates of midnight,
Dream of sunrise.

ONE

ON THE WHITE BEACH OF HIVA OA, WHICH looked toward the moonrise and the breakers on the outer reef, Kaloni Kienga the Navigator squatted under a palm tree and drew pictures in the sand. He was an old man and sacred—more sacred even than the chief—because he knew all the secrets of the sea; how the wind whispered before a big blow, how the currents bent when they passed this atoll or that, how the *te lapa,* the underwater lightning, shone, ten fathoms down, even when the sky was black and starless at midnight.

The pictures which Kaloni drew in the sand were mystic signs like those tattooed on his arms and his breast. Their names were spoken only in the ritual language of the ancestors. The rising tide would wash them away. The wind would jumble their syllables, so that none but the sacred men would ever comprehend them.

For Kaloni Kienga the drawing of the pictures was no mere idleness. It was an act of making, a creation of that which had been destined, dreamed, called to happen long, long before the seed of himself had been planted in his mother's belly. The events which he traced in symbol must be, would be; and he could no more change them than he could lift his finger from the sand until the whole design was complete.

The moon which rose this night would be a dying moon. One day, when it rose new and young, the ship would come with it, ghosting through the channel, sails spread like a seabird's wings, running before the night wind. He would hear the clout of her canvas as she came up into the breeze, the rattle of her hawser as she dropped anchor in the lagoon. He would see her, stripped black and bare against the sickle moon, as she lay back on her anchor, her lights yellow on the slack water. He would hear the voices of her crew and the silence afterwards as they settled to rest from the long swing of the ocean. Then, out of the silence, out of the water, sleek as a silver fish, a man would come to him: the promised one, the fellow voyager who would lead him on the last seaway, to the last landfall, the home of the trade winds.

His coming was as certain as the rising of the moon. The landfall was certain too: the haven of all navigators, the homing place which lay below the orbit of the dog star, below the shining black path of the god Kanaloa. Kaloni Kienga drew the last symbol in the sand, the symbol of the guardian spirit who would greet him on his arrival, and hold him forever safe against invasion. Then he bowed his head on his knees and slept until the incoming tide lapped about his footsoles.

On the same night, two thousand five hundred miles to the northeast, James Neal Anderson, Dean of Oceanic Studies at the University of Hawaii, stood in his garden and watched the same dying moon rise over the Wahila ridge. The soft damp air was heavy with the scent of ginger flowers and jasmine and frangipani. There was a gleam of green and gold and scarlet where the light fell among the leaves and the trailing orchids. Once he had loved this place, the cloying sweetness of it, the profusion and the privacy it afforded from the bustle of the campus, and the politics of a large, polyglot university. Then it had become a lonely place, dangerous to a man suddenly widowed after twenty years of contented marriage. Tonight it would be a place of execution.

It was a mistake to have invited Thorkild here. There were matters best dispatched formally, in the Dean's office, close to the merciful distractions of telephones and secretaries and student visitors. But Gunnar Thorkild merited something better than a curt delivery of the warrant and a swift bloodless killing. He was too big a man to be dismissed with brief regrets and barren courtesies.

True, he was thorny, and contentious, too loud in argument, too impatient of the opinions of his elders, too little versed in the diplomacies of a large and sensitive institution of learning at the crossroads between Asia and the West. He had risen too fast and too young. He had too much charm for women students, and faculty wives, and too little thought for their consorts who were less free, less handsome, and less brilliant than himself. Nonetheless, he merited respect, and from James Neal Anderson he would have it.

Tanaka, the houseman, came into the garden with a tray of drinks, and set them down on the wicker table beside the folder in which was recorded the past and the present of Gunnar Thorkild, Ph.D., and the publications which bore his name: *Phonic Variables in Polynesian Dialects, A Comparative Study of the Myths and Legends of Oceania, A Handbook of Polynesian Navigation with an Appendix on the Cult of the Navigator.*

"Shall I pour you a drink, Doctor?"

"No thanks, Tanaka, I'll wait for our guest."

"He just telephoned. He'll be a few minutes late."

"It doesn't matter. I'll wait."

Waiting for Gunnar Thorkild was no new matter. He was late for lectures, staff meetings, parties, campus ceremonies; and when he did arrive it was always in turmoil and disarray with a lopsided grin and a toss of his blond mane and a booming apology that set everyone's nerves on edge. As the Chancellor had once commented dryly:

"Thorkild always looks as though he's just tumbled out of bed."

To which his wife had added the tart rejoinder:

"And he generally has, my dear. I wonder whose it was this time."

They might have been more generous to him, Anderson reflected wryly, had the record been less specific about his origins. He was the son of Thor Thorkild, a Norwegian master mariner, and a Marquesan woman called Kawena Kienga, who had died giving him birth in the general hospital in Honolulu a week before Pearl Harbor. His father had handed himself and his ship to the United States Navy and his child to the Sisters of St. Joseph with a sackful of silver dollars to pay for his Christian upbringing. When neither the father nor his ship returned, the Sisters and the Government of the United States financed the boy's nurture and education. They found to their mutual surprise that they had on their hands a prodigy who devoured learning faster than it could be fed to him.

After the Sisters, the Jesuits took him, and he graduated magna cum laude six months before his eighteenth birthday. The day after graduation he shipped out as a deckhand on a French freighter bound for the Marquesas, and came back five years later to matriculate to the School of Oceanic Studies. At twenty-eight he was appointed junior lecturer in Pacific Ethnography. At thirty-three he was an assistant professor. Now he presented himself as one of five candidates for tenure, and the Chair. It was Anderson's job to tell him that his candidacy had been rejected. . . .

"Why, James? Why?" Gunnar Thorkild sat slumped in his chair, a six-foot hulk of anger and misery, with a glass of whiskey clamped in his fist, while Anderson sat a safe distance away with the folder open on his knees. "Goddammit man! By what norms do they judge me? If it's academic record, you know mine's twice as good as Holroyd's and ten times better than that bloodless bitch Auerbach's. As for Luton and Samuels, they're good men, sure! But their field work is weak. They're theorists, pure and simple. I've been there, James—from the Tuamotus to the Gilberts! I've lived what I teach. You, of all people, must know that!"

"I do know it, Gunnar. You were my candidate! But you know how these appointments are made—by consensus of the faculty with all the Civil Liberties groups looking over our shoulders. The sad fact is that the consensus is against you."

"Who cast the votes?"

"You know I can't tell you that. But I'll give you the words, without the names. Before I do, are you sure you want to hear them?"

"You're damned right I do!"

"Pour yourself another drink. You're going to need it."

Gunnar Thorkild splashed liquor into his glass. Dean Anderson opened the folder and read in neutral monotone:

". . . Mr. Gunnar Thorkild is a stimulating lecturer, popular—perhaps a little too popular—with his students and with junior colleagues. His theories are often brilliant; his conclusions, too hastily published, are less than reliable. He is more poet than scholar, an inspired dreamer perhaps, but certainly a flawed scholar.

"He is a passionate collector and a skillful editor of island legends; but when he founds upon these legends a new land, a kind of Polynesian Hy-Brasil, he lapses into bathos and absurdity. What all the great cartographers have missed, what even the satellites have not recorded, Mr. Thorkild posits as fact: an undiscovered island, a graveyard for chieftains and navigators, somewhere between Pitcairn and New Zealand.

"He is still young, so there is hope that time and experience may mellow his judgment. We should therefore be prepared to accept him as an associate professor for a trial period of three years. However, we are not prepared to endorse him at this stage as a candidate for tenure in the Chair of Pacific Ethnography. . . ."

The Dean closed the folder. Gunnar Thorkild sat a long time, staring into the lees of the liquor. Then he asked quietly:

"Is that a majority report?"

"Yes."

"How many names on it?"

"Seven."

"No way to fight it then?"

"I'm afraid not. You'd betray me if you even hinted that you'd heard it."

"I wouldn't do that, James. But, Christ! Did they have to be so rough? 'Bathos and absurdity . . . a flawed scholar . . .' With that in the record I'm a dead man!"

"Not quite. They still accept you as an associate."

"The hell they do! They cut my balls off and then ask me to eat them for dinner! No way, James! No way in the world! You'll have my resignation in the morning."

"It's only a month to the end of this semester. You can't quit before then, without making a fool of yourself and a scandal for the whole campus. Then there's three to four months of the summer vacation. No appointments will be published until the end of August. That's breathing space. Use it! To set your thinking straight, add up whether it's worth throwing away your whole career for one first rejection—no matter how roughly it's been phrased. . . . No! Sit down! You owe me some courtesies, Gunnar. That last monograph of yours on the Polynesian navigators—I read it. It was good. It was clear, logical, beautifully documented. But you fouled it up in the appendix. You lapsed out of scholarship and into speculation. You claimed for fact that a place exists which is only, could only be a theory. You say your colleagues cut your balls off—but you handed them the knife. Why?"

"Because I know it exists."

"How?"

"The man who told me is my grandfather, Kaloni Kienga. Everything else in that paper he taught me."

"And proved to you?"

"Yes."

"But he didn't prove this—or if he did, you didn't

prove it in publication. You flung it in the face of the scholarly public and said, 'That's it! Take it or leave it, because I say it!' Once again, why?"

"Because—can't you see?—somewhere, sometime, something has to be taken on faith. Kaloni Kienga is a great man. He has a thousand years of knowledge and tradition locked in his head. I believed him. I still do. Isn't every man entitled to his act of faith?"

"He is. But he can't complain when other people ask for proof and crucify him because he can't or won't produce it. I'm sorry, Gunnar, but I'm a lot older than you are and that's the way I read what's happened to you. Now, what are you going to do? Blaspheme or give witness?"

Gunnar Thorkild set down his glass carefully, wiped his hands and his lips, and gave a long whistle of amusement.

"Oh, James! James Neal Anderson! You're a rough man! Blaspheme or give witness. That's good! That's thunder from the pulpit. Now tell me how you think I should give witness. The truth now! No hedging."

"And no complaints when you hear it?"

"None, I promise."

"Two ways, and I'll accept either one. The first: you accept the verdict of your peers, take the appointment they offer and thereby admit a defect—a remediable defect—in your scholarship. The second: ask for six months' study leave, which I'll guarantee will be granted, and go prove your point. Find your island. Bring the bearings, map the contours and photograph the features. Then you'll have your Chair and your tenure—even if we have to subsidize a new one to accommodate you."

Thorkild sat a long moment, sunk in a brooding silence, then abruptly he heaved himself to his feet. "One more question, James."

"Yes?"

"Why should you care at all, either way?"

"Because," said James Neal Anderson, "I believe you're a sounder scholar than the others, and a bigger man than you've shown yourself so far."

"Do you mind if I think it over?"

"Not at all. So long as you let me know before the end of June."

"Thanks, James."

"For nothing. Would you like a dram for the road?"

"Better not," said Gunnar Thorkild ruefully. "One more driving offense and I lose my license."

He walked away, a shambling, puzzled giant, his blond head brushing the plumeria tree, his shoulders flecked with yellow blossoms, leaving James Neal Anderson to finish his drink alone, in the scented garden under a ragged dying moon. . . .

For all the disorder of his personal appearance, and the occasional uncouthness of his manners, Gunnar Thorkild's apartment on South Beretania was spartan in its simplicity and order. He had taken an old clapboard house and divided it into two separate areas, one containing a kitchen and huge living area, the other a study and sleeping quarters. The first was open to all comers, students, friends, lovers. The second was reserved to himself alone, an open space lined with books and box files in which the only furnishings were a bed, a chair and a desk meticulously ordered. Here no one intruded but old Molly Kaapu, who lived two doors away and came in daily to clean and cook for him. The windows were shuttered, the ceiling and the floor were soundproofed so that he could work with no other sound than the low hum of the air conditioner. It was his boast, but a truth as well, that he never came here drunk or in heat, and that if he slept with his boots on or a woman beside him, he slept downstairs in the living room. Even there, however, the same order prevailed. His visitors could lounge where they wished, sing, shout or dance —but if they fouled the place with spilled liquor or scattered ash or neglected the courtesies of cleaning before they left, they were never asked again. "I've lived on ships," he would explain in gentler moments. "If you didn't keep your bunk tidy and your cabin clear, it became unlivable in a week."

Molly Kaapu was devoted to him, because he talked the old language and made her laugh till her sides ached with his scandalous tales. When he was sick of his own or others' company he would call her over, and they would sit for an hour gossiping over a glass of tea, and then she would roll up her sleeves and massage the muscles of his back and neck before he went upstairs to his books and his students' themes. She was the only one who knew and used his native name, Kaloni, the only one to whom he cared to tell the tales of his wandering years in the islands. When he came home from Anderson's house, she was waiting for him, clucking and frowning.

"Ah-ah. I know it. Something bad? Take off your shirt, Kaloni. Let Molly give you *lomi-lomi*. Then you tell me, eh?"

As she kneaded and pounded at the tense, balled muscles, he told her, fumbling sometimes for the words to compass the alien thoughts of the *haole* in the language of a simpler, older people. To Molly it was all a madness. The *haole* complicated everything. If a thing was, it was. Why did they have to prove it? The old ones *knew*. They sailed the oceans by the stars and the shape of the clouds and the flight of birds. They didn't write things down, they remembered and told them or sang them. Why worry about the *haole* at all? Why not go back to his mother's people?

Why not, indeed—except that he could never go, all of him in one piece; because he was split in two and split again by knowing and again by dreaming and wishing, until there was no self at all but only scraps and fragments blown like dead leaves in the trade winds. Old Molly understood that too, but she still believed she could put him together again, kneading him like dough in her big hands, crooning old songs out of a forgotten time.

When he slept at last, she drew the covers over him, switched off the light and left him. When she reached her own house, she found her daughter, Dulcie, drowsing by the television. She handed her the keys to Thorkild's house and admonished her gently:

"Kaloni has a black cloud on him tonight. Go to him, girl. Make him forget what the *haole* have done to him. Make him remember that he is still a man."

When the girl slid into bed, naked beside him, Gunnar Thorkild stirred and smiled and drew her to him, murmuring a single sleepy word, *Ka'u*—"O breast that comforts me."

However he came by it—and it was not in his nature to ask—there was a piety in him, a sense of dependence and of duty. He did not feel it a burden, he accepted it as simply as he accepted the ministrations of old Molly and her daughter and the casual friendships of bar and waterfront.

On the last Sunday of each month, punctually at eleven he drove up to the door of the Jesuit Center on East Moana to collect what they had agreed to call the corpus delicti, being the body of Michael Aloysius Flanagan S.J., onetime mentor of Gunnar Thorkild, onetime Roman Catholic chaplain of the Faculty of

Oceanic Studies, and now a wasting marmoset in a wheelchair with a pair of useless legs and a perennial taste for intrigue and the lower roads to salvation. The body once stowed, they drove down to the old Moana Hotel, to sit under the banyan tree and drink planter's punch and eat grilled *mahi-mahi* and set the world to rights, or on its ear, no matter which.

For Michael Aloysius Flanagan, sixty-five years old, twenty years in the Islands, five in a wheelchair, creation was a bloody mess and God a puzzled architect trying to make the best of a botched job. For Gunnar Thorkild, Flanagan S.J. was the man who came nearest to the father he had never known, the man who had boxed his ears and wiped his snotty nose and stood between him and the bullies, and taught him the beauties of logic and the concordance of even the most contradictory notions. Flanagan had long since come to a confused conclusion: you couldn't save the world, you could only love it. So, being a celibate in a barren cause, he had centered the last of his loving on Gunnar Thorkild. Which love, he averred, gave him a certain large freedom of speech, which he used without restraint.

"Gunnar Thorkild, you're a bloody idiot!"

"I am, Father."

"At a critical time in your career you've exposed yourself naked to the ungodly."

"I have, and I know it."

"And what did they do?"

"Just what you might expect."

"So there you stand, bitched, buggered and bewildered, and what do you expect me to do about it?"

"Nothing. I was just talking. Drink your liquor and let's order another."

"Hold your tongue, boy, and let me talk. James

Neal Anderson is a good man and he had you to rights
—for all that he's a Methodist with no joy in him at
all. So now what are *you* going to do?"

"I wear it or take a job slicing pineapples for the
Dole Company."

"You could put your money where your big mouth
is and go out and prove what you wrote. How much
money have you got, by the way?"

"Ten thousand dollars, clear in the bank."

"It's more than you deserve and a hell of a lot less
than you need."

"How would you know what I need?"

"Because I do my homework—which you had to be
driven to do, Gunnar Thorkild. If I were you—and
thank God I'm not, because you've got a load of grief
coming to you!—I'd buy me an old island trader, I'd
refit it and stock it and crew it, and I'd put some
guests on board to pay the bills and be witnesses to
my exploits. I'd pick up my old grandfather, and sail
away, and I wouldn't come back until I'd found my
island."

"And if you did find it?"

"I'd look at it, and if I found it good I'd scuttle the
ship and stay there! The world's gone mad, boy!
Bombs in the streets and terror in the sky, and politics
a gibbering bedlam! So I'd stay there!"

"Two more drinks," said Gunnar Thorkild to the
hovering waiter. "And hold the fish. I'll tell you when
we're ready."

"I am not aout to get drunk," said Michael
Aloysius Flanagan. "I am about to instruct you in the
black art of patronage."

"You know what old Samuel Johnson said about
patrons, Father."

"Sam Johnson was a pompous old ass and a Protes-
tant to boot! Any shavetail novice in the Jesuits could

run rings around him. Now hear me, and hear me well. You need a ship. For a ship you need money, and on these sweet islands there are people with money running out of their backsides. . . ."

"And not a dollar of it rolls my way!"

"No reason why it should. You get an adequate salary and enough leisure to enjoy it. Nobody owes you a dime."

"So why raise the question?"

"Because, my boy, if you put your imagination to work, you could find yourself a sponsor for any sort of madness—from pole-sitting to the conversion of the penguins. Now hold your tongue, because I am about to make a sermon about money and the people who make it. . . ."

. . . From which sermon and much scribbling on paper napkins, it emerged that Michael Aloysius Flanagan S.J. had several friends, any one of whom might, for certain commercial advantages like world-wide publication rights and television rights and film rights, be prepared to sponsor a new voyage of discovery in the South Seas. If Gunnar Thorkild had an ounce of faith left, which at three o'clock on this bibulous Sunday he obviously had not, he would begin a novena to the Blessed Virgin and leave the rest of it to his old friend Flanagan, who had a lot of time on his hands, and a list of donors he hadn't tapped for at least five years.

It was a generous thought and the old man was as elated as if he had the money in his pocket. Gunnar Thorkild was a mite more skeptical. In his day Flanagan S.J. had raised millions. He had built two churches, an orphanage and a house of studies; but in the autumn of his days he still had to wait for Gunnar Thorkild to take him out to dinner.

When he had delivered the old man safe to the Jesuit house, and settled him to doze in the garden, Thorkild drove out to Sunset Beach where the young bloods went to ride the big surf that came rolling in from the North Pacific. He was too old for the game now, a first-class candidate for a broken back or a split skull; but he loved to watch it, understanding it as a ritual thing, like bull-leaping or swinging from treetops by an ankle thong, with big risks and no rewards but the rhythm of the act itself, the explosive orgasm of accomplishment, and the afterglow of acclaim from the initiates.

There was a sullen majesty in the great waves, fetched all the way from the Kuriles and the Aleutians, curling slowly, folding in upon themselves and toppling in a ruin of foam at the surf line. There was a heart-stopping beauty in the sight of a man-figure, balanced on a spear-blade of wood, riding down the slope with a wall of water collapsing behind him. There was terror when he was tossed like a fleck of foam high in the air, with his board flying an inch from his brain box, and then buried in a welter of foam and shingles. Girls and boys, they looked like sea gods out of some ancient fable, happy and proud and yet somehow cruel, because they were so private and so heedless.

A girl, in a shapeless muu-muu, with the colours almost bleached out of it, trudged down the beach and flopped on the sand beside Thorkild. Her blond hair was a tangled mess, her childish face puffy, her lips cracked with sun and windburn.

"Hi, prof!"

"Hi, Jenny. Long time no see!"

"Uh-uh."

"I missed you this semester. Where've you been hiding?"

"Around."

"Dropped out?"

"Yeah."

"Where are you living?"

"Around."

"Eating?"

"Enough for two—or hadn't you noticed?" She moulded the muu-muu round her swollen belly. "Pretty, eh? Five months of it."

"Do I know the father?"

"You used to. Billy-Jo Spaulding. He split as soon as he found out. Big Daddy shot him off to New York. He sent me a thousand dollars and the address of a doctor who would do a nice clean job."

"But you didn't want that?"

"I wanted to have Billy-Jo's baby. I still do. Crazy, huh?"

"Not by me. Who pays the rent now?"

"I do."

"How?"

"Oh, you know. . . . My father still thinks I'm attending courses. He sends me the money for that. I do things, run errands, baby-sit. . . . Gopher Jenny, that's me."

"Have you got a habit?"

"Can't afford one. . . . Grass sometimes."

"I could get you a job and a room."

"Gee . . . I dunno. What sort of job?"

"Let's go look. No likee, no takee. What do you say?"

"You're sweet, prof, but . . ."

"You could use a dinner, couldn't you?"

"Two, even."

"Let's go."

He hauled her to her feet and they walked slowly back to the car, hand in hand. Before they were halfway there, he was sure he had made a mistake. He had never been attracted to her, as he had to other girls in his classes. She had always been a lumpish one, laconic, vague, irritating, but somehow pathetic in her compliance with anyone who paid her the simplest attentions. As a student she had been an eager but indifferent performer, one of those for whom learning, like life, was always a jigsaw with pieces missing. He asked her:

"Have you told your parents about the baby?"

"Hell, no! They've got their own troubles. It's too complicated."

"I guess it is."

"Where are we going, prof?"

"To see a friend of mine. We'll stop at a supermarket on the way and pick up some things for supper. Lieberman's is open on Sunday, I think."

"I guess so. But listen, won't it look a bit funny?"

"What?"

"Me like this." She giggled childishly. "And you with your reputation?"

"I didn't know I had one."

She giggled again. "Oh, Professor! You know what they used to say. 'Gunnar Thorkild has the biggest gun on the island and he shoots on sight.' You must have heard it. That's why you got so many women in your classes. That's why I signed on."

"Pity you didn't stay."

"Are you mad at me now?"

"No. I just wonder what else they said, whether they learned anything except the details of my sex life. Did you ever learn anything, Jenny?"

"You mean about the Polynesians and their voyages and their life and all that? I learned something, I guess. But I could never see the point of it."

"Why not?"

"Well, you know . . . What did they do that amounted to a row of beans? What are they now? They don't even own the islands they live on. There's us here and in Samoa and the French in Tahiti. . . . Here in Hawaii they're nothing—waiters and beach boys. . . ."

"And what are we, Jenny, you and me?"

"Well, I mean, at least we're civilized. We've made progress. We . . . Oh, Christ! I really walked into that one, didn't I?"

"You did, baby. You opened your mouth and shut your mind. Try it the other way sometime."

She was silent then as they drove downtown. She would not go into the market but sat huddled in the car, tousle-haired and shapeless like a rag doll. Gunnar Thorkild shopped angrily and recklessly—plank steaks and salads and fruit and wine and pâté and frozen desserts. He was a big-mouthed idiot who couldn't mind his own business. Why he had to pick this particular lame duck he would never know; and what would Martha Gilman say when it waddled into her kitchen on this Sunday evening? As if she didn't have enough problems of her own: a husband who had killed himself with Chinese heroin in Saigon, a towheaded hellion of eleven who had to be fed and educated, a thirty-year-old figure that was no man's dream of delight, stringy brown hair, a gamin face that was always smudged with poster paint and printer's ink, a studio full of work in progress—wahines on black velvet for the tourist shops, picture maps for the land developers, silk-screen prints, wood blocks and charcoal sketches—and a string of customers shouting down the telephone for undelivered work. . . . Oh yes, she would adore to have lumpish, pregnant Jenny dumped on her doormat!

When they arrived at the old frame house, in an

unfashionable street off Nuuanu Avenue, Thorkild marched ahead like a tribal legate loaded with gifts for a threatening chieftain. The door was opened by Mark, the hellion, who ran, shouting, to announce him.

"Hi, Ma! Uncle Gunnar's here with a dame! They've come for supper!"

Martha Gilman, her hair a mess of snakes, her smock stained as if with spilled blood, appeared at the end of the hall. She was armed with a palette and a paint knife and she demanded ominously:

"Gunnar, what the hell is this? I work weekends like every other day! If you want to come visiting, you telephone. I can't afford the time to . . ."

"I know, my sweet." Thorkild smiled at her gorgan image over the celery tops. "So I've come to make your supper. Martha, this is Jenny. As you see, she's pregnant."

"By you?"

"Not this time. But she needs a job and a place to sleep, and you need someone to baby-sit that monster and clean up the mess you live in. So why don't you both sit down and discuss it, while I start supper."

Holding the packages before him like a breastwork, he marched into the kitchen and barricaded himself with a chair shoved under the door handle. He spread the preparations over an hour with another twenty minutes added for safety, wondering at the silence outside, bracing himself against the whirlwind that must surely hit him when he emerged from his sanctuary. When, finally, he got up enough courage to announce the meal, he found the table laid, Jenny dressed in a fresh muu-muu with a ribbon in her hair, playing checkers with the hellion, and Martha Gilman in house gown and gold slippers, lighting the candles. As he stood gaping, with the wine bottles clutched in his fists, Martha said sweetly:

"Why don't you go and freshen up, Gunnar? Jenny and I will serve."

He had never been noted for discretion, but this time he had the grace to keep his mouth shut and be grateful in silence. It was only after the meal was over and—miracle upon miracle!—Jenny and Mark were washing dishes in the kitchen that Martha Gilman said the words of absolution:

"You're a clown, Gunnar. But a sweet clown. If she wants to stay I'll keep her. I could use some help and God knows she needs somewhere to nest for a while. So, we'll see . . . Now, what's this I hear about your appointment?"

"Hey! Whose phone have you been tapping?"

"None of your business. Now tell me."

"They've offered me a three-year appointment as associate professor. But tenure and the Chair—no! Anderson's offered me six months' study leave to prove my thesis—which is great; except nobody's come up with the money to finance the kind of expedition it needs."

"You're a whore, Gunnar Thorkild!"

"That's not funny."

"It isn't meant to be. I read your thesis, remember. I drew the maps and the illustrations. I believed what I read about your ancestors: how they paddled and sailed without lodestone, without charts; how they lived on island fruits and ocean fish and made landfalls on tiny atolls and big islands like this one. I be lieved the voyages you yourself had made on the luggers and copra boats and alone with your grandfather. Now I hear you talking about sponsorships and expeditions and all the dreck that goes with them. You weren't sponsored then. Why do you need it now? Or have you lost your nerve? You've sat here in this room and I've seen dreams in a small boy's eyes when you talked. I've heard your students—even that poor dumb chick in there—tell how you've opened up horizons they had never dreamed in their lives before. Now—what are you? Some kind of sophomore sex symbol, talking high and acting low and playing out your little games of benevolence like this one today! Where has the big man gone—the son of the daughter of Kaloni Kienga, the sacred navigator? Will he go home to prepare his grandfather for his voyage to the island of the trade winds?"

The vigor and the venom of her attack stunned him for a moment. He had known her in tempers and tantrums, and had always found words to coax her out of them; but this was cold anger, contemptuous and lethal. She was thrusting for the kill at crotch and heart and jugular; but he would not give her the satisfaction of engaging in the duel. He said curtly:

"Shut up, Martha! If you're in the dog days, I'm sorry. If you're in trouble, I'll try to help. But don't play bitch games with me."

"You're a bastard, Thorkild."

"That's not news, sweetheart. It's on my birth certificate."

"You're so damn prodigal. You waste so much that other people would give their eyes for—talent, opportunity, freedom."

"And since when do I have to account for my life to you, or anyone else?"

"Because you are accountable . . . that's just the point. Today, on an impulse, you've changed three lives, Jenny's, mine and Mark's. . . . I'm not grudging what I've done. I think it will turn out fine. My point is that *you* made the change without asking. You've imposed a situation on us all, yet when you've finished here tonight you'll walk away whistling 'Dixie' as though nothing has happened. It's the same in your lecture room. Every lesson you teach is consequential for someone. Every time you cock your hat at some new girl there's a consequence for her. But you don't seem to care. You're . . . I don't know . . . You're . . ."

"*Haphaole*," said Gunnar Thorkild quietly. "Half-white, and all adrift. That's really what you're trying to say."

"No!"

"Yes, Martha. Yes! . . . Oh, I know it isn't a colour thing or a race prejudice. But it does have to do with what I am, and what seems to you a lack of—what's the fashionable word?—commitment. I'm a tribal man, not a group man. In a tribe you don't make commitments, you are committed, from birth to death, to sharing and loving and suffering and relationships that go back to the old gods. You fish together and you share the catch. Families exchange their children with no loss to the child and no shock to the order of things. In a *haole* group it's different. The family's destroyed or wilted. You have to insist on what you are, prove your identity and then dedicate all of it or part of it as the price of admission to the group. I'm not a team man, a faculty man, a company man. I refuse to work at conformity. I'm just me. . . . You're hating me because I seem to have a freedom that is denied to you. But you let me come and go because I don't make demands on you, and you can shut the door in my face. My colleagues damn me because they say I'm uncomfortable to work with. The truth is, I have no past they are interested to share and no future I'm prepared to mortgage to their demands. So I'm an oddity . . . like a man who's lost his shadow. Nothing will change that. Not even if I strip mother-naked and walk like Christ on the water from Diamond Head to Pukapuka!"

She was near to tears, but she would not be silenced. She pleaded with him desperately.

"I understand what you're saying. You can't let your personal peace reside in other men's mouths—in their gossip and hearsay. But this is different. Your integrity as a scholar is in question. Your authority as a teacher is under challenge. You must answer the challenge, or abdicate."

"Which means a voyage of exploration, right?"

"Right."

"Which means a ship and crew and supplies—in other words, money."

"You've got money."

"Ten thousand dollars in the bank."

"And salary, and a house, and a valuable library and a car . . ."

"And you think I should gamble all that on this single enterprise?"

"I think you must, otherwise the record stands against you. You're finished as a teacher and a scholar, and you will have discredited your mother's people."

"Why the hell should you care about me or my mother's people?"

"Because I'm fond of you and Mark adores you—and I'd like to know there was one man in a dog's world we could both respect! Now will you please go home. I don't think I can take any more tonight."

He woke next morning, red-eyed and unrested, at his desk in the soundproof room, with a note pad full of scrawled figures under his hand. The figures showed that if he borrowed against his assets, he could come up with forty thousand dollars in cash and it would take him ten years of bone-poor living to pay off the loan. His first lecture did not begin until eleven, so he shaved and showered, drank half a pint of orange juice and drove down to Red Mulligan's boatyard at Ala Moana.

Red was an ex-marine, with a beer belly and a blasphemous tongue and a shrewd eye for a sucker, who ran the best yard and the soundest brokerage business in the Islands. His wife was a bustling, roly-poly woman who looked after the office and chivvied the painters and riggers and carpenters and kept Red sober during working hours. They were an ill-assorted couple, but good friends, pawky and generous and full of the salty gossip of the waterfront. Over a mug of coffee in the carpenter's shop Gunnar Thorkild laid out his first tentative plans:

". . . I know what I want, Red. Something like a Baltic trader or an island lugger, three hundred tons, a hundred feet overall, three-masted with one square sail for the trades. I want a slow-revving engine, one of those old thumpers that will keep going even under water! I want basic accommodation for thirty people, students and crew. And I want you to sign in blood that her hull's got no worms and her spars and rigging are sound."

"You're talking about an antique," said Red Mulligan. "And if you want one that's safe for the big seas out there, you're going to have to pay for it. How much can you afford?"

"Thirty thousand—tops."

Red Mulligan looked at him with the pity which the Irish keep for drunks and spoiled priests and congenital idiots. He shook his head slowly from side to side while his belly gurgled in protest at the insanity. Finally he stretched out two arms like tree trunks and laid his hands on Thorkild's shoulders. There were geniune tears in his voice.

"Doc! For thirty thousand here's what you can do. You can go to any travel agent, pick up two first-class tickets for a round-the-world tour. You can phone up Helen's Dating Service and she'll give you a choice of fifty broads to take along. You can have yourself lodged, laid and liquored for six months and still come home with money in your jeans. But a Baltic trader—forget it! You know what a boat like that is, doc? It's nothin' but a big hole in the sea for suckers to pour money into and smart guys like me to take money out of. Do you read me, doc? Do you read me?"

"Loud and clear," said Gunnar Thorkild. "But you've told me yourself that boats change hands like used cars. People find they can't afford the upkeep, so sometimes the yards attach them for unpaid bills. Why don't you see what you can find?"

"It's not a question of finding her," said Red Mulligan slowly. "I know where she is right now."

"Where?"

"Two miles from here at Mort Faraday's Marina."

"Who owns her?"

"Carl Magnusson."

"The cannery man?"

"The cannery man, the freight-line man, the you-name-it-he's-in-it man, the God-us-and-the-Dillinghams man . . . Yeah, that Magnusson."

"How much is he asking for her?"

"Two hundred and twenty-five thousand."

"What will he take?"

"Two hundred and twenty-five thousand."

"Like that, eh?"

"The hardest nose in the business, buddy boy."

"I'd still like to see the vessel."

"I'll call Mort Faraday. When do you want to go?"

"Now, if possible."

"Do me a favour, eh, doc? Make like you've got the money and you're just being careful about spend-

ing it. Mort and I do a lot of business together and I
don't want to spoil a beautiful friendship. . . ."

Fifteen minutes later Gunnar Thorkild was standing
on the deck of the *Frigate Bird*—three hundred tons
of Baltic trader, barquentine rigged, powered by twin
MAN diesels, converted from North Sea freighter to
a cadet training ship and finally to a rich man's yacht,
with teak decks and gleaming brightwork and sails
immaculate as table linen and cordage white as the
day it was bought. The engine room was like a surgi-
cal theater and the wheelhouse was a navigator's
heaven. For Gunnar Thorkild it was love at first sight
—and despair the instant afterward.

At the price—if one had the price—the vessel was
a gift. But to man and maintain her in this pristine
splendour would require another fortune. Mort Faraday, the broker, commented hopefully:

"She's a beauty, eh?"

"How does Magnusson run her?"

"Skippers her himself—at least he did before his
illness—and crews her with island boys from his place
on Kauai."

"Has she ever been chartered?"

"Never and nohow! We've had big offers from big
names. Magnusson would as lief rent you his wife as
this beauty."

"Why's he selling then?"

"Like I said, he had an illness last year—a stroke.
He's recovered, but it's left him with one gimpy leg
and an arm that's not as good as it used to be. I guess
he's just decided the *Frigate Bird*'s one thing too
many."

"Any chance he'd shade the price?"

"Would you, if she were yours?"

"No, I guess not."

"Tell you what, though. At this price, which is a

steal, our finance company would come through with
a seventy-five percent loan, over a five-year term. If
you bought her and exploited her for charter, you
could manage that easily."

"Let me think about it. Is Magnusson in town?"

"Far as I know. He doesn't go far from home these
days. But if you're thinking of a private haggle, forget
it. He'll chew you up like popcorn—if you ever get
to see him, which isn't too easy."

"Thanks for the tip. How long to get her ready for
sea?"

"Man! As long as it takes you to buy fresh stores
and load 'em. Her tanks are full, there's dry goods
and a deep-freeze full of meat and a full inventory of
spares and duplicate systems. All you have to do is
press the starters and motor off the mooring. I swear
to you, you'll never find another buy like this
one. . . ."

"I believe you, Mort," said Gunnar Thorkild amiably "I'll be back. Take care now."

"You take care, Professor. I hate to lose a sale. . . ."

As he drove slowly out to the University through
the press of morning traffic, Gunnar Thorkild was already composing the letter which would be delivered
by messenger that same evening to Carl Magnusson.

The house of Carl Magnusson was like the man
himself, separate, discreet, privileged, a low-built bun-
galow of teakwood and volcanic stone, set in a tropic
garden where lawns and shrubberies rolled down to
the water's edge. There were wrought-iron gates and
a guardian to open them. Who came here came by
grant and never by right; and high secrets of state and
of commerce had been talked in the drawing room
and on the lanai that looked out over the pool and the
horizon beyond the reef.

Carl Magnusson himself was a character of forbidding reputation and singular personal charm. He was a big man, sturdy as a tree, white-haired and ruddy, with a soft voice and an air of rapt interest in the most banal talk of his guests. His angers were formidable and on occasions destructive, but they were never raucous or violent. It was a matter of public record that he had married four times and begotten six children. All the children were grown and gone away. Since his illness, he had lived in seclusion with a Filipino staff, his fourth wife and a resident secretary.

He received Gunnar Thorkild on the lanai, seated him at a table on which were laid his letter and a complete set of his publications, waited until coffee was served and then put him to the question:

"Thorkild, I've read your letter and your publications. I've also informed myself of your personal and academic background. I'm impressed. I'm also puzzled."

"Why?"

"At a critical moment in your career you made a mistake—a big one."

"It wasn't a mistake. It was an act of faith in a great man, my grandfather."

"An act of faith—that's an interesting point of view. One of your colleagues, to whom I spoke yesterday, described it as a surrender to a fairy tale, a dream out of folklore."

"It is a dream, Mr. Magnusson; but it's the dream of a whole people. You hear it in one form or another all over the Pacific, from the Gambiers to the Gilberts. The substance of it is always the same: there is an island, a sacred place where the *alii,* the great chiefs and the great navigators, go to die. . . . Now this is not the small dreaming of one man. It is what Jung called the great dreaming: the mythos of a whole race dispersed over the biggest ocean on the planet. Behind every great dreaming is a great truth—or even a small one that has assumed a fundamental importance."

"And you really believe this island exists?"

"Yes."

"And you believe you can find it?"

"I know I will find it."

"How do you know?"

"My grandfather will tell me. The knowledge must pass to me and he must pass it. That is the way things are."

"Come now, Mr. Thorkild! It must happen because that's the way things are! From a scholar, that's too much!"

"How long have you lived in the Islands, Mr. Magnusson?"

"We've been here four generations, Thorkild!"

"Then you shouldn't mock 'the way things are' and the things that are handed down. A few miles off the Pali pass there are sacred places, lost for centuries, but if you stumble across them, you will find yourself surrounded and warned away by the guardian families. You know that the trust and the meaning are still transmitted—and if you don't, you should!"

"I know." Carl Magnusson grinned. "I just wondered if you did. For a fellow who wants a favour you're damned prickly."

"I don't want favours. I want a deal."

"What sort of deal?"

"I want to charter the *Frigate Bird*."

"She's for sale, not for charter."

"I was hoping you'd consider a charter offer."

"No. She's a thing I love, not a commodity."

"I understand the loving," said Gunnar Thorkild

wryly. "I fell in love with her myself. There's no use pretending I can afford her."

"Suppose you could. What would you do?"

"I'd skipper her myself, I'd get a good crew, and a bunch of boys and girls, and sail her down to Hiva Oa. I'd put my grandfather and his canoe on board and let him navigate me as far as he was willing. Then I'd put him overside in his own craft and say good-bye to him. After that I would have a choice to make. . . ."

"What choice?"

"A hard one. I would know by then how to reach the island. I could turn back, and keep the knowledge to myself. Or sail on, find the place, chart it and then come home and vindicate my reputation as a scholar."

"And how do you think you would choose?"

"That's the problem. I'm *haphaole,* you see—two men in one skin."

"There's a third choice."

"I've thought of that too," said Gunnar Thorkild. "Find the one secret place left on the planet and stay there. It's a tempting thought."

"I could be tempted."

"Away from all this?" Gunnar Thorkild was skeptical.

"Let me tell you something, Thorkild. When you're flat on your back and you can't move and you can't talk, and the vultures are waiting in the boardroom to pick your bones clean, you get a new slant on living . . ." He broke off and sat a long moment, staring at the liver spots on the back of his hands. Then he said flatly: "It's an interesting idea; but you're snookered, aren't you? I won't charter. You can't afford to buy. What do you do now?"

"I keep looking for a vessel I can afford. If I don't find it by the end of the month I leave and go to my grandfather on Hiva Oa. I have the feeling his time is running out. I must be there to prepare him for his last journey."

"I wonder," said Carl Magnusson sourly, "I wonder if our grandchildren will have the same thought. . . ."

Gunnar Thorkild said nothing.

The old man frowned. "You're embarrassed? Why? A family like ours—we build empires and dynasties and then have to call in the mercenaries to protect us. When I die the mercenaries will take over—trustees, bankers, boards of directors, lawyers. What do they know or care about the old pieties . . ." He thrust a long, thick forefinger at Thorkild's breastbone. "As I said, you're snookered! So I'm going to make you an offer. I'll finance your expedition: yourself and ten bodies of your choice—the rest I'll choose. I'll sail the *Frigate Bird* with my crew, and you direct the operation from the time we pick up your grandfather until we mutually agree to break off and come home. I pay all bills and you assign to me all rights of publication and other exploitation of all records and discoveries, financial rewards therefrom to be split sixty to me, forty to you. One more thing. It's a take-it-or-leave-it deal. No haggling. No whys or wherefores. And you decide now! Well, Thorkild, what do you say?"

"I leave it," said Gunnar Thorkild flatly.

The old man gaped at him. "You what?"

"I leave it."

"Why?"

"Because if it's a good deal, it will stand reflection and discussion. If it's a bad one, it won't; and besides, there are things I can't trade, Mr. Magnusson, because they don't belong to me, but to my mother's people. You're being very generous. I know I'll never get an offer like this again. If you'll excuse me, I won't waste any more of your time."

"Sit down," said Carl Magnusson harshly. "Let's

start again! Even before I had your letter, I'd heard about you—from your Jesuit friend Flanagan. I trust him, because like me, he's living on borrowed time. . . ."

On the white beach of Hiva Oa, Kaloni the Navigator sat and watched the rising of the newborn moon. He was not alone now, because this was a night of feasting, when he took his rightful place beside the chief, and called alternately with him the genealogies that linked them to the old high gods: Kane the supreme, Lono the fruitful, Ku the powerful and Kanaloa, Lord of the deep sea. Alone, he intoned the hymn to Kanaloa, and all the guardian spirits beneath him. Then, when the dancing was done, the chief called for silence, and Kaloni stepped forward to pronounce his own obit:

> "The high gods have told me,
> One moon more,
> I shall stay with you.
> When Hina shows herself again
> I shall go,
> Like the white seabird.
> Kaloni Kienga the Navigator
> Will make his last voyage.
> You will not follow me,
> But when I go,
> You will throw flowers into the sea,
> The waves will carry them to me,
> Beyond the path of the shining one,
> Beyond the black path of the god Kanaloa."

When he had finished there was silence again, and out of the silence the maidens came one by one to hang leis about his neck, and the young men, after

them, to pile fruit at his feet. Then, when they retired
the chief himself came, carrying a paddle, carved
with the symbol of the god Kanaloa, and gave it into
his hands and blessed him:

"May Kanaloa protect you,
  And Hina shine on your passage,
  And may the high chiefs and the navigators
      receive you,
  In peace and with joy."

Kaloni closed his eyes and let the blessing flow over
him. When he opened them again the beach was
empty. There were only the flowers and the fruit and
the cook-fires, for a memory of what had happened.
He was dispensed now from human commerce. He
was consigned to the ancestors. He was ritually dead.
He had only to wait for the next new moon, when
the black ship would come to carry him to the home
of the navigators, the island of the trade winds.

TWO

Gunnar Thorkild had demanded discussion; he got it in gluttonous measure—a rude lesson in the usages and consequences of power. He wanted clear terms and definitions. Carl Magnusson gave them to him, phrase by hammered phrase:

". . . What we want to do and what we say we want to do are two different things. . . . Why? Because we're mounting a voyage of maritime discovery, to find an island which exists so far only in legend. If we reveal our true intent, we become objects of political scrutiny. We'll be cruising at first in French territorial waters, where they have a large naval force and an intelligence screen to protect their atomic experiments. We'll be sailing in my ship and I am known to have certain affiliations in the State Department and the Navy. Suppose we do find our island. An interesting question then arises: who owns it? In theory we do. We can annex it to ourselves by a unilateral act and demonstrable possession—provided, of course, we can defend it against other claimants, which we obviously can't. . . . So we annex it in the name of the United States and claim land rights to ourselves. . . . You never thought of that? Imagine what the press would make of it, especially with the Magnusson name involved. And I'm damn sure the French would have a destroyer on our tail, tracking us by radar every mile from Hiva Oa! So whatever you've said to anyone, up to now, my dear Thorkild, we're going to retract and replace with a fiction that the press and your colleagues will accept and hopefully embellish. They've laughed you out of court already, so that helps!"

Gunnar Thorkild thought about it for a moment and then nodded agreement. "The simpler the story, the easier to tell. Local philanthropist Carl Magnusson invites assistant professor Gunnar Thorkild and a group of senior students on a summer cruise of the South Pacific. Students will trace the migrations of the early navigators, study local dialects and customs, and collect folk music . . . period."

"Fine! Except I'll have my public relations people dress it up. We might as well make some profit out of it! Now, you and me. You've told me a moment may come when you feel obliged, for reasons of tribal loyalty, to keep certain information secret. I accepted that, provided you accept that I am free to proceed on the basis of my own information and my own deductions, even if it means violating the secrecy or possession of a place which is sacred to you."

"If that situation arose," said Thorkild, "I would have to separate myself from you and from the enterprise."

"And from any further participation in its profits or advantages?"

"Agreed. But I might also feel obliged to oppose you, actively."

"I'm a rough man to fight," said Magnusson. "Just be warned. Now let's talk about personnel. It will be a long voyage. We'd better be damn sure we can all live together. The crew first. I'm the skipper. You move in as mate and navigator. I have four boys from Kauai with my cook and a galley boy. That's eight bodies and it's ample, provided the guests share cleaning and serving."

"That's eight males," said Thorkild with a grin. "It's Navy style, traditional but tedious. I prefer the tribal way: men, women and children with a litter of pigs for good measure."

"No pigs!" Magnusson laughed. It was the first time. Thorkild had seen him genuinely amused. "The women, yes. The children . . . well, that depends whose they are. My wife won't come. She hates the sea and she"ll be glad of a rest from my company. So I'm inviting Sally Anderton. She's a physician of merit and a damned attractive woman as well. I'd like to get Gabe Greenaway, who's a naval hydrographer, and Mildred, his girl friend, who used to be a marine biologist at Woods Hole. They're old friends and good shipmates. . . . That's all so far. What are your thoughts?"

"None, yet. But I think we need a community that has some shape to it."

"Why do you say that?"

"Because the moment we slip our moorings and head south we're a group in hazard. We're navigating in dangerous waters. We face storm and shipwreck like any other mariners. We'd reduce the hazard if the group had some sort of shape, some look of family. For instance, you want to have the passengers in some kind of sexual balance, yet you accept without question six boys from Kauai with no sexual companionship at all. I think that's dangerous. It needs rethinking. . . ."

For a moment it seemed as though Magnusson would explode into anger, but he recovered himself and pronounced flatly:

"Let's get something straight, Thorkild. On my ship it's two worlds: the forepeak and the afterdeck, and the captain's the only bridge in between. There's courtesy, but no community high-jinks. The crew are there to work the ship, the passengers to enjoy it."

"That I understand, in the circumstances that obtained before. For your crew, the ship was an extension of their home and their employment with you. For your passengers, it was a pleasure cruise. Now the definitions have changed. The passengers are participating in an enterprise which entails stress and risk, an enterprise whose real purpose may be only half revealed to them. So we can't think of them as joyriders. They'll have to function very quickly as a community. For the crew the definition changes even more abruptly. . . ."

"I don't see that at all!"

"Give me time to explain it. Whether you admit it or not, there is, de facto, a barrier of class and race aboard your ship!"

"Nonsense!"

"Is it? All the crew are Polynesians. I would guess all your guests were *haole*. . . . No, hear me out, Magnusson! From the moment we pick up my grandfather in Hiva Oa the situation changes dramatically. A sacred man comes on board—a *kapu* man—making his last journey to join the ancestors. Your boys will recognize him as such, even though his dialect will be different and there are two thousand miles of sea between Kauai and Hiva Oa. All you will see, all the

others will see, will be an old, white-haired man, tattooed on breast and back and arms, who won't have
very much to say to anyone. Now, how you treat this
man, the accommodation you offer him, the respect
you pay him, will be a matter of note and concern to
your crew. . . . There's more yet. When Kaloni Kienga
leaves us—and he will, because he must make the
last part of his voyage alone—I will be the sacred
man, the *kapu* one. That will be known too, almost
from the beginning. And all my relationships will be
dominated by it. . . . So let's take our time over this
part, eh? Let's be very open and flexible. If you don't
think you can tolerate what it entails, socially, then
let's call off the arrangement, with no hard feelings. . . ."

Carl Magnusson was patently unhappy. He limped
away across the lanai, grunting and muttering,
splashed water into a glass, tossed it down at a gulp
and then stumped back to face Gunnar Thorkild. He
was stony-faced and hostile.

"You're a subtle bastard, Thorkild! You throw
me an argument like that, knowing I have no way to
answer it. I know what *kapu* means. but it doesn't
concern me. It's outside my culture pattern. . . . That's
been my stand all along, on the whole race problem.
You live your way, I'll live mine- -and you marry
yours, I'll marry mine. Let's build good fences and
we'll all be very happy neighbours."

"In this case," Gunnar Thorkild snapped back
savagely, "we'll be living on the same small ship, in
jeopardy on the same big ocean. And—for God's
sake!—is it too much to ask you to respect a man who
has two thousand years of history and knowledge at
his command? On the *Frigate Bird* you've got every
damn navigational aid that her electrics will carry. I
tell you, Kaloni Kienga will sail you to any Pacific

landfall you name, without even a compass! God Almighty! What's at stake for you? Are you afraid he'll smell? He will. He eats taro root and that gives a man bad breath! But for the rest, you'll be meeting a man ten times your size with a longer history than either the Magnussons or the Dillinghams—for all the pineapples they've dumped on the world. Is that what you're afraid of?"

Carl Magnusson's trap mouth twitched into a thin smile.

"No, Thorkild. That's not it. I'm afraid of what happens on the day when you can claim—truly or falsely, we can't know—that all his knowledge and his power have passed to you!"

It was a brutal attack, but Gunnar Thorkild made no move to counter it. He sat a long while, lips pursed, eyes half closed, nodding like a porcelain buddha, as he pondered the import of Magnusson's words. When finally he spoke, it was with a curious humility and detachment:

"You're right, of course. It's one thing to claim power. It's another to possess it truly. And of course there's no guarantee I won't misuse it. I don't really know what to say. I won't know what to say until the *mana* of my grandfather passes into me. . . . Forgive me, you do understand what *mana* means?"

"It means 'spirit,' 'soul' . . . something like that."

"Like, but yet unlike. It means the emanation, the endowment from the high gods, which makes the chief what he is, the great navigator what he is. I have not received it yet. I cannot say what it will do to me. So you're right to be afraid, but I was not wrong when I told you the rest of it. I believe in my bones that we have to give ourselves the chance to grow together. On the other hand, it's your ship, your money. Only you can decide whether you want to commit them on these conditions."

Magnusson hesitated a moment, then held out his hand to Thorkild.

"The bargain stands. I'm not a flexible man. You're not an easy one either. We'll need some patience with each other. Let's wrap it up for today and meet again later in the week."

"Come to my place, Mr. Magnusson. There are things I'd like to show you. People I'd like you to meet."

"Bring them here. I rarely go out these days."

"Maybe it's time to make a change," said Gunnar Thorkild evenly. "Among my people, it's a shame on the house if a stranger refuses to enter and share the food."

"Among my people," said Carl Magnusson with a grin, "good manners are rare—and getting rarer. Give me a call. I'll be glad to come."

When he passed by the Jesuit house to offer his thanks to Flanagan, he found the old man uneasy and dubious about the whole affair. Pressed to explain why, he fussed and fidgeted, turned on the brogue and the blarney, and in ten minutes managed to say nothing at all. Then he fell prey to a migraine so fearsome that even a whisper was like a blacksmith's hammer in his head. A silent turn around the garden, with Thorkild pushing, relieved him somewhat, and finally he consented to explain himself.

". . . Gunnar, my boy, it's like this. In the old days, when I was raising cash for good causes—collecting dowry money for the bride of Christ, as one of my pious superiors put it—I always went straight after the big fish, the fellow with the power. He didn't have to be a Holy Roman. In fact it was better if he wasn't.

He could skip the message and write the check, and then enjoy feeling benevolent afterwards. . . . There was wisdom in the tactic, and it almost always worked, because if you're rich and potent you can do what the poor man can't—spread your investment over the board: so much for gilts, so much for equities, so much for patronage, and a flyer on each of the going Gods—Jewish, Episcopalian, Roman, Unitarian! After that you'd lay a little on the horses, and some on the fillies—and even a side wager on the syndicate in case they might be useful one day. . . . So all I needed was a good spiel and a thick hide and I generally came home with the bacon—which is exactly what I did for you with Magnusson. I've tapped him before. We've been nodding friends for a long time. Sure, he said, it was the kind of adventurous project he liked to back, and now it had a special appeal for him. . . . Are you with me, Gunnar Thorkild? Are you attending?"

"I'm with you, Father. I'm just wondering why you're worried."

"Well, he told me what had happened to him—the stroke and all that—and it was as if I were looking into a mirror and reading my own tiny mind. You see, when first you're stricken, you wilt; then you fight. It's a matter of the testicles—the little witnesses you invoke to prove you're a man. Now the fight's good—until the day when you realize you'll never really win it. You're damaged. The clock is running against you. Then you start plotting for continuity—invoking love and friendship, buying allies, making leagues and treaties—all of which will terminate the minute they put pennies in your eyes and pull the sheet over your face. You know that. So you turn inwards, looking for that little, bland, vagrant soul which, until now, you hadn't thought about very much. Then you're scared and sometimes desperate; because at first you see only darkness, and after that shadows and folly-fires and sometimes monsters that raise the hackles and make you feel most wondrous cold. . . . I know it all, because I've been there. You're dangerous then, because you're cornered and you're envious and resentful, and sometimes you can turn destructive. . . . Now that's what troubles me about you and Carl Magnusson. I know he's in the dark country. I'm not sure you're the man to handle him. . . . Maybe this is all double Dutch to you, but . . ."

"I know what you mean." Thorkild was suddenly withdrawn and thoughtful. "I sensed some of it today, but I didn't define it as you do. He had to display his power. He wanted to set all the terms of an alliance. I wasn't prepared to accept them. Then he was afraid of what would happen when the *mana* of Kaloni the Navigator passed to me. . . ."

"You say he was afraid? Are you sure?"

"No. He *said* he was afraid—which is different. I thought he was just warning me about getting too big for my breeches; but that wasn't the whole of it."

"You're damn right it wasn't!" said Flanagan with sudden vehemence. "Not by a long chalk!"

Thorkild was suddenly afraid for the old man. He was so excited, so vehement, that it seemed his frail body could not support the strain. Thorkild tried to calm him with a smile and an offhand word.

"Easy now, Father! It isn't so important."

"You say so! But I tell you it's the root and core of the matter! I know about *mana* and the handing down of power. I started from nothing—a Boston Irish kid with the backside out of his breeches. I got my education the hard way: fistfights in the alleys and a black strap around my backside at home. I joined the Society. Suddenly I was a sacred thing—*kapu!* I couldn't marry. It was a sacrilege to touch my dedicated person. I studied; knowledge was handed to me, year after year. Then I was ordained. . . . A sacred man, the bishop, who got his *mana* from the Pope, who got his *mana* from Peter the Fisherman, who got his from Christ, laid his hands on me and said, 'Now you are a priest forever according to the order of Melchizedek. . . .' Now I'm a big *kapu*! I welcome the newborn and send home the dying. I make God out of bread. I remit sins and give rescripts for salvation. Your wife—if you had one!—tells me what she does with you in bed, and I tell her if it's good or bad. You kill the Dean one fine summer night, and if I judge you're sorry enough, I send you away, clean in conscience, safe from pursuit by God, and still secret from man. That's a big endowment. That's God and Flanagan in a private duet! So what happens to Flanagan? Either he gets so holy and high and mighty that he thinks he's God himself, or he can't take the strain and takes to drink and seducing his female penitents! Or he tries to get rid of the *mana* altogether—makes himself good-boy-Joe, jolly-club-counsellor, Mr. Nobody, so broad-minded his brains fall out of his earholes. . . . Don't laugh! That's the truth. A fellow like Magnusson, with all his millions, can't come near that sort of power. So he tries to buy it with a donation, command it with an exuberance of charity; and I—God help me!—can pretend to share it with him. That's what he'll try to do with you. He'll carry you so far, with money and influence; then one day you'll find him on your back, like the old man of the sea, begging to be carried just one league farther. . . ."

"And then?"

"Then you'll try to do it, because you think the *mana* is strong enough. But it isn't—and it can't be; because the reed is not the wind that blows it, and you will find that Gunnar Thorkild is just a man, with a failing heart and an over-worked prostate and a brain that's bursting with complications and confusions."

"So what are you telling me, Father? Call it off?"

"You won't do that, because you're already committed."

"What then?"

"Gunnar Thorkild, I love you like a son, but I don't know what to tell you. The *mana* will come; but you'll suffer for it. People will lean on you and you will fall under their weight. They will lift you up and you will hate them for the faith they have in you. You will try to flee them, but they will not let you escape. What you do then, God only knows. And you'll die begging Him to tell you; or you'll live, begging Him to die, because the burden is intolerable."

"Easy, Father, easy now! You're making a big fuss over a very little matter."

Flanagan made a shaky effort to recover himself. "Sure, boy! That's what the doctors told me, isn't it? I'd have crises and explosions. . . . Pay me no mind. I'm just purging my vile humour on you. You'll have a wonderful voyage—and I'll be here to welcome you at the end of it! Take me in now. It's almost time for chapel!"

The old man's outburst troubled him. It raised old, haunting memories, specters out of an antique time. He was glad of the brusque, commonsensical reasoning of James Neal Anderson, who saw the whole affair as tidy solution to a diplomatic crisis.

"Frankly, Gunnar, I couldn't be happier. Magnusson's been a notable benefactor to the University. So it's easy for me to arrange your study leave without making it appear a sop to your wounded pride. . . .

The fact that you're publicizing the affair as a study cruise, instead of a sensational attempt to vindicate your reputation, also takes the heat out of the campus situation and, quite frankly, puts you in better grace with the administration."

"Patronage is a wonderful thing, isn't it, James?"

Anderson was relaxed enough to enjoy the joke. "Provided you can keep the patron happy. Which reminds me—how are you choosing the students for the cruise?"

"Equally from both sexes on the basis of scholastic merit, capacity for original research, and ability to adjust to abnormal social situations."

"And who's going to judge that?"

"I am."

"Is that wise?"

"It's necessary."

"Advice, from a man with scars on his back. You make the decisions; but let someone else take the responsibility."

"In this case, who?"

"The patron—Magnusson."

"And how do I get him to do that?"

"Call for applications; make a short list of a dozen candidates, pull their records and present them to Magnusson. Make sure he picks the people you want, and then let him announce the chosen."

"Great—if he'll do it! If he starts to play games— I'm in schtuck!"

"Why would he want to play games?"

"To teach me my place!"

Anderson laughed immoderately and choked on his whiskey. "That's rich. . . . You're learning at last. . . . I've been trying all these years to teach you diplomacy and Magnusson does it in a single lesson!"

Thorkild gave him a lopsided grin. "Let me show

you how well I've learned it, James! I call for applications. I make the short list. You, the Dean, choose the final candidates for Magnusson to approve—and you make sure they're all my nominees."

"And why, Professor Thorkild, should I fall for that little ploy? While you're off cruising happily, I'll be left here carrying the can with students and faculty."

He said it with a chuckle, but Thorkild was no longer amused. His answer was deliberate and somber. "You're a good friend, James. I don't want to embarrass you more than I can help. But one way or another I must get the people I want. Why? Because the sea's big and treacherous; because now that I'm committed, I have to face a tribal mystery that I can't explain even to myself. . . . I'm afraid of what I'm doing, even while I know that I have to do it. Because I'm afraid, I need all the support I can get—people I know, people I'm fond of and can trust because they've stood with me before, in intimate situations. They have to know they're at risk, even though I can't tell them what the risks are because I don't know all of them myself. James, I'm saying this badly, but . . ."

"You're hedging." Anderson was terse. "You owe me better."

"There's nothing to tell. It's all just a cobweb in the mind."

"Tell me about the cobweb then."

"I think I'd like another drink."

"After you've paid for it."

"At least make me a promise."

"What?"

"Because it's a cobweb, and I'm a fool to be afraid, it stays a secret between you and me."

"Agreed."

"I believe the island exists. I believe, more strongly

every day, that we'll find it. It's what happens then that scares me."

"Why?"

"Of all the great navigators who have gone to this place, none has come back. That's all! Period! And if you laugh at me, James, I'll break the whiskey bottle over your head."

"I'm not laughing. I'm wondering how and when you tell that to the people who go with you. . . . And when you do tell them, how will they take it? And if they take it badly, what will you do with them?"

"That's why I need an even chance to choose the right candidates."

"You've made your point."

Gunnar Thorkild gave a long sigh of relief. "At least you understand."

"Why shouldn't I?"

"God knows. I guess, until now, I'd rather taken you for granted. You were a friend. You were there. . . . I'm sorry."

"My wife used to keep a scrapbook." Anderson was suddenly remote, as if the whole subject had become irrelevant. "She used to write down things that interested her. She wrote a beautiful hand, a kind of gothic script. It was a joy just to look at it. When she died, I couldn't bear to keep the book. I burned it. I remember things, though, snippets, phrases, a verse or two. There was one she copied only a couple of months before she died. How does it start? . . .

"Strange, is it not? that of the myriads who
    Before us pass'd the Door of Darkness
        through . . .

. . . I always liked the phrase: the Door of Darkness.

It seemed to promise a light on the other side. But old Omar didn't say that at all. The verse ends:

"Not one returns to tell us of the Road,
Which to discover we must travel too.

"That says it all, doesn't it?"

"Not for me, James. Not for my people. The road is known. The place is known. The knowledge is not sent back; it is transmitted from the high gods who are the beginning of everything. It's the happening which is not told—the afterwards."

"The afterwards is what you make it." James Neal Anderson was harsh and impatient. "I learned that when my wife died. You live one minute after another, one hour, one day. The future is what you dream. The reality is only now—the heartbeat moment. The rest is a cobweb in the mind."

"I never knew it had been so rough for you, James."

"Something else you never knew, Gunnar. I've envied you. I still do. In my world we live in plastic capsules, wanting but not daring to get out."

"Don't kid yourself," said Thorkild curtly. "We're all prisoners, of our genes, of our history, of our long, ancestral dreams. I guess that's why I was so eager to have the Chair and tenure. I could escape my past, and shut it out behind a plastic wall. Now I have to confront it, receive it into me like a vapour from an old man's last breathing. . . . Do I get my drink now?"

"I'll join you. And before we both get drunk you'd better write me the names of your candidates."

There was one more encounter which he had to face, and it was the one for which he was least prepared. James Neal Anderson might live in his plastic capsule; Flanagan S.J. had emerged from his dark country into a twilight of resignation; but Martha Gilman had locked herself in an ice palace, from which no tenderness and no argument would tempt her. Everything in her life was designed as a defense: her compulsive work, her dishevelled look, her trenchant talk, the rasping discipline she imposed on a rebellious boy-child. She endured life like a hair shirt, a secret penance for the man she had married too soon and surrendered too abruptly to addiction and death.

Yet there was passion in her and a haunted yearning which made her at times vulnerable and afterwards deeply resentful. To Gunnar Thorkild she had presented herself first as a possible conquest, then as an object of sympathy and, only much later, as a companion of quiet hours. Once, only once, had they come near to being lovers; and then it was he who had drawn back, suddenly aware and afraid of the burdens each would lay on the other. She needed to be bound. He had to be free. She demanded to be conquered. He wanted the free-and-easy loving of the island people—moon games and beach games and a smile of greeting for the morning. The end of it was a truce, uneasy but tenable, affectionate, but always a little abrasive, guarded yet mutually protective.

Martha Gilman forced him to recognize and to value the reality of his other self—the *haole* half of him. It was she who demanded engagement, a discharge of his contract with the society which paid his stipend and put young minds in his care. What he gave to her was harder to define: a warmth in the ice palace, a window open to the sun, a wink for the woman hiding in the black armour of the working widow. To the boy Mark, he gave a male companionship, an offhand counsel, an occasional sharp rebuke, which he accepted without resentment. He might have given more; but Martha was swift to reject any intrusion on her authority.

It was an odd relationship, ready-made for gossip and party jokes; but he could not absent himself from it curtly and without a backwards look. So at the end of the day's lectures he telephoned Martha Gilman and invited her to dinner. She protested, as she always did, and then allowed herself to be persuaded, provided it wasn't a heavy night or a late one, and there was a number where Jenny could call her, if necessary. He swore to all of it, and promised to pass by at seven for a cocktail and allow her to drive if he had one drink too many. Then he telephoned Anna Wei at the Manchu Palace, ordered a private booth and her best dinner—and wondered ruefully why he was taking such a long way round to get a very small clutch of eggs.

It was Jenny who opened the door to him—plump and cozy and domesticated—with curlers in her hair, a chocolate bar in one hand and a paperback in the other.

"Hi, prof! Come in. Martha's dressing. Mark's doing his homework. He doesn't get to watch television until he's finished."

"How goes it, Jenny?"

"Great, just great—now that I've got Martha organized."

"Come again!"

"We've got an understanding. I don't tidy her studio and she doesn't muss the house. Mark's mine from breakfast until he's finished his homework. After that, Martha has him."

"Not sorry you came?"

"Glad. I've discovered I'm a domestic cat really. What will you drink?"

"I'll get it. How does Mark like the new arrangement?"

"Fine. I'm big sister. And now that Martha's given over nagging him, the kid's showing a brain and he's much easier to handle. Martha says I can come back here and bring the baby if I want."

"And do you?"

"Maybe. We've got a joke going. Two one-parent families make one two-parent house. I—I'm just comfortable, prof. I don't want to think too much about the future."

"I'll drink to that, Jenny girl."

"Hi, Uncle Gunnar!" Mark Gilman marched in with an offhand greeting and held out his exercise book for inspection. "Check it, will you, Jenny? The program starts in five minutes."

Jenny rumpled his hair affectionately. "Haven't you forgotten something, Junior?"

"Like what?"

"Like, 'Please, Jenny.' "

"Please, Jenny."

As he sipped his drink, Gunnar Thorkild watched them, child-mother and boy-child, bent over the book, and he felt a sudden lurch of emotion at the sweetness of the moment. Then Martha came in, and he marvelled at the change in her too. Her hair was set in a modish style, her dress was new. The old half-welcoming, half-wary look was gone. There was a softness in her smile and her greeting that he had never known before. She flushed at his stare and said:

"Well, do you like it or don't you?"

"Which? The dress or the girl?"

"Either."

"Both. . . . A drink?"

"Please."

He took his time making it, careful lest an offhand

word destroy the fragile harmony of the moment. Martha asked him:

"Where are we going?"

"The Manchu Palace. Anna Wei is making us her number one dinner."

"What is this—a celebration?"

He raised his glass towards Jenny and the boy. "It's a sort of occasion. You look better than I've seen you in years."

"Thanks to Jenny—and you."

"All part of the service, ma'am."

"What about your plans?"

"Oh, they're coming along. I'll tell you later."

"Sounds mysterious."

"No mystery. It's a long story, easier to tell over a meal. How's your work?"

"Still plenty of it—but it's simpler to handle now. I owe you an apology for the other night. I was rattled and unhappy. I had no right to say the things I did."

"I didn't hear them."

"Next time I'll shout! I'm a woman who demands to be heard."

"Tonight, Martha Gilman, you're going to listen— and if you talk at all, there must be honey on your lips. A promise?"

"I'll try."

"Drink up. Say good night to the family and let's go!"

As they drove through the soft night, she sat, relaxed, eyes closed against the glare of oncoming lights, talking in musing desultory phrases, so alien to her normal fashion that she seemed like another woman.

". . . A funny week altogether. . . . That Jenny, she looked like a nothing, a dumpling; but in one day she took over my life. You don't think about it, until you see it in close-up. . . . It takes guts for a girl to bear a

child without a father. . . . I tried to fight with her, but
she faced me down. . . . She wasn't a waif, she said.
It's such an old-fashioned word! If she wasn't welcome, she'd leave. If she stayed, she had to work; and
she couldn't work if I kept getting under her feet. . . .
She made me laugh. And when I saw her with Mark
she made me cry. . . . When Mark's father died, I
swore I'd never cry for anyone or anything again. . . .
I hope she stays. It would be good for Mark to have
another child in the house. . . . Me too, I guess. . . .
I was beginning to feel like the Dragon Lady; but I
couldn't help myself. I didn't know how to. . . . You've
been a good friend, Gunnar, and I've never once said
a real thank you. . . ."

"I'm glad you can cry." Gunnar Thorkild mocked
her gently. "But dry your eyes and powder your nose.
Anna Wei is very critical of my women, and tonight
I'd like to prove I have good taste."

The alcove was dim and private. Anna Wei's dinner
was long and leisurely, and by the end of it he had
told Martha everything about the impending voyage
—except his own fears for its outcome. She kept her
promise. She listened and said very little until he was
talked out. Then she told him, in quiet, formal words,
that she was pleased for him, and wished him the best
of all good luck, and that she would miss him when
he was gone. She raised her glass and made a toast to
the voyage. Then they sat over the last of the wine,
each waiting for the other to speak.

Finally Martha Gilman said, "It's a crazy thought.
But I wish I was coming with you."

"You could."

"I couldn't and you know it. There's Mark and now
there's Jenny. And I've spent four years building a
business that keeps us in reasonable comfort. If there

were only me, I'd toss it away tomorrow. But I can't, and that's the end of it."

"You're frowning again, Martha. I like you better when you smile."

"That better?"

"Much. Look at me!"

"I'm looking."

"Now be quiet and listen!"

"I'm listening."

"This isn't party talk and wouldn't it be wonderful if . . . This is truth, Martha. If you want to come on this voyage, I'll take you. I'll take Mark and Jenny too. The places are mine to dispose of—so the offer's clear and open. When we come back I'll stake you to a new start in business. If we don't come back—and I'll read you all the risks and possibilities—then all I can say is, I'll share what happens with you, good and bad. . . ."

She gaped at him in utter disbelief. She shook her head slowly from side to side as if to clear it of mists and noises. Then she began to laugh, softly and uncontrollably.

"My God! . . . I just don't believe it!"

"I told you—it's the truth."

"But why? Why should you of all people saddle yourself with a widow, an eleven-year-old boy, and a pregnant girl? It's—it's madness!"

"All the rest of it could be madness too—the old gods, the island of the navigators, Magnusson's dream of finding a new land before he dies, me the inheritor of the *mana*. . . . But just suppose it isn't, eh? Suppose we make our landfall and find the last new place on the planet? I'm carrying a whole future with me—a woman, a boy, a girl with tomorrow in her womb. . . . They travelled like that in olden times. The migrant peoples do it still—with plants and livestock and children. . . . Even without you, my sweet, there'll be a whole tribe aboard the *Frigate Bird*. Why not join it? Why not give the boy an adventure he'll remember all his life? Why not let the girl have a cherishing she'd never get in any city midden?"

"She may not want to come."

"Ask her. The question is, do you want to come?"

"Why me? Why not any of your other women?"

"Because you're a good artist and a good cartographer and I need someone to keep my records. Is that reason enough?"

"No. There are other artists better, cheaper and childless."

"Give me another reason then."

"It's a long voyage. You need a mistress."

"There are others, cheaper and childless."

"You're a bastard."

He laughed and clamped his big hands on her wrists, holding them hard against the tabletop.

"Don't let's play games with each other, Martha. For whatever it may mean, you and Mark are the nearest I've got to family—and I'm not talking about a small selfish cellule, but the big, neighbourly, loving and quarrelling thing, where all doors are open and everyone's fingers are in the *poi* bowl. I know it isn't exclusive enough or possessive enough for some— maybe it isn't for you—but it's all I know, the only situation in which I'm comfortable and happy. . . . It isn't something I've dreamed up for you. I've said the same to Magnusson. It's very simple."

"Is it, Gunnar?"

"You asked for reasons. We gave already. What more do you want?"

"You could say you loved me."

"I could—and then you'd want to know how much and why and what's the difference between you and the other women and what do I want to do about it? ... And I won't know what to say."

"Because you're scared?"

"No! Because there's two of me. One is going back to the ancestors—and it's a long, dark journey and he can't answer to anyone for what may happen on the way. The other me is here, with all the girls for playmates and no woman to hold and call his own. For what it's worth—and it may not be very much— you're the nearest and the dearest."

"And you've never once invited me to sleep with you."

"Would you have said yes?"

"I'm not sure. I'd probably have used you like a fetish doll and stuck pins all over you."

"You may feel like that tomorrow."

"I know. I've been so screwed up for so long—it's hard to break the habit. I nag at Mark, I snap on the telephone, I lay little traps for men to walk into and then wonder why I'm making the living pay for the dead."

"I'm offering you the oldest cure in the world—a long sea voyage."

"Let me think about it, talk to Mark and Jenny."

"I can't give you too long. If you're not coming, I'll have to choose others."

"When do you want to know?"

"Tomorrow night. I'm giving a party at my place. If you're joining the *Frigate Bird,* be there, all three of you. If you decide against it, there's no harm done, and we'll still be friends. . . . Well, I promised you an early night. . . ."

"I think I'd like a nightcap somewhere."

"Sure. Where would you like to go? The Barefoot Bar?"

"Why not your place?"

"Because if you weren't so screwed up, Mrs. Gilman, you'd know there was no charge for family. Some other time, eh?"

"Thank you, Mr. Thorkild. Thank you very, very much!"

On the night of the party Carl Magnusson arrived an hour before the other guests. He had things to talk about, he said, and besides, he hated to barge in on a whole crowd of people. He needed to take them slowly, one by one. Molly Kaapu and Dulcie were already there, laying out food and liquor, and there was a moment's comedy when Molly stood staring at the visitor and then burst into a long, wheezing chuckle.

"Now look at him! Little Carlie! My, my, how he's grown! Don't you remember me, Carl Magnusson? I used to work at your place when you was half grown and you used to chase me round the house!"

Magnusson stared at her in disbelief and then he too burst into laughter. "My God! Molly Kaapu! What the hell are you doing here?"

"I work for the man. And this here's Dulcie, my daughter. Just as well I could run fast or she might have been yours!"

The encounter put the old man in a good humour. He cast an approving eye over the room and its furnishings and commented.

"You've got a pleasant place here, Thorkild."

"I like it."

"I hate mess and clutter."

"So do I."

"That's a good drink."

"Cheers!"

"These people coming tonight—they're your choice for the voyage?"

"Right."

"What happens if I don't like any of 'em?"

"You say why and we talk about it in private, afterwards."

"Fair enough. Do you want to tell me about them?"

"You've seen the student records. There are three outsiders you don't know about. I'd rather you meet them cold, and make your own judgment. Anything I said at this moment would sound like special pleading."

"Let's talk about the island."

"Sure."

"I've been studying your documents, and your source references, and making some guesses of my own. I'd like to check them with you. Have you got any charts of the Pacific?"

"Several. I'll bring them down."

"No, I'd rather not have anyone else know what we're discussing. Can we work upstairs?"

"Well . . . sure."

Thorkild led the way to his bedroom and held the door open for the old man to enter. Magnusson marched to the center of the floor and stood a long moment, surveying the sparse, cell-like chamber. He said soberly:

"So you live alone, eh?"

"Here, yes."

"And I'm intruding. I beg your pardon."

"You're a guest. My house is yours."

"Thank you. What charts have you got?"

"French Navy, U.S. Navy and a British Admiralty routing chart. That's the one that makes most sense for this discussion."

"Why?"

"Because it demonstrates how easy it would be to miss a small land mass."

He crossed to the farther wall and, from under a

pelmet, pulled down a canvas-backed chart of the Pacific Ocean. The superscription read 5128(6) June —Routeing Chart, South Pacific Ocean. The chart was a maze of lines, each of which indicated a shipping route and the distance in nautical miles: Suva to Panama, 6,323; Honolulu to Valparaiso, 5,912; Apia to Tahiti, 1,303. . . . The crisscross of routes made a variety of geometric shapes, small and large, across the surface of the map. Magnusson studied it for a few moments and then turned to Thorkild:

"Now show me where you think your island lies."

Thorkild picked up a pencil from the desk and laid the point of it on Papeete in the Society Islands.

"Start from there. Southest there is the route from Papeete to Wellington. Southeast, the route from Papeete to the Magellan Straits. Between those there's a big blank triangle where no routes are shown until you hit the line from Panama to Sydney . . . that line there running just south of Marotiri Island. Are you with me so far?"

"I'm with you," said Magnusson. "I'm waiting to hear the arguments."

"O.K. First argument—very general. A large blank space on the map, off the shipping and air routes. Second argument, more interesting. All the legends say the island lies beyond the path of A'a, the glowing one. That's Sirius, the dog star, whose orbit is about seventeen degrees south latitude. It lies also beyond the shining black path of the god Kanaloa, which is the Tropic of Capricorn—twenty-seven degrees south. Look at the center of the empty triangle. That's about thirty degrees south, so it fits the legend. Now . . ." Thorkild began to trace a series of lines on the chart. "These are some of the known routes of the island navigators. All of them go through that empty triangle. . . ."

"So why no record of colonization or settlement?"

"Wrong question, Mr. Magnusson. There is a record—but in oral legend, because the Polynesians had no system of writing. What's missing is an account of its life or its people. But the same applies to Pitcairn. When Fletcher Christan arrived there with his mutineers, they found no inhabitants but many relics of an older occupation . . ." He broke off and faced Magnusson with a quizzical challenge. "You said you had some conclusions of your own. How do they match with mine?"

"Near enough to make me believe our voyage is worthwhile."

"Good! That's one thing we won't be quarrelling about."

Magnusson gave him a sharp sidelong look. "And why should we quarrel at all, Mr. Thorkild?"

"We shouldn't, but we're the sort of men who will. We might as well get as many contentious matters as possible out of the way before we start."

"Can you think of any at this moment?"

"Specifically no, but let's try a few subjects. If I understood you correctly, it would be your intention to annex this island to the United States, occupy it, and claim land rights to ourselves."

"Right. And unless some *kapu* there intervenes, you would go along with that?"

"Yes. I've chosen the people to that end, young ones, men and women who I believe would be open to a new life and capable of continuing it if they were left alone."

"Colonists in fact?"

"But not takers. If this place is already occupied by an indigenous people, we claim no rights at all over them, because we will have none."

"I think," said Magnusson slowly, "I think I'd like another drink while I take that under advisement."

When Thorkild came back with the drink, he found Magnusson sprawled in the chair, reading one of the manuscript volumes of his lectures. Magnusson took the glass, absently mumbled a word of thanks and went on reading. After a while he looked up and said:

"Is this stuff all original?"

"Unless it's marked otherwise, yes."

"This piece for instance." He turned back to the manuscript and began reading. ". . . The oceanic horizon is vast. The island habitat is small. Its frontier is the outer reef. The community is confined and in-bred. Its activities are traditional, and repetitive, modulated to the tones of the weather and the rhythm of the ocean. Prowess is acclaimed—the strong swimmer, the clever fisherman, the chanter or the skillful navigator. But there is no question of attainment, as continental man, metropolitan man understands the term. What is there to attain? Rank comes by birth. Privilege belongs only to the high-born. And what is there to possess, when what is grown or caught is consumed at the next meal? Of course, if you intrude into this system new and alien elements, the changes are swift and sometimes catastrophic. . . ." Magnusson broke off the reading. "I like that, Thorkild. I begin to like you too. I'll buy your argument. We don't intrude where we have no rights."

"Thanks."

"I've thought about the crew question. Two of my boys have wives. I've told them they can bring them, provided they work. The other two are only interested in each other. There's a minor problem though. I've lost my cook. He'll sign on for a cruise, not for a long voyage."

"Molly Kaapu's a good cook."

"She's a rowdy old bawd and she takes up a lot of room. Still, she'd be easier to live with than a stranger. Let me see what I can find first. If no one better turns up, you can offer her the job." He grinned with impish amusement. "It looks as if you'll get your wish, Thorkild. We'll soon be a bloody Noah's ark! Still, it'll make a change from some of the bores I've carried."

Wary though he was, Thorkild could not refuse the old man a salute for his skill. He was like an expert fisherman, who let the marlin run, and then brought him up, short and surprised, with the barb snagged deeper in his jaw. There was no malice in the game. It was a conscious art, a duellist's exercise, precise, determined, self-satisfying and quite ruthless.

For the party, therefore, Thorkild had devised his own tactic, simple and elementary. He knew from experience that the impact of young animals, the thrust of personalities eager to affirm themselves, was strong and often disconcerting. He would let Magnusson take the full brunt of it, translate for himself the gestures and the jargon, wait out the silences, answer the challenges, blunt or subtle, from the young bulls and their attendant females. He himself would intervene only to present the drinks and draw off the garrulous to let the quiet ones speak. Only for Martha Gilman and Jenny would he stand as advocate, and then plead if he had to, softly but tenaciously. In the end, Magnusson must tire first. He was maimed and ageing. He was on strange tribal ground. The newness and the numbers were against him. The students themselves were an exotic group with some formidable attainments.

There was Franz Harsanyi, son of Hungarian immigrants, a gangling, shock-haired youth with pebble spectacles, who was working on a comparative study of the sixty and more Polynesian dialects. There was Adam Briggs, a Negro from Alabama, studying under the G.I. Bill of Rights, who had—for some secret reason—interested himself in land rights and their transmission by verbal memory among the archipelagoes.

There was Hernan Castillo, part Malay, part Spanish, whose father brewed beer in Manila. He was a low-level student but a beautiful craftsman who had made, with his own hands, a collection of miniature island seacraft, perfect to the last detail. Last of the male contingent was Simon Cohen, who looked like a ragpicker and was in fact an ardent musicologist, a scavenger of chants and songs and dances, whose work had earned him a Unesco grant.

The three women made an equally incongruous group: Monica O'Grady, a sad-eyed, horse-faced woman from San Francisco, with a bawdy tongue and a passion for prehistoric pottery and stone artifacts; Yoko Nagamuna, a doll-like Okinawan who studied nutrition and the marriage market with equal fervour; and for a final surprise, Ellen Ching, half Chinese, half Hawaiian, who danced hulas for the tourists to pay for her studies in the botany of the Pacific.

Some of them were friends. None of them, so far as he knew, were lovers. Each of them had a chameleon talent of conformity and contradiction. All of them had the quality he prized, a continuing curiosity, a zest and enjoyment of the things they did. How they would react under the stress of enforced companionship and the discomforts of sea travel he did not know. In an odd fashion he wanted to rely on Magnusson's judgment of them, yet could not and would not concede his right to make it.

Before the party was an hour old, he was forced to admit that Carl Magnusson was a master of social strat-

egy. In spite of his infirmity, he moved freely round
the group, never fumbling a name or a personal detail. He smiled, was gracious, never condescended,
was always interested and ready with a joke to take
the weight off the talk. By the time the meal was
served he was perched on the divan like a satrap,
with Mark Gilman curled up beside him, and Jenny
squatting at his feet, feeding him morsels from her
plate, while he engaged the whole company in a running debate on the geopolitics of the Pacific Basin. It
was a conductor's triumph and, on the stroke of
eleven, he finished it with a flourish. He held up his
hand for silence and announced, with a laugh of dep-
recation:

"I'm an old man and I've got to get to bed. I guess
we've all been on trial here tonight—me as well as
you. So let's wrap it up quickly. I'll be very happy to
have all of you aboard the *Frigate Bird*. But you've
got to feel happy to come. So let's have a show of
hands. Who's ready to sign on?"

Every hand was raised. Magnusson grinned and
nodded approval. Then he went on: . .

"Good! Now let's settle the protocol once and for all.
A ship's a dictatorship. There's only one boss. That's
me. Professor Thorkild's your teacher, but he's my
mate. He'll try to turn you men into seamen, and I'm
sure you women know enough about housekeeping to
run a clean and tidy ship. You'll need valid passports
and visas for French, British and New Zealand Pacific
territories. You'll need all the normal shots and a doctor's certificate that you're free from any communica-
ble disease. Which reminds me . . . Your private
relationships are not my concern; but if you're drunk
on board or catch clap ashore, you're flown home
from the next port of call. Any questions? . . . Good!
We sail in two weeks. I hope I'll learn something

from you all. Thanks for your company. Stay and finish your party. If you wouldn't mind driving me home, Professor . . . ?"

They gave him a small affectionate ovation and he went out with handshakes for the men and kisses for the women, leaving behind him an aura of patriarchal benevolence. As Thorkild drove him through the city he was cheerful and complimentary.

"That was a good party, Thorkild."

"I'm glad you enjoyed it."

"They're an intelligent group—much brighter than we were at their age."

"I guess they have to be."

"Interesting to see how they'll pair off."

"Yes."

"That young girl, Jenny; is it your child she's carrying?"

"No."

"I wouldn't mind if it were."

"It's not."

"That makes you a kind man, and Mrs. Gilman an understanding woman."

"It wasn't a big thing. The girl was adrift. Martha and I are old friends."

"She's very fond of you."

"It's mutual."

"Going to marry her?"

"No."

"You could do a lot worse."

"I know."

"I was just thinking, we'll have a real multiracial society on board. Curious in a way."

"Why curious? Hawaii's a melting pot, and it functions comfortably with fewer tensions than New York."

"I wasn't suggesting it wouldn't work. I was just

interested in the genetics. After all, it was you who raised the question. What did you call it?—'some shape of family.' That must have been in your mind when you selected your students. Otherwise why bring a pregnant girl on board? Not that I mind. On the contrary. I'm debarred from sexual commerce. They tell me I'm likely to die in the middle of it—which would be pleasant for me but not for the woman. But I haven't lost interest in the matter."

"You've been very generous," said Gunnar Thorkild awkwardly. "There's no way I can repay you. I'd like you to know I'm deeply grateful."

"Don't bend to me, man! I'm borrowing from you too, and from those kids back there. Youth and a new horizon—something I can't buy! I'm jealous of you, Thorkild. Never forget that!"

"Why should you be jealous?"

"Because I'm a perverse old son of a bitch who can't get laid and whose time's running out. If you give me half a chance I'll rub your nose in the dirt."

"I'll keep it in mind," said Thorkild amiably. "When do you want me to meet your guests?"

"Oh hell! I'd forgotten to mention that. Sally Anderton can't get here until the day before we sail. Gabe Greenaway and Mildred have dropped out. Gabe's found a new girl apparently; and Mildred's off to Europe to get him out of her system. So I've made a little deal with the U.S. Navy. They're lending us some rather special communication equipment and a trained officer to run it. . . . He'll have no authority, of course."

"He won't need it. He'll have the Commander-in-Chief, Pacific, for a godfather."

"You don't like the idea?" Magnusson was surprised as a virgin hearing her first vulgar word.

"I think it stinks," said Gunnar Thorkild curtly.

"Why not go the whole hog and call in the Marines?"

When the last of his guests had gone, and the house was clean and silent, he stripped and bathed and locked himself in the upper room. From the drawer of his desk he took a sandalwood box in which, wrapped in cotton wool, lay a long wedge of polished obsidian. It was the most precious thing he owned, a gift from his grandfather, the blade of the stone adze with which Kaloni the Navigator had built his first canoe.

The blade was a sacred thing. On the night before building began, the blade was put to sleep in a holy place where Tane the land god would infuse it with his *mana*. In the morning it was dipped in the sea to waken it and set the *mana* working. Before the adze was laid to a tree Tane's permisson must be asked. When the axe grew hot with labour it was cooled in the sap of a banana plant. Thus the wood and the tool and the man and the god were all at one and the *mana* would pass to the boat that was built upon the land to ride upon the sea.

Gunnar Thorkild took the blade in his hands, sat cross-legged on the floor, closed his eyes and waited for the *mana* to flow into him. It was a quiet thing and very simple. The stone warmed in his hand so that it seemed part of his body. The air in the soundless room wavered into the rhythm of a far-off chanting. The syllables made themselves heard, clear and comforting as nursery rhymes to a child.

> "Hold my hands as I steer,
>   Hold the hands that ply
> The high-rising, low-sweeping paddles.
> The sky goes away,

All the time;
But the power comes to meet us,
All the time.
This is the way
No man has taken,
This is the sacred way
Of all the high ancestors.
This is the way
Of those before
And those who follow
Kaloni Kienga,
The understanding one,
The scanner of birds and clouds,
Who looks into the eyes of night,
And sees the land of tomorrow."

When the chant died away, he sat a long time, rested and tranquil. Then he rose, kissed the stone and laid it back in the box. When he sailed, the box and the stone and all the memories that it held would sail with him. He closed the box and put it back in the drawer and said in the old language, "Good night, Grandfather. I will see you soon." He knew that, even as he spoke them, his grandfather would hear the words and would rest quietly on their promise.

THREE

I T WAS THE TIME HE LOVED: THE LONG, QUIET swing of the middle watch, with the wind fair abeam, the vessel loping comfortably across the swell, the wake a runnel of phosphorescence, the stars so low that he could reach up and pluck them like silver fruit.

They were reaching southeast, across the trades and the north equatorial current into the doldrums, where the winds dropped and the counter-current ran eastward and they would churn along under motor until they picked up the southeast winds and began beating down to the Marquesas. It was the traditional route of his ancestors when they made the passage from Nuku Hiva to Hawaii, and home again, sailing northward towards the zenith of Arcturus and south towards the rising of Sirius.

They had sailed in a craft, miraculous in its beauty, the *Va'a Hou'ua,* a great double-hulled canoe whose sternposts were carved into long, graceful sweeps, and whose sail was like the wing of a seabird. When the wind dropped, they paddled, chanting to the sea god to send them wind, and rain to fill the water gourds. They carried the fruits of the land, taro and coconut and breadfruit paste and bananas. They brought figs and fowl and little dogs which had no bark, and ate vegetables, and which could be eaten in their turn. They fished the sea with sennit lines and hooks made of clam shell, and dried their catch by hanging it to the mast.

Why had they travelled so far and at such perils? The answers handed down were always embroidered with legend, but the facts were fundamental: a quarrel among the clans, a shortage of food, a sudden plague which decimated a small island and left it accursed. . . .

From his place at the wheel, Gunnar Thorkild looked down across the canted deck where the Kauai men and their wives sat singing softly to Simon Cohen's guitar. On the foredeck, braced against the stays like some giant figure out of a legendary past, Adam Briggs, the dark man from Alabama, kept watch for passing ships. They could relax tonight. The swell was regular, the wind was light, but steady. The *Frigate Bird* was sea-kindly. The cadence of the music was like the cadence of the old life, languid, monotonous, infinitely soothing.

The voyage had begun well. Magnusson's welcome to his motley contingent had been cordial; but he had left no doubt about his own command, or the kind of ship he ran. On every bunk there were laid three sets of uniforms, provided at his expense, white cotton T-shirts, white shorts for the men, blouses and skirts for the women. With the clothing was a formal request that uniforms be worn on entering and leaving harbour and at the evening meal. There was a printed

roster of watches and other sea duties, a note about
the conservation of fresh water, the care of the ship's
plumbing, the disposal of waste, and precautions
against sunburn and heat exhaustion. The ship's officers were listed as Carl Magnusson, captain: Gunnar
Thorkild, mate; Peter André Lorillard, communications; Sally Anderton, medical; Martha Gilman, writer
to the captain; the bosun was Charles Kamakau. The
captain requested that his officers meet him each evening for drinks at seven and dinner at eight, weather
and sea duties permitting. It was old-style, and formal,
but shrewd management as well. The young ones had
made jokes about it at first; but after four days at sea,
they had settled to the routine and were open in their
praise of the old man and his methods.

The newcomers were a curious pair. Sally Anderton
was a tall, statuesque woman in her middle thirties,
handsome rather than beautiful, who seemed to survey the world with good-humoured irony. In the day-
time, Magnusson monopolized her; and she, for her
part, was clearly the captain's consort, a little withdrawn from the rest of the company, careful to raise
no jealousies. Peter André Lorillard, Lieutenant, U.S.
Navy, was Old South, agreeable but formal, with a
ready smile, a nicely calculated deference and an un-
shakable faith in the civilizing mission of the Service.
Martha Gilman found him attractive. Thorkild found
him more than a little of a bore and was vaguely irri-
tated by his arch secrecy about what he called his
"boxes of tricks."

It was too early yet to see how the community
would shape itself. Some were still queasy with motion sickness. The languor of the sea had settled on
them all, and their attention was dispersed over a
huge, empty horizon where a cruising shark or a
school of porpoise provided the only focus of interest.
Still, there were changes. Magnusson had assumed a

grandfatherly interest in the boy, Mark, and was teaching him the rudiments of helmsmanship and navigation. Franz Harsanyi, the linguist, and Cohen, the music man, had made friends with the crewmen from Kauai. Yoko Nagamuna was setting her cap at Hernan Castillo, the Filipino. Adam Briggs had developed a consuming passion for the arts of seamanship and a touching solicitude for Jenny, who seemed perfectly happy to spend her days peeling potatoes and slicing vegetables for the galley.

For Thorkild himself it was the season of seadreaming. There was nothing to plan, nothing to decide. He had only to run the ship and sail her and open his mind and wait for his past to flow into him and his future to declare itself through the mouth of Kaloni Kienga the Navigator.

Sally Anderton came up the companionway carrying two cups of coffee and a plate of sandwiches. It was the first night she had appeared after midnight and Thorkild was mildly surprised at the visit. She explained it without embarrassment:

"Carl's asleep. I was restless. I thought I'd make supper for the helmsman."

"Thanks for the thought."

"Do you mind if I sit with you awhile?"

"Please. It's a long watch."

"What's the song they're singing?"

"It's a very old one. I think it comes originally from Puka-puka. It starts, *'Ke Kave 'u i toku panga.* . . . I shall sleep on a pandanus mat outside her father's house. . . . Thus we promise ourselves to each other, my special woman and I.' Old island custom signifying betrothal."

"That's beautiful. . . Like the Bible. . . . 'I sleep but my heart watches.' Did you spread your mat too?"

"No." Thorkild gave her a boyish self-conscious

grin. "I played with the unmarried, which was fun, but something different."

She laughed then and quoted lightly:

" 'What was left of soul, I wonder, when the kissing had to stop? . . .' "

"So far it hasn't."

"Bully for you. . . . Would you like me to take the wheel while you have your coffee? I know what to do."

"Sure. . . . The course is one three five."

"One three five. Aye-aye, sir!"

As he ate and drank, he watched her and approved what he saw: the easy stance, the steady hands, not fussing with the wheel but nursing it quietly, eyes intent on the luff of the sail and the set of the waves under the bow. She was wearing a long cotton muumuu, green and gold, and her hair was tied back with a green ribbon. She was fresh as if she had just stepped out of a bath and her perfume was like lemon flowers, faint and astringent. She was silent for a space and then apropos of nothing at all she said:

"I'm worried about Carl."

"Why?"

"I advised him against this trip; but he insisted on making it. His blood pressure's very high. If he has another incident, on board, it could be the end of him."

"Perhaps that's the way he wants to go."

"Perhaps. . . . What would happen if he died at sea?"

"I'd enter it in the log, you'd sign a certificate. We'd bury him overside."

"And you'd assume command?"

"Right. . . ."

"That's comforting."

"It's the way of the sea."

"I suppose you wonder what we mean to each other, Carl and I."

"It's none of my business."

"He thought he was in love with me once. After his third wife divorced him he asked me to marry him."

"Obviously you didn't."

"Not so obviously. We were lovers for a while, but he's a very dominating man, and I'm not made for the kind of possessive relationship he wanted. We parted but remained good friends. I treated him during his illness. When this trip was mooted he offered me a year's earnings to come and hold his hand; I was due for a long vacation. It meant I could put in a good locum. So, here I am . . . . Problem is, Carl still thinks I can put the clock back for him. I can't. No one can."

"What about his wife?"

"His wife is a cool, intelligent lady, who does everything a good wife could be expected to do, and stands to inherit ten million dollars."

"And you never married?"

"Oh yes. I married a boy who graduated with me from medical school. It turned out he had a passion for football players."

"That's tough."

"It happens. One recovers. From what I hear you have no interest in football. . . ."

"None at all, madam."

"But you sleep alone and always take the middle watch."

"The middle watch is the mate's job. You need a good man on the bridge if the rest of the ship is to sleep quietly."

"And you're a good man, Gunnar Thorkild?"

"I'm the son of a sea captain, the grandson of a great navigator."

"You're very proud of that, aren't you?"

"Yes, I am. . . . You're letting her head fall off. Bring her up."

"Yes, sir. One three five."

"And steady as she goes."

They both laughed then and the momentary tension relaxed. Thorkild reached across and snapped out the binnacle light.

"Steer by the stars for a while. That's Procyon, the little dog, halfway up the forestay. Hold on him for a while. He's a little east of our course, but we'll make up some leeway while you're on him."

"You've told me why you take the middle watch. You haven't told me why you sleep alone."

"I'm a guest on another man's ship. I'm responsible for the safety and discipline of a mixed bag of people, most of them with no sea experience at all. I can't afford to play hole-and-corner love games."

"You're the damnedest academic I've ever met!"

"I stopped being an academic the day I walked on board the *Frigate Bird*."

"I believe you. I was just wondering how Martha Gilman feels about your sea change."

"I've got no claims on Martha Gilman."

"If you have you'd better press them. Our friend Lorillard is mighty interested. And she's not blind to his douce southern charm."

"Why don't you stick to your physic bottles, Doctor?"

"You've never had to fight for a woman in your life, have you?"

"No. And I've never wanted to."

"Oy-oy! Aren't you the smug one, Mr. Thorkild!"

"You're shivering. There's a chill in that wind. If you want to stay topside, go and put on a wrap."

"I'm not cold, I promise."

"Do as you're told, like a good girl. We can't have the doctor going down with the grippe. . . . Oh, and while you're below, how about making more coffee for Briggs and the rest of the deck watch?"

"I thought they made their own in the forepeak galley."

"They do. But they might appreciate a thought from Lady Bountiful. . . . If you want to join the middle watch you have to pay for the privilege. On your way, woman!"

She went, with a laugh and a toss of her ribboned hair, but her perfume lingered and he wondered what kind of wounds Sally Anderton nursed in her own night watches, and whether she was content to sit holding the hand of an old pirate with the clocks set against him.

Two days later, as they were running down into the doldrums, he had his first real quarrel with Magnusson.

He should have been prepared for it. He had been at sea long enough to know that doldrum weather was tetchy and unpropitious. The wind, the steady, cheering wind of the northeast trades, had fallen away to light and fickle airs. The ground swell was long and greasy. The decks were like oven plates and had to be hosed every hour to make them tolerable to the feet. The *Frigate Bird* was under motor, with only steadying canvas to damp the roll; and the smell of diesel wafted across the deck from her exhausts.

Awnings were spread across the main boom, and, as he made his afternoon round, Thorkild handed out salt tablets and issued new warnings to the unwary about the dangers of sunburn and heat exhaustion. At four in the afternoon, when the dogwatch took over, he was summoned for a conference with Magnusson and Peter André Lorillard.

Magnusson's cabin was air-conditioned, and after the swelter of the open deck, the cool was grateful. Lorillard's mint juleps were made with an expert hand. Magnusson was relaxed and cordial, and the discussion began in a desultory, informal fashion, with no hint of danger at all.

"Well, gentlemen, it's been a pleasant run, so far. Everything's shaken down nicely. Anything to report from your watch, Thorkild?"

"No. We're on course and on time. The engine room's O.K. We've filled the batteries and they're charging evenly. We're making almost enough water for daily consumption. Oil pressures are steady."

"Let's talk about schedules then. Today's Wednesday. We're making twelve knots under motor. So Saturday morning we're in Nuku Hiva. We're pratiqued into French Territory. We take on fuel, water and fresh food. From Nuku Hiva it's a twelve-hour run down to Hiva Oa, where we pick up your grandfather. Then it's Papeete, which is our real starting point for the enterprise and our last port for bunkering and topping up supplies. After that we're on our own, until we find our landfall . . . or we break off the expedition and head for home. So . . . let's talk about what happens from Hiva Oa onward. . . . You first, Thorkild. Your grandfather will come on board. He will tell you where he wants to go . . ."

"Let's be clear." Thorkild cut him off in mid-speech. "What my grandfather tells me, and how he tells it, will be quite different from what you imagine. He will not lay a course, as we do and tell the helmsman to sail it. He is a *kapu* man, dealing with a secret thing, a privileged knowledge. He will take the wheel and set his own course. When he tires he will call me, and show me where to steer until he wakes. He will explain nothing, give no reasons. We have to trust him.

He has to know that we trust him. . . . You talk about going to Papeete. He may not choose to take that route. We cannot, we must not interfere."

There was a moment's silence before Lorillard interposed:

"With great respect, Professor. It's a lot of ship and a lot of people to trust to an old man."

"It's the deal I made," said Magnusson calmly. "It's the deal I'll stand on. However, we do have certain insurances. We have on our navigational aids, radio, radar, direction finders, the log and our daily sun-sights. While the professor and his grandfather are sailing their course, you, Lorillard, and I will be plotting it on our charts. We won't interfere, but we won't be blind either. . . . Fair enough for you, Thorkild?"

"Fair enough."

"Which brings me to Mr. Lorillard here and what he'll be doing for us, and for the Navy. He's got all his boxes of tricks set up, and he's ready to start work. First, he'll work a daily, coded, radio schedule with the Navy; he'll be reporting our positions, sightings of French naval units, and more especially on the incidence of radioactive atmospheres in the areas of the Tuamotus and the Societies. Second, he's brought some very sophisticated gadgets in the shape of marker buoys which emit a radio signal over a long range. When your grandfather leaves us to make the last leg of his voyage, alone, we want you to persuade him to carry one of these markers, and drop others along his course. That way, both we and, when the time comes, the Navy can home on them. Even if your grandfather were lost at sea, we'd have his last position. . . ."

"I'd like to know"—Thorkild was ominously calm —"why the Navy was prepared to involve itself with expensive hardware and a ranking specialist like Lieutenant Lorillard."

"Let me read you something." Magnusson leaned back in his chair, pulled a volume from the bookshelves and opened it at a marked page. "This is Hall on International Law: 'A state may acquire territory through a unilateral act of its own, by occupation, by cession consequent upon contract with another state or with a community or single owner or by gift, by prescription through the operation of time, or by accretion through the operation of nature. . . .' Now!" He closed the book with a snap and set it down on the table. "That's a nice clear definition of what we're going to do. We're sailing in my ship, under my command, to find and take possession of an island, which we shall occupy, and whose sovereignty we shall cede by contract to the United States of America, in the person of Lieutenant Lorillard here. In return for that promise of cession by contract, the Navy will aid, comfort and protect us on our voyage and guarantee our safe possession of such lands and territories as we may chance to find. Objections?"

"Plenty!" Thorkild slammed his fist down on the table. "But I'll make them to you, in private."

"You'll make them now." Magnusson was cold as a hanging judge. "Before a witness."

"Let's have it in writing then, by Christ!"

"If you want."

"Do you write shorthand, Mr. Lorillard?"

"No. I've got a tape recorder. We could record the talk and certify a typescript later."

"Would you get it, please?"

When he had gone, Magnusson held out his glass to Thorkild.

"Would you mind making me another drink? You look as though you could use one yourself."

"The same?"

"No. Bourbon on the rocks. . . . You're making a big mistake, Thorkild."

"You've already made yours."

"Have I? Let's wait till we get it down on the record. And by the way, let's be clear that this is the record, Thorkild; and I'll hold you to every goddam word of it, right up to the Supreme Court!"

Lieutenant Lorillard came back with the recorder and loaded it with a cassette.

"Ready when you are, gentlemen."

Thorkild looked at Magnusson. "Do you want to start?"

"No. It's your case, Thorkild. You make it. I'll cross-examine as we go along."

Lorillard switched on the recorder. Thorkild waited a moment and then began:

"The matters under discussion on this tape were transacted during the month of June of this year between Carl Magnusson and Gunnar Thorkild of Honolulu in the State of Hawaii. There is no contention as to date, only as to substance and interpretation. Do you agree that, Mr. Magnusson?"

"Yes."

"I, Gunnar Thorkild, approached Carl Magnusson to charter his vessel, the *Frigate Bird,* for a voyage to the South Pacific to confirm the existence of an island, called in legend the island of the Trade Winds or the Island of the Navigators. Mr. Magnusson refused to charter the vessel but agreed to accept me and guests nominated by me and to defray the costs of the voyage. It was agreed that, for political reasons, the voyage should be called a study cruise, but its original intent remained the same. Correct?"

"Correct."

"Mr. Magnusson raised the question of the annexation and colonization of the island, if we should find it.

He suggested that we should annex the island to the United States while claiming land rights to ourselves. I agreed this with the proviso that no attempt at annexation or colonization should be made if the island were occupied by an indigenous population. Mr. Magnusson accepted this. I reserved also my right to withdraw from the enterprise if it should appear that I were infringing upon any *kapu*, affecting my grandfather or his people, who are also mine. Mr. Magnusson reserved his right to continue the enterprise and to use, to this end, any knowledge which he had acquired, directly or by deduction, from me or my grandfather."

"Correct. Now will you agree that our arrangement involved a partnership in which I would supply the vessel and the physical resources of the voyage, while you would provide the knowledge and information which were the basis of the expedition? Will you agree also that you disposed to me certain rights of publication and exploitation of information arising out of the voyage, and that you would share in the rewards, if any?"

"Yes."

"You also agreed that I should captain the vessel, and that you would serve as mate?"

"Yes."

"Thereby giving me sole responsibility under maritime law for the safety of the vessel and the souls who travelled in her?"

"Yes."

"Thank you, Professor Thorkild. Go on, please."

"Four days out from Honolulu. You, Mr. Magnusson, announced to me that you had made an arrangement with the U.S. Navy, whereby certain equipment was installed on board and an officer to run the equipment. You further informed me that you had made, unilaterally, a deal whereby the U.S. Navy would receive, in the name of the United States, a contract of cession of sovereignty over any new land which we might discover."

"Correction. I informed you before our departure that I had asked the Navy to supply personnel and equipment."

"And I protested that."

"You protested but did not object it."

"Agreed. But I had no idea, then, of the scope of the activity proposed."

"Did you ask for details?"

"No."

"Now that you have heard them, would you not say that they offer an additional safeguard to the ship and the passengers?"

"They could, yes."

"And that such safeguards are the captain's normal responsibility?"

"Yes."

"As to the act of cession, we had already agreed this, subject to your original reservation."

"Yes. But I ask now, in the presence of the naval representative, was my original reservation communicated to the Navy?"

"It was."

"Do you confirm that, Lieutenant Lorillard?"

"I'm sorry, sir. I'm a junior officer under orders of secondment. I have no knowledge of upper echelon communications."

"So I ask you now, Mr. Magnusson, did the Navy agree my reservation?"

"No. The Navy is a service, not a sovereign state. They supplied facilities on the basis of our intent to make a contract. The contract would still have to be ratified by the State Department."

"Which could act unilaterally and annex without contract?"

"It could, yes. I doubt it would."

"Therefore, Mr. Magnusson, I submit that you have acted without due consultation or regard for my rights as a partner, and have in fact placed those rights in jeopardy. I state now that I reserve my position and may in fact withdraw from the expedition."

"And I state, Professor Thorkild, that by the non-exercise of your rights you have passed the responsibility for their exercise to me. I further state that, should you withdraw before your rights have been actually infringed, I shall sue for recovery of the costs of this expedition, and for contingent loss and damage."

There was silence then. Lorillard switched off the recorder and looked from one to the other.

"Is there anything more, gentlemen?"

"Not from me," said Carl Magnusson.

"I'm finished." Thorkild stood up. "Do you want one of my girls to type it?"

"Martha Gilman will do it. No point in spreading our quarrel round the ship. I'm sorry, Thorkild, but I did warn you. I play rough when I'm pushed."

"Go play with yourself!" said Thorkild bitterly. "Life's too short for children's games!"

Lieutenant Peter André Lorillard said nothing at all. The Navy had taught him well. The silent ones got the stripes, and the talkers ended with a mouthful of bilge water.

That evening Thorkild absented himself from the dinner table. He scribbled a brief note of excuse to Magnusson, ate a sandwich with Molly Kaapu in the galley and returned to his cabin to read and rest until midnight. His anger had subsided. He had humour enough to know that he had allowed himself to be gulled into a trap. What troubled him was his own

confusion, his almost pathological sensitiveness to anything that touched his tribal relationship.

In all logic and legality, Magnusson was right. Any
territorial discovery must involve the sovereign state of
which one was a citizen. Every expedition, to the top
of Everest or the bottom of the sea, was a testing
ground for new equipment; and the custom of the
trade, the usages of patronage and sponsorship, pru-
dence itself, dictated a close cooperation with the services which controlled the funds and the gadgetry.

The roots of the dispute went much deeper. They
were tangled in his own psychic life, that shadowy
domain of dreams and memories and legends in which
his identity—if he had one—ultimately resided. It was
this domain which Magnusson had invaded and whose
confines he would continue to harry, until Gunnar
Thorkild could define and defend them adequately.
So far the definition had eluded him. For all his scholarship he lacked the words or the images to make it
clear even to himself. As he lay on his bunk, listening
to the throb of the engines, the creak of timbers, the
chatter of the wash along the skin of the hull, he felt
like a man groping through a fog, blind, half deaf,
choked with dank emanations.

Then, slowly, the fog solidified two shapes: two
men, very much alike, yet quite different, one from
the other. Both were old, both had reached that moment of life when death stood plain before them, not
beckoning but waiting, patient and inexorable, for
them to come forward to the encounter. Both were
committed to make the last passage by sea. Each
stretched out a hand to Gunnar Thorkild, inviting him
to join them in the final rite; but for each the rite was
different, and the pieties they demanded were in contradiction.

Carl Magnusson was rich, skeptical, proud, a taker

and a ruler. He had fought for power all his life. He had surrounded himself with its panoply. He would hold it, until it dropped from his dead hands. Even then, his testament would bind his heirs and assigns; his will would dominate their dispositions long after they had sealed him in the vault.

Kaloni Kienga would go out, naked, in a small boat, which he had built with his own hands. He would carry nothing but food for the last journey. He would leave nothing but a knowledge which he had received in trust from the high gods, and which he would pass on in trust to blood kin.

To each of them Gunnar Thorkild was bound: to Magnusson by gift and largesse, which must be repaid; to Kaloni Kienga by blood and the *mana* that flowed with the blood. But how to reconcile the duties, when Magnusson, with his politics and his perversities, intruded into a spiritual relationship which he did not understand at all? Conclusion for Professor Thorkild, scholar and ethnographer: how the devil can he understand it if no one has the grace or the time to explain it. . . ?

There was a knock on his door and Martha Gilman came in with a handful of typescript. She was unhappy and abrupt.

"Mr. Magnusson asks you to read and sign these. One copy for him, one for you."

"Leave them. I'll do it later."

"Is this why you didn't show up for dinner tonight?"

"Part of the reason, yes."

"Gunnar, I'm ashamed of you."

"Martha, mind your own damn business!"

"This is my business. You invited us on this trip. Magnusson accepted the three of us without question. He couldn't have been more generous. He's so kind to

Mark. And you . . . you start this sordid little feud that can poison the whole ship."

"Did Magnusson say that?"

"Of course not! Whatever else he is, he's a gentleman. But Peter Lorillard was there and he told me. . . ."

"Did he? Now there's a real gentleman for you!"

"It wasn't like that!"

"What was it like, sweetheart? Tut-tut-tut and a lift of the eyebrow and dear madam, don't let these vulgarities distress you? Grow up, Martha!"

"You're the one who should grow up! You're like a big selfish child who wants everything his own way. Carl Magnusson's given you the chance of a lifetime and you . . ."

"I thought we were talking about Lorillard."

"O.K., let's talk about him. He's a pleasant, friendly man who's paid me some attention. Which I'm glad to have; because I've had damn little from you on this trip."

"From where I stand, you haven't needed it. You've got a Navy doll to play with."

"That's not true."

"Isn't it? You burst in here like the angel of the Lord and deliver your little judgment on matters you know nothing about, except by hearsay. I don't need that. Certainly not from Peter bloody Lorillard, U.S.N.!"

"You're jealous of him!"

"On the contrary. I think you'll be good for each other. To me he's just a stuffed shirt—and, through no fault of his own, a bloody nuisance."

"And to hell with you too, Gunnar Thorkild!"

"Aloha, sweetheart!"

When she had gone, he got up, signed the documents, tidied himself and walked along to Magnusson's stateroom. The old man was still up, playing gin rummy with Sally Anderton. His greeting was less than cordial.

"Oh, hullo, Thorkild. Over your tantrums?"

"I'd like a few words with you—alone if possible."

"I have no secrets from my lawyer or my physician. Sit down. Drink?"

"No, thanks. I won't keep you from your game. First, I've signed the papers, so that there can be no question I'm ducking the issue between us. Second, I want to apologize. I was hasty and rude. I forced us both into an argument which was irrelevant to the real matter of contention. I had never defined it properly to myself. I had certainly never exposed it clearly to you. I want to try to do so now—if only to avoid further dissension and discomfort for other people. May I?"

"Go ahead."

"There are two aspects to this venture. I have confused them—for myself and everyone else. We're all embarked on what we hope will be a voyage of discovery, which, if it succeeds, will have certain consequences: for me the vindication of my scholarship, for you a territorial acquisition, for my students a chance to participate and learn. In respect of all those things, what you have done is advantageous and proper. I might wish it otherwise, but I have no real ground of complaint. The other aspect is more difficult to explain. In respect of my grandfather and my people, I am engaging in a ritual act. I have no right to invite or procure the intrusion of any other parties into that sacred area. Nevertheless, I have done so by the mere fact of accepting your generosity. The idea of asking my grandfather, in his last days, to participate in a naval exercise is as repugnant to me as it would be for a Christian to defile the sacrament. So I am in dilemma. I cannot ask you to resolve it. I do not yet know how to resolve it for myself. So, if I infringe your rights, you have the right and the document to call me to account. You may not understand my motives. I hope you will accept that they are not base. That's it, I guess. Again, I apologize."

Carl Magnusson gathered up the cards with his one good hand and pushed them across to Sally Anderton to shuffle. His tone was flat and formal.

"Thank you, Thorkild. I'll think about what you have said. Your apology is accepted. While you're on watch tonight would you have Charles Kamakau check the injectors? We seem to be running a bit rough on the port engine."

"He rubbed my nose in it," said Gunnar Thorkild bitterly. "He sat there, let me go through it all, and then rubbed my nose in the muck. Oh, brother. . . . !"

Briggs was at the wheel and Thorkild was standing at the midships rail with Sally Anderton, staring down at the luminescent wash that curled away from the planking. Sally Anderton linked her arm in his and drew him away.

"Walk me awhile, please!"

"If you like."

As they paced the deck, grateful for the silence, they passed Malo and Tioto, the men-lovers from Kauai, stretched on the hatch cover, talking in low tones, embracing sometimes, giggling like children over some private joke. They saluted Thorkild without embarrassment and assured him that they were awake and watchful. See! The sails were stowed neatly, halyards were cleated, sheets were coiled and tidy.

"A good run, eh, mister?"

"Sure, a good run."

Sally Anderton smiled and said ruefully, "There's all kinds of living. I wish I'd realized it sooner."

"You're lucky. Some people never learn. They live all their lives in one idiom, one little set of convictions. . . . Like tonight, with Magnusson. . . . I might have been talking Urdu for all he understood."

"No! You're wrong—terribly wrong."

"For God's sake, Sally! You were there. You . . ."

"I was there, afterwards too—long afterwards. I saw a stubborn old man who knew he had missed a beautiful moment, because he'd never learned to bend, even for an instant in his life. When you left we played one hand. Then he threw down the cards and burst out, 'Hell, Sally! Does he have to think I'm a monster? Does he want me to cut my heart out and show it to him on a dish? I know what he means— better than he does, maybe. But he throws a goddam document in my face, and says he'll answer to it if I want! Why does he have to be so formal? Why doesn't he call me Carl? He's a man in his own right. He's got more of everything than I've got, except money. And what the hell does that mean. . . ?' I settled him down and dosed him. I lay down beside him and held him till he was calm. He wanted me to make love to him, but I couldn't and he shouldn't. He's so lonely sometimes, my heart bleeds for him. That's the penalty of power. He knows it; but the payment comes heavy. . . . Don't ever let him know I told you all this. He'd never trust me again."

"I won't tell him. . . . And thanks, Sally."

"You're welcome. . . . Would you like some coffee?"

"You go ahead and make it. I'll join you in the galley when I've finished my rounds."

He made his tour of the deck, talked a moment with Adam Briggs in the wheelhouse and then went down to the engine room to check the gauges and write up the engineer's log. On his way back to the galley he passed through the cabin area and heard Martha Gilman's voice and, after it, a man's suppressed laughter. He stopped in his tracks, then shrugged and passed by, frowning. A moment after, he saw the humour of it and grinned sourly. The sea change was working and there was no mate or master who could stop it.

In the galley, Sally Anderton was cutting sandwiches and waiting for the coffee to percolate.

"All's well, Mr. Mate?"

"All's well, topside and below."

"Here's something else for the log . . . I'm signing on for the middle watch."

"You'll be welcome."

She put down the knife, wiped her hands on a paper towel, then leaned against the bench, looking at him.

"There's something I want to say, Gunnar."

"Say it."

"When I saw you face Carl tonight, I saw a man I could respect and maybe love. But whatever it is, respect, love, friendship, I don't want to play out the whole silly scene. I loathe coy women. I don't like bitch games. So let's get the flirtation over and done. There's something good between us. I feel it. I think you feel it too. Whatever grows out of it, I want it easy and open. And so long as Carl's alive and I'm his doctor, he has to know. . . .

"The rules of the game, eh?" Gunnar Thorkild stretched out his hands and drew her to him. "This time, I spread my mat outside her father's door?"

"Or you tell me good night and pass by; but let's be able to smile at each other when we meet."

"There's also ritual rape." Thorkild mocked her gently. "The lover anoints himself with coconut oil, creeps into the hut, lies down beside the girl and hopes she's willing. If she screams, he bolts for the door and his pursuers can't hold him for the oil on his body."

"Have you ever tried it?"

"Not yet. I'm not a very fast runner."

"And I don't have a very big scream."

He kissed her then and the kissing was warm and easy with the taste of love in it; and, when he went back on deck to resume his watch, he found himself singing the chant of the young bachelors:

> "Today my son is happy.
>   He has bound his body with sennit cord,
>   He is hard in bone and flesh
>   And full of a man's seed. . . ."

They had cleared Nuku Hiva and were coasting down past the atolls to Hiva Oa before he found the words or the courage to talk to Carl Magnusson. It was a bright morning, but the wind was already fresh and they could see the surf piling up on the distant reefs. Magnusson was at the wheel, and Thorkild was working over the chart tables. Magnusson was raw-tongued and irritable.

"These blasted French. They kept us two hours late with their paper work and charged us an extra day's harbour dues for the privilege. Now we won't make Hiva Oa until dark, and we'll have to stand off all night. There's no way we're going to run the reef in darkness."

Thorkild looked up from his calculations. "The new moon rises at eight. We'll be off the channel at eight-twenty. I'll take her in for you, Carl."

Magnusson gave him a swift sidelong look and said

emphatically, "No way! Not with that surf. And it'll be bigger by nightfall."

"Relax, Carl. I know the channel like the back of my hand. Besides, my grandfather will be waiting for us. He'll have beacon fires lit on the beach, like they do for the homing fishermen. . . . What's the alternative? Twelve hours' running up and down waiting for sunrise, and an uncomfortable night for everyone. Come on, Carl! You know me. I'm not going to risk your ship or your passengers!"

Magnusson hesitated and finally nodded a grudging assent. "Very well. I trust you. . . . But how can your grandfather possibly know you're arriving tonight?"

"He knows. He'll be waiting. And, Carl, when we've dropped anchor, I'm going ashore, alone. I want you to hold everyone else on board until morning. This meeting is important to me, and to him."

"Afterwards," said Carl Magnusson deliberately, "I want to meet him in private. What languages does he speak?"

"His own and island French. He has very little English."

"You'll have to interpret then. And, Gunnar . . ."

"Yes?"

"This is important to me too. Would you believe I'm scared? . . . Me, Carl Magnusson, scared to meet an old boatman on a little island in the middle of nowhere!"

"There's nothing to be scared of, Carl. It's a moment for respect. That's all."

"I have respect. I have it for you too, though I've been a long time saying it."

"Thank you. . . . There's something else I wanted to say."

"Yes?"

"Sally Anderton . . ."

"I know. She told me. Are you in love with her?"

"Yes, I am."

"She was mine once." Magnusson was suddenly harsh and abrupt. "She's had other lovers and a no-good husband as well. If that matters, you'd better come to terms with it now."

"Among my people," said Gunnar Thorkild quietly, "there was never a cult of virginity. In the old days the maiden was deflowered, in a public act, by the chief, and sometimes by her own father. It wasn't a damage. It was a rite of passage to womanhood."

"That's not all of it. I want—I need her close to me!"

"I owe you a debt. Maybe I can pay it this way. Keep her close."

"I don't understand you at all, Gunnar."

"I think you do. I'm nearly home. I was begotten on my father's ship, in the lagoon where we'll drop anchor tonight. It's another world, with other ways. The high man is respected, and his rights are accepted without question. You're a high man too, Carl. I think you and my grandfather will understand each other."

"Get off my bridge!" growled Carl Magnusson. "Before I make a goddam fool of myself!"

On the white beach, under the sickle moon, Gunnar Thorkild sat with Kaloni Kienga the Navigator. They had eaten together, fish cooked on the hot stones of the pit. They had drunk whiskey, which Thorkild had brought from the ship. The old man had sat in silence, while Thorkild laid out for him, in words and symbols, the story of his coming, and the why and the how of the bargains he had been forced to make to ensure his arrival.

When he had finished, he too fell silent, because it was proper to wait upon the judgment, and not plead for it or pre-empt it. If he had spoken the truth, the old man would know it from his communion with the ancestor gods; if a lie, then the gods would dispose of the liar in their own fashion.

Kaloni the Navigator seemed to be asleep. His eyes were closed, his head sunk on his breast, his hands slack upon his knees. But Thorkild knew that he was not sleeping. He was closing out the land and the sea, and opening himself to the timeless past. Finally he raised his head and opened his eyes and said simply:

"It is well. It would not have happened if it had not been disposed."

Gunnar Thorkild gave a long exhalation of relief. It was as if a storm cloud had lifted and the sea was bright again and the landfall in sight. He said gratefully:

"I'm glad. You will come with me?"

"I will come. And afterwards I will leave you."

"And I may follow—with the people who are on board?"

"It is so disposed. You will follow."

"Will I come to the island?"

"You will come to it."

"And afterwards?"

"I shall be dead and you will find me in the high place. That is all I have been told."

"And the people with me?"

"They will be yours, not mine. I have no people now, only you; and, when you send me to the ancestors, you will be alone. . . . Now there is a thing to be done. Come!"

He stood up and, with Thorkild at his heels, walked down the beach and through the coconut fringe, past the taro patches and along a narrow path, scarcely discernible in the tropic undergrowth. The path rose steeply along the shoulder of a valley, deep as an axe-cut in the hills, and then it opened suddenly into what had once been a clearing, but was now a kind of chamber, arched with living trees, and floored with moss and rotting leaves and low undergrowth. When his eyes became accustomed to the near-darkness, Thorkild saw the shapes of tumbled carvings, with great heads and stumpy bodies, and short dwarfish legs. Beyond the carvings were the stone platforms from which they had fallen.

Kaloni Kienga pointed to one of the platforms. "Sit there."

He sat down, and ran his hands over the surface of the stone. It was clear of moss, and the surface was covered with glyptic symbols which he could feel but could not see.

The old man came and sat beside him. "Take my hands."

Thorkild took the old man's hands in his own. They were cold and clammy as chicken skin; he felt himself shivering at the touch.

"Now," said Kaloni Kienga, "we will wait."

"For what, Grandfather?"

"For that which comes and abides. For that which passes from me and is given to you."

"I'm afraid, Grandfather."

"In this place there is nothing to fear. . . . Afterwards, we will go down and put to sea."

As with all else, there was ceremony. Thorkild, the inheritor, must be presented to the chief and the villagers. Kaloni's boat must be loaded with provisions for his journey: with water, dried fish, bananas, coconuts and breadfruit paste wrapped in pandanus leaves. No matter that there was food and water on the *Frigate Bird;* the navigator must carry his own viaticum. He would not share quarters with anyone; he would sleep on deck, on his own mat, in the belly of his own boat, sheltered from the weather by a covering of woven palm leaves. Because he would be a guest, he must bring a gift for the captain—a wooden bailing scoop whose handle was carved in the shape of a kneeling woman. . . .

When they paddled out to the *Frigate Bird* they were accompanied by a flotilla of small craft and a score of swimming children. While the canoe was being hoisted inboard and lashed on deck, Thorkild presented his grandfather to Magnusson and the rest of the group. It was a moment, curiously grave and formal, in which the old navigator seemed to measure each man and woman, before delivering the greeting for Thorkild to translate.

When Magnusson thanked him for his gift he said, "Tell him I am grateful that he has brought you to me; that I shall remember him when he makes his own journey." To Jenny he said, "One day you will bear a chief's son," and when she blushed and giggled, he smiled gravely and said, "There is more than one fruit on the tree." With the boy, Mark, he was strangely moved. He looked at him a long moment, then laid a hand on his head, looked up at Thorkild and announced: "Hold this boy close. He is the one who will remember. . . ."

Franz Harsanyi, who was standing close by, gave a small gasp of surprise and said, "He's right, by God! The kid's got a memory like a computer."

The old man turned to him and addressed him directly:

"You of the tongues! Teach him!"

"I hear you," said Franz Harsanyi. "I will teach him!"

To the others he offered only a simple greeting; but when Adam Briggs was presented he said to Thorkild, "This one will read the water," and when Lorillard nodded a greeting the old man murmured a phrase of contempt: "Sucker-fish . . . the little one who swims with the big shark."

"What did he say?" asked Lorillard.

"Just a greeting," said Gunnar Thorkild. "He recognizes you and salutes you." He turned to Magnusson. "Do you want to talk with my grandfather now or later, Carl?"

"Forget it!" said Carl Magnusson. "He needs no words from me. Lash down and secure for sea. That wind's getting up and I'd like to get the hell out of here."

It was Kaloni Kienga who took them out, through the boil of the channel and the big rollers beyond it, until they could set sail and head south across the wind to the tail of the archipelago. Standing at the wheel, grey-haired, naked except for his skirt of *tapa* cloth, he looked like an apparition from the great past, the past of Kaho, the blind one, and Tutapu, the fierce pursuer, and the men of the high family who were called *fafakitahi* the feelers of the sea. Gunnar Thorkild felt a surge of pride and elation as he watched the *Frigate Bird* settle to the sea, and heard Carl Magnusson's aside to Lorillard:

"Relax, man! He's nursing her like a baby! It's beautiful."

As he made his round of the deck he heard the Kauai men gossiping and caught the awe in their tones as they described the aura that hung about the old man. Martha Gilman, who was propped against the mast, sketching, looked up as he passed and asked calmly:

"Are you happy now?"

"Yes. I'm glad he's come. By the way, I'm sorry about the other night."

"Forget it. I should have minded my own business. What did your grandfather say about Mark?"

"He said I should hold him close, because he is the one who will remember."

"What did he mean by that?"

"I don't know. It will come clear in time."

"What did you do ashore last night?"

"I stayed with my grandfather."

"I didn't mean that."

"I know you didn't." He grinned at her and laid a hand on her hair. "It was . . . an event, a psychic event. Before it, I was afraid. Afterwards, very calm. . . . Can I tell you something?"

"If you like."

"You're still family. I hope Lorillard will make you happy."

"Thanks. . . . I hope Sally Anderton will do the same for you."

"Does it show?"

"It shows. . . . Now do you mind? I'd like to finish this before lunch."

The most curious reaction came from Monica O'Grady, the horse-faced girl from San Francisco, who came up to smoke a cigarette with him on the afterdeck. She said in her brusque bawdy fashion:

"I've never seen you look so relaxed, Professor. Did you get laid last night?"

Thorkild laughed. "No. Did you?"

"No, but I wish to Christ I had—or could. I don't know what it's doing for anyone else, but the sea air makes me randy."

"Sorry I can't help."

"I know. You're bespoke. It's all over the ship. Anyway, I didn't come up here to talk about my sex life. . . ."

"What's on your mind, O'Grady?"

"That old man, your grandfather. When I shook hands with him, I had the strangest feeling. . . . I can't shake it off. It's the Irish in me, I guess. My own grandmother was supposed to have the second sight. . . . But it was almost as though he were warning me about something—some threat, some danger. It reminded me of a thing my father used to say, which always gave me goose bumps: 'Never come to land when the seabirds are leaving it. . . .' Don't laugh at me now, or I'll spit in your eye."

"I'm not laughing, girl," said Thorkild soberly. "I spent last night in a sacred place, where the *mana* of the ancestors is very potent. I, too, felt things that I can't put into words, for all the scholarship that's been drummed into me. But I can tell you, from my own experience, the feeling's one thing and the meaning may be quite, quite different. Don't brood on it; otherwise you'll haunt yourself with phantoms out of your own head."

"Maybe you're right; but don't bullshit me, Professor! Do you believe in *mana* or not?"

"Yes, I believe in it."

"And you've experienced it?"

"Yes."

"Then hold my hand and tell me there's nothing to worry about."

"There . . .I'm holding your hand."

"Now tell me."

"Monica O'Grady, there's nothing to worry about."

But what he could not tell her, what he could hardly admit to himself, was that her hands were cold as his grandfather's; that, even as he spoke, his mouth was full of the salt taste of blood, and in his ears was the echo of the old chant:

I see her among the stars,
Dancing,
Dancing with voyagers long dead.

Three days' sailing, with stiff winds and a favourable current, brought them past the Islands of Disappointment and down among the Tuamotus, that long string of coral reefs and low islets and atolls whose names were made of music: Mataiva, Kaukura, Taharea, Nengonengo. It was a region of sudden beauties and small surprises, the shape of clouds, the flight of seabirds, the flurry of shoaling fish. There were dangers too. The currents that set around the atolls were strong and irregular, and there were reefs and shallows still unmarked on the charts.

Kaloni the Navigator used neither chart nor compass. For him, the journey was plotted by other symbols, written in the sky, and in the sea itself. The high gods had made an orderly world. The sun, the moon, the stars, moved in courses that were set from the beginning of things. The sea, calm or turbulent, had a law of its own: the currents were bent in a regular fashion by each island they encountered; the ground swells told the path of storms, near or distant; driftwood told of land to windward; seaward spoke of a reef, upcurrent. The light itself was at the service of the knowing ones. The green of a distant lagoon was reflected from the base of a cloud and back again to the sea. The clouds that were pulled by the updraft were better landmarks than mountains. The birds themselves, terns and frigates and boobies and migrating curlew, pointed the way to land.

Withal, the navigator himself must cooperate. He must be confident in the high ones, but never arrogant or boastful. He must observe the rituals that indicated his respect for the gods and his dependence on their favour. He, too, had his place in the order of things; and, if he ruptured the order, he must inevitably perish.

While Kaloni the Navigator sailed his own course, Magnusson and Lorillard plotted it on their charts by their own mathematic of sunsights and radar and radio. Even Lorillard was forced to admit that the difference was minimal, and that the margin of error was generally against him, because the Pilot Book would not tell him how the current ran round a small atoll or how the updraft swung the wind from hour to hour. Still, he had the grace to admit it, and his attitude to Thorkild and to the old navigator took on a new shade of deference.

Magnusson, too, had changed. He was less abrupt, less irritable, more withdrawn, as though the presence of the old navigator were a constant reminder of his own mortality. On the evening of the third day, when they had passed Makemo Island and were reaching down to Motutunga, he came up to join Thorkild at the wheel. He asked:

"What time do we make Motutunga?"

"About four in the morning."

"What's our heading?"

"Two hundred and ten magnetic. There's a big compass variation here, nearly twelve degrees."

"If we stay on this course, that's the last land we'll see for five hundred miles."

"I know."

"We're coming down into your empty triangle. Has your grandfather said when he wants to leave us?"

"Soon. That's all he's said."

"How are our supplies?"

"Water, fine. Fuel, we're almost full. We've sailed most of the time and the generators don't eat much. We're a bit light on fresh fruit and vegetables; but there's plenty of canned and frozen stuff. The boys have been catching enough fish for one meal a day all round. . . . Something on your mind, Carl?"

"In my bones, more like. Everything's been too easy so far, too placid."

"We've been lucky. The farther south we get, the more chance of a big blow."

"I didn't mean that. I mean . . . Oh hell! What's the use of hedging? Everything you told me about your grandfather is true. I've seen it, sensed it. Now I have to believe that the island is true, too. Has he given you a course for it yet?"

"No."

"Talked about it?"

"Not a word, except that night on Hiva Oa, when he promised that we would come to it."

"Does he ever talk about his own death: how it will be, when it will come?"

"He wouldn't, Carl. He came to terms with it long ago. Now, in a sense, he's already involved in the act."

"I wish to Christ I could come to terms with mine."

"It's a long way off, Carl!"

"Maybe. Maybe not. But I'll tell you, my boy, I'm so goddam jealous of every day; I hate to see the sun go down. . . . Sometimes I'm so resentful of those young ones down there on deck, I can hardly bring myself to be civil. Crazy, isn't it? It might be easier if I had some of my own brood around. But, then again, it mightn't. I'd be riding herd on them the way I always did. . . . Anyway, I didn't come up here to sing you a jeremiad. I want to tell you something. When your grandfather leaves us, I want you to take command of the *Frigate Bird.*"

"Why, for God's sake!"

Magnusson gave a small, sour chuckle. "In the log we'll show medical reasons. In fact I'm tossing you a hot potato. Blame yourself. You told me you found something obscene about turning your grandfather's death into a naval exercise. Now I find it that way myself. I can't break faith with my friends in the Navy; but you have no commitment to them. When you're in command you can order Lorillard to break off communications and resume them at your discretion. . . ."

"Carl, you're an old monster!"

"I know it. I used to enjoy it. . . . There's another thing. If anything should happen to me, you'll find money in the ship's safe, enough to complete the voyage home."

"Nothing's going to happen to you!"

"Shut up, man, and listen! You'll also find a sealed envelope addressed to you. It's a deed of gift, signed and witnessed. The *Frigate Bird,* and everything in her, will belong to you."

"That's madness!"

"Why? She's mine. I can do what I like with her. I'd rather you have her than anyone else."

"I couldn't take her, Carl. She's worth a fortune."

"It's done. There's no discussion. How you dispose of her afterwards is your own business."

"Does Sally know about this?"

"No. And you're not going to tell her."

"Why not?"

"Because she'll make the same fuss you did. She expects me to be bright and breezy and Jack-me-hearty, every day and all day. I don't feel like that. I feel bleak and old; and I'd give every damn dollar I've ever earned to go out the way your grandfather's going, with no enmities, and one of his own blood to set him on the way. . . ."

"Carl, what can I say? If you want friends, you have them: Sally and me. If you want a shoulder to lean on, use mine. But for God's sake, man! It comes free. . . . Believe that!"

"For a man like me, that's the hardest thing in the world to believe. Here! Let me have the wheel for a while. They're making music on deck. Go find your woman and join them."

He was glad to go, glad to be freed from the plague of pity and the shame that a man should be reduced to buy it with a gift. Then in a rush of recollection the words of Flanagan S.J. came back to him:

". . . The *mana* will come; but you'll suffer for it. People will lean on you and you will fall under their weight. You will try to flee them, but they will not let you escape."

When he walked forward, he saw his students and the Kauai men gathered round Ellen Ching and Molly Kaapu and Yoko Nagamuna, who were dancing a hula to Simon Cohen's guitar. They shouted for him to join them. He peeled off his shirt and stepped into the ring, beating his hands to the rhythm, feeling the sap rise in his loins, glad to shut out the lone gull-cry of age and discontent.

FOUR

THE FOLLOWING DAY, KALONI KIENGA AN-
nounced the time and the manner of his going.
When night fell, and the first stars came, they would
heave to and put him overside in his canoe. He would
sail southward, they would cruise northward, until he
was lost beyond the horizon. Then, and only then,
might they come about and set their own course for
the island. He begged that there should be no con-
course and no ceremony. Only Magnusson and Charlie
Kamakau and Briggs and Thorkild should be on deck
to cast him off and wave him away. Thorkild should
explain the sacredness and the privacy of the act, lest
he, Kaloni Kienga, should be deemed discourteous or
ungrateful.

As for Thorkild, when he turned south again, he
should sail all night on the guide-stars which would
be shown to him, and all the next day on the same
course. When night fell again he would be in the east-

ward current, and must sail against it, watching the flow of the *te lapa,* the underwater lightning. At dawn he would see the cloud, under which lay the Island of the Navigators; and, if the sky were overcast or confused, the *manuvakai,* the lookout bird, would show him the way. All this was long in the telling, with a wealth of image and detail that only a feeler-of-the-sea could understand. He made Thorkild rehearse it, over and over, until every point was clear as if it were written on his palm.

Then he told of the island. It was not like the low islands, a hump of sand and coral. It rose high and steep out of the sea. It was round like a *kava* bowl, and on one side the lip of the bowl was broken. In front of the broken lip there was a small beach and, before the beach, a reef, out of which rose a single, sentinel rock, the crag of a submerged mountain. To make the channel, one must keep the rock on the left hand and drive close into it. Outside the reef there was no anchorage, because the coral and the rock fell away into enormous deeps inhabited by monstrous fish. The rock itself was inhabited by the guardian spirits of the island, relatives of the sea god, upon whose favour a safe entry depended. . . . If he passed the rock and came safe into the lagoon, then he could approach the island without fear, and climb to the high place, where those who had arrived before him sat where they had died, looking out to sea. That was where he, Kaloni Kienga, would be found, if the gods permitted him a safe arrival. . . . This was what he had been told by his own father. More he could not tell, because he did not know. Now, since he must sail all night, he must rest; and, as there would be movement on deck all day, he would be glad to rest in Thorkild's cabin.

As they went down the companionway they came

face to face with Sally Anderton, who was coming up on deck. The old man stretched out a hand to stay her. He turned to Thorkild.

"This is your woman?"

"What's he saying?" asked Sally Anderton.

"He asks if you are my woman."

"Tell him yes. And tell him I want to make a son for the grandson of Kaloni."

Thorkild translated. The old man nodded gravely. "It is good, if the gods approve. Say that I wish her well."

"I wish him well too," said Sally Anderton. "Before he goes, he should speak to Carl. He's very depressed."

Thorkild explained. Kaloni hesitated a moment and then agreed.

"Let me speak with him now. Afterwards I must rest."

"I'll see you on deck, Gunnar."

"Do me a favour, Sally. Explain to the others that my grandfather wants to go quietly. He asks that there be only four people on deck when he leaves. That's Briggs, Charlie Kamakau, Magnusson and myself. I'd be greatful if they'd respect that wish."

"They will." She took the old man's hand and held it to her lips. "I pray you have a good voyage, Navigator."

"And for you," said Kaloni Kienga, "I pray a safe sleeping with my daughter's son. . . ."

Carl Magnusson received the news calmly. He begged the old man to be seated and offered him whiskey and made a toast to his journey. Then he turned to Thorkild. "Tell your grandfather I wish I were going with him."

Kaloni Kienga smiled and shook his head. "Every man goes to his own gods by his own road."

"Can you read my road, Navigator?"

"I do not know your gods."

"I have none," said Carl Magnusson.

"Even when the stars are hidden, they are still there. The gods wait, even for the unknowing."

"How will they receive us?"

"They neither receive us nor reject us. We are always in their hold, like fish in the sea, like birds in the air."

"Why are your gods different from others?"

"They are not different; we give them different names."

"Why are there so many for you, for others only one?"

"Because we see the many and we tell the many, even while we dream the one which we cannot see. Why do you trouble yourself with these things?"

"Because I am afraid. Have you never been afraid, Navigator?"

"The fear is what keeps us alive. In the dying there is no fear. I am already dead. . . . Rest easy. My grandson will do for you what he has done for me."

"He is my captain now," said Carl Magnusson.

"Trust him," said Kaloni the Navigator. "He has the *mana*. . . ."

When Thorkild went up to the bridge, Charlie Kamakau was at the wheel, and Peter André Lorillard was at the chart table, preparing his coded transmissions to the Navy. Thorkild announced calmly:

"The old man's asked me to take over command of the *Frigate Bird*. Charlie, will you inform the crew when you come off watch?"

"Sure, Mr. Thorkild—Captain!"

Lorillard gaped at him. "Am I to understand this is official?"

"It's official. The old man will sign the log."

"I have to inform the Navy."

"Of course. And tell them we're closing down transmissions until further notice."

"What?"

"You heard me, Mr. Lorillard. We're closing down all transmissions until further notice. That will be logged too."

"But why? What reasons do I give?"

"Two reasons. First, we're making a scientific experiment, closing down all navigational systems, radio, radar, even covering the compass, to follow the methods of ancient Polynesian navigators. If that isn't enough, then you fall back on Captain's orders. The Navy will understand that one, I'm sure."

"The hell they will! There's a contract for my services and the equipment."

"I haven't seen the contract. I didn't make it. If you can't take orders from the lawfully appointed skipper, you're suspended from duty until operations are resumed."

"I'm under Navy orders."

"You're under mine—as crew, passenger or in the brig. Take your pick."

"I don't accept that. I shall continue to operate my schedules."

"If you try it, Mr. Lorillard, I'll confine you to quarters—and I'll put a fire axe through your equipment and toss it overside. Is that clear?"

"Carl Magnusson's the owner. I'll take it up with him."

"You do that. Do it now, Mr. Lorillard!"

When he had gone, Charlie Kamakau chuckled and said happily, "I get the feeling he doesn't like you, Captain."

"He'll get used to it. . . . My grandfather leaves us tonight."

"I heard."

"I want the decks cleared before we put him over-side."

"I heard that too. My boys understand. And, Captain . . ."

"Yes, Charlie?"

"They know about the old ways. They'll be glad to serve under you. They like Mr. Magnusson too. He's a good master; but it's not the same thing, is it?"

"No, it's not the same thing."

"Funny. . . . Back home we've got all the one label on us. We're all citizens of the great United States of America; we carry the same passports, live under the same Constitution, get slugged with the same taxes. Out here, suddenly, it's different. The past comes up and smacks us in the teeth. . . . All the stories the old people used to tell us, the customs we used to laugh at, they mean something now. Even you. . . . I heard the kids joking and calling you 'prof,' and telling about your lectures and your love life. Then, all of a sudden, you're changed. You're the high one—and we know it, even if the others don't. Yeah, it's sure funny. . . ."

The tropic dusk lapsed swiftly, and night came down star-bright over the empty sea. Carl Magnusson swung the *Frigate Bird* into the wind, and she lay there, rocking in the ground swell, while Adam Briggs and Charlie Kamakau checked the stowage and the water gourds and then unlashed the canoe and hooked it on to the davit blocks.

Kaloni the Navigator stood apart with Gunnar Thorkild and pointed southwards where Hadar and Rigil Kent, the two bright stars of Centaurus, pricked out from a velvet sky. He showed Thorkild the path they would follow and how he should steer on them. As Thorkild opened his lips to speak the words of farewell, Kaloni silenced him with a gesture and a simple, grave admonition:

"It is all said. All done."

Thorkild drew the old man to him and embraced him. Then, together, they went to the rail to watch the canoe being swung out over the side. Kaloni climbed down into it, and they watched as he raised the mast and stayed it, thrust off and paddled out into the wind and raised the birdwing sail.

They saw the wind catch him, heard the twang of the sennit rope as the stays tightened, the suck and splash as the outrigger lifted out of the water. They watched the old man stand, not painfully, but proud and confident, with the sheet in his hand, one foot braced against the steering paddle, riding the waves like a sea god. Gunnar Thorkild felt salt tears pricking at his eyelids, and a great cry was wretched out of him:

"Ai-ee, Kaloni! Ai-ee, Son of the Sons of Navigators!"

As if he were another man, he heard the cry blown away on the wind, and saw Kaloni and his frail vessel fade into the darkness. Then a hand was laid on his shoulder, and Magnusson's voice challenged him back to reality:

"He's gone, Thorkild; and you've got a ship to sail."

Next morning, while Charlie Kamakau was at the wheel, Thorkild gathered the ship's company around him on the deck and told them:

". . . You understand, now, what we are doing. We are sailing as the old ones did, without charts or compass. Whatever else happens, you will know you have done that. . . . If the legends are true, and I have followed my grandfather's sailing directions properly, we shall come on our island tomorrow. If we find a safe anchorage, we'll stay there long enough to examine its features and record them. If it's uninhabited, we establish possession of it. If it will support a human community, then some of us—or all of us—may be interested to establish such a community. . . . Curious possibility, isn't it? All of us, at one time or another, have said or thought that we'd like to stop the world and get off. Suppose, tomorrow, we find we can do just that? . . . Now remember we're free either way. The *Frigate Bird* guarantees that freedom. We can stay or sail away, some of us, all of us."

"Can we sail away, Professor?" Yoko Nagamuna asked the question in her small, birdlike voice. "You said we're not using charts or compasses. How will we know where we are?"

"Of course we do—at least approximately enough for us to set a course and sail to New Zealand or Tahiti. I'll lay even money, Lieutenant Lorillard has us pinpointed on the chart right now."

"You're damn right I have!" said Lorillard emphatically.

"You see!" Thorkild dismissed the matter with a laugh. "The frames of reference are different. The result is the same. We know where we are now. We'll know where we are tomorrow."

"Even if we didn't have the *Frigate Bird,*" Hernan Castillo added his mite of encouragement, "we could still build our own boat, and sail her."

"Provided we had the tools, buster." Ellen Ching was skeptical. "And the skills, and the materials."

"Which brings up another point." Monica O'Grady thrust herself into the talk. "The professor talked about 'some of us or all of us.' I don't think it could work that way. We've fragmented our knowledge so much

that we're like . . . well, for Christ's sake!—like
flightless birds or three-legged horses, or—or Vestal
Virgins in a whorehouse. We don't know how to do it
anymore."

"At which point," said Gunnar Thorkild with a grin,
"I leave you, ladies and gentlemen. Question for discussion: how does a Vestal Virgin make out in a
whorehouse—or how do you win at Hialeah with a
three-legged horse?"

"Or what," asked Peter Lorillard with a rare flash
of humour, "what do you make of a mariner who
sails by the bones of his arse?"

"You make him a cook, mister!" Molly Kaapu
stood over them like a great hen shepherding her
chicks. "And if some of you girls don't start peeling,
no one gets lunch!"

Later, while they were having a pre-lunch drink
in Magnusson's stateroom, Sally Anderton added a
postscript to the discussion:

". . . I've never heard them so lively. After you'd
gone, Gunnar, even the crew joined in. But here's the
odd thing. It's still theory in their minds. None of
them regards it as a concrete possibility. . . ."

"I'll tell you why," said Carl Magnusson. "When
you've been aboard awhile, the ship becomes a womb.
You're warm; you're fed; and, once you're used to
the motions, you're so comfortable you never want to
leave it. Watch any sailor. Two days before landfall,
he's rearing to get ashore. Two days after, when he's
had his woman and a skinful of liquor, he can't
wait to get back on board. It's the only reality he
knows. . . ."

"Fair enough." Gunnar Thorkild was suddenly
moody and distracted. "I was just trying to bring them
to grips with the idea. You see . . ."

"What's on your mind, Thorkild?"

"Something my grandfather said. The rock that rises out of the reef is guarded by spirits. . . ."

"And that means?"

"Specifically, I don't know. Neither did he. But every legend has its base in fact. So I have to think of possible hazards. The problem isn't the hazard, but the haunted area that surrounds it in one's own mind. Reason falls out of gear and tribal memory takes control. . . . How did you make out with Lorillard?"

"He was upset. That's natural. I pointed out that your experiment in primitive navigation could be of value to the Navy. I urged him to record it, which he's doing. However, he's got troubles of his own."

"Oh?"

"He's moved in on Martha Gilman."

"I know."

"He thinks you're jealous."

"I hoped she'd do better; but I'm not jealous."

"You tell him that."

"Why should I bother?"

"Because," said Carl Magnusson, "now that you're skipper, you get to see his personal record. It shows he's married, with a wife and two children in San Diego."

"Oh, Christ!"

"Exactly. . . . Try picking the bones out of the stew, Captain Thorkild."

"If you take my advice"—Sally Anderton was empathic—"you won't say or do anything about it. Let them enjoy each other while they're on board and sort the rest out for themselves later."

"But if Martha doesn't know . . ."

"She won't thank you, Gunnar Thorkild, for telling her."

"And that," said Magnusson with cheerful malice,

"that disposes of Lieutenant Peter Lorillard, U.S.N. Now, what about you two?"

"What about us?" It was Sally who asked the question.

"Are you going to get married?"

"We are married," said Gunnar Thorkild. "I've spread my mat. The elders approved. The woman has walked to my house. That's the old way. Do you know a better one?"

"No, I guess not. I've tried four times: twice with a minister and twice with a judge. Your way seems as good as any."

At three in the morning they were running westwards, before a ten-knot wind under a sky full of stars. Adam Briggs was at the wheel, and Gunnar Thorkild was on the foredeck, watching the *te lapa*, that strange luminescence, which flowed, deep down, with the eastward current. Even through the broken water he could see it, long streams of greenish light like flashes of lightning, flaring and parting under the bows.

The spectacle was hypnotic; and, every little while, he had to avert his eyes and refocus them on the familiar objects of the deck. Then, gradually, he became aware of a change in the pattern. The sharp flashes began to shimmer and break up, as though a shock wave had passed through them. It was a phenomenon he had never seen before, and his grandfather had never mentioned it to him. It puzzled him, but it gave him no cause for alarm. The wind was fair, the glass was high and the sea was comfortable. All he felt was a sharp pang of loss, because Kaloni the Navigator was not there to explain the strangeness.

When the sun rose, he could see, far down on the western horizon, the shape of the promised cloud, the pile of white vapour formed by the updraft of sea winds over a land mass. An hour later, he could make out the land itself: a high truncated cone, bright under the climbing sun. He felt a wild surge of elation, and he yelled to Adam Briggs:

"We made it, brother! We made it! Go below and rouse 'em all up! Magnusson too. This is what we came for! Let 'em all see it!"

They came tumbling up, excited and chattering, to crowd the foredeck, and watch the distant shapes grow and harden, until they could make out the folds and fissures on its flanks and the first hint of colour from the reef and on the land. In the wheelhouse Sally Anderton was like a child, caught between tears and laughter. Magnusson was flushed and stammering with triumph:

"I can't believe it! This . . . this is the best moment of my life! Dammit! I'm only the carrier. You did it, Thorkild! . . ."

As they came close, Thorkild could distinguish all the features which his grandfather had described: the break in the lip of the bowl, through which a cascade of green foliage poured down to the beach, the sentinel rock, and the channel which ran past it into the lagoon. The tide was low and the swell was light, both good omens for a safe passage. He called Charlie Kamakau to the wheelhouse.

"Let's have the sails off her, Charlie. I'll stand in to about a quarter of a mile, then I'll heave her to. You take the whaler with Malo and Tioto and sound me that channel. It looks narrow; but with water under us, we should make it easily enough. . . . Also see what water we've got in the lagoon. It's quite wide, but I want to be able to lay out enough chain to hold us in a blow. . . ."

Half an hour later Charlie Kamakau was back with

his report. "The channel's about twenty yards wide, deeper towards the rock. . . . You've got at least eighteen feet of water all the way in. The current's about two knots. As you go in, you'll get a lift from the swell that swings you towards the big rock, so bear away from it a bit. Once you're inside the lagoon you're O.K. It's low tide and you've still got eighteen feet and enough swinging room for a long chain. The bottom's sand and coral. . . ."

"You saw no hazards round the rock?"

"None, except the way the swell skews into the channel. . . . But with today's sea, there's no problem."

"O.K. We go in!"

"See those three palms on the beach? Line yourself up on the middle one. . . ."

"Got it, Charlie!"

Thorkild swung the *Frigate Bird* in a wide arc and headed at half speed towards the entrance. A cheer went up from the watchers on deck and he waved a hand to acknowledge it. They were about a cable's length from the channel when Charlie Kamakau gave a warning and pointed astern. Thorkild looked back and saw a great wall of water, like the surf on Sunset Beach, rolling down towards them. Recognition was swift and terrifying. It was a freak wave, like those which the Japanese called *tsunami,* the product of some underwater upheaval.

He could not turn back. If he did, the wave would broach him onto the reef. If he could get through the channel he might have a chance, because the reef would fracture the wave and dissipate its force. He slammed the throttles up and headed straight for the entrance. For one wild moment, he thought they were through; then the swell lifted under the hull and they were slammed hard against the rockface. He heard the timbers rend, saw the decks buckle, and bodies tossed

and tumbled like dolls in a water chute. Then he, himself, was caught by a giant hand that plucked him
from the wheel and flung him against the bulkhead.
The last thing he remembered, before he slid into
blackness, was the green light of the *te lapa* and how
it had shattered under the water as if a shock wave
had passed through it. . . .

When he woke, he was lying on green leaves, with
Sally Anderton and Adam Briggs bending over him.
His scalp was split in a long, bloody furrow. His hands
were torn. But he could see and hear, and after a while
he could sit up and begin to understand the dimen-
sion of the tragedy.

The *Frigate Bird* was a total wreck. Her back was
broken; her ribs were stove in. Her decks were awash
and she was wedged sidelong in the channel, where
the surf would batter her to pieces. Malo was drowned.
Monica O'Grady was dead too, her neck snapped when
she was flung against the mast. He himself would have
died had not Tioto hauled him, unconscious, to the
beach and pumped the water out of his lungs. Magnusson was alive, but with a broken shoulder. The rest
were scarred and shocked but safe. The great wave
had come, and gone; and, most monstrous of ironies,
the sea was calm again.

In spite of Sally's warnings about concussion and
collapse, Thorkild made them hoist him to his feet
and steady him until the first dizziness had passed.
Then he made them walk him inland, through the
break in the island wall, until they found a place where
a cascade of fresh water flowed down over moss-
covered ledges into a small rocky pool. They rested a
moment and drank, and then went back to the beach
to join the others.

Some were huddled under the palm trees, an abject

misery, staring out at the twisted hulk of the *Frigate Bird*. Others were prying aimlessly among the debris on the beach, or bathing their cuts in the shallows. Magnusson, grey and listless, was propped against a pandanus bole, with Molly Kaapu fanning his face. He gave Thorkild a grimace that was meant to be a smile and said:

"Well, Thorkild! You couldn't have made a better job if you'd scuttled her yourself. What happened?"

"Tsunami—like the big one that hit Hilo. They come out of nowhere."

"So we're stuck here."

"Looks like it."

"We made a mistake, Professor. We should have let Lorillard have his way. At least the Navy would have known where we are."

"We made the mistake. We live with it! Round 'em up, Adam. I want to talk to them."

They came, shabby and straggling, stunned by the spectacle of each other's misery. Thorkild snapped at them brutally:

"Wake up! Pull yourselves together! You're alive! Be glad of it! That wave could have killed us all! Where's Hernan Castillo?"

"Here, Professor."

"A hundred yards inland, you'll find fresh water. Just near it, there's a flat, open space. We'll make a camp there. We need a windbreak, shelter and a fire-pit. Franz, Yoko, Martha, you go help him. As soon as the shelter's prepared, make a place for Mr. Magnusson. Ellen Ching?"

"I'm here."

"You're a botanist. You know fruits and plants. Take Charlie's wife and Molly Kaapu and see what else is growing around here, besides coconuts. We need a big meal as soon as we can get it. Now you, Charlie and Adam and Tioto . . . if you're ready for another swim, get yourselves out to the ship and see what you can salvage before she gets her first battering. Fire axes and tools first, canvas, cordage . . . after that whatever you can lay your hands on or dismantle. Wrench off the hatch covers and use them as rafts to float things back. . . . Simon, you take Jenny and Mark and Sally and scour the beach. Pick up anything that's been washed overboard—I mean anything—bits of wood, cans. . . . Pile it all in a big heap near the campsite. Don't overlook anything. Willy Kuhio, you're the fisherman. You and your wife start prodding round the pools and see what you can find that's eatable. Lorillard and I will be the burial party. . . ."

It took them two hours to scrape out the shallow graves in the coarse sand at the head of the beach, to lay out the bodies, cover them with stones and sand and build a small cairn. By the time they had finished their backs were aching and their hands were raw and bleeding.

Lorillard said, "We ought to give them a prayer."

"May they rest easy," said Gunnar Thorkild. "May they speak for us, wherever they are."

"Amen. . . ." Lorillard sat down on the sand and buried his face in his hands. "What a mess! What a bloody stupid mess!"

"We'll survive."

"So what? We've dropped off the edge of the world. We'll be reported missing—they'll search for a while and then they'll write us into the book of the dead."

"You can say that to me." Gunnar Thorkild's tone was threatening. "But not to the others. We need hope —not a doomsday man!"

"You don't have a very high opinion of me, do you, Thorkild?"

"Mr. Lorillard, I don't have a high opinion of myself. . . . Look! We've just buried our dead. Let's call a truce, eh?"

"Fine! A truce! Now what?"

"For the moment everybody's busy. Tonight the reaction will hit—and they'll be deep in the miseries. We'll have to keep jolting them into action."

"You take it all on yourself." Lorillard was bleak. "You assume no one else is as fit or prepared as you are. That's a mistake. If you'd listened to me, we'd have the Navy steaming out to find us right now. . . ."

Thorkild was seized with a sudden nausea. He turned away and retched and then pitched, face down, in his own vomit.

. . . There was smoke and there was fire. There was a wind that chilled him to the marrow and a heat that burned him. There was earth under his hands and then a sea that lifted him up and carried him away. There were stars, and then a blackness. There were ghost voices and bird cries and the sibilant wash of waves on the beach. There was a foulness in his gullet and hammers beating at his skull, and then a vortex that swirled him, like a leaf, into nowhere. Then there was a woman's breast and his cheek against it and water, cool on his parched tongue and, after it, a long tranquillity. When he opened his eyes, he could see nothing. Panic-stricken, he struggled to sit up; but Sally Anderton's hands forced him back to the sand and her voice admonished him in a whisper:

"Lie quiet! You're all right."

"Where am I?" It was not his own voice but a crow's croak out of nowhere.

"You're here with me."

"What happened?"

"Nothing. . . . A touch of concussion."

"What time is it?"

"After midnight. . . ."

"Where are the others?"

"All here. They're asleep."

"Was there food?"

"Plenty. . . ."

"Briggs and Charlie . . . are they back from the ship?"

"Yes. They found useful things. Lie quiet now. You'll be better in the morning."

"I'm cold."

"I'll make you warm."

When he woke at first light, he was himself again, weak but clearheaded and in control of his faculties. He eased himself away from Sally, sat up, stood and surveyed his tatterdemalion tribe, huddled in sleep under the windbreak which had been their shelter for the night. The fire pit was still warm, and the remains of the evening meal were scattered around it: scraps of coconut, shells, banana peelings. A little farther away was a pile of what looked like rubbish, the scourings of the beach, and the first salvage of the *Frigate Bird*. He did not stop to examine it. There would be time enough later—interminable time. He walked to the spring, sluiced his face, drank a few mouthfuls of water and walked slowly down to the beach to void himself, native-fashion in the shallows. The surf was higher this morning, and the waves were tossing over the decks and around the broken spars of the *Frigate Bird*. Then he saw a thing that left him gape-mouthed with shock. At the far end of the lagoon, where the reef swung in to join the land, he saw Charlie Kamakau and Adam Briggs sitting in a canoe, fishing. He shouted to them and ran, weak-kneed and stumbling, along the beach. They saw him and came paddling inshore, using their bare hands for propulsion.

As they came closer he saw that it was his grandfather's craft, dismasted, the outrigger torn off, but the hull still sound. They had found it high on the beach, they told him, tossed among the pandanus palms by the big wave. Charlie had made a line from the sennit cords and a hook from a seashell; and there were fish for breakfast. For a crazy, confused moment, they clung to each other on the beach, babbling, shouting congratulations to each other on their vast good fortune. Adam Briggs said:

"So you see, he got here! He must be alive!"

"No." Gunnar Thorkild pronounced it like an epitaph. "He's dead. We'll find him up there in the high place."

"Do you know where it is?" asked Charlie Kamakau.

"Somewhere up there. Later on, I'll go up and find it. We'll do our own work first."

Adam Briggs looked at him with odd concern. "Are you O.K., Professor? You had us worried last night."

"A bit weak, otherwise fine. How are the others?"

"Bewildered, mostly. Young Jenny was sick. And Magnusson was in a lot of pain. None of us got to sleep till very late. Today could be rough, I think."

"That's the truth," said Charlie Kamakau gravely. "You're the high man now, Kaloni. We look to you to make the rules."

"We talked about it." Adam Briggs pressed the point in his sober, quiet fashion. "Lorillard and Simon Cohen and Yoko were making a lot of words about sharing decisions and avoiding the mistakes of one-man rule. . . . Mrs. Gilman said that what goes on a ship doesn't work in a land-based community. Charlie and I disagreed. But we thought you should know about the division of opinion."

"We'll cope with it." Thorkild was thoughtful. "Let's feed 'em a good breakfast and then we'll talk it out."

The talk proved longer and more difficult than he had expected. The easy comradeship of shipboard was gone now. Gone, too, was the unquestioning respect for Gunnar Thorkild as the fountain of knowledge about all things Polynesian. He was the man who had lost a ship and, as the result of a colossal imprudence, had put its survivors beyond all hope of early rescue. Whatever he offered now was only an inadequate reparation. None of it was said. All of it was plain to read in the closed and cautious faces that surrounded him. His preamble was brief and blunt:

"Like it or not, we are here for a long time. We have all the means of survival. We share enough skills to make our life more than tolerable. We can, with much time and much patience, build a vessel that will take us away from here. To accomplish these things we have to plan and work together. . . . So let's establish some priorities. Who wants to speak first?"

"I do," said Sally Anderton. "I'm a doctor with certain skills and no medicines at all. So I'm going to give you a couple of simple lessons in preventive medicine." She held up her hand, palm outwards. "See those? Coral cuts. They're already infected. Most of you have them. If you neglect them, or any other wounds, they'll turn very quickly into rodent tropical ulcers which spread rapidly outwards and inwards. So cleanse them constantly. Keep them dry. . . ." She pointed down at the litter of food scraps around the pit. "That rubbish will bring insects and gastric infections. Burn it after every meal. I noticed all of you going into the bushes to urinate and stool. Don't! Go down to the far end of the beach. Do your business at the edge of the water. The tide will carry out the refuse. That's all for the moment; but remember, it's important. Later on, with Ellen's knowledge of botany I may be able to build up a simple pharmacopoeia; but for the present, I'm pretty helpless. . . ."

They understood that and approved it. The next question came from Simon Cohen, and there was a certain aggressiveness in the matter of its phrasing.

"You said we had all the means of survival. Medically it's clear that we haven't. What about food? Are we sure we can survive with what's here?"

Adams Briggs was swift to answer him. "The lagoon's swarming with fish. We spotted a pair of turtles. We've got a boat. The tackle we can make ourselves. No problems there. What did you find, Ellen?"

"There's coconuts and breadfruit and there's taro growing up the valley. We can cultivate that later. We'll certainly have enough to eat. We can even make liquor if we want."

"You're the nutritionist, Yoko. Do you agree?"

"I agree." She was very short about it, as though there were other things much more important to discuss.

"Next question?"

"Tools," said Franz Harsanyi. "There's one fire axe, a couple of screwdrivers, and four seamen's knives between us. . . ."

"We make the rest." It was Hernan Castillo who spoke now, firmly and positively. "We make scrapers and knives from shells. There's enough stone around to make primitive hammers and axe heads. It'll take time; but we've got plenty of that. Which reminds me, we've got two waterproof watches that are working—and the ship's chronometer, which is broken."

"We're going to need proper shelter!" Carl Magnusson cut in brusquely. "We can't camp out in the open like this. It hasn't rained yet. But when it does it will come down in buckets. I say shelter's a first priority—one big house with a floor and a roof to keep out the rain. We should start that today—as soon as possible."

They agreed with that too. Then there was a short uneasy silence until Martha Gilman spoke.

"This question was raised last night. It should be resolved now. How do we organize ourselves? Who says what is to be done and by whom?"

"There can only be one boss." Carl Magnusson spoke again, harsh and imperative. "We're a tribe, not a goddam municipality. So let's name him and get it done with."

"I nominate Lieutenant Lorillard," said Simon Cohen.

"And I nominate Professor Thorkild." It was Jenny's voice, tremulous but defiant.

"Any others . . . None. Then let's have a show of hands. For Lieutenant Lorillard, how many?"

Martha Gilman, Simon Cohen, Yoko Nagamuna and Hernan Castillo raised their hands.

"Seems you're in the minority, Mr. Lorillard." Carl Magnusson smiled. "I'm sure you'll concede with good grace. You're elected, Thorkild."

Thorkild sat silent a moment, gathering himself for a moment critical to all of them. Then he heaved himself to his feet and stood looking down at the small shabby assembly. His face was grim and unsmiling. His voice was solemn as if he were calling the genealogies, like the old high ones of the past.

"I meant to tell you something; and then you will vote again, this time understanding what you do. We have all stepped back in time. We're twentieth-century people, reduced at one stroke to a primitive situation. So, relative values change. Some of the things we know are useless junk. Knowledge that we counted as trivial may be vitally important. Personal roles change too. And relationships that were once exclusive have

to be widened to include a whole group. If you elect
me, you make me a chief, not a puppet. You put your
lives in my hands. You engage yourselves to obey. I
will seek counsel from each and all of you. I will engage to act on it only if I deem it wise. You will engage to obey what I order. That was the way of my
people, the people who came to this island in olden
times. It is the only way I know to be a tribe: one
people caring for the many within it. Think about this.
Speak to it if you want. Then vote again. If you
choose Mr. Lorillard or anyone else, I will give him
the same obedience that I should expect from him.
Think of another thing. Should there not be two of us,
a man and a woman, so that each sex has its own recourse? . . . I see you smile as though I have said
something amusing. Is it really a matter of humour? I
am not thinking of a consort, a wife, though the question of how we mate and breed will come very soon.
I am thinking of a wise woman, who can be the high
mother of this community—the *kapu* one to whom
other women may turn for their special needs. I am
going to leave you while you discuss and decide these
things, but I want you all to decide—you, Charlie,
and your wife and Tioto, and you, too Willy, and Eva
Kuhio. One last word. Like it or not, you are one people now, in one small land from which we cannot de-
part for a long time yet. Try to think like that. Try to
act like that. . . . And take your time, because tomorrow stretches a long way." He relaxed then and moved
away and tapped Mark Gilman on the shoulder. "You
come with me, young fellow. We'll go look for a place
to build our house. . . ."

It was a relief to leave them with their fears and
their jealousies and plunge into the green tangle that
grew where once, centuries ago, the lava had broken
through the lip of the crater and flowed down into a

boiling sea. The vegetation was dense, the ground covered with a thick, spongy layer of rotting leaves and decaying tree trunks; but after a while they became aware of contours, a series of wide, flat terraces, where giant bamboo and pandanus and *fei* trees and papaya and red hibiscus and blue and green *tapo-tapo* thrust themselves up in wild profusion. The air was heavy, and full of insects and the sunlight filtered down through a thick lattice of leaves and branches and palm fronds. Sometimes they heard birdcalls and caught the iridescent flash of wings. When Thorkild reached up to pluck a plantain from the *fei* tree, a tiny fruit rat scuttled away from his touch.

The fourth terrace was wider than the others; and, as they hacked their way across it, Thorkild's foot caught under a projecting stone and he fell forwards, clouting his shoulder on the trunk of a large tree. He recovered himself and bent to examine the obstacle. It was a long ledge of stone, overgrown with moss and fern. As he scraped away the growth he turned up a shard of pottery, large as his hand, with a curious reticulated pattern around the edge. He cleaned it carefully and showed it to the boy.

"Look at this carefully, Mark. It's very important. What does it tell you?"

"I don't know. What is it, Uncle Gunnar?"

"Pottery. Lapita pottery—the oldest thing you find in the islands. This sort of thing was made and carried through the Pacific nearly a thousand years before Christ."

"What does it mean?"

"That people lived here a long time ago. They made these terraces and planted them."

"What happened to them?"

"I don't know. They died out. They went away. But their memory remains in the memory of my people. The thing is, my boy, they lived here, just as we're going to do. This is where we'll build our first house—with those bamboos over there, and those palms—and we'll plant our first garden around it. We'll name it for you: Mark Gilman's dwelling place. Go on, carve your name on that tree, while I chop out the first clearing. Then we'll mark a path as we go back. . . ."

"Gee, Uncle Gunnar, there's so much of everything. How will we ever get it cleared?"

"Listen to me, Mark! There's an old Chinese saying: 'The journey of a thousand miles begins with one step.' That's the step you need guts to make. . . . How do we clear it? We cut one bush, then another, and another, until we've made room for a house and a garden. Then we'll clear another terrace and another, and by the time you're a man the whole valley will be a garden."

"By the time I'm a man! You mean we're going to be here that long?"

"Well, if we want to get off, we have to build the kind of big boat my ancestors did. That takes time too. We have to find the trees and fell them, and clear a slide to get them down to the beach to work on them. . . . Tell you what. Why don't we pick out a tree or two on the way back?"

"I'm scared, Uncle Gunnar. This place is creepy."

"Hold out your hand."

The boy held out his hand and Thorkild laid the shard of pottery in his palm.

"Look at that. Feel it. It's pottery. A thing people make to hold food and water and liquor that makes them sing. Those are good things, happy things, and we're going to make Mark Gilman's place happy too. Right?"

"I guess. . . . Can we go back now, please?"

They were waiting for him, uneasy at his absence, shamefaced at what they had to tell him. They had made Carl Magnusson their spokesman, and he delivered their verdict in his habitual blunt fashion:

". . . The discussion was free and open. The decision was unanimous. You are appointed leader. Molly Kaapu is the consort you asked for. However, no one was completely happy to have you rule absolutely in the old tribal way. We're in a primitive situation, yes; but we're twentieth-century people and all of us are scared of absolute power, even if it's exercised for a common good. So we've appointed a council to advise and assist you. The council consists of five members: Charlie Kamakau, Peter André Lorillard, Franz Harsanyi, Ellen Ching and Martha Gilman. If the matter is in dispute, you and Molly Kaapu vote with the council. A majority decides the issue. We review the whole situation in a common council from time to time. I am asked to say that your competence is not in question. The final issue was this: the community wished to set the terms by which cooperation and harmony could be best established and preserved. We all hope you will accept these terms. If you can't, we'll appoint someone else in your place. Please feel free to ask any question of anyone."

It was a strange, mystic moment. The *mana* that he felt within himself was challenged by another, not hostile but more potent, an emanation from other gods, other high ones, out of other histories. He could fight it or he could acknowledge it and in so doing receive part of it into himself. The outcome of conflict would be disaster, a worm eating at the rooftrees of their small new world. He waited, trying to measure the cost and the consequences of his first, critical surrender. Finally he announced calmly enough:

"I'd like to ask questions first."

"Go ahead."

"If a matter is decided by me and the council agrees it, will you all obey?"

"Yes." The answer was a unanimous murmur.

"Will you enforce obedience on one another?"

"Yes."

"Will you agree to communicate openly, either directly to me or through the council, any problems or objections, and to refrain from forming cliques or cabals among yourselves?"

"Yes."

"Do you consent that our labour and the fruits of it and anything we possess or may possess be regarded as a common trust for the good of us all?"

"Yes."

"And that the only privilege of any person shall be that dictated by need?"

"Yes."

"Good. What you have just done is set down the law by which we undertake to live. Do you all understand it in that sense?"

"Yes."

"Then on that understanding, I accept to lead you and to hold myself accountable."

They cheered him then and came crowding around to shake his hand and wish him well and make their private fealties. After a few moments he silenced them and held up the piece of pottery he had found on the upland terrace.

"See this! It is a piece of Lapita pottery that Mark and I found up the hill. Understand what it means. Other people did live here long ago. The fruits they planted have reproduced themselves. We can cultivate them again. We'll clear the terraces and build houses and make gardens. That will take time. So, first, we build ourselves a house down here near the beach.

There's bamboo for the frames and palm thatch for the roof and the walls. Everyone can help but Carl, and two people for the fishing and two for gathering food on the land. Peter Lorillard and Charlie Kamakau will organize the work parties. Molly, you come with me. You, too, Carl. Get 'em started, Charlie! I'd like to see us in shelter before sunset. . . ."

Carl Magnusson was in distress. His limp was more pronounced. His shoulder ached with every movement. His face was grey and his breathing laboured. They propped him against a palm bole and sprawled on the sand beside him. He told them, painfully:

". . . I've had some rough meetings in my time—proxy fights, board-room wrangles, injunction proceedings—but today's parley was the roughest of all. Everything boiled up at once—race, religion, political attitudes, personal prejudices. Even the ones who supported you had fears and reservations. The tribal idea was new and sometimes repugnant. They didn't like the thought of rules and orders. They wanted a kind of round-table religious dedication, a hierarchy based on talent, a benevolent anarchy. We arrived at a compromise, but we spilt blood trying to get it. If you hadn't accepted, Gunnar, we might have had bad trouble."

"Be sure of it. We'll still get trouble," said Molly Kaapu dolefully.

"What sort of trouble?" Thorkild asked the question. "Don't they understand we've got to pull together?"

"Sure they do—with their heads. But past their heads and down to their toes they feel different. Look what we've got! Ten men and a boy—and Mr. Magnusson here is out of the running. So that's nine men. Other side we've got eight women—one pregnant and me too fat and old for a man to fancy. That's nine to six. Bad enough. Then there's Mr. Lorillard that doesn't like you, and Martha Gilman that's jealous of Mrs. Anderton, and Simon Cohen that's hot for the Japanese girl but she wants Castillo and Castillo's got his cap set for Ellen Ching, and Charlie Kamakau's wife that needs more than Charlie gives her—and Tioto that's lost his friend and thinks he'd like to try girls again. . . . Put 'em all in one little house on one little island, you got trouble with a capital 'T.' You're fine, Kaloni. You're the big chief. You got your own woman. Mrs. Gilman goes to Lorillard. . . . The rest you shake up in the box and they never come out even."

"Molly's right," said Carl Magnusson with a grin. "Read it one way, it's a dirty joke. Read it another and there's blood on the beach. Any ideas, Gunnar?"

"Give me time, Carl. Give them time too. . . . What do the women say about it, Molly?"

"What women say and what they do is two different things. You know that, Kaloni—and if you don't, you should. But in the end, they're the ones that's going to decide. Me . . . ? I'd put 'em all in one big house and let the men come visiting. Them that want one man, have him, them that want more make their own arrangements. If they make children—and they will—the children belong to everybody. One thing I'm sure of, Kaloni . . ."

"What's that, Molly?"

"You keep your big nose out of it. Let me handle the girls until I ask different. O.K.?"

"It's good advice." Carl Magnusson laughed painfully. "That was one thing everyone agreed. They wanted Molly Kaapu as mother of the tribe."

"Mother, hell!" Molly Kaapu exploded. "I could still give some of those babies a tumble they'd never forget. You too, Carl Magnusson, if you hadn't worn yourself out chasing dollars and fancy wives."

"Maybe you should see me off that way, Molly. One big bang and then bury me with a lei round my neck."

"Maybe I will," said Molly Kaapu tartly. "But there's one that might go off before you."

Thorkild was instantly wary. "Who's that, Molly?"

"That little girl of yours, Jenny. She won't say so, but she got hurt when we hit the rock. She's just dragging herself around. If she carries to her full time, I'm a millionaire's playgirl."

"Has Sally Anderton had a look at her?"

"Sure. But she only says wait and see."

"Then the girl shouldn't be working."

"So what should she do, lie in the sun all day, scared and sorry for herself? Grow up, Kaloni! This is women's business. Leave it to us! You got plenty else to worry about."

"Like the *Frigate Bird*. . . ." Carl Magnusson pointed to the channel where the breakers tossed high over the hulk and sluiced white foam over her decks. "There's a hell of a lot more we could salvage before she breaks up."

"Not in this sea, Carl. We'll wait for the next low tide, take a party aboard and swim around inside her. Now that we've got the canoe we can ferry stuff back and forth quite quickly."

Carl Magnusson gave him an odd sidelong look and said deliberately:

"You might, just might, be able to salvage some of Lorillard's radio equipment: the signal buoys, for instance, or enough parts to put a transmitter together."

"We could try."

"How hard?" asked Carl Magnusson coolly. "And before you answer, let me say I haven't raised the question with Lorillard or anyone else. I figure if he's Navy-trained he should think of it himself. On the other hand, you're the high chief. So maybe it's your duty to do something."

"Or it could be a higher duty to concentrate all our efforts to establish this community and make it self-sufficient before we distract it with faint hopes. . . . I'll think about it."

Carl Magnusson turned to Molly Kaapu. "What do you say, Mother Molly?"

"I say mind your own business, old man. You got a judgment coming up and you don't want to answer to any more mischief. You do what your head tells you, Kaloni. Pay no mind to anyone else."

"That's fine." Carl Magnusson grimaced as the pain took him again. "But back there, you made a contract. Your labour and the fruits of it belong to the community. You breach that bargain at your peril."

A long hour before sunset, the house was finished and the whole group stood and surveyed it with triumph. It was no palace; they would admit that. A great architect—but only a great one—might cavil at certain defects. The craftsmen of other islands might note that the bamboo frames were slightly askew, and the palm roof was roughly laid and the walls were not woven but simply laced against the frame like a brushwood fence. Still it was, beyond dispute, a house that would keep them dry, and filter the wind and even afford a certain privacy, because it was divided by a rough screen so that the women might be private to themselves and sleep together if they chose. Outside, there was a space, swept clear of debris, with a cooking pit and a raised oven of stones, and a rough shelter to keep their firewood dry and house their miscellany of salvage. They were proud of their handiwork, eager as children to be praised and, for a moment, solemn at this first small promise of permanence and continuity.

"It deserves a blessing," said Martha Gilman. "The chief should speak."

"This is our first home," said Gunnar Thorkild simply. "We have built it with our own hands in a sacred place. I pray that we may live in it safely and at peace. Amen."

"We should make a feast tonight," said Molly Kaapu. "We should put flowers in our hair and sing and dance."

"I haven't got a darn thing to wear," said Ellen Ching.

They laughed then, a high, happy laughter that released, for the first time, all the tensions of the last two days.

"Let's go swimming," said Franz Harsanyi. "I stink like a polecat."

"Leave your clothes here," said Sally Anderton. "I'll soak them in fresh water. If you get salt in them they'll never dry."

There was a brief self-conscious moment when they peeled off their clothes and trooped down to the beach, laughing and shouting like children let out of school, while Jenny, swollen and awkward, waddled behind with Adam Briggs at her side.

Carl Magnusson growled approval. "I wondered how that would happen. Bright girl, Sally!" Then he added: "Do you think you could do something with this shoulder? It hurts like hell."

"Not much I can do, Carl, except immobilize it better. Here, let's try . . ."

"It's my good arm, dammit! I feel helpless as a baby. Everyone else is working. I'm limping around like the village idiot."

"There . . . is that better?"

"A little. Thanks. . . ."

"You stay here with me, Carlie boy," Molly Kaapu told him firmly. "You can talk to me while I make the fire and start supper. You and me aren't made for skinny-dipping."

Sally Anderton gathered up the pile of cast-off clothing and carried it over to the spring. Gunnar Thorkild followed her and watched as she took off her own clothes and tossed them into the pool.

"Give me yours too, Gunnar. Then you can help me rinse and wring them."

Thorkild obeyed, laughing. "Now we're really back to nature, aren't we? These rags won't last long. Then we'll be down to loincloths."

"Sooner the better. The sooner we throw off the past, the better we'll be. . . . Do you think you could stop being a great chief for a while and make love to me?"

"The way you are, woman, I'd have to clean you up first."

"Clean me up! Look at yourself, you're smutty as a sweep!"

They played like children under the waterfall. They teased and tumbled each other in the pool. They made love hungrily on the mossy bank. They lay together afterwards, calm and content, dappled by the late sun, lulled by the water music and the long whisper of the wind through the tufted palms.

"I'm happy now," said Sally Anderton. "This morning I was very afraid."

"For God's sake, why?"

"After that first vote, when you stood up and made that big, solemn speech, you looked so remote, so different. It was as if you weren't part of us at all, as if you'd come from some other world. I thought I knew you, every limb and every pulsebeat. Suddenly you were a stranger—threatening and dangerous. It wasn't only me. The others felt it too."

"Is that why they changed things—limited my authority?"

"Yes."

"And was it unanimous, as Carl said?"

"It was. I agreed with the others."

"I'm still the same Gunnar Thorkild."

"Oh no, dear heart. You're not. Not since the night you went ashore in Hiva Oa to find your grandfather. Before that you were half a dozen men, rolled into a bundle and tied with string. Now there's only one of you, and I haven't learned all of him yet. . . . So long as we can be like this, I'm not sure that I want to know any more."

"Do you know I love you, Sally?"

"That I do know."

"Do you love me?"

"Can you doubt it?"

"No. I only hope I don't make you carry too heavy a load."

"Like what?"

"Like me, and all that's behind me and all that lies ahead. For the first time in my life I've found a woman to whom I can surrender myself absolutely and truly. I've done that. I did it the first night we made love on the *Frigate Bird*. Now there are other claims on me. There will be more and more; and every claim I pay leaves less for you. All I can promise is to make up as much of the balance as I can. . . . Do you understand what I'm trying to say?"

"I hope I do. We may have to learn to share each other. But not now. Hold me, darling. Hold me close."

FIVE

THE NIGHT CAME DOWN ON A SCENE OF TRIBAL simplicity. Molly Kaapu had marshalled the *pake* women about the fire pit and was teaching them the arts of making breadfruit paste and broiling *fei*, the thick red plantains that cooked sweeter than bananas, and baking a groper fish in a wrapping of leaves. The two wives from Kauai were shredding palm leaves and plaiting lines for the fishermen. Tioto and Willy Kuhio were shaping shells into hooks. Simon Cohen was notching a bamboo tube into a simple flute. Hernan Castillo was trying to make an adze from a chunk of basalt and a gnarled tree root. Adam Briggs and Charlie Kamakau were making a pair of paddles for the canoe while Franz Harsanyi, Carl Magnusson and Mark Gilman were engaged in some complicated memory game from which all others were excluded. Apart, in the shadows, Gunnar Thorkild sat with Jenny, who was tearful and full of miseries.

"I feel so lousy, prof. I get these pains. It's like I was all knotted up inside. Then they go away and I just feel sick. I know I'm a drag. Everybody's kind and careful; but it's not fair to them. . . ."

"It's good for them, Jenny. They need you to take their minds off their own problems. Besides, you're important to them for another reason. You're carrying the first new child that will be born on this island. You're a precious thing and your baby will be a pride for everybody."

"I never thought of it like that."

"Then you should, because it's true."

"I'm scared, prof. I mean how it will happen, how much it'll hurt. There's no medicine here, no anaesthetic, nothing!"

"Jenny love, women were having babies long before medicine was thought of. You've got Sally and Molly Kaapu and Martha. They'll give you more help than you'd get in most hospitals today."

"I know that. They've been talking to me, trying to explain things. But I'm still scared."

"When your time is over, you'll have to help the others, because there'll be more babies born here for sure."

"I wonder whose they'll be."

"Ours, Jenny. They'll belong to all of us. The children will be the luckiest kids in the world."

"I wish I belonged to someone. I really do."

Thorkild put his arm round her shoulder and drew her close to him.

"Well, girl, I guess you belong to me and Martha. I picked you off the beach. Martha took you in."

"Why didn't you and Martha get together?"

"I don't know. The chemistry didn't work."

"She's still in love with you."

"No, she isn't. We were made to be friends. Not lovers."

"Will you make it up with her? Say something kind and gentle."

"Sure, if it would make you feel better."

"It would make both of us feel better. Lorillard's all right, I guess. Some ways he's good for her, but she doesn't get much support from him."

"She's not tied. There are younger and better ones. Franz Harsanyi, for instance, or Adam Briggs."

"Funny that! . . . Here we all are, and nobody's tied to anyone—except you and Sally. This afternoon we all were swimming together without a stitch on, but it was like a fraternity picnic. I wonder how it'll work out in the end."

"I wonder too. Feeling better now?"

"Yes, thanks. I'm sorry to be such a mess. Will you do something for me, prof?"

"Sure, what do you want?"

"Promise you won't laugh?"

"Promise."

"Before I go to bed, will you . . . will you just kiss me good night?'

"I'll kiss you now, chicken—and for bedtime too. Dry your eyes and let's join the party."

As they walked over to the hut Hernan Castillo beckoned to Thorkild and held up the adze on which he had been working.

"Take a look at that, chief. What do you think of it?"

"It looks great. Have you tried it yet?"

"You try it."

Thorkild walked over to one of the large palms that fringed the clearing and cut a series of notches in the trunk. The stone blade bit deep but still held firm in the shaft. The little Filipino let out a whoop of joy.

Thorkild strode back to the fire pit to display the miracle.

"Look at this! Hernan made it!"

Castillo was bubbling with explanations:

"Now we know how to do the notches and the binding, we can make other things—knives, hammers. Next thing we have to learn is how to flake and chip the stone to put a good edge on it. If any of you see pieces of basalt like this, pick 'em up and dump them outside the hut. . . . If anybody wants to learn how to do it, I'll show 'em."

"Pity we haven't got a drink, to celebrate," said Carl Magnusson.

"Find me a can for the mash," said Adam Briggs, "and I'll make you the best moonshine you've ever tasted."

"And I'll test it first." Sally Anderton gave a smiling caution. "To make sure you don't go blind or rot your livers."

When they sprawled round the fire pit to eat supper, they were all elated, full of plans and prospects, great and small: to weave fish traps and fruit baskets, to find the bark that would make *tapa* cloth, to make an outrigger and a sail for the canoe, a kneading trough for the women, a press for the oil of the coconut. It was good talk, eager and boisterous and full of hopes.

When the meal was done, they tossed the scraps into the pit, built up the fire and, led by Simon Cohen, began to sing, raggedly at first, and then in more tranquil harmony. It was an hour of strange, sad beauty, with the moon path on the empty sea, the cadence of the voices rising and falling against the boom of the distant surf and the shoheen-ho of the wind in the palms. They drew close to each other, holding body to body, swaying to old rhythms, sharing wordless memories and untellable fears. Led by Ellen Ching,

the Kauai girls and Molly Kaapu danced, while the
men chanted the old melodies, hackneyed once for the
tourists, but now filled with a new beauty, the nostalgia
of a vanished paradise. When they had sung themselves
out, Molly Kaapu gave them her own bawdy good
night.

"See that house there? . . . That's where we sleep.
It's boys on one side, girls on the other; because us
ladies like to be private sometimes. Those that have
other things in mind can dig a nice warm hole on the
beach. . . . But watch out for land crabs which can
give you a nasty nip in the wrong places. And when
you come home, don't wake the rest of us. Good night,
all. . . ."

As they dispersed slowly into the darkness, Gunnar
Thorkild sat alone, staring into the glowing embers
of the fire pit. Jenny had had her good-night kiss.
Sally had gone to settle Carl Magnusson. The others
would dispose themselves in their own fashion in their
own times and seasons. For himself there was the
problem, which tomorrow would become immediate,
of Peter André Lorillard and his gadgets. The radio
did not trouble him. There was no hope of raising
the generators, and without a power supply the radio
would not function. The signal buoys were another
matter. If they could be raised and if they were still
serviceable, then clearly there was a means, however
chancy, of communication with the outside world.
Equally clearly, he had no right to refuse that chance
to a single one of his castaways. And yet, caught in
the magical afterglow of the evening, he found the
idea repugnant, as if he were inviting the armed invasion of a sanctuary. Remembering the eager talk, the
sudden surge of creative impulse in the whole group,
he wondered whether it would have taken place had
they still had hopes of a mechanical intervention by

a bleating object drifting in a wilderness of sea. Besides, even if he left the damned things to be eaten by the coral, he was not denying hope, only deferring it to a time when they could build their own vessel and send it voyaging with a trained crew. . . . He was still wrestling with the thought when Martha Gilman's voice startled him out of his reverie:

"Gunnar, can you spare a minute?"

"Sure." He scrambled to his feet. "Something wrong?"

"No. I've just settled Mark to sleep. Peter's waiting for me down on the beach. I wanted to say something."

"Let me say it." Thorkild's tone was gentle. "We've been friends too long to go on fighting. If I hurt you, I'm sorry. Can we pick it up from there?"

"Of course. And I'm sorry too. But there's something else. Peter's told me about his wife and family in San Diego."

"And . . .?"

"You knew, didn't you?"

"Yes."

"Thanks for letting him tell me. But, Gunnar, I have to know this because it changes everything. What are our chances of getting off the island?"

"Now? In the immediate future? Almost nil. Later, when we're settled and can design and build a boat—maybe."

"Still only maybe?"

"Right."

"You see what I mean, don't you? If we're stuck here, well, Peter and I can make a new life. If we're not and I have a baby and . . ."

"What do you want me to say, Martha?"

"I want you to tell me what to do."

"Can't Lorillard tell you?"

"He says he'd be willing to stay here forever with me."

"That's the answer then—if you believe him."

"Do you?"

"I don't know yet. I've never seen him tested. But if you believe him, go ahead. You can't keep juggling oranges all your life. You have to let 'em drop sometimes."

"Thanks, old friend." She took his face in her hands and kissed him on the lips. "I'm sorry I used you for a fetish doll. Sally Anderton's a lucky girl. I hope she knows it. Good night, chief."

As she hurried away towards the beach he asked himself, with bleak irony, what Peter Lorillard would say when he raised the question of the signal buoys.

Somewhere in the small hours of the morning, Thorkild was awakened by the sound of scuffling and women's voices, behind the partition. A moment later, Sally was beside him, strained and urgent.

"Jenny's going to abort. The water's broken, the labour will begin very soon. Stoke up the fire. Get us some kind of light. Get me some water."

"We've got nothing to boil it in!"

"Oh, Christ! Spring water then. . . . And give me a sterile knife to cut the cord. But we need light. . . ."

"Bring her outside. We've still got the moon and the fire."

"We can't!"

"She'll be warmer and you can see what you're doing. I'll call you when I'm ready."

He hurried outside, cursing the new madness. He piled brambles on the dying fire, snatched up the axe and went charging through the jungle fringe to the *fei* trees. He hacked down a whole plant, dragged it back to the fire pit and spread the broad green leaves like a coverlet on the sand. He went down to the beach and began gathering armfuls of seaweed and driftwood and the husks of coconuts to pile on the fire. He went to the spring and filled half a dozen coconut cups with fresh water. Then he went back inside the hut, where Jenny was already groaning with the first spasms. He waited until the spasms had passed, then carried her out, with the women trailing after him. He laid her down on the leaf mat beside the fire. Molly Kaapu squatted at her head, making a pillow of her lap. Martha Gilman and Charlie Kamakau's wife knelt on either side, gripping her hands. Sally Anderton knelt between her spread legs. Ellen Ching and Yoko braced her feet.

When the spasms began again, Jenny screamed, and the men came tumbling bleary-eyed out of the hut. Thorkild shouted at them to get inside and stay there. He whittled and cleaned a piece of wood and held it to Jenny's mouth so that she could bite on it as she wrestled and thrust, to the urgings of the women. The labour was long and difficult, and when birth came it was a tiny boy child, dead before its entry into life. Sally Anderton was bloody to the elbows, sweating and exhausted, but she completed the operation, silenced the weeping women and told them brusquely:

"Take her inside. Wrap her in your clothes. Lie with her and keep her warm. And for Christ's sake stop blubbering. It doesn't help her one bit!"

When they had gone she herself wept with savage anger, beating her fists into the sand. Thorkild laid a hand on her shoulder and tried to comfort her. She rejected him fiercely.

"Don't touch me! Just bury it. Bury it quickly!"

Gunnar Thorkild wrapped the tiny, bloody corpse in the *fei* leaves and walked down to the beach. Before he was half-way there, Adam Briggs fell into step beside him. He helped to dig the grave and pile the stones. He sat with Thorkild while he wept, bitterly, silently, until no more tears were left. Then he helped him to his feet and said calmly:

"Enough's enough, man! You can't carry us all—not all the time! Let's go home and catch some sleep."

He could not sleep. He cleaned up the mess by the fire pit. He prowled about in the false dawn, gathering fuel and fruit. He pushed out the canoe and fished for an hour, so that when the camp was roused he could offer them food and bustle them about the day's tasks before they felt the full impact of the omens. He could lend them no pity. He could not afford to let them pity themselves. He told them:

". . . Last night was a sad thing, but it's done, finished. Jenny is alive and will bear other children. We have to go on with the business of living and help her to do the same. . . . The tide's low this morning. I want to mount a full-scale salvage operation on the *Frigate Bird* before she breaks up altogether. Peter Lorillard will be in charge. Pick the men you want, Peter, but make sure they can all swim and dive, because you're going to have to submerge inside the hull and grope about for whatever you can find. Do you think your signal buoys would still be serviceable?"

"Possibly, yes."

"Make those a priority. See if they can be got out without risking anyone's neck. Where were they stored?"

"In a box in the hold. We may not be able to get down that far. Besides, they're quite bulky."

"Try anyway. What about other radio gear?"

"Useless without power supply."

"Forget it then. Next priority, metal containers. Last

night we didn't even have a vessel to boil water. After that tools and metal"—he managed a pale joke—"and if you can lay your hands on any of Carl's liquor, bring that too! . . . For the rest, strip the ship. But if the sea gets up and she starts to move, quit. It's my guess she'll be sucked back into the big deep. Understood?"

"Understood."

"Hernan Castillo?"

"Here!"

"I want you to start making as many tools as you can—adzes, simple cultivators, anything you can devise for clearing and building and planting up on the terrace. . . . Molly, Eva, we need baskets, and mats for sleeping and for the walls of the hut. We need fiber for binding. Some of you know how to make these things. Teach the others and get all the women working. . . . Except Ellen Ching. I want her with me today. I want you too, Tioto. Bring a knife. We're going to start exploring the island. We'll be back before sunset. . . . Any questions?"

"Just one, chief." It was Franz Harsanyi who spoke. "Shouldn't we try to salvage books and charts and papers as well? I know they'll be water-spoiled, and some will be useless, but we've got to find some way of preserving the knowledge we hold between us. We can't let it die. I want to say more about this later, but while we're working on the ship . . ."

"Agreed, Franz. So long as it's understood that the means of survival come first. We'll talk later, as you suggest. Anyone else?"

"The medicine chest," said Sally Anderton. "It's in Carl's stateroom in a cupboard under his bunk. It's a large squarish metal box. I'd like that given high priority."

"I'll see to it," said Peter Lorillard. "It's a sight

more important than the signal buoys, which may not work anyway."

Thorkild said casually:

"You're in charge, Peter. Make your own assessment when you get on board. Sort yourselves out quickly. Time and the sea are against us. Ellen and Tioto, be ready to leave in ten minutes. I want to see you first, Sally."

As she walked with him towards the hut, she said, "Darling, I didn't mean to hurt you last night."

"I know that."

"I felt so horribly futile and helpless. I wish you'd take me with you today."

"I can't. I need Ellen because she's a botanist. I want Tioto because he's a gossip and a scandalmonger. If there are social problems brewing—and I think there may be—I'll hear about them. When you're working with the women I want you to keep your ears open too."

She stopped dead in her tracks and stared at him.

"My God! You're a real politician. I've never seen this side of you before. I'm not sure I like it."

"Don't judge me!" He was harsh and strained. "I've buried three dead in forty-eight hours, and there are eighteen living souls depending on me still. I've put Lorillard in charge of salvage so that he'll have to make a decision that I don't want to make; because if it's the wrong one it will damage my authority and the people who depend on its exercise. If that makes me a politician—so be it! Here or in Honolulu, man's still a political animal; and until he's learned to govern himself, faith, hope and charity aren't enough. I don't ask you to approve what I do, only to understand it. I can't fight on two fronts, Sally."

"Don't shut me out then. Help me to understand."

"I'll try. How's Jenny?"

"Miserable. But, unless there's a big infection, she'll live."

"Can I see her?"

"Of course. She's been asking for you. Do me a favour, Gunnar. Meet me by the waterfall before you go."

"Sure. I won't be long."

Lying on the floor of the hut, wrapped in the clothes of the other women, Jenny, the dumpling child, looked like a rag doll, discarded after playtime. Her face, framed in lank hair, was pinched. There were dark hollows under her eyes. When she saw him she gave him a tearful smile and held out a limp, clammy hand.

"Hi, prof!"

"Hi, Jenny!" He squatted on the ground beside her and smoothed back the hair from her forehead. "How do you feel?". .

"Lousy. I'm sorry I gave you such a bad night."

"All part of the service."

"Where did you bury it?"

"Down on the beach, with the others."

"Will I be able to have another one?"

"Sure you will. Several probably."

"Your grandfather promised that, didn't he? He said there was more than one fruit on the tree."

"So he did. I'd almost forgotten."

"And he said I'd bear a chief's son."

"That too."

"I'm glad this one's dead. Billy Spaulding's baby wouldn't really fit with us, would it?"

"Well, the old people used to say whatever happens is good, otherwise the gods wouldn't allow it. You rest now. I'll be back to see you later. Is there anything you want?"

"No. I'll sleep. Will you kiss me?"

He bent and kissed her and she held him for a moment and then lay back with a little sigh of contentment.

"I'm so glad you're here. I remember you carrying me out last night, and how you held me, just like my father when I was tiny. I'll be better soon, won't I?"

"Very soon. Sleep tight."

He drew the ragged covers about her and walked out to meet Sally Anderton by the waterfall. As they kissed and clung together, she begged him:

"Don't let them eat you up. Keep something for me, please!"

"Hush now, sweetheart. I love you."

"You're my man, but you're their lifeline. Their hold is stronger than mine."

"Sally, look at me! Don't be scared. Love's the one thing that grows as you spend it."

"But life isn't! Time isn't! If you don't use it right, you turn round one day and look back at a wasteland."

"What do you want me to do?"

"Nothing. That's the terrible thing. I see you standing there with the group, and you're taller and stronger than any of them, and I'm proud of you and I wouldn't want you to be anything else. But I'm scared too, because I know you can never be wholly mine. I know it's selfish and stupid—and I'm old enough to know better, but that's the way I feel and I can't help myself. Don't blame me, please!"

"I don't blame you," said Gunnar Thorkild somberly. "But I can't escape what I am either: what the ancestors made me, what these people have chosen me to be and do. You're the first woman I've truly loved. You're the haven I turn to out of every storm. . . . But if that isn't enough—God help us both!"

The purpose of the journey, as he explained it to Ellen Ching and Tioto, was twofold: to examine with an expert eye the animal and vegetable resources of the island, and to find, if possible, the high place of which Kaloni the Navigator had spoken. He had already established the fact of a previous habitation of the island, and there was probably an animal population, pigs or dogs descended from their original imports. These could be dangerous if met unaware, so they armed themselves with bamboo staves sharpened at one end. They would go first to the terrace where, with Mark Gilman, he had found the pottery shard. From there they would climb to the level of the crater rim and begin to circle it, marking a route for others to follow at a later time. They would time their journey by the sun, turning about just after midday to avoid being overtaken by darkness in the upland rain forest.

His companions were a useful pair. Tioto was intelligent, resourceful and witty. He had been a sailor, a hairdresser, a nightclub singer, a barman and a gymnast. He was strong as an ox, and a colourful talker in the old language and in English. Ellen Ching was an agreeable blend of Chinese pragmatism and island humour. Her mind worked like an abacus, clickety-click, and the mathematics of her own life had always been meticulously ordered. As they began their march towards the uplands, she talked freely and openly about the future.

". . . I don't know how far you've thought ahead, chief, but once you open up land for cultivation, you'll have a whole set of new structures."

"In what way, Ellen?"

"Let's start from the beginning. The soil's decomposed lava. It'll grow most things we want; but the growth here is so rapid, it's a full-time job to cultivate and harvest and hold back the jungle."

"So?"

"So you're going to need a settled agricultural community. At the same time you need fish for protein, and people to build your boat. . . . That's a shoreline group, pursuing different arts, making another kind of adaptation—even climatically. Feel how different it is up here—sticky, humid; the higher we climb, the more we're dominated by that big cloud."

"I don't see, Ellen, why the division has to be so rigid."

"In the beginning it won't be. We'll all be sharing the same labour. Later, as skills and aptitudes define themselves, the divisions and differences will become clearer. You'll have to work harder to hold people together."

"She's right, chief." Tioto chuckled. "You got bananas. I got fish. How many bananas for one fish, eh? You know how long it takes to make a piece of bark cloth? Remember how much it cost in the tourist market? You're not going to give it away, are you? Then you got a man making tools. How much for an axe? Not now, but later, everyone will want to trade. It's in the blood. . . ."

"Then we've got to get it out of the blood, Tioto, because it'll destroy us, like a disease. Remember the agreement we made: everything is held in common?"

"Easy to say, chief. Hard to do. Unless you make like the old chiefs and bury people alive or beat them with stingray barbs. . . . And what about the man-woman thing? Do we have that in common too?"

Ellen Ching laughed. "And I never knew you cared, Tioto!"

"Sure I care!" Tioto was nettled. "Charlie Kamakau's my friend. What happens when Charlie's wife makes bedroom eyes at one of the *haole* boys, and they go off into the bushes together? I've seen Charlie break a man's head with a marlinspike just because he came drunk on board and talked dirty. . . . And what happens if I get horny one night and chase Miss Ching up the beach?"

"I'll kick your balls off, Tioto."

"If you kick everybody's balls off, sweetheart, you'll have a long, lonely life."

"Then let's run a sporting house together, Tioto. You greet the customers—I'll take the cash."

"Lay off, you two!" Thorkild laughed. "Let's take a breather. This is the terrace where I came the other day. Give us a rundown on what you've seen so far, Ellen."

"Well, plantains, bananas, coconuts, breadfruit, taro. We know about those. There's mango and guava. That bush over there is a pepper plant. You make kava out of the roots—provided your teeth are strong enough to chew them in the first place. We've seen husk-shell tomatoes, and sugarcane and wild pineapples. That big tree is a paper mulberry. You strip off the inner bark to make *tapa* cloth. . . . The fruit rats that eat the bananas are clean animals. We can eat those too if we're pushed to it. . . . There's everything we can ever want, even if we just forage for it. If we cultivate, then we're so much better off."

"There's pig, too," said Tioto. "Listen!"

In the thicket to the left they heard snuffling and grunting, and a moment later, a big black sow, with a piglet at her heels, trotted across the small clearing. Tioto raised his stave to strike at the piglet, but Thorkild stayed his arm.

"Don't! If there's a boar back there, he'll tear the

shanks off you. Enough that we know there's meat to be had."

"You're right, chief." Tioto relaxed and watched the animals disappear into the undergrowth. "How come you think quicker than me? Is that what they teach you at university?"

"That's what my grandfather taught me, Tioto."

"Oh yeah! I forgot." He shivered involuntarily and looked uneasily about him. "Can we move on now? I don't like this place."

It was the second time Thorkild had heard the same thought. This time he was not prepared to dismiss it with a platitude. He asked quietly:

"What's wrong with it, Tioto?"

"Something bad, something cruel."

"I don't feel anything," said Ellen Ching in her downright fashion. "I see it's a fertile place. It would be good for us to work!"

"Do you feel anything, chief?"

"No, Tioto. I feel nothing."

"You're a high chief and a navigator. You have the *mana*. Maybe it doesn't touch you; but I wouldn't live here for a sackful of dollars."

"There are other places," said Thorkild easily. "Let's push on."

The ascent was steeper now, the terraces narrower, the sunlight less and less intense, until finally, when they reached the rim of the crater, they were groping through long, ragged curtains of mist. As they paused to recover their breath and wait for a break in the mist, Ellen Ching pressed home her point.

"You see what I mean, chief. The working altitude is obviously critical. The old terraces stop about two hundred feet short of the cloudline. That place where we saw the pig was obviously the principal tribal area. It also had the greatest variety of edible plants. . . ."

"Maybe that's what I felt." Tioto was still broody and uneasy. "Too many people, too much fighting. At home they make all sorts of pretty stories for the tourists; but our ancestors were rough and bloody warriors. They ate each other. They made human sacrifice. They used sorcery and torture."

"The mist's clearing," said Ellen Ching abruptly. "Let's push on while we have the chance."

The bowl of the cater was still invisible, covered with a deep lake of cloud, but the rim was clear, a razorback of black lava where nothing grew but coarse tussocks. For the first time, however, there was a clearly defined path—a narrow, moss-grown track winding round the inner lip. Thorkild took the lead, and they made easy progress for about half a mile, and then the track ended abruptly, in front of a high wall of lava. The wall was pierced by a tunnel, high as two men, at the end of which light was visible. The air that funnelled through it was fresh, with the taste of salt in it.

"I think this is your place," said Tioto.

"I know it is," said Gunnar Thorkild. "From here, I go alone. Wait for me."

He hesitated a moment, touched by an ancient dread, then he took a deep breath, drew himself erect and strode into the tunnel. It was empty for its whole length. The floor was rough with loose stones and sharp outcrops. It was more than a hundred paces long; but the distance seemed interminable. Ten paces from the opening he stopped, gathering himself against the terror that might confront him in the place which was the end of all journeys. Then he stepped forward into the light.

He was greeted by the scream of a thousand sea-birds that rose in clouds from the hollows in the rocks. Before him lay a boundless ocean, dazzling in the sunlight. He closed his eyes against the glare and the vertigo, and when he opened them again he saw that he stood on a broad platform that ran, on either hand, along the outer rim of the crater. Around the platform, against the wall, were set small blocks of stones. On each block was the skeleton of a man, the bones tumbled into disarray as the flesh and the ligaments that held them had dissolved or been eaten by the seabirds. Beside each skeleton was a wooden paddle, carved, some simply, some more ornately, with the symbol of the god Kanaloa.

Slowly, painfully, like a man in a fever-dream, Thorkild passed along the row of skeletons, not daring to cast his eyes ahead lest his courage desert him and he flee from the final encounter with his grandfather. The journey seemed to take a lifetime. One stone, one pile of bones, one paddle; pause a moment to give reverence to the nameless spirit; pass and look again; wait for the stink of corruption to strike the nostrils, and pray for courage enough to look at the face of a loved one in the horror of dissolution. The panic grew and grew until it seemed to choke him; but still he moved on, pace by slow pace, to the moment of revelation. When it came, he was stunned by the serenity of it.

Kaloni the Navigator sat cross-legged upon his stone, his face upturned to the sun, eyes closed as if in sleep, the paddle held across his knees. There was no mark on him, no scar of discoloration. When Thorkild reached out a trembling hand to touch him, the flesh was still warm and pliant as if the last pulse-beat had gone only a moment before. Then it was as if his own heart burst inside him. He turned his face to the sea and threw out his arms and in the tongue of the high ones shouted his grief to the sun:

"Ai-ee!
Kaloni the Navigator is dead.
Kaloni from whose seed I sprang
Is dead!
I am alone.
I am blind.
I cannot read the sea.
I cannot see the stars.
O Kaloni,
Speak for me to the high ones.
Send me their answer on the wind.
Ai-ee! Ai-ee!
Roll back the dark, Kaloni.
Make me see. . . !"

As they worked their way back down the jungle slope Ellen Ching said:

"You look strange. Are you sick or something?"

"Leave him be." Tioto rebuked her quietly. "Was he there, chief?"

"He was there. All of them were there."

"O my God!" It was a whisper of awe from the girl. "It was all true, then?"

"It was all true. But there's nothing to fear. It's peaceful now . . . peaceful and terribly lonely."

"Can we help?"

"No one can help." Tioto was grave and strangely tender. "I know . . . when Malo died, the stars went out for me. Was it like that for you, chief?"

"Very like, Tioto. I never knew my father or my mother. Kaloni Kienga was all the family I had. Whatever's best in me came from him."

"The *mana* too, chief. Don't forget that."

"I can't forget it," said Gunnar Thorkild. "I wish I could."

"The *pake* don't understand it."

"Don't be too sure!" Ellen Ching was suddenly angry. "We may not understand it; but we feel it, whatever it is. Not all of us maybe, not always in the same way, but it's there. It's like this cloud, it changes every moment, but it's always here. There's something of the same thing in the Bible too. We learned about it at school: the Israelites in the desert followed a pillar of cloud by day and a pillar of fire by night."

"Are you sorry you came with me?"

"I am." Tioto was blunt. "If I hadn't come, Malo would still be alive. But I don't blame you. Don't think that. It's just the stinking way things turn out. Like that poor kid last night. Rough, very rough."

"I'm a fatalist," said Ellen Ching. "The fortune-teller casts the wands. You can't change the way they fall. Can I say something to you, chief?"

"Whatever you like."

"Don't worry too much about what we think or say. Don't bend too easily. No one will thank you for it."

"Are you afraid I'll be too weak?"

"No. But once we're settled, with full bellies and a rhythm of life, we'll start to think for ourselves again. The things that Tioto says are in the blood will come out. You'll have to be very strong then."

"This woman's got brains." Tioto said a grudging tribute. "You listen to her, chief. That's good Chinese talk. Money in the bank, land under the feet and the old ones holding the family together. That's the rough part . . . how you hold us together."

"Let's rest awhile," said Thorkild. "We're making good time."

They propped themselves against a tall tree, which Tioto remarked was the kind from which their boat should be made. Ellen Ching took the knife and began to loosen the earth round the roots of a big pepper plant. Tioto plucked a few hard husk-tomatoes, tiny red globules, handed some to Thorkild, squatted down beside him and began to talk quietly in the old language:

"Chief, this business of the women . . . you got to do something about it. Eva Kuhio, she's a fine smart girl. She and Willy make out fine. But Charlie's wife—ay, ay! She's hot for every man but Charlie. That one over there . . ." He jerked a thumb towards Ellen Ching. "She's a steady one too—Hakka blood, all head and not much fire down below—but steady. Your little Japanese, now, she's a troublemaker. Oh, I know she's sweet as sugarcane, and pretty as a china doll; but— oh, man!—you cross her and she'll put poison in the poi bowl. I know I'm right, chief. I'm closer to women than you'll ever be. So you better start thinking, before Charlie Kamakau runs mad with the fire axe."

"What do you suggest, Tioto?"

"Go back to the old way. The married woman is *kapu* to every man but her husband. The unmarried play what games they like; but the high chief has to approve any marriage or permanent arrangement."

"It sounds easy, Tioto, but I'm not sure it would work. These people come from a different society."

"But they're back in an old one, and they're going to stay in it! Listen, chief, I don't care that much . . . except for Charlie. I could make him happier than his wife does. But if he breaks out . . . then I tell you there's more grief than you can guess."

"Thanks for telling me, Tioto. I'll think about it."

"Can I ask you a favour, chief?"

"What, Tioto?"

"Keep me down on the beach. Don't ask me to work up on the mountain."

"All right. But don't mention it to anyone else. If it's bad *kapu* for them, let them find out for themselves. . . . Now you can do something for me, Tioto."

"Anything. You know that."

"I'll spell it. You lose someone you love. You see all the others playing ring-a-rosy. That's bitter and hard to swallow. . . . It makes a man sour sometimes and cruel. . . . So! Don't you be the one to put poison in the poi bowl."

Tioto gave a little nervous laugh. "So I bitch a little. What's the harm? Still, you got a deal. . . . You never treated me like a funny man. I appreciate that."

Ellen Ching came back and tossed them each a handful of roots.

"Here, carry these back. We'll make ourselves some happy juice."

Thorkild chuckled and shook his head. "Kava isn't happy juice—far from it. It's yellow and its tastes vile and after about twenty minutes you feel sad and drowsy. That's why they used it for big occasions, like meetings of chiefs and divinations of the future. It makes you solemn and important. Try it if you like; but leave me out of it. I feel solemn enough for ten drunks. Come on, let's move! There's a two-hour walk ahead of us."

The campsite was like a junkyard, piled with blankets, waterlogged books, oilcans, cordage, cutlery, tools, bottles of liquor, metal fittings, wooden panels, cabinet drawers, rigging wire, broken spars, scraps of sail track, pots, pans, odd shoes, articles of clothing, cans of food—a miscellany of booty, which was being sorted and stacked under the vigilant eye of Carl Magnusson, while Willy Kuhio and Charlie Kamakau and Adam Briggs worked on a rough shelter to house it all. Peter Lorillard was glowing with satisfaction as he made his report.

"They worked like dogs. We must have made a

dozen runs, back and forth, before the tide came up. We salvaged the compass and most of the charts. We got Sally's medicine chest. There's a lot more stuff on board, but I doubt we'll get much of it. She's moving a lot; seems to be slipping seaward. The next big sea will finish her, I think."

"What about the signal buoys?"

"No way. We couldn't even get into the hold. I went down first and Willy Kuhio went down after me, but it was too dark to identify anything, and we couldn't stay submerged long enough to work. It's damn dangerous out there."

"Well, you tried. . . . I'll make sure everybody knows it."

"Thanks. I've got something of yours."

He hurried over to the hut and a few moments later came back carrying the box which contained Thorkild's personal treasure, the adze head of Kaloni the Navigator. Thorkild was deeply moved. He asked shakily:

"How did you know about this?"

"Sally asked me to find it. Apparently you showed it to her one night."

Thorkild held out his hand. "I owe you a big debt. . . . I'll try to pay it one day."

Lorillard shrugged. "It was there. I brought it. Simple. . . . How did you make out on the mountain?"

"Fine. There's good ground up there and everything we need for cultivation. There's pig too. We'll need two settlements though. So we'll extend ourselves here before we open up the high ground."

"Sounds wise. Anything else?"

"I found the high place. My grandfather was there."

"That must have been a bad moment."

"Bad enough. There are thousands of seabirds nest-ing in the ledges round the crater. That means eggs, if we want to climb for them."

"It's another plus in the ledger. I felt good today, Thorkild. Better than I've felt in a long spell. By the way, you've got to believe we tried for those signal buoys."

"I believe it," said Thorkild easily. "Why shouldn't I?"

Franz Harsanyi called to him. He was sitting amidst a pile of books and charts, with Mark Gilman beside him, separating the pages, trying to dry them in the late sun. He held out a black volume.

"Here's your log, chief . . . and I found a few pencils in the wheelhouse. Don't handle the book until we dry it."

"Thanks, Franz."

"It's important, chief—for young Mark here and those who come after us. We've got to record things, hold them in memory. We can't let two thousand years of learning blow away, just because we've got shelter and full bellies. You agree with that, don't you?"

"I agree, Franz. I'll help as much as I can."

"I'll look after the books if you like—with Mark here. He and I have been trying some experiments."

"What kind of experiments?"

"We'll give you a demonstration when we're ready, Uncle Gunnar."

"You say when, partner. Have you seen Sally?"

"She's down at the waterfall with Molly. They're washing blankets or something. Want me to fetch her?"

"No. I'll wait till she's finished."

As he walked towards the hut, he passed Hernan Castillo, squatting on the ground with a pile of stones on one side of him and a mess of wood chips on the other. He held up the results of his labour, a single basalt wedge, with a serrated blade about four inches wide.

"I've got the knack now, chief. There's a day's work in that, but I can work faster now. That's a damn good blade, even though I do say it myself. The hafts are easy. See? . . . When the others go out to cut wood, they should look for shapes like this and bring them to me."

"I'd like to show you something," said Gunnar Thorkild gravely.

He opened the box, peeled off the sodden wrappers from the stone and handed it to Castillo. He held it in his hands with a kind of reverence, turning it over and over to examine every detail. Then he looked up.

"It's beautiful. Where did you get it?"

"From my grandfather. He made it himself; built his first canoe with it."

"Thanks for showing it to me. I appreciate it."

"Keep it," said Gunnar Thorkild. "I don't need it anymore."

"You can't mean that. This is a sacred thing."

"You're the toolmaker now. That's a sacred art. Please keep it."

Hernan Castillo stood up and held out his hand.

"Want to know something, chief? I never felt so lonely in my life as I did sitting here all day, chipping at stones while the others were working and laughing together. This tells me what it means. . . . Funny. . . . It's like seeing you and myself for the first time. You're a big man, Professor. I'm proud to know you."

Thorkild shrugged off the compliment. "Don't rate me too high. Otherwise you'll want to pull me down one day. . . . Could you make spearheads too? There's game up there on the mountain."

"Spearheads, bow and arrows—easy!"

"Can you forge metal? If you can, we've got a lot of scrap over there."

"I don't know. I could try. But let me work this thing out first. I've got a one-track mind. That's why I was never a good student."

"That's why you're such a good artisan. Stay with it."

Thorkild gave him an offhand salute and walked into the hut to see Jenny. She was dozing; but she woke at his footfall and sat up to greet him. She felt better. She had eaten a little. She had walked a few steps. She would like to try again. Would he take her outside? He helped her to her feet, supported her to the door and called to the others to witness her triumph. They gathered around her, excited and solicitous.

Then Adam Briggs pushed his way to the front and took possession of her. "I'm going to carry you down to the beach, young lady."

He swept her up into his arms and carried her away to the applause of the little group. Peter Lorillard added a laughing postscript:

"He damn near drowned himself on board, trying to find her dresses and a brush and comb!"

"Love, it's wonderful!" Barbara Kamakau was deliberately provocative. "All my Charlie thought of was tools and oilcans!"

"And liquor," Carl Magnusson cut in swiftly. "We'll crack a bottle tonight, just to celebrate. . . . That is, if the chief approves!"

"I approve." Thorkild played out the comedy of diversion. "Unless you'd like *kava* instead. Ellen brought back the makings." He held up the roots with the earth still clinging to them. "You chew these up and spit the juice into a bowl and brew it up afterwards."

"Thanks," said Sally Anderton. "But I'll have bourbon. . . . And I need you, Barbara, to help lay out the washing. Those blankets weigh a ton."

As the group dispersed Charlie Kamakau exploded:

"That Barbara! Always pinching and pricking. Nothing is right! Nothing is enough! One day I'm going to beat the hell out of her."

"Take it easy, Charlie!" Thorkild drew him away from the group. "It's been a long day for everyone. I'm going down for a swim. Join me?"

"Sure. Give me ten minutes to finish the shed. I'll meet you down there."

When he was out of earshot, Carl Magnusson growled his disapproval.

"Damn fool! He'll never learn! He's forty years old. He picks up a pretty girl in a waterfront bar, marries her in a week, goes to sea with me—and expects to come home and find her darning his socks! . . . If I were Charlie I'd get rid of her and keep my self-respect. Mind if I walk to the beach with you, Thorkild?"

"Please! How's the shoulder?"

"Better today—probably because I found something useful to do. How did you make out?"

Thorkild recounted his day. Magnusson was strangely moved by the story of the last resting place of Kaloni Kienga and the Navigators. He said broodingly:

"I remember having a long argument with your priest friend, Flanagan, about the nature of faith. He made the point that I'm only now beginning to understand: that religious faith provides man with what he called the arithmetic of the cosmos . . . a means to harmonize himself with the mysterious universe in which he finds himself. He went further and said that, without that arithmetic, we were idiots living in a bedlam. I couldn't see it then. I see it now. I never knew a man so complete and harmonious as your grandfather. That's why his end seems so—so proper. . . . Our group, now, is quite different. So far, you're doing the right thing, holding them together with a single, simple ethic—work together to survive. But that won't carry you far enough. Even now, it's clear that we've got more than we need, and more time than we can cope with. So, tomorrow and the days after, the rhythm is going to slow down, partly because of the climate and, according to Sally Anderton, partly because of the monotony of our activities. You'll slow down too, Gunnar. Inevitably your grip will loosen, as mine has. What then. . . ?"

"If I think that way," said Gunnar Thorkild, "I'll never do anything. I've got to work from day to day, proposing limited goals—the salvage, the upland farm, the building of our vessel. Right now, it's the social situation that bothers me. Charlie Kamakau and his Barbara are just the first symptoms."

"I know. Molly Kaapu and I talked about it today. We listened too—mostly to the women. They talk about things much more freely than men."

"How were they talking, Carl?"

"Well, let's start from the beginning. . . . They've all got preferences among the men." He laughed. "They've got us all weighed off, Thorkild—even you —as providers and protectors and sexual partners; and their preferences aren't confined to one man. They know they themselves are vulnerable. There's no pill, no condoms; so any one of them can fall pregnant. Which is why most of them are being careful right now. They're still not convinced that we're going to spend a lifetime here—and they don't relish the idea of going home one day with a parcel of kids that once belonged to nobody. There's no law here that protects them: no marriage, no divorce, no property right, no framework that will continue if they ever leave here. Sure, when they come to that, they'll mate and to hell with the consequences. They'll bury their fears and live from day to day; but the uncertainty will always be there. . . . At first sight the married ones like Barbara Kamakau and Eve Kuhio are better off; in another sense, they're worse, because they're bound, while the others are free. . . . Am I making sense?"

"Very good sense, Carl. Except I don't yet see what to do about it."

"Are you open to a proposition?"

"Anything."

"Well, go back to the argument you and I had before we set out: annexation of this territory to a sovereign state, the United States of America. Now, at first sight that's a meaningless formality. However, if we agreed to it, we'd set ourselves under a code of laws to which we're all accustomed—with enough flexible variations to enable us to administer a kind of frontier justice, and make it stick if we ever returned home—which I'm sure I won't. We could solemnize marriages, register land rights, agree divorces, permit cohabitation but protect the rights of the women and their issue. . . . I may be wrong, but I think we'd do a great deal that way to stabilize relationships. As it is, murder could be done here, and no sanctions could be applied against the murderer once he or she was off the island."

"Who's talking about murder?" Charlie Kamakau flopped down on the sand beside them. "I feel like breaking a few heads myself."

"What's the trouble, Charlie?" asked Thorkild.

"That woman of mine!" said Charlie Kamakau. "I just walked over to the waterfall, and there she was, washing herself, mother-naked, with Yoko and Simon Cohen and Franz. I told her I didn't think it was right for a married woman. She just laughed at me. I hauled her out and slapped her and sent her back to the camp."

"There's no harm in it, Charlie." Thorkild tried to placate him. "She's young and high-spirited. Besides, everyone's bathing naked now."

"She was a whore when I married her." Charlie was bitter. "She's still a whore."

"Then let her go, Charlie," said Magnusson firmly. "Why tear your tripes out?"

"Because she's mine and I'll make an honest woman out of her if I have to beat her black and blue —and I'll kill any man that lays hands on her!"

"That's bad talk, Charlie," Thorkild snapped at him. "Bad and dangerous. I'll have no more of it."

"She's my woman!"

"And you're both my people! You made me a chief. You know what that means, better than anyone."

"Then you talk sense into her, chief!"

"All right, I'll try. Now let's go for a swim and cool down." He helped Magnusson to his feet. "You go back to camp, Carl. We'll finish our talk later. And break out two bottles of liquor. I think we could all use a stiff drink at supper!"

That night there were torches round the fire pit, bundles of fiber, soaked in oil and bound to bamboo stakes. The smoke drove away the insects; the light made a circle of security and domesticity, a wider frontier against the dark that encroached at nightfall on body and spirit. At the end of the meal, Thorkild made a great ritual of pouring the liquor, a single tot for everyone and one tossed into the fire for a libation of thanks to that which was the Beginning, the Foundation of all things. He made the toast:

"To all of us, and to the future!"

"I'd say the future looked pretty bright," said Carl Magnusson. "I'm only sorry mine looks shorter than yours. With the permission of the chief here, I'd like to say a few words—and if they're not the right ones you'll remember that I'm a cross-grained old bastard who's lost everything he ever owned and gained himself a family and isn't too unhappy with the exchange. . . . Well, chief?"

"You have the floor, Senator," said Thorkild with a grin.

"I'll stand," said Magnusson. "I think better on my feet."

Simon Cohen and Willy Kuhio helped him to his feet. In the glow of the torches he looked like some old warrior, hoary and battle-scarred, but full of strength and dignity. He began slowly, choosing his words with care:

"I want to talk to you about two things: who we are and what we may become. We are a mixed group of men and women, most of us citizens of the United States of America, cast away on an unknown island, off the trade routes. We have, at our disposal, all the means of survival. We have the hope and the skill to build a vessel that will bring us back into contact with the outside world. We have the navigators who can sail it. . . . But this hope brings its own danger for us. It can distract us from the tasks at hand. It can prevent us from perfecting those relationships —of sex, friendship and, let me say it, love—on which our tribal living will depend. . . . As it stands now, because we are outside any jurisdiction of state or law, any one of us could repudiate whatever has happened on this island. Now, if we were all perfect, that wouldn't matter; but we're not perfect. We're jealous, possessive, mismatched in one way or another to the natural harmony. . . . I'm an old man. I've lived rough and fought hard. I can tell you these things honestly because none of you can think that I have any claims on you, except for kindness. . . . So I have a proposal to make, a proposal which I believe would supply a necessary continuity between our past, our present and the future we hope to achieve. I propose that, as a group of citizens, we annex this territory to the United States of America, and in so doing, place ourselves under its Constitution and live under the generality of its laws. If we do this, several things happen. Our children retain the citizenship which we enjoy. Our social acts, of marriage and, if need be, divorce, have a legal character. Our individual rights under a common land tenure can be adjudicated, if need be. Our elected leaders have an authority beyond dispute. . . . Now that's the good side. The bad is that we admit that we are in need of an overriding state and a system, with all its defects, already established. We may provoke contention instead of avoiding it. We will limit our personal choices, and our capacity to conform them, by compromise, one with the other. It may be that some of you, or all of you, want a more flexible society than the one I have described—a more open marriage for instance, a sexual relationship less restrictive and more adapted to the life we have here, so that tensions can be abated more easily and jealousies avoided. I'm beyond all that; so I have chosen to raise the question which must be in your minds. I do not suggest that this question be resolved quickly by a campfire vote. I do say it must be settled soberly and after reflection and deep discussion in public and in private. . . . As our old preacher used to say: 'Brothers and Sisters, thank you for your patience.' "

He sat down to a prolonged applause, after which Martha Gilman spoke up, in her jerky, no-nonsense style.

"I'd like to thank Carl Magnusson for saying things that needed to be set in the open. . . . I don't quarrel with his argument. I see problems in both situations; because you can't adopt a set of laws and then abrogate them at will. . . . For instance, under the laws of the United States, private property is sacred, the fruits of labour belong to the individual. We agreed to a completely different system—communal ownership of labour and its fruits. I think we all see that's right for us; so half the laws made under the Constitution are already out the window—if we had a window! . . . Now, the other thing, marriage, sex, what you will . . . I think we owe it to each other to be absolutely honest about that, too. After all, we're working, side by side, all day. We're trotting around half naked, we're bathing and playing together. There are no possible secrets—and I don't think there should be. There are two married couples. They made their contracts long before they met the rest of us. Peter's my lover. Sally and the chief are lovers too. . . . But how exclusive do we want these things to be? How long can they remain exclusive in this kind of group? These things are very personal, I know. They touch intimate areas of our lives—personal feelings, private and public moralities. But this beach, this island are our world now. We've got to run it the best way we can. . . . I'm a woman. I'm the vessel that bears the child, the body that nurtures it. I want to be free to bear a child to the father of my choice. If I want more than one man, that's my choice too—good or bad. I want to be free to accept or reject for myself. We women talked about these things between us. Whatever happens, we don't want to be chattels or slaves to a contract that doesn't bind everybody— because in this community it's hard to see how it can. . . ."

"Are you saying"—Charlie Kamakau was glowering and angry—"that Willy's marriage or mine doesn't mean anything; that we hand over our wives as common property?"

"Not at all, Charlie," said Martha Gilman calmly. "I'm saying that our relationships should be as exclusive or as open as each of us may decide. I don't want to be invaded and you don't want to be a stud stallion for any woman who demands to be serviced, whether you like her or not."

Surprisingly it was Eva Kuhio who stepped into the argument. She was a big quiet girl, with a slow smile and a meek, compliant manner that made her the least conspicuous member of the group. She asked:

"Is it all right for me to say something, chief?"

"Sure, Eva. Speak up."

"Well, as Martha says, we did talk about this. I talked to my Willy too. I love him and so long as I've got him, I'm happy. . . . But suppose we all pair off, there's still men left with nobody to love or lie with when they're lonely. That's a sad thing for them and a bad thing for us all. I was brought up religious and I still believe what I was taught at school and in church. But I don't believe God wants to send any man to prison for life; and I don't believe any of us women has a right to put him there. So maybe we all have to loosen up a little and give some loving where it's needed."

"I agree with Eva," said Sally Anderton.

"I too," said Yoko Nagamuna.

"I don't," said Charlie Kamakau. "No way! No-how! If I wanted to go whoring around I'd have stayed single."

"We're talking about loving," said Franz Harsanyi.

"You're sailing the wrong tack, Charlie." Simon Cohen was patently hostile. "And none of us likes to see a woman slapped around."

Charlie Kamakau lunged towards him, hand up-raised to strike. Adam Briggs and Thorkild wrenched him back to his place.

Thorkild rebuked him. "This is tribe talk. You give it respect. If you have something to say, stand up and say it."

"Let her say it!" Charlie Kamakau thrust an ac-cusing finger at his wife. "Let her tell you who she's played with, here and on the *Frigate Bird* and before that! Let her tell me now what she wants."

"Okay then!" Barbara was on her feet, savage and defiant. "You asked for it. Here it is! I'm sick of you, Charlie Kamakau! You're jealous and you slap me around because you can't do what a man ought to do with a woman. I chase around to get what I don't get in bed with you. That's the truth and you know it! So here and now, I'm finished. I don't want any part of you anymore!"

There was a long, wary silence as they faced each other across the fire pit. Then Charlie Kamakau laughed, a high animal sound, horrible to hear.

"You say that? You, a waterfront tramp I picked out of a bar? You know why I can't touch you? You stink! You stink of every man that's ever had you, every rotten bed you've ever been laid on! Okay, it's finished!"

. He stood up and spat in the fire. Then he swung round to face Thorkild.

"You hear me, chief. She's not my woman anymore!"

"I hear you, Charlie. So be it!"

Charlie Kamakau turned on his heel and strode away towards the beach.

Tioto got up to follow him. "Leave him to me, chief. I know how to handle him."

"I'll bet you do, lover!" Barbara Kamakau shouted at his back. "I'll bloody bet you do!"

"Go to bed, woman," said Molly Kaapu wearily. "You've made enough grief for one night."

Later, when the others had retired to sleep, and she walked with Thorkild on the beach, Sally Anderton summed it up in sober, clinical fashion:

". . . It's like a boil. You have to lance it; but it leaves a nasty mess."

"A dangerous mess, sweetheart. Charlie was stripped down and castrated tonight. How are we going to restore his self-esteem?"

"Only a woman can do that."

"I doubt any woman will get close to him for a long time yet—if any one would want to after tonight. Goddammit. He's the most useful man we've got, and that little bitch . . ."

"Don't blame her too much, my love. She's had a rough time too. Charlie's got a violent streak in him."

"I know. That's what worries me. I'll have to work hard to hold his loyalty and get him to see things in perspective. That was a gruelling session tonight, and in the end nothing was accomplished."

"I think we accomplished a lot." Sally was very definite about it. "There was a real encounter between us all. Issues were faced and resolved at least in part."

"Like the women calling the tune, and . . ."

"And being willing to share themselves. That's what you wanted to say, wasn't it?"

"I guess so."

"Was the idea repugnant to you?"

Thorkild shrugged and gave her a rueful grin. "No. It's a part of the old life I understood and approved; but when I heard you say it—yes, I was jealous."

"That makes two of us, doesn't it? I don't like sharing you. You don't like sharing me."

"Don't play games with me, Sally."

"It's not a game, darling. It's a fact of our life with which we're all trying to come to terms. I have no wish to go necking on the beach here with another man; but—how can I put it?—if I thought I could give Charlie Kamakau back his manhood and bring him back into the group again, I'd do it. Would you hold me back?"

"I'm not sure. I'm not sure of anything anymore."

"Tired?"

"Hungry."

"What about the land crabs?"

"People are more dangerous," said Thorkild. "Let's sleep down here tonight."

SIX

NEXT MORNING THEY WOKE EARLY, TO A LOWER-
ing sky and an oily sea, and a windless hush
that presaged a big blow. Charlie Kamakau and Tioto
were already out, fishing the inner reef. Thorkild
hailed them and they came paddling in, displaying
their catch: pawns and an octopus and *mahimahi*
and a big crayfish. He helped them drag the canoe
high up on the beach and, while Sally walked back to
the camp with Tioto, he himself lingered on the beach
with Charlie Kamakau.

Charlie was calm now and very respectful, but
oddly empty, like the biblical man whose devils were
purged out, but who found himself lost and lonely
without them. He was sorry for the scene he had
made, but determined and indeed content that the
break between himself and his wife was final and ir-
revocable. He had a request to make. He hoped
Thorkild would grant it.

". . . I don't know how I can say it, chief. I feel better this morning; but I'm all broken up inside. I don't want to go back there and face all those people who heard me shamed last night. I don't want them looking at me and wondering whether what Barbara said is true, and I'm no good with a woman. I am, chief. I was before I met her, and she started running around, and only coming home to cut me up. . . . Anyway, I want to get away by myself for a while. I'd like you to give me some tools and let me go up and start clearing the terrace."

"That's a hell of a job, Charlie."

"I know. That's why I'd like to do it. It would prove something maybe."

"It's pretty lonely up there."

"Tioto told me. He doesn't want me to go; but I'd be a lot lonelier down here, watching Barbara waving her tail for everyone but me. You could visit me, chief. You could send people up. Besides, it wouldn't be forever, just until I get the maggots out of my skull."

"Charlie, I hate the idea of your running away. Why not sweat it out here? Two or three days and the worst will be over."

"And I'll have that bitch under my eyes everywhere I turn. It's too much. Let me go, chief!"

There was no good reason to refuse, one very good reason to consent: it would spare the community the embarrassment of a bitter divorcement. Thorkild agreed and added a caution:

"If you're sick, Charlie, or you find it too lonely, come down. People don't care as much as you think about you and Barbara. They're too busy with their own concerns. Promise?"

"I promise, chief. I'll put a few tools together and move off."

"Good luck, Charlie. Don't stay away too long."

Before the rest of the camp was astir, he was gone. Tioto was grim and dubious. The terrace was a bad place. For a mixed-up man like Charlie it was doubly dangerous. It would have been better to keep him on the beach, make him a fisherman, let him work away from the others until he was ready again for human companionship. Thorkild shrugged off the argument. Better to let him go his own gait until he was ready to walk, straight and strong again. There was a big blow coming; they had best secure the camp before it hit.

The storm lasted all day and half the night, fifteen hours of high winds and driving rain, and thunderous seas, during which they huddled inside the leaking hut, keeping themselves busy with handwork: plaiting sennit and palm fiber, weaving mats and baskets, scraping shells into hooks, making spears and traps for the fishing. It was simple, satisfying labour, enlivened by small jokes at the expense of the fumblers, and easy, discursive talk about their future plans.

Franz Harsanyi and Mark Gilman gave their demonstration. The boy had a prodigious memory, both aural and visual. He could read a page of print and recite it back, word perfect. Call him a list of names and numbers, or the verses of a poem, and he would chant them over, without a hesitation or an error. He had a natural ear for languages and was already picking up dialect talk. Franz Harsanyi, in a long burst of eloquence, developed the theme he had first broached to Thorkild.

". . . We've all got certain specialized knowledge which we're not using now, but which may be enormously useful later on. . . . Dr. Anderton, for instance, and Peter Lorillard and Ellen Ching with her botany. We can record some of it, on the backs of charts or in the margins of books; but for the most part we'll have to preserve and transmit it in the old way, by memory. Simon Cohen can help, by setting it to simple melodies and rhythms, which make it easier to remember. But we should all work at it. At night, when we're sitting round the fire, each one could contribute a piece of his own knowledge. We set it in mnemonic form. We chant it, call it over, test each other on it. It's like a game; but it's a very important game, and it's been played for centuries. Young Mark here is a genius at it, as you've seen. . . . Well, what do you say, chief?"

"I say it's a great idea. It puts us all back to school. It keeps our minds alive. It gives us a pool of knowledge on which we can draw if any one of us—God forbid!—drops out or becomes incapable. We should try to develop a situation where we're all teaching one another, just as we're doing now with this handwork. We'll make it a regular thing—an hour every night after supper."

"Just a minute!" Yoko Nagamuna piped up from the corner where she was working with Hernan Castillo. "That's another regulation on top of everything we've got already! I register an objection, chief."

"Do you mind telling why, Yoko?"

"It seems to me we're getting back to the very thing some of us have been trying to escape, even at home: a totally regulated society. That's what caused the fuss last night. You want rules and timetables for everything—even for sex. You're not leaving us any room to grow as ourselves."

"She's got a point." Simon Cohen was swift to confirm the protest. "Me, for instance, I'm happy to do my share of the work; but I'm damned if I want to spend every evening making up nursery rhymes about medicine and navigation. . . ."

"But if you get sick," said Thorkild evenly, "you'll still expect medical attention. And when we try to sail away from here you'll still expect someone to lay a course and identify the stars and know how the winds blow and the currents run."

"Sure, but that's a specialist function."

"What happens," asked Franz Harsanyi, "if the specialist gets washed overboard or breaks his neck?"

"Agreed," said Yoko. "But my point is that there should be an element of personal choice. I'm a nutritionist. I'd be happy to understudy Sally in medicine or Ellen in botany; but I don't want to wear Peter Lorillard's hat, because I don't have the head for it."

"Seems to me"—Carl Magnusson was testy—"we'd all like to eat the omelette, provided someone else makes it."

"I think we need regulation," said Adam Briggs bluntly. "Otherwise our efforts will be so diffused we'll get nothing done. . . . This house, for instance, it's shaking over our heads right now. It gives us no privacy. We've got to build other and better ones. That means our labour's got to be marshalled and directed."

"I've accepted that," said Simon Cohen.

"You've accepted the part that suits you!"

"Let me try to explain something," Sally Anderton cut in quickly. "You may not be aware of it. As a doctor I see it plainly. Since our arrival here, our diet has changed radically. We're losing a lot of salt, because of the humidity. Our mineral intake and our protein intake are lower than before, because we're eating tropical fruits and fish instead of hard meats. Unconsciously, we're all slowing down, to compensate for the new situation. There's a psychological side effect too. There's a Greek word for it—*accidie*. It means torpor, or indifference. It's compounded by monotony, a limited and repetitive series of activities. Now that's precisely what Gunnar Thorkild is trying to avoid. He's lived this island life. He knows the traps and the pitfalls. He's not trying to regulate your lives like some petty tryant. He's trying to keep you active and interested and ready for the big tasks ahead: farming our land, building our boat. . . . It's no secret that I love him; but I'd face him down if I thought he were wrong or unjust. In this case he isn't. . . ."

"And I'll say the rest of it," said Molly Kaapu. "You're *haole*. You don't know how to live the way we do. If you don't learn, you'll end up on the beach staring out to sea, with flies crawling out of your sores!"

Yoko Nagamuna was not to be put down so easily. "I still say . . ."

"Don't say it, kid!" Hernan Castillo gave a big theatrical yawn. "Write a book about it when you get home. Now for God's sake help me with these bindings."

Sometime during the high fury of the storm, the *Frigate Bird* disappeared, sucked down in the great deeps beyond the sentinel rock. Nothing was left to show that she had ever been there except a few balks of broken timber and miscellaneous rubbish thrown up on the beach. Thorkild was the happier for her going, because now the channel was open and the tragic reminder of their voyage and its ill fortune was removed from sight. Now they could navigate their canoe beyond the reef, explore the farther coasts of the island, and, when their big vessel was built, float it into open water.

For the present, there was other, more urgent work. After the ravages of the wind and rain the big hut was barely habitable; so with Tioto and Lorillard and Adam Briggs, Thorkild pegged out the shape of a permanent, beach-side village. In all there were eleven men and eight women. But Charlie Kamakau was away, so he decided that they should build eight small huts and a larger storehouse, which could also be used as a sleeping place.

This time the labour would be more systematic. The men would cut and erect the bamboo frames. The women would prepare the bindings and weave the palm thatch and the mats for the walls. Willy Kuhio and Eva and Mark Gilman and Jenny would be detached for the fishing and the food gathering, and the cooking.

The design he proposed for each house was simple in the extreme—four main posts with cross members to hold them firm, a skillion roof, pitched sharp enough to throw off the rain, with bamboo slats and a thatch of palm fiber and walls of palm matting, which could be raised or lowered to let in the breeze or close out the rain. No nails or cleats would be needed. The members would be lashed, the wall and roof coverings laced with fiber. The dwellings would be set, four on each side, facing each other across the mouth of the valley, where it debouched onto the beach. The storehouse would be set crosswise between them, leaving a space for a log slide down which the trees for their boat could be brought to the beach. The open ground between would be the place for the fire pit and their communal work.

About this project at least there were no arguments. They were all beginning to chafe at their enforced confinement in a single dwelling. Tempers were frayed and they were beginning to gibe at each other's personal idiosyncrasies. This one snored, that one belched, another took up twice the normal sleeping room. As the first pegs were being driven, Carl Magnusson drew Thorkild aside. He was stammering and self-conscious as a schoolboy.

"Uh—Thorkild . . . I thought I'd tell you—uh . . . When you're set up here, I'm—uh—moving in with Molly Kaapu."

Thorkild was hard put to suppress a smile, but he managed an offhand answer. "Sure, Carl. Pick any house you want."

"Hell! It doesn't matter which. It's just that, well, I can't do much for myself and Molly's a kind soul and . . ."

"You don't have to spell it, Carl. I understand."

"I guess you do. Queer though, isn't it? Here am I, the big taipan, best name, biggest money in the islands, shacking up with an old girl who used to scrub my mother's floors . . . And what's more, I'm glad of it—damn glad!" Suddenly he was shaking with laughter. "I wonder what my wife would say if she could see me now?—or James Neal Anderson or your friend Flanagan?"

"I think those two would envy you, Carl."

"They probably would at that. Tell me, how are you going to arrange the rest of the housing?"

"Well, there's a place for Sally and me, one for Lorillard and Martha. Mark can bunk with the boys. The others can make whatever combinations they choose. It'll be interesting to see how they work it out."

"You're damn right it will be." Carl Magnusson snorted irritably. "I can't figure how their minds work; but Sally Anderton gave them a real come-uppance—and you showed more patience than I ever gave you credit for."

"I'm learning, Carl, but we're still only at the beginning. I'd better get back to work now. There's a lot to be done. By the way, what colour curtains would you like?"

"Go to hell!" said Carl Magnusson, and stamped off to join Molly Kaapu and the weavers.

At the end of five days, all the huts were framed and the thatching had begun. They were working in rhythm now, steadily and cheerfully, so Thorkild decided to leave them for a day and go up to visit Charlie Kamakau on the mountain terrace. This time he took Sally Anderton, with the halfhearted excuse that Charlie might need some medical attention. Tioto gave him a pair of fish, fresh caught and wrapped in leaves, for a gift to Charlie; and on a last-minute impulse, Thorkild took a bottle of whiskey as a peace offering from the whole group.

As they made their way up the first slopes, Sally was as excited as a child at the profusion of fruits and flowers and the orchids that grew from the crannies of rocks and trees. Later as the air grew heavier and the insects began to plague them, she became quiet and thoughtful. Thorkild asked her:

"Something's the matter, Sally. What is it?"

"There's an awful lot of mosquitoes."

"That's not unusual."

"I know. . . . How long would you say it is since people lived here?"

"Hard to say. The pottery we found is very old. As we open up the land here, we may find other relics that will give us a better idea. Why do you ask?"

"Mosquitoes carry the disease of filariasis, which is endemic in certain Pacific islands. Prolonged exposure to it produces the condition we call elephantiasis—enormous swellings of limbs and other members."

"I know. I've seen it. Horrible."

"In this part of the world the filariae are usually

carried by a day-flying mosquito. . . . So if we're going to have people working up here, we'll have to be aware of the danger and try to combat it."

"How, for Pete's sake? We don't have mosquito nets. We've got no drugs."

"We'd really have to try to kill the mosquitoes themselves."

"Impossible. That would mean spraying all the breeding places, clearing miles of tropical vegetation!"

"Don't snap at me, darling. I'm just pointing out a danger."

"Of course. . . . I'm sorry. We're really helpless, aren't we?"

"Wherever we are, we're at risk. The best we can do is recognize the risk and minimize it as much as possible. . . . Is it much farther now?"

"About half a mile. Smell the smoke? He's probably burning off."

For a man working alone in a tropic jungle, Charlie Kamakau had accomplished a minor miracle. With no other tools but the fire axe, and a seaman's knife, and Hernan Castillo's stone adze, he had grubbed out an area nearly twenty yards square, leaving the fruit-bearing trees and the big trunks standing and piling the undergrowth into great heaps, which he burned with the diesel he had hauled up from the beach. He had built himself a rough shelter of bamboo and a small oven of stones. His once bulky body was honed down to bone and muscle. He was filthy with dust and ash. There were suppurating sores on his arms and legs, but there was a fierce, fanatic triumph in his bloodshot eyes.

"Look at it, chief! They say Charlie Kamakau's not a man! I'll bet you three of those young *haole* couldn't have done it in the same time!"

"It's wonderful, Charlie! But don't kill yourself!"

"Kill myself? Look at me! Do I look like a dying man? Give me a month, and we'll be ready to make our first gardens. You tell 'em that, chief."

"I'll tell 'em, Charlie. They'll be very proud of you. They sent you up some presents. The fish are from Tioto. The whiskey's from all of us!"

"Not from Madam Barbara! Don't tell me that!"

"From her too, Charlie." Sally tried to placate him. "She's . . . well, she's been very quiet since you left."

"I don't want to hear about her!"

"We're setting up the beach village now, Charlie," Thorkild told him quietly. "As soon as that's done, I'll send you some help up here."

"Not before I say so, chief!" He was instantly on edge. "You hear that? Not before I say I'm ready. They've got to know what Charlie Kamakau can do."

"They know it already, Charlie. They miss you down there."

"That's good! They have to know they can't insult a high man. And that's another thing, chief. When we build our place here, I want to run it."

"Let's talk about that when the time comes."

"Talk about it as much as you like, but I'll run it. This is a very special place—there's a big *kapu* here. I'm the only one that knows it and understands it."

"How do you know it, Charlie?" asked Sally Anderton innocently.

"I'll show you." He disappeared into the shelter and came out a moment later carrying a parcel of *fei* leaves. He laid it on the stone, and before he opened it, made them step back a pace, and warned them, "Don't touch. Just look."

He opened the parcel and spread the contents on the rock: a small stone mortar with a pestle of polished greenstone, a war club of hardwood, finely carved but pitted and scored with age, a human skull, yellow as old ivory, with a gaping hole in the front temporal bone. He gave them a mocking wolfish grin and said:

"Big, big *kapu,* eh, chief? That's a priest's bowl, to mix the magic plants. This stone was for sacrifice and this was the club that killed the victims. That's right, isn't it, chief?"

"Probably," said Thorkild quietly. "Where did you find these things?"

"Right here beside the platform. I found the club first, then the head. The day after, I dug up the bowl. They wanted me to find it, because they wanted me to be the guardian of this place. You understand that, don't you, chief?"

"I'll try to understand it, Charlie. Would you like us to cook the fish for you?"

"No. I never eat till night. I've got to get back to work."

Sally Anderton moved a step closer to him. "Charlie, you've got bad sores on your legs and your arms. They'll get worse if we don't treat them. Would you let me have a look at them, please?"

"No! They're nothing. I clean them at the end of the day! Thanks for the food and the drink. You take her home, chief. I'll tell you when I'm ready."

"All right, Charlie. I'll be back soon."

"Just you, next time, chief. We talk, high man to high man, eh?"

"Sure, Charlie. Take care now!"

As they turned away and plunged into the undergrowth, they heard him singing in a high, cracked voice the song of Kaka and Koko, who fell into the sea and were swallowed by a great shark so that never again could they mate with man or woman.

"He's halfway round the bend," said Thorkild gloomily.

"He's right round," said Sally Anderton firmly. "And he'll stay there, unless we can bring him back and hold him in contact with reality for a while."

"And how do we manage that, my dear doctor—with his girl a constant mockery?"

"I don't know, darling." Sally teased him with rueful humour. "What did they do in the old days with casualties like that?"

"If they were harmless," said Gunnar Thorkild, "they were cherished as objects of amusement. If they were dangerous, they were sacrificed to placate the gods."

Later, back at the encampment, they talked to Tioto and Carl Magnusson. Tioto's prescription was clear: ". . . You get him back to camp, chief. I can look after him. I'll keep him calm, take him out fishing and sailing and make sure Barbara stays away from him. But up there, in that place, I can't do anything; because I'm scared and he knows it. I know what's happened to him. He's gone back—back to the dreamtime we lived in when we were kids and the old people still remembered the past. It happened to me when . . . well, when I was still trying to find out who and what I was. It could happen again if I stayed too long in a *kapu* place."

"*Kapu* means nothing to me," said Carl Magnusson. "And Charlie Kamakau knows that too. He'll talk to me in another way altogether. There's a good chance I could coax him down; then Tioto could take him in hand."

"I'd like you to try, Carl," said Thorkild. "I'd take you up close to the terrace and then let you go in alone. But let's reason the whole thing out. Suppose he refuses to leave?"

"Then," said Sally firmly, "you'll have a sick, crazy hermit wandering the uplands until he dies. I say you've got to coax him down. I could tranquillize him, and keep him that way for a few days until my drugs run out. After that, perhaps, Tioto could nurse him back to normality."

"Suppose he resists, tries to escape into the bush?"

"Then you've got a manhunt," said Carl Magnusson, "which is dangerous and destructive to the whole community. I'm against that."

"Why not leave him there a while longer?" Tioto persisted. "He wants that anyway. He wants to finish the work, then call us up and make a big show of what he's done. He may be sick, sure; but when the work's done he'll be high and happy—and just that much easier to handle."

"That's the best sense we've heard so far." Magnusson was emphatic in his approval. "When in doubt, do nothing. There's a chance he'll survive his own crisis and find his own way back to sanity."

"I've got big doubts about that," said Sally Anderton. "We're not talking about pneumonia. We're talking about a psychic aberration, the pattern of which may become confirmed and deepened until it's irreversible."

"And then what?" Gunnar Thorkild put the last bleak question, but no one was prepared to answer it.

As they sat around the fire pit that night Lorillard raised once again the issue of their social identity. He put it clearly and bluntly:

"Some of us would like this question resolved quickly. Do we or do we not agree to annex this island and place ourselves by common consent under the jurisdiction of the United States? Carl Magnusson put the case clearly for and against. He asked us to think about it and discuss it. We've had time to do that. Can we put it to the vote now?"

"What's the hurry, Peter?" asked Thorkild quietly.

"I'm going to have a baby," Martha Gilman answered him. "Peter wants to be a gentleman about it. He wants a divorce and a marriage that will hold under the laws of the United States."

"Let me recall our original intention." Lorillard was well prepared. "Carl Magnusson financed the expedition and contracted for my services on that basis. The other night he pointed out that a formal act would—or might—give us a certain sense of security and continuity. For myself, for Martha and Mark, I'd like to have that."

"There's a problem." Gunnar Thorkild spoke earnestly and deliberately. "We're nineteen people in all. At this moment Charlie Kamakau is absent and medically incompetent. Young Mark is a minor without a vote. Hernan Castillo is a Filipino national. That leaves sixteen. If we vote now, Charlie's deprived of his franchise. Shouldn't we wait at least a reasonable time, to see if he becomes capable of exercising it?"

"I don't see that." Simon Cohen was still the contentious one. "It's normal voting procedure. Incompetence, whether permanent or temporary, disqualifies the voter."

"Then," said Thorkild, "I'd like to take the proceedings in two motions. Will someone move that the vote be taken now instead of being deferred to a later date?"

"I'll move that," said Lorillard.

"I'll second," said Simon Cohen.

"All in favour?"

The vote was nine in favour, five against.

"The next motion, please."

"I've written it." Lorillard held up a water-stained page, the flyleaf of a pilot book. "We don't have much paper, so I'll read it first and pass it round. . . .

'Moved that this community, composed, with one exception, of citizens of the United States of America, annex this island and place it under the jurisdiction of the said United States, and engage themselves to live under the jurisdiction of that Commonwealth according to its Constitution, and such laws as, under that Constitution, they may frame to meet the special and peculiar circumstances of their lives.' "

"I second the motion," said Yoko Nagamuna.

"When you've all read it," said Thorkild, "I'll hear discussions for and against. You first, Peter—it's your motion."

Lorillard waited until the paper had been passed from hand to hand, then he began to speak, simply and dispassionately:

". . . I want to tell you three things which, in my view, make this step necessary. First, any children born on this island now are born stateless, and must attempt to acquire citizenship by a legal act at a later date. Second, we have no legal means, other than custom—and custom is still undeveloped among us—to establish marital status and conjugal rights. Third, we have no legal recourse—in theory or in practice—against the invasion of individual or minority rights by a majority, or even by a forceful group. We are living by fact and not by law. We cannot, obviously, apply to ourselves all the provisions of existing law, either of the States or the Commonwealth. We can, however, adopt the principles of that law, judge ourselves against them, and, if ever we escape or are rescued, have a continuing recourse in our homeland. That's as clear as I can make it. I beg you to support the motion."

There was a moment's silence, then a murmur of surprise as Jenny got unsteadily to her feet. She gave them an embarrassed smile and began:

"You all know I was a dropout. I ended up on a beach, pregnant. The Professor and Martha picked me up, dusted me off and—here I am. I'm not doing so well here either, but I've learned something. When you get so far down that you need someone to own you, you're in bad shape. When you have to lean on the law, you find the law is a lot of words that everybody reads to suit himself. The law busts you. The law punishes you. The law cleans up the mess when you hurt each other. . . . But that's where it stops. It wasn't the law that gave me a home. It was a kind woman. I'm scared when I hear people talking like Peter. It's like . . . like they had believed in some kind of magic, the flag and the Constitution and all that. Our boys in Vietnam died under the flag for a lost cause. Martha's husband killed himself with heroin—because the Constitution and the President sent him to do something he hated. I don't need the flag and the law and all that. I want us to go on doing what we're doing now, with each other and for each other. And I don't want what Peter calls recourse. . . . Hell! If today's bad, I want to wipe it out, kiss and make up and start again tomorrow. You can't do that if you've got a policeman with a gun, or someone with a big black book and a lot of long words! . . . If you're worried about the kids and us women, we'll make out better with loving than with a gunboat out in the bay. . . . I guess it's a question of how much we trust each other; but if we don't, how can any government do it from thousands of miles away?"

She was weeping when she sat down. Adam Briggs put his arm around her and kissed her. Franz Harsanyi clapped loudly and called:

"Bravo, kid!"

The talk went round and round, sometimes harshly

reasoned, sometimes fumbling and confused, but always passionate and concerned. At the end of it Gunnar Thorkild said:

"I'd like to vacate the chair for a moment and express a personal opinion. May I?"

They assured him they would be happy to hear him. His argument was brutally simple:

"What does it add to our existence if, right now, we raise the Stars and Stripes on this beachhead? Nothing. What does the law tell us that we don't know already: that we have to deal simply and honestly and kindly one with another? What do we need from government that we cannot find among ourselves? . . . And if it's a question of record, we can supply that. We can solemnize marriage for those who want it; recognize divorcement if they find it impossible to live together. As for recourse, how can any court in the future judge of what we do here? Up there on the mountain is a sick, sad man, a burden to himself, a potential danger to this community. . . . He's our problem. We can't claim proxy from some distant authority. We—just we—have to look after our own. . . . Now I'll resume the chair. And I'll take a show of hands. All in favour?"

Six people supported the motion: Martha Gilman, Lorillard, Yoko Nagamuna, Simon Cohen, Willy and Eva Kuhio.

"Motion defeated," said Gunnar Thorkild. "We're on our own. The meeting's adjourned."

"Hold it a moment." Lorillard was on his feet instantly. "That's not the end of it, surely. Opinions may change. We must be able to bring the matter back again."

"There's nothing to stop you."

"Except this." Magnusson challenged the group. "Keep scratching a sore and you get an ulcerous infection. The last thing we want is nuisance tactics. Let's go about our business and see how well or ill we manage. I'd say no new motion on this matter for at least a year."

"Six months," said Lorillard.

"Six months then." Thorkild closed the argument. "If we're not settled down by then, this place will be bedlam."

Whatever their conflicts over law and sovereignty, there were none on the question of their domestic arrangements. The older couples paired off immediately. Magnusson and Molly Kaapu, Martha and Lorillard, Thorkild and Sally, Willy and Eva Kuhio. Yoko and Jenny shared one hut, Barbara Kamakau and Ellen Ching moved in together. Franz Harsanyi took Mark Gilman. Adam Briggs and Hernan Castillo occupied the last hut while Simon Cohen and Tioto installed themselves at either end of the store building. If Charlie Kamakau came back, a new hut would be built.

From the moment they took possession of their separate dwellings, a change became evident in the pattern of their tribal life. They began to make simple furniture, beds and bamboo tables and stools. Tools were passed from hand to hand, skills exchanged, simple stores distributed—a plate, a knife, a piece of sail canvas . . . a cup of fuel oil to prime a shell lamp. The single group broke into small cells. A rule of privacy was established without a word spoken: no one entered another's hut without an invitation. Food was cooked and shared at the fire pit, but might be eaten in common or apart. The tensions of propinquity relaxed. Talk became less assertive and more ruminative. Companionship became easier and less demanding. The women were sup-

portive of each other. The men had their own clubbish
interludes.

Carl Magnusson seemed to take a new and stronger
hold on life. His shoulder was mending. He could do
simple tasks. His limp was less pronounced, and he
could be heard all over the camp, shouting amiably
at Molly Kaapu, as she bullied or cajoled him. Soon,
Thorkild judged, he would be ready to make the long
walk up the mountain to reason with Charlie Kamakau. He himself had already made two more trips up
to the terrace, each time alone, to carry fish and
cooked food and try to establish a dialogue with the
eccentric recluse. Each time he had been encouraged,
albeit faintly, by what he found.

Charlie Kamakau was still working prodigiously, but
he seemed to have fallen into a less desperate rhythm.
He had consented to use the dressing which Sally sent
for his sores. However, he was still obsessed by the
notion that the old ones had chosen him to rule his
part of the mountain, and he displayed a whole miscellany of artifacts, each one of which was a new
proof of election and mystic favour. He rejected utterly the proposal that he return to the shore settlement. He would receive Carl Magnusson; but no one
else must come until the whole terrace was cleared
and planted. He would go down part way to leave
fruits and vegetables for the camp and receive fish for
himself, provided only the men came. He was done
with women; and any mention of Barbara set him off
into a gibbering frenzy of threats and obscenities. As
for Tioto, he was beginning to be suspicious of
him too. Tioto was afraid of the *kapu,* which meant
that the high ones were displeased with him. . . .
They were nerve-wracking interludes and Thorkild
was glad to leave and turn his face to the seas, where

at last there was a vestige of reason and laughter and happy talk.

It was not all gaiety, however. Jenny had begun to mope and several times she had been found, by the cascade or in a far corner of the beach, weeping miserably. Sally Anderton put it down brusquely to postnatal depression and tried, in vain, to coax and scold her out of it. Adam Briggs, who was still courting her assiduously, was in a state of quiet desperation. One day he asked Thorkild to make the round of the fish traps with him, and as they went he opened his heart:

". . . I love that girl, chief. I love her so much it hurts all the time. I know what she needs too, better than any doctor—a man to love her and give her the baby she lost and make her feel safe and secure. I could do all that. I'd be happy to spend my whole life doing it. But the way it is now, I can hardly get near her. She hates to be touched, she says; and in the next breath she says she likes me better than anyone. I ask her if it's because I'm black, and she swears it isn't and cries and says she just can't help herself. . . . I'm worried, chief. You don't see as much of her these days; but I tell you she's going away—far and fast."

"What can I say, Adam? I want to help. You know that. Have you thought she might be keen on one of the others—Franz, for instance—and doesn't want to tell you?"

"No way! I thought of that too. They've all invited her down to the beach. . . . The only one she'll go with is me. I even asked the other girls what they thought. They just shrugged and said women went that way sometimes."

"Do you mind if I tell Sally what you've just told me?"

"Hell, no! If it helps, I'll walk up the mountain on my hands. What I don't want is to see her go like that poor crazy coot, Charlie. . . . Anyway, thanks for listening. Let's talk about something else. You saw what we did with the canoe. We fitted a new outrigger and the girls are working on a palm mat for the sail."

"It's great, Adam. She rides beautifully."

"When the sail's ready you and I could take her round the island."

"Say when, Adam. I'll be there."

"When are you going to start on the big one?"

"Pretty soon now. I wanted to get everyone settled down first. And we'll need a lot more tools than we have yet."

"How long will it take us to build?"

"Twelve months. More, maybe. It's a big job."

"And you'll teach me to handle it first? I want that, chief. I want it very much."

"You've got it already. My grandfather named you. Remember?"

"Every day and all day."

"Hold the thought, man. We can't let the race of navigators die out."

"Could be you'll have a son of your own now, chief."

"Could be." Thorkild laughed. "We're a long way from campus, aren't we, man?"

"Would you like to go back?"

"To what?"

"Like you say, chief: to what? We've got our own little world down here—no pollution, no atom bomb, no muggers. It's so close to the Garden of Eden, I keep wondering when the snake pops up."

"He's here already," said Gunnar Thorkild wryly. "I sit higher than you. I've already seen him."

That night, as they lay together listening to the distant boom of the surf, and the soughing of the wind through the tall palms, and the plaintive distant piping of Simon Cohen's flute, he told Sally of his talk with Adam Briggs. She listened in silence, then rolled away from him and lay with her hands behind her head, staring up at the slats of the ceiling. When he tried to draw her to him again she pushed him away and said:

"Please! This isn't easy. Let me think for a while. . . . How far she'll go, how long she'll stay in this kind of fugue, I don't know. I'm a physician, not a psychiatrist. Postnatal depression is common enough. Most women get over it fairly quickly. But in Jenny's case there's a long and complicated history: a broken home, indifferent parents, a boyfriend who rejected her when she fell pregnant, a brief period of security with Martha and you, then a late and very traumatic miscarriage. Now Martha's pregnant and you've got me and she's hacked about inside and feeling miserable and insecure. . . . Not a very promising prognosis, is it?"

"So what can you do about it?"

"Me? Very little. If I were home I'd probably put her on euphorics for a while, and then, if she didn't pick herself up, recommend a course of supportive therapy with a good psychiatrist. Here I've got nothing except the basics you find in a ship's medicine chest, a few tranquillizers and the anticoagulants I was using for Carl. I'm like a magician without his wand and his little box of illusions."

"What's the answer then?"

"We support her as best we can, make her feel cherished and wanted."

"She's getting that already, from us—and much more from Adam Briggs."

"And it's not enough?"

"Obviously."

"Have you ever thought, my dear, dear man, that you care too much?"

"I have to care! You know that! Just the same as I've got to care for Charlie Kamakau. A sickness in one member—is a sickness in us all."

She rolled back to him, raised herself on one elbow and ran the tips of her fingers over his taut, stubbled cheeks. She said, very softly:

"You still don't see it, do you?"

"See what?"

"Jenny's in love with you—has been from the day you picked her off the beach."

"That's nonsense! I'm old enough to be her father."

"That's part of it, probably."

"Then it's . . . it's damn near incest!"

"Call it what you like, sweetheart. It's very real. She can't have you. She doesn't want anyone else. So, as Adam put it, she's going away—far and fast."

"Why did you have to tell me?"

"Because I love you and I owe you the truth; and other people see it, even if you and Adam don't!"

"Oh Christ! What a mess! What a stinking, bloody mess! The crazy part is I've played around with all sorts of women, all my life, and the one I've never, never been drawn to, sexually, is Jenny. I'm fond of her, yes—the way I'm fond of a child who's alone and in need of protection."

"I know that. You know it. Jenny sees it differently."

She bent and kissed him on the lips; he clung to her in desperation.

"It's what Flanagan said: everyone leans, everyone clings, everyone wants me to set their world to rights. I can't do it. There's not enough of me!"

"There's two of us, darling. Remember?"

"What do I do? Tell me!"

"Go to Adam. Tell him you talked to me, and what I said."

"Why Adam?"

"Because he's as blind as you are. And one day he's going to wake up to the gossip; and then you'll lose the best friend you've got in this group. You need him. You'll need him more and more as time goes on. Do it now. It's not late. People are still stirring. Get it off your mind. Then come back and make love to your wife. . . ."

He found Adam Briggs knee-deep in the shallows, trying to spear flatfish by torchlight. They walked up the sand together, and perched themselves like seabirds on a flat rock. Briggs listened in silence as Thorkild laid out the story, flat and plain, without gloss or embellishment; then he said:

"I'm glad you told me. Thank Sally for me. She's a wise woman. . . . It's hard to know what to say. First, though, this makes no difference to you and me. I like you. I admire you. Always have, always will."

"Thanks."

"And I still feel the same way about Jenny. She's not to blame. She's done no wrong. She's just got to where she can't help herself."

"That's about the size of it, Adam."

"But I'm not going to let her lose herself. . . . You understand that?"

"Sure."

"No matter what I have to do. No matter what I've got to take."

"You may have to take an awful lot, man."

"You think I can't?"

"I know you can. If I can help, I'm always around. No place else to go."

"That's my last point, chief; so I'll make it and then you can spit in my eye or feed me to the sharks out there. . . . If it would help Jenny, to have you mate her and give her a baby, I'd be agreeable and I'd take 'em both and love 'em both ever after."

"That's a crazy thought, Adam. I don't feel that way for Jenny."

"I know you don't. All I said was 'if'. . . . Just so you know where I stand. Love's a terrible thing, chief; terrible and beautiful and . . ." His voice cracked into a sob of utter anguish. "And just so goddam unfair!"

"Did you know," asked Sally sleepily, "did you know that doctors make lousy lovers?"

"Statement or question?" Thorkild drew her close, to shield her from the first flurry of the land breezes, searching through the matting wall.

"Statement."

"I've got no complaints, so far."

"That's because I'm an exceptional doctor. No drugs, no books, no pretensions. But seriously . . ."

"At this hour? It's nearly sunrise."

"So rise up, my love, my dove, my beautiful one, and come . . ."

"No way, Josephine! You've had me awake all night."

"So listen! Why do doctors make lousy lovers? Because their trade is mortality—with Latin names. They know all the parts and all the functions and all the pathology—and not one of them has ever seen a soul under the microscope. If they get mixed up with metaphysics—which some of them do—they tend to fall short on medicine. If they pin their faith to *corpus hominis,* they'll become like breeders and butchers, totting life up by weight and market price. . . . That's why, in an odd way, I'm glad to be helpless here. I can just be a woman for a change."

"And forget the parts and the functions?"

"No . . . the mortality. You're dealing with that now."

"And hating it."

"Not all of it. You're a high man because you're made for it and called to it. I like it too, because I was made to mate with high men—though this is the first time I've fallen in love with one. And I like to know that I'm the one he needs when he topples off his perch. It's all beautifully selfish, but not so selfish that I don't know you're my last and only."

"Why don't you go to sleep?"

"Because I haven't finished. You told Carl once and he told me that you didn't care about my past, because you understood the old way, where the chief or the father deflowered the virgins in a rite of passage. . . . Now, I tell you. I don't care what you do or with whom or why, so long as I'm the chief's woman, and I wait for him in his house."

"Still Jenny?"

"Still. . . ."

"Don't you think she might have something to say about it?"

"As much as she wants—just so she says it and does it and gets it out of her system."

"Do you know what I'm going to do tomorrow—no, it's today already?"

"Tell me."

"I'm going to take the canoe, all on my sweet lonesome, and paddle out through the channel and circumnavigate the island."

"You can't. That's dangerous."

"For the grandson of Kaloni the Navigator?"

"Take me with you?"

"Not this time."

"Why not?"

"Because, lover, I just want to be alone."

"Is it so bad?"

"So bad. Not with you, but with all the others. I'm like a kindergarten teacher dreaming up new games each day to keep the kiddies amused. Now you want to turn me into a stud for the lovelorn."

"I didn't say that! I didn't mean that!"

"Whatever you meant, I mean this: for one day, just one single day, I want to be me—alone! No demands, no debates, no problems. Is that too much?"

"Little enough." Sally Anderton's voice was small and tremulous. "Come back safe, that's all."

"Tell them I've gone," said Thorkild harshly. "Tell 'em why, if you want."

"Please, don't go like this!"

"Sally, sweetheart, it isn't you. It's this—this whole goddam tribe. Whether they know it or not—and some of them do know—they're playing me like a fish, running me out, hauling me back for this problem or that debate. Even mad Charlie up on the mountain, he's doing the same thing in his own way; give a little, take a little, snap when I say the wrong thing. Well, they'd better learn now! I'm only human. The *mana* dies with me unless I choose to pass it on. Let 'em show a little respect. Let them give me some cherishing for a change."

"I've heard that before," said Sally dryly. "From Charlie Kamakau. So you go, Gunnar! Go out and get clean and let me see you walk back like a king—not like some pint-sized executive with peptic ulcers!"

Half a mile offshore he ceased paddling and let the

tiny craft lie, rocking like a piece of driftwood in the long swell. He was on the far side of the island, where the sides of the crater rose sheer into the cloud and plunged downwards in vast blue deeps. The sun was noon-high, the sea like a vast undulating mirror, save where the swell broke against the black walls and surged around the narrow inlets, between the humps of the old lava flow. Behind him and on either hand the sea was empty, save for a gaggle of seabirds, squabbling over a shoal of fish, which were being harried by a brace of cruising shark.

The small drama of predation intrigued him for a moment; then he grew bored with it. He was not here to provide food, or to celebrate his manhood by the capture of a shark and shout it afterwards to the bucks and the women. He was here to restore himself, as his grandfather had taught him, long ago in the past, by a conscious act of withdrawal, a gathering-in of all the diffused and distended faculties, a shutting out of all intrusive sights and sounds.

Once, after a great storm, which overtook a lugger full of people on their way to Raiatea, he had seen the old man perch himself on the foredeck, and sit there for nearly six hours, closed in by a silence that was tangible as a wall. Afterwards the old man had explained it to him:

"It's like the making of sennit rope. Each fiber is weak—so weak that a child can snap it. Plait them together, they will hold a mast against a hurricane. . . . After a long, rough passage, I am like a rope that is strained and frayed. I sit and plait myself together again with new threads—I stare and dream and remember the counsels of my father and the words of the song-makers, and the cries of all the birds. I do not speak, because each word is a thread torn away. No one may touch me, because each touch robs me of a piece of myself. You too must learn this. Learn to be silent. Draw a circle around yourself and let no one step inside it. . . ."

It was for this reason that he had built the sound-proof room in the house in Honolulu. It was for this that he had fled today, confining himself, yet opening himself in the vast circle of the sea. He was weaker than his grandfather, very much more vulnerable; and his need for renewal was the more urgent. The cosmogony of Kaloni Kienga was essentially fixed and simple. For all the multitude of gods and guardian spirits, everything was rooted in and related to *Te Tumu*, the Foundation. The roots were many, but the tree was one. The relationships were complex, but fixed and unalterable.

For Gunnar Thorkild, there was not one cosmogony, not one morality, but many. His tribe was not a tribe, but demos, the people, hydra-headed, each head howling and snapping at the other in a cacophony of words, whose meanings changed with every whim and surge of passion. He himself was divided and subdivided. One part of him trapped by reason and the specious logic of scholarship, another lost and wandering among the expatriates of a twentieth-century city, another clinging childlike to a legendary past, another still, armed and watchful against the encroachment of anarchy on a beachhead in the middle of nowhere. Each part was threatened by a different menace: the scholar by irony and skepticism, the wanderer by a babel-madness of voices in conflict, the child by a terror of ridicule, the guardian by a draconian devil tempting to tyranny.

Out here, at least, he was whole: a tiny man in a frail cockleshell, alone, untrammelled, at one with the vastness of sea and sky and a small land, thrust up from the deeps, unchanged since the first voyagers

saw it, a long millennium ago. The harmony of the
moment crept over him, and through him, grateful as
sleep after long labour. He knew without knowing,
saw without seeing, what had drawn his people out,
centuries ago, from their island havens into immensity.
He understood something else too: that for a small
people, fragmented by migration and enormous distance, bound to a monotony of simple, concrete things,
the fountain of dreaming was always the secret ones,
the remembering ones, the high men and the magical
and the knowing. No matter that they were privileged,
proud, tyrannical; they were set at the navel of things.
Through them the past joined the present and the future was determined by the dead.

He began to paddle again, steadily, rhythmically, to
breast the current and follow the contour of the land.
The seabirds rose screaming at his approach and the
two sharks left the shoal and began cruising near the
canoe, circling wide at first and then coming closer,
so that he could see the bluish sheen on their dorsal
skin, and as they turned, the white flash of their un-
derbellies. They were big fellows, twenty feet long at
least; but they were gorged on the shoal and they
would not attack, though more than one lone fisherman had had his paddle snapped when he struck, im-
pudently, at a cruising monster.

For Thorkild it was a reminder that the community
was still unpracticed in the skills of the big sea, still
huddled on a small beachhead and feeding from the
inner reef and the near hinterlands. Even the Kauai
men were not as practiced as the far islanders. They
too had been civilized and citified and made depend-
ent on store-bought comfort. It was time to push them
all out, further and further, and practice them in the
harsher arts of survival. The problem of Charlie
Kamakau must be solved too, because he was an im-

pediment to their outward thrust. He might become a
threat to their safety. He would certainly become an
object of fear and superstition, like a night prowler or
a denizen scavenger.

The problem was what to do with him if he could
not submit or respond to the therapy of normal community intercourse. Whether the community could
provide such a therapy was another and more fundamental question. If Charlie proved an incurable and
eccentric recluse, banishment was a possibility. He had
enough skills to maintain himself. The problem was to
find a place sufficently removed to debar him from
any future contact with the group. Remembering the
old horrors of Molokai, the leper lazarette, Thorkild
felt a sickening disgust at the brutality of the remedy.
Nonetheless, he changed course and began paddling
inshore to see if there might be another bay or beachhead where a lone man might survive. There was
none. The coast was ironbound, no haven for any
creature but the seabirds.

The current was stronger at this end of the island
and the noon wind was springing up and blowing
against it. This, with the rising tide and the backwash
from the cliffs, forced him to paddle harder, to round
the point with sea room and make passage home to
the reef channel. There was a heady joy in the exercise, a feeling not of mastery but of complicity with
the elements. He remembered the old chant which
Kaloni had taught him, the song of the sea-feelers
to the sea itself.

> I know you,
> O sea,
> Home of the sea god.
> I do not fight you
> Like a warrior,

O sea.
I do not sing to you
Like a woman,
O sea.
I swim in you
Like the white shark.
I ride on you
Like the fisher-bird,
O sea.
I live in you
As I live in the house of my father,
O mirror of Hiva and the night-eyes.

It was midafternoon before he lay off the reef again, a long way out, now seeing, now losing the beach and the huts and the small ant figures moving between them. Their diminishment pleased him. They were removed, unreal, like manikins in a primitive picture. They were bound, locked between the mountain and the reef. He was free, large, strong, the king that Sally dreamed and he had almost forgotten.

He paddled inshore, steadily, easily, watching how the current swirled through the channel, and how the reef was buried under the high tide, and where the rollers broke evenly and where they crashed, turbulent and destructive, over the coral outcrops. . . . He would show them something now! He would not run the channel. He would ride in over the reef itself. If he misjudged the wave, if it failed to run right—so be it! —he would never know! If he made it, then, by God, they would know why a feeler-of-the-sea was different from other men!

It was a wild, drunken moment, but he surrendered himself to it, shouting with exultation as he paddled to the spot where the big rollers shaped themselves before the surf line. He hung there a while, backing against the swell, feeling the surge and the lift, waiting for the fractional moment in which he must commit himself.

When it came, he gave a shout and plunged his paddle and felt himself heaved and carried, up and up, on a great hump of water. For one heart-stopping moment he thought it would break too soon and capsize him; but it held and curled like a long drum roll under the hull, and carried him forward over the reef, and weltered into a foam that swept him fast as a running horse onto the shingle!

There should have been paeans and a chant of women welcoming the *Koa*—the superman of the sea. Instead there was only a rasping shout from Lorillard!

"You're an idiot, Thorkild. You could have broken your bloody neck!"

They had not been idle in his absence. Indeed, as Sally told him with a lover's malice, they had been glad to be rid of him for a while and tend to their private business. Willy Kuhio and Tioto had walked inland, found the trees he had marked, rejected them as too big and hard to work, chosen others and slashed out a track for the log slide. Franz Harsanyi and Hernan Castillo had completed a small assortment of tools—adzes, scrapers, fish spears and even a primitive pump drill made from wood and cord and a pointed piece of basalt.

Adam Briggs was boiling up a foul-looking mess of coconut, breadfruit, bananas and assorted fruit scraps, which, he claimed, would ultimately ferment into drinkable spirit—though Lorillard averred skeptically that it would make fusel oil look like medical alcohol. Eva Kuhio and Barbara had finished the matting sail for the canoe and were now lacing it to the bamboo frame. Lorillard himself, with Martha and Mark, had made a small, rough kiln in which wood charcoal could be made for a forge—and even, God willing, to filter the witches' brew which Briggs was cooking. Yoko and Ellen and Jenny had found a new taro patch and were transplanting some of the tubers to the soft ground near the waterfall. Simon Cohen and Barbara Kamakau had gone out to gather fruit and were not yet returned. Thorkild frowned over this last piece of news; and when they came back, an hour later, laden with papaya and mangoes and a big head of bananas, he accosted them and read them a quiet lecture.

"Barbara, until I give the word, I want you to stay down here on the beach. So long as Charlie's up there, the mountain's a dangerous place for you."

Simon Cohen protested:

"We didn't go far. I had a knife."

"And Charlie's got a fire axe and he's twice your size and crazy as a coot where Barbara's concerned. Don't give me an argument! Just do as I ask, eh?"

"Don't blame him, chief." Barbara grinned at him provocatively. "I suggested it. Where else would we go in daylight, eh?"

"Anywhere you like—but not up the mountain."

Tioto, who had been hovering in the background, stepped into the group. "You listen to what the chief says, woman! He's seen Charlie—you haven't. Besides, he's not always up on the terrace. He's moving around now."

Thorkild swung round to confront him. "Say that again, Tioto!"

"He's moving around, chief. The last tree we marked is about halfway up to the terrace. I found this caught on a thornbush." He held out a scrap of white gauze, stained and discoloured. "That's a piece of bandage, like the doctor has in her medicine chest!"

"What does it mean?" Barbara was visibly shaken.

"What Tioto says. Charlie's prowling, closer to the camp." He turned to face Simon Cohen. "What about you two? Are you pairing off?"

Cohen grinned sheepishly. "Well, sort of, I guess."

"Fine! Barbara moves into the storehouse with you and Tioto. Then there'll be two of you to protect her."

"You mean. . . ?"

"You heard me, sonny boy! I don't give a damn about your sex life. I do care about keeping your woman alive."

He turned away and walked briskly across to Carl Magnusson, who was reading Adam Briggs a lecture on moonshine and the making thereof. Thorkild asked him:

"Feel like a long walk tomorrow, Carl?"

"To see Charlie? Sure, I'm as ready as I'll ever be."

"You come too, Adam. You and Willy Kuhio. I may need you."

"Expecting trouble?"

"I'm hoping Carl can help us avoid it."

Carl Magnusson gave him a shrewd, speculative look and grunted. "Don't expect too much, Thorkild. When Charlie was a simple sailor, I could handle him; but madness and magic are way outside my territory. I'd like to get Sally's advice."

When she heard the plan, Sally Anderton raged at them in total exasperation.

"You men! You stand on your wooden heads and read the world upside down! There's a poor devil, crazy because he's lost his wife, working his guts out on a tropic mountain, all alone, surrounded by the ghouls and ghosts of the past—and, suddenly, he wants to come home! He can't do it all at once, because he's haunted and scared. So he comes halfway and turns back, leaving a rag of himself hanging to a bush. Then, all of a sudden, it's the Oxbow Incident —three bullies and Carl Magnusson for spokesman, striding out to subdue him. You make me sick!"

"Easy, Sally! Easy!" Carl Magnusson reached out to hold her. "What's the shouting for? We came to ask your medical opinion."

"So I'll give it to you!" She stood straddled-legged in the middle of the hut, challenging them. "There's four of you—Gunnar, Adam, Willy and you, Carl. Why so many? That's no way to make a parley, even with a sane man! How would you feel, Carl, if you invited me to lunch, and I turned up with three attorneys and a stenographer? Madness! Pure madness!"

"What do you suggest, ma'am?" Adam Briggs was meticulously polite.

"For a start, Adam, you stay home. You're wise enough to know why. You're more foreign to a Polynesian than you are to a Connecticut Yankee. I'm not insulting you. It's a fact of life."

"I know it, ma'am. But when the chief gives an order, I obey. That's the deal."

"When a life's at stake, all deals are off. Gunnar?"

"You're the doctor, Sally. We're waiting for the prescription."

"You go, Gunnar. You take food and liquor. No weapons. No threats. Nothing but soft words and gentleness. . . . Talk him down, as they do a pilot lost in high weather. If he panics, let him go back, and try again another time. . . . God! Why do I have to spell it out like this?"

"Because we're dumb," said Willy Kuhio with a grin. "It's like when my Eva asks me to hold the knitting wool. I'm all thumbs and tangles. But put me and her on a boat, she wouldn't know a clove hitch from a running bowline."

"You're not a psychiatrist, Sally," said Gunnar

Thorkild flatly. "You said that yourself. You can't in-
sure us against all the risks. So Willy and I will go up
with Carl and try to coax Charlie down. If he won't
come, we bring him back by force. We've got to start
working that mountain, for food and timber. More!
We can't have this whole community living in fear,
with Charlie free, and the rest of us pinned down to
a beachhead like the goddam Marines on Iwo Jima!"

"Why can't we?" Sally faced him, flushed and furi-
ous. "What do we lack? What do we need that we
can't have?"

"Security," said Thorkild. "People safe in their
beds."

"Balls!" said Sally Anderton. "Have they been
threatened yet?"

"No. But . . ."

"But what? They could be drowned by another tidal
wave, strangled by a giant octopus! . . . But they won't
be. You're fighting phantoms. I pray you don't end
killing a man!"

"Sally, please. . . !"

"I've said it, sweetheart. I've said it all, backwards
and frontwards. Now I've run out of words. Why don't
you three men walk down to the beach and think it
out together. I'm tired. I'd like to go to bed."

"One last word, ma'am, if you'll be so kind."

"What's that, Adam?"

"Your husband . . . the chief here . . ."

"Let him speak for himself."

"Ma'am, a man can't do that. What does he say?
He's right? You're wrong? Or maybe you're both right
and wrong at once? But because he's the chief he just
can't bet everything on the nose. He's got to lay off,
up and down the card. He can't think just about
Charlie, or just about himself. It's you, and Barbara
and Jenny . . . all of us! When you had a patient dying,

you had to think of the ones left, just as much as the one going. Or maybe you didn't—I wouldn't know. But you see what I mean. . . ."

"Don't plead for me," said Thorkild brusquely. "It's settled."

"When a man does you a kindness," said Carl Magnusson gruffly, "you tell him thank you. And when a woman says hard words with love, you listen with respect! Come with me, Mr. Briggs. Let's look at that mash of yours!"

SEVEN

THE TERRACE WAS CLEARED, THE LAST BRUSH-wood burned away, the ground open for the cultivators; but Charlie Kamakau was gone. His hut was empty; the ashes of his fire were long cold, the food scraps decomposed. His tools were gone too, and, with them, the relics he had uncovered and cherished as signs of his sacred calling. Only the skull remained, shattered now and strewn in fragments on the sacrificial stone.

Thorkild and Kuhio combed the terrace and the surrounding bush, but the undergrowth was too dense and lush to show traces of his passing. They shouted for him over and over again, but the only answer was a flutter of wings and the shrilling of startled birds. Thorkild was troubled. The last vestiges of logic had been destroyed. Charlie Kamakau had achieved his aim. The clearing was a monument to his prowess and endurance, but he no longer wanted to demonstrate

233

it. Or was his flight only another anguished cry for help? "See! You need me! Come find me!" The smashed skull spoke of violence; but whether it was a symbolic act or a simple outburst of anger, there was no way to tell. Where was he now? Had he retreated to higher ground—even to the place of the navigators itself? Or was he hovering round the lower slopes, too afraid—or too hostile—to rejoin the group? Carl Magnusson summed up the situation tersely.

"No point in beating around any longer, Thorkild. You could have the whole camp looking for him and still lose him in that jungle. Let's go back. You can set a night watch, and instruct everybody to treat him gently if he's seen. When you put work parties up here, and on the timber slide, you give them the same instruction. . . . If he's gone bush for good then there's nothing more to be done. If he's working his way home, he'll communicate in his own time. . . . Sally's right in one thing. He hasn't committed any hostile act. You're right in another. We can't immobilize ourselves any longer."

"Why not leave him a message?" asked Willy Kuhio in his mild fashion.

Thorkild took out his knife and scratched on the surface of the sacrificial stone: "Great work, Charlie! Come down and celebrate—Thorkild, Willy, Carl!"

"That say it, Willy?"

"That says it," said Willy unhappily. "We can't know whether he'll believe it."

"We'll go home, then."

"Let's take it easy on the way back," said Carl Magnusson. "I'm not as young as I used to be."

"There's no hurry, Carl. I want to have a look at the timber they've marked."

As they plodded down the hillside, it was a relief to talk about simple, concrete things. The boat, they agreed, should be designed by Hernan Castillo, who had made models of almost every craft in the Pacific: the *Pahi* of the Societies, the *Ndrua* of Fiji, the *Waka Taurua* of the Cook Islanders. But before they chose the craft they must decide, in concert, the nature of the voyage. Would they commit the whole group in a single attempt to return to the nearest known port? Would they send out a small party, two or three, to make the perilous voyage and send back rescuers?

If they chose to set out, all together, they would need a large vessel, double-hulled and decked, to carry them and their water and provisions. To build it would take a long time, much longer than the year that Thorkild had projected. If they chose to send out a small advance party, they must consent to lose skilled and valuable manpower, and resign themselves to a long period of uncertainty about their fate. As they sat, resting under one of the marked trees, Carl Magnusson made a comment which gave Thorkild matter for long reflection.

". . . Once the goal is clear, and is recognized as attainable, I think it's important to forget the time element altogether. How can I put it? The work is more important than what it produces. The journey is more important than the arrival. It's an art of living we've lost in our mechanic age. I've rediscovered it too late, I'm afraid. Even Peter André Lorillard—God wash his starchy soul—has begun to want it. . . . That argument the other night, about too much regulation, is part of the same pattern . . . people wanting to grow instead of accomplish. They're beginning to feel, however vaguely, that they could fulfill themselves quite happily on this island. . . . Have you been down to the graves lately, Thorkild?"

"No. Why?"

"There are fresh flowers on them every day."

"Molly Kaapu and my Eva put them there," said Willy Kuhio. "When they go to bathe or look at the fish traps. It's a pleasant thing. A kind of prayer, I guess."

"That's what I was coming to." Magnusson plucked at an overhanging orchid and held the small purple bloom in his hands. "The thing that's happening to us all. Time is stopping; life is flowering. We're beginning to contemplate the mysteries. Some of us anyway. I keep wondering who will be our first prophet—and what will waken him and set him speaking?"

"I hope he doesn't come too soon." Thorkild laughed. "I've got enough troubles in my plate."

"That's queer. . . ." Willy Kuhio seized on the thought. "My Eva said the other night, the one thing she misses is church and the prayer meeting on Sunday. I told her we were all different religions, and some people had none at all, so it was best to keep it a private thing."

"I haven't been near a church in twenty years," said Magnusson lightly. "But I wonder sometimes about what Kaloni Kienga said, the day he left us, that each man goes to his gods by his own road; but all the gods are images of one. . . . What do you think, Thorkild?"

Thorkild shrugged and toyed a moment with the thought before he answered.

"I rejected Christianity when I left the Sisters. Mostly, I guess, because I didn't want to live up to it. With my grandfather I was drawn back to the old ways—but that's an emotional, a poetic thing if you want, although the *mana* is something very real to me. In that sense, I suppose I'm still a religious man. I have reverence. I have respect. But I don't think I have anything to teach anybody. However, if Eva or anyone else wants to pray or meet or meditate, I'll join them, gladly."

"It helps a lot of folk," said Willy Kuhio simply. "A hymn to lift up the heart, a prayer against the dark. There's always a fear in people—and sometimes God is the only one they can tell it to."

"I'm rested now." Carl Magnusson heaved himself to his feet. "Reach me down those orchids, Thorkild. We'll take some flowers back to the ladies."

The news of Charlie Kamakau's disappearance made everyone uneasy; but Thorkild took pains to abate their fears. So long as people were moving about the camp there was no danger. A watch would be kept from midnight until dawn, two men dividing it between them. No knives or other evident weapons would be carried, but a bamboo stave could be kept handy for any unlikely emergency. If Charlie were seen, he should be addressed calmly and invited to eat and drink at the fire pit. He should not be challenged or pursued, but made to feel free to come and go at will. Barbara Kamakau's movements were restricted to the campsite and to the beach. If, after a period, there were no signs of Charlie, the precautions might be relaxed. The first night watch would be split between Lorillard and Tioto. . . . Thorkild would share the roster with the rest. It was agreed that, with these simple precautions, everyone could relax and sleep quietly at night.

Franz Harsanyi profited by their good humour to press for a trial of his memory game. So Thorkild began with a simple lesson on the stars of the southern hemisphere, their movements and the legends associated with them in the folklore of the Polynesians. He made them cover their eyes and then draw the constellations in the sand, then lift their heads and identify them and name the stars in the order of their magnitude. By the end, even Simon Cohen had joined the game, singing the names into a pattern which they chanted in unison.

> "Aldebaran, Alrilam,
> Betelgeuse and Bellatrix,
> Pollux and Procyon. . . ."

As Ellen Ching remarked afterwards, it was strictly a kids' game, but it beat hell out of mugging or campus cocktail parties. Yoko Nagamuna, who had done well at the recognition, made a prim little lecture about the long tradition of geisha games, and how people—especially men!—were always children at heart. Thorkild nodded and smiled and then walked down to the beach with Sally. They pushed out the canoe and paddled across the lagoon, away from the inrush of the channel, and into the slack water where they could lie, cradled in the wooden shell, drifting slowly under the stars.

"Last night," said Sally drowsily, "I was so miserable I wanted to dig a hole in the sand and bury myself. You and I were fighting about poor Charlie Kamakau. I was jealous of Martha Gilman, because she's started a baby to Peter Lorillard, and so far I haven't been able to give you anything but sex and arguments. I was so mad with Jenny, I wanted to shake her and tell her, for God's sake, to go out and get laid and come back smiling for once! And to add to it all I had the curse and had to improvise napkins —which is one of the problems the great chief ignores in this primitive kingdom! . . . But today, everything was different. For the first time I found myself singing, and gossiping like a housewife with Molly Kaapu, and making jokes with Adam Briggs. I felt all cuddly and domestic; and I couldn't wait for you to get home. . . . Silly, isn't it?"

"Not to me, girl. When I took off around the island yesterday, I was desperate, chewed up like shark bait. Now I'm better too."

"Tell me something, honestly. Would you really like a child of your own? I mean here, in this place."

"Yes, I would. Better here than anywhere, I think. He'd have so much love spent on him. . . . Did I ever tell you how it was in the old days?"

"Tell me now."

"Well, you know, in spite of all the violence and the cruelty and the tyranny, there was always a sense of grace and beauty and generosity. . . . Strangers came; you invited them to food and drink. At the meal, no one must talk of sour or sad things. Troubles, like food, must be shared. . . . They called it "putting together again." If a woman couldn't have a child, she was given one by another family. . . . As for sex, it was the most natural thing in the world. It was everywhere, even in shells and stones. A pregnant woman looked for a female god-stone on which to give birth. If a man-child was born, his *piko*—the navel cord and the afterbirth—were buried in a cave, so that he would remain bound to the ancestral earth. When he was circumcised they tied a flower to the wound, to say that he was a man and his maleness was beautiful. . . . One of the things I've never understood is the madness that makes us demand to kill the unborn. At the same time, I understand the anarchist who wants to blow up our midden cities and let grass and trees grow through the ruins. Rousseau's noble savage wasn't just a romantic fiction; but we've put men on the moon and elevated torture to a fine art. . . . Yes,

I'd like our child to be born here! And I'd like to keep him and his mother here, always."

"It's a beautiful dream, my love; but don't build too much on it."

"Why not?"

"Because once we make contact with the outside world everything will change—even thee and me!"

"But we'll never be the same people again."

"I'll still be a doctor. You'll be the great scholar, with tenure and a chair and a worldwide reputation."

"And my heart always flying southward like the frigate bird."

"Mine too! . . . Why do I fight you so hard, when I love you so much?"

"One man failed you. Now you want to know how much the new one can take."

"And the answer?"

"There's no answer. I'm lying out here and looking at you and thinking that your eyes have stars in them, and your breasts are beautiful and you're warm to lie with and easy to laugh with—and a bitch to fight! . . . Also that we've got through one more day, and who's going to cut timber and who's going to work on the plantation terrace and how the hell will we cope with day-flying mosquitoes. . . . And if you don't start paddling we'll be on the reef!"

"Gunnar Thorkild, you're impossible! The next time I . . ."

"Hold it a minute!"

"What's the matter?"

"I thought I heard a shout. Let's go back!"

By the time they reached the beach, the crowd was waiting—shocked and sinister and angry. Peter Lorillard gave him the story. They had just dispersed to their huts. He had taken up his post by the fire when he heard a cry from the store hut. Charlie

Kamakau had cut his way through the matting wall and was waiting in ambush behind the pile of salvage. He had attacked Barbara with a knife. She was badly wounded but alive. Tioto and Simon Cohen had disarmed him. They, too, were hurt. Charlie Kamakau was bound and insensible after his beating.

The scene around the fire pit was a gory one. Barbara was slashed on breasts, arms and belly and was bleeding profusely. Tioto's hands were cut and Simon Cohen was torn along the neck and the jawline. Sally Anderton organized the women quickly to cleanse the men's wounds and stanch their bleeding, while she set to work, with Thorkild, on Barbara Kamakau. It was fast, rough surgery: cleanse and clamp and sew; then start on the next lesion. It would leave scars. There would be no cosmetic treatment to obliterate them afterwards; but the girl would live, and the boys would mend quickly, except that Tioto would be maimed afterwards, because the tendons of his left palm were severed.

When Sally had finished, the wounded were dosed with the last of the ship's morphine and put to rest in the huts, with the women to nurse them during the night. Then Thorkild, Sally and Peter Lorillard walked over to the store hut where Willy Kuhio was standing guard over Charlie Kamakau. He was trussed like a chicken, in cordage salvaged from the ship. He was bruised and bloody, but conscious now, and uncannily calm. Sally Anderton sponged his face and gave him water and spoke to him gently:

"Charlie, do you recognize me?"

"Sure, I recognize you. You're Mrs. Anderton."

"Do you know what you've done?"

"Yes."

"Why did you do it?"

"I had to, I was told. Nothing would go right until she was dead."

"She's not dead, Charlie."

"They won't blame me for that. I tried. I can try again afterwards. Could you take these ropes off me? I'm very tired. I'd like to sleep."

"I'll give you something to make you sleep, Charlie; but the ropes must stay on. Otherwise you'll do more harm."

"I didn't mean harm—only to Barbara!"

"You wounded Tioto, who is your friend, and Simon Cohen, who used to play music and sing with you."

"Only because they tried to stop me. They shouldn't have done that! Barbara was the bad one."

"All right, Charlie. I'll be back in a moment to give you something for sleep. Stay quiet now. No one will hurt you."

She walked out of the hut, signing to Thorkild and Lorillard to follow her. She answered their question before they uttered it.

"He's gone—far gone. I'll fill him up with barbiturate and let him sleep. He may be more rational in the morning, though I doubt it."

Lorillard said flatly:

"You put him to sleep and let Thorkild and me take him out to the deep water and dump him. It would be a mercy for him and everybody else."

"It would also be murder," said Thorkild. "If he's lucid in the morning, he must answer for himself. If he's not, we'll discuss, in full meeting, what's to be done with him."

"I'll get the tablets," said Sally Anderton.

When she had gone, Lorillard rounded on Thorkild. He was bitterly angry.

"Listen, man! You're the big chief. I'm one of your

counsellors and I'll guarantee you the votes of the others. Why don't we settle this thing now, cleanly and mercifully? Why put everyone through another agony? Haven't you ever heard of triage? You get a mess of wounded. You sort 'em out—one, two, three —those you can save, those you might and those that already have the mark of death on them. You let them go as painlessly as possible. . . . I've been through it. If you haven't the stomach for it, I'll do it myself."

"You won't—and here's why! We're one tribe with a sick member. Our responsibility is both personal and collective. We'll face it together; because, whatever is done, we'll all have to live with it afterwards. We'll have no heroes and no scapegoats. Clear?"

"Crap!" said Lorillard.

"If you like." Thorkild was grim. "But you dispose of other people's lives too easily, Lorillard—your wife's, your kids', ours too! Those signal buoys weren't all in the hold. Two at least were in your cabin! You were testing them the day I took command."

"You can't prove that! I put them back in the hold afterwards."

"I don't want to prove it. I left you to make the decision. I'm not complaining about it. But I don't trust you enough to have you as judge, jury and executioner. . . . You've finished your watch, mister! Now go to bed, for God's sake!"

Sally Anderton's prognosis proved wrong. When they saw him early in the morning, Charlie Kamakau was lucid, if still a long way from normality. He remembered what he had done; but he spoke of it as if there were two men concerned, the one possessed and driven by the other. He spoke of himself as Charlie and of the other as the *kapu* man. When the *kapu* man held the club and the magic pestle in his hands, voices spoke to him in the old tongue: big, commanding voices, telling him that the fruit would wither and the land lie sterile unless blood were poured to make it fertile. He believed the voices, because he knew how it was in the old days. . . . Charlie still hated Barbara, but not enough to kill her. He would like Thorkild to tell everyone Charlie was sorry for their trouble—Barbara too, because she was punished now, and she would not be able to flaunt herself and destroy other men. Charlie understood he must be tried; but he did not want to be present or to speak, in case he should be shamed again. If Carl Magnusson and the chief would explain things, that was all he asked. He didn't really care whether he lived or died. One day everyone would eat from the land he had opened up. He had proved, hadn't he, that he was a man? He could not understand why he was still bound. Charlie meant no evil to anyone; but the *kapu* man must be obeyed.

Outside, while the others were still moving sluggishly about their waking tasks, Gunnar Thorkild briefed Sally Anderton on her part in the council. He, himself, would ask her some questions which she would answer to the best of her ability. For the rest, she was free to join in the discussion or abstain from it. What were the questions? In fairness to the group, he must reserve them. She agreed, wearily. The sooner the whole mess was cleared up the better. Barbara was too sick to be present. She was still in shock and there were disquieting signs of infection. She warned Thorkild he would face a hostile and demoralized assembly. To add to their joys, Carl Magnusson was not well. The long walk up the mountain and the night's disturbance had sent his blood pressure soaring; but he still insisted on attending the meeting. She herself was holding up, but she would be glad if Thorkild would take a swim with her before the assembly.

As they walked down to the beach, Martha Gilman joined them. She was worried about Mark. She had asked him to look after Barbara while the discussion was going on. He had refused sulkily and Lorillard had slapped him. Then she and Lorillard had quarrelled and he had accused her of destroying his necessary authority over the boy. Thorkild grinned sourly at this last gratuitous mess. He told Martha:

"I think the boy should be at the meeting, Martha. He'll get a rough lesson in tribal morality; and—who knows?—he may even have something to contribute to the discussion. You don't have to back down. I'll just tell him I've overruled your decision, because I think it's time he learned to behave like a man."

Half an hour later, they were all gathered, some sitting, some standing, others sprawled on the sand, with Thorkild seated on an upturned can facing them, as if he and not Charlie Kamakau were under indictment. He waited until they were settled and silent, then rose to address them.

". . . We are here to decide the fate of a fellow human being, a comrade of our voyage and our misfortune. We must decide it together, with all the wisdom and compassion we can command. I stress 'together,' because we cannot make any single one a scapegoat for our decision. Some of you know, and some of you do not, the history of the *Bounty* mutineers on Pitcairn. Every today, that tiny community is haunted by the memory of murder and violence perpetrated by its founders. We must spare ourselves and our children such a horrible burden. We must make our decision in common, and bear, in common, the responsibility for it. Everyone must speak. Everyone must vote—even the boy, Mark Gilman here, because he will inherit the consequences of what we now decide. As your chief I shall begin; then, as each one speaks, all of you must feel free to challenge or interrogate. Have I made myself clear? . . . Dr. Sally Anderton, will you stand, please?"

She stood, stony-faced, but calm and erect.

"Have I informed you of my questions or prompted your answers?"

"No."

"Do you understand that you can answer freely?"

"Yes."

"First question. In your opinion, is Charlie Kamakau a sane man?"

"No."

"Is he responsible in a legal or moral sense for what he has done?"

"No."

"Again, in your opinion, is he competent to answer for what he has done before this assembly?"

"No."

"Can you specify the nature of his condition?"

"I don't think I'm competent to do that. I'm a physician with a very limited experience of mental diseases."

"Could you tell us, or even guess, whether the condition is curable?"

"I simply don't know."

"Is he or is he not still a risk to this community?"

"In my opinion, he is still a risk—to himself and others."

"Should we ask him to plead before this assembly?"

"Definitely not."

"Thank you, Doctor. Now"—he was very calm, very judicial—"the question is clear: what do we do with a sick and incompetent man who has committed violence, who may repeat it, for whom the best opinion we have offers no guarantee of cure? You may specify by statement or amplify the issue by questions. Carl Magnusson?"

"A question for you, chief. Can we separate him permanently and securely from the rest of us?"

"From what I know of the geography of the island, that's impossible."

"To you, then, Sally: what would happen if we confined him permanently in or near the camp?"

"It would drive him into permanent insanity and demoralize the rest of us."

"Thank you. I reserve my conclusion. Back to you, chief."

"Molly Kaapu?"

"I say Charlie had a bad run. He did bad things, sure; but I think he would come back, if we hold him quiet awhile."

"Can you suggest how we might do that?"

"Well . . . no, I can't. I'd like to think about it while the rest of you talk."

"Mr. Lorillard?"

"I've already stated my opinion. The man is, unfortunately, beyond help. I think we should dispose of him mercifully."

"In fact, kill him?"

"Yes."

"Yoko Nagamuna?"

"I agree with Peter Lorillard. It could be done quickly and painlessly."

"Who would do it?"

"I hadn't thought about that."

"Would you like to consider the question, while we continue? Simon Cohen?"

"I pass. I'm a victim and prejudiced."

"Tioto?"

"Charlie's my friend. Everybody knows that, eh?

But if we can't cure him and can't separate him, I say we put him to sleep quietly."

"Martha Gilman?"

"I don't know . . . I just don't know."

"Willy Kuhio?"

"Can I speak for Eva too?"

"Certainly."

"We talked about this all night. We think—but we can't promise—if we took Charlie away, not back to the terrace but higher up or lower down, and we worked with him and looked after him, maybe he'd come good again. Trouble is, we couldn't lock him up, we wouldn't. But we'd be willing to try—if the rest were willing to take the risk."

"Thanks, Willy. Thank you too, Eva. . . . Now I think we should hear from Mark Gilman."

"I'm like my mother. I don't know. All I say is we got no right to kill someone, just like that, because it stops everything. I mean, there's no afterwards. It just finishes there. Besides, who's going to do it? And what do we say to them afterwards?"

"Thank you, Mark. Those are important questions for all of us. Ellen Ching?"

"Pass. I'll wait for the vote—which, by the way, should be secret."

"Point taken. Franz Harsanyi?"

"If you accept Willy and Eva's suggestion, I'll go with them and help. It's a long chance, but I'd be willing to take it."

"Hernan Castillo?"

"Let me put it this way. If you can't work a stone, you throw it away. If you can't work a tree, you fell another one. I'm for a quick, clean solution; and in the end I think Charlie Kamakau would be grateful for it."

"Jenny?"

"I'm with Willy and Eva and Franz. If you'll let them look after him, I'll help."

"Adam Briggs?"

"I'm with Jenny."

"Sally, you answered opening questions. Do you want to speak for yourself?"

"Yes, I do." She was obviously under strain, but her voice was steady and she chose her words with singular care. "The abstainers simply duck the issue and hide themselves behind a secret vote. They help us not at all. They wash their hands like Pilate and give themselves an easy option for afterwards. Two solutions only have been offered. Death, or a kind of open therapy in a volunteer community. I have to say, with the deepest regret, that I do not believe that solution will work. Our group will be split and will become so much more vulnerable. Those who have the custody of Charlie will have a responsibility that none of us dare lay upon them. I think he may be curable. I cannot, in any good conscience, promise that he is. So we come to the next solution: death. It can be quick. It can be painless. It may well be the most merciful solution. Let me show you." She held up the hypodermic syringe from the ship's medicine chest. "All you have to do is inject a bubble of air into a vein. The patient will die, in a brief spasm, as soon as the bubble reaches the heart. There's only one question: who will do it? I will not, because I swore to cure, not to harm. Will you, Peter? You, Yoko? You, Hernan? Any of you abstainers? If that's the way the vote goes, someone has to do it."

No one spoke. No one raised a hand. She passed the syringe to Thorkild and sat down.

A moment later Tioto announced, "We've all spoken—except one. What do you say, chief?"

Gunnar Thorkild stood up, tall and grotesque

against the flare of the lamps. He said in a flat, toneless voice:

"I agree with everyone who has spoken here tonight —with those in favour of a merciful elimination, those who would offer themselves as voluntary custodians, those who, for whatever reason, abstain from offering an opinion. None of us must blame another for any thoughts expressed here tonight. Banishment is impossible—and even if possible, it would be an inhuman torture. Death, administered as Sally Anderton describes, would be a discreet mercy. Custody would be an intolerable and corrupting burden on the custodians, and might expose us all later to recrimination and dissension. So what do we do? Kill a man we cannot cure? Attempt, dangerously, a cure beyond our small resources? There is no argument that does not carry long and dangerous consequences. I therefore have decided to use the authority with which you have invested me, and the *mana* with which my ancestors have endowed me. Here is what we will do. Adam Briggs, you will rig the canoe, with mast and sail, paddles and fishing tackle and a knife. Molly Kaapu, you will provision it—with water and fruit and whatever else we have. We will give Charlie the boat and let him sail wherever he can. He is a good navigator. He has a better chance of survival than most, if he wishes to take it. Nothing that he has done here can touch him anywhere else in the world, because we are beyond the jurisdiction of any state or law. The sea has given new life, new hope to other men, perhaps it will do the same for Charlie Kamakau. Will you agree by vote?"

"I agree," said Tioto swiftly. "If Charlie wants, I'll go with him."

"He goes alone," said Thorkild curtly.

"What do we do for a boat?" asked Yoko Nagamuna.

"We build another one—and live from the traps until we do."

"And why"—Peter Lorillard was bitter as wormwood—"why didn't you propose this solution at the beginning?"

"Don't be angry, Mr. Lorillard." Eva Kuhio reached out to touch him. "None of us knows what bread costs until we do our own shopping."

"I reject that!" Lorillard was shaking with fury. "I say the man we elected as our chief has deliberately trapped us into a series of admissions or opinions, that damage our esteem of one another. He did this in order to cement his own authority, by offering a simple solution of which he was already aware. I say this was a crude and cruel political trick, and that a man who would perpetrate it is unfit to lead us."

"Those are hard words, Mr. Lorillard." Adam Briggs was instantly on his feet. "I don't deny your right to state any case before this group. But, now you've put this one, I'd like to examine it. You say the chief deliberately trapped us. How?"

"By the oldest trick in the book—procedure! He knew that by following the formality he could force us to disclose our opinions and withhold his own."

"And the disclosure of our opinions lessens our esteem for one another?"

"Yes."

"I fail to see that. I have great respect for anyone who can confront a harsh decision with courage. I've seen more combat than you. I've had to weigh one man's death against the safety of others—and decide to kill him or let him die. . . . Even our abstainers helped us—and here I disagree with Sally Anderton— because they preserved a necessary attitude of caution. . . . Also, to submit to this open encounter over an issue of life and death was—as the chief stated it to be—vital to us all."

"I still believe it was divisive and damaging."

"Two more points then. You called this a simple solution. I don't see it as simple, either for the man who proposed it or for Charlie Kamakau. It involves a deprivation of one of our big assets, a seaworthy craft. It commits a sick man to an enormous risk—even while it appears to offer him a hope of cure and of safety. It takes one burden off our backs—but leaves us with another one: the knowledge that we cannot, as yet, cope with aberrants and misfits—which any of us could still become."

"You're on my side now, Briggs!" Lorillard seized on the thought. "The solution was made to look simple. In truth it isn't. Its only virtue is that it makes the chief look humane and compassionate, and the rest of us either cowards or cold-hearted executioners. Now, what's your last point?"

"Procedure again," said Adam Briggs calmly. "The solution was not imposed, it was proposed for a vote."

"Then let's stick to procedure, eh? We've got three different proposals before us—death, community therapy, or this . . . this buccaneering gesture of sending a ship's Jonah off in an open boat! I insist all three be put to the vote."

"Before we do that," said Carl Magnusson heavily, "some others of us might like to speak. Me, for instance. I reserved a position. Now I'd like to state it. There's one point on which we all agree. We confess that we cannot guarantee safe custody or adequate therapy for Charlie Kamakau. Some of us want to try it, without guarantees. The rest want Charlie eliminated from the community. . . . I say it's time we stopped talking about him as an absent cipher. I'd like us to see him, sick or well, in this assembly."

"We'd frighten him to death," said Tioto.

"I think we're all scared," Martha Gilman cut in quickly. "We've never really looked at ourselves before."

Thorkild thrust himself to his feet and faced them.

"I'm going to end the discussion. My integrity has been called in question. I cannot serve you without full confidence. So I resign, here and now. I'm no longer your chief, just Gunnar Thorkild. I'm going to rig the canoe, which, I remind you, belonged to my grandfather. I'm going to load it and put Charlie in it and let him go. If any of you want to stop me, you're welcome to try. . . ."

He left them and walked over to the store hut. A few moments later he came out, with Charlie Kamakau, stooped and shambling, beside him. They looked neither to right nor left, but headed straight for the beach where they began stepping the mast on the canoe. Then Molly Kaapu got up, and with Jenny at her heels gathered up a half-dozen water gourds, and set off for the cascade. A moment later Adam Briggs and Tioto set off into the bush with knives and hatchets. Peter André Lorillard said with wintry malice:

"Well! So much for sweet reason and democracy."

"I've got a patient," said Sally Anderton. "Lend me a hand, please, Ellen."

"I guess we start thinking about a new election," said Yoko Nagamuna amiably.

"You think about it, sweetheart!" Carl Magnusson climbed wearily to his feet. "I'm going to say good-bye to a friend."

Charlie Kamakau had not uttered a word from the moment Thorkild had entered the hut and explained his situation. Thorkild made no effort to engage him in talk, but as they worked he kept up a simple, toneless monologue.

". . . From here, Charlie, you head north, making as much easting as you can. You'll end up either in the lower Cooks or the Austral Islands. . . . You've got fishing tackle. You'll need to conserve water, but you'll make it if you're careful. . . . Now keep in mind, no one, no one in the world, can touch you for what's happened here. But you don't even have to mention it. . . . When you make your landfall, explain that you were bosun on the *Frigate Bird* and you volunteered to make a single-handed journey to bring help. . . . I'll confirm that, so will your other friends. . . . The only thing is you must never, never come back here. . . . You keep going, north by east, and at night you steer on the dog star, between the rising and the zenith. . . . You forget everything, except that you're going home. There are no voices, no *kapu* . . . nothing but the new landfall. . . ."

There was no sign that he heard or understood, except that all his movements were seaman-like and purposive. Watched by the little group of helpers, he tested the rigging for strain; he raised and lowered the sail; he stowed the food and the water gourds and the tackle neatly to his hand. Tioto went to him and embraced him. He stood rigid as a tree and made no response to the gesture. Carl Magnusson held out his hand and said:

"Good-bye, old shipmate."

Charlie Kamakau ignored him. He squatted in the shallows, voided his bowels and his bladder, then pushed the canoe into the water, hauled himself inboard and, without a backward glance, paddled away towards the channel.

"Why?" Tioto begged dolefully of no one in particular. "Why did he go like that? We were his friends. He knew that much."

"We failed him," said Gunnar Thorkild. "Lorillard and the others were right. He wanted us to kill him."

Now that it was done, he felt empty and aimless, craving like an alcoholic for strong liquor and solitude. The others sensed his mood and huddled away from him, talking in low tones among themselves. For want of anything better to do he went in to see Barbara Kamakau. Sally had just changed her dressings and was bathing her face with cool water. She was feverish and in much pain, but she held out a limp hand in greeting.

"Has Charlie gone?"

"He's gone."

"And he'll never come back?"

"Never."

"Don't let them hate me, please!"

"Nobody hates you, girl. We want you well and smiling. We've ordered flowers and chocolates by the next flight!"

"You're crazy, chief."

"Crazy like a fox!" Sally was tart and unsmiling. "Now get out of here and let the girl rest."

He walked over to the store hut, picked up a hatchet, a seaman's knife, an auger and a bundle of lashings and headed out of the camp towards the uplands. Half a mile from the camp he found what he was looking for: a fresh stand of bamboo growing near a large, flat rock. With more simple satisfaction than he had felt for a long time, he settled down to work, choosing the canes, testing them for strength and flexibility, cutting and grading them. It was nearly nightfall when he completed his project—a simple canoe frame, large enough to carry two men. When the frame was lined with palm matting and covered with sail canvas, it would make a craft serviceable enough for fishing the lagoon and the reef.

He gathered up his tools, hoisted the frame onto his shoulders and walked back to the camp. He set the frame down near the fire pit, brought out a length of sailcloth and a few pieces of matting, and, by the light of the fire and the torches, demonstrated how the covering should be done. It was a day's work at most. They would not be too long deprived. As he walked back to his hut, Sally fell into step beside him and announced acidly:

"Before you start playing lone ranger, my love, give a thought to the little woman back at the ranch."

Thorkild was unusually contrite. "I didn't think. I'm sorry. I wanted them to have that damn boat today. . . . It's rather neat, don't you think?"

"Very. But they won't turn out the band for you."

"Have I asked for it?"

"No. But that's the problem. No one knows what you're asking for."

"Nothing."

"Then why did you resign? There were good things happening at that meeting. Hard things were said, sure! Lorillard was certainly insulting—but no one else. And you had eloquent and faithful defenders. I have to say this, my love—you disappointed me. You put yourself and everyone else in a false position. . . ."

"I'm sorry; but I don't see it like that. I'm an old-fashioned man. I was taught to give respect. I expect to get it."

"You didn't give it today. You breached the bargain you made at the beginning—open talk, decisions in common. And do you know why? Because you weren't prepared to trust us to make a decent, human decision. You robbed us all—yes, me too!—of a fundamental right. . . . It's a terrible thing to say to the man I love. But I mean it, Gunnar. I mean every word of it."

"What should I do? Call my lawyer?"

"Don't be flippant. It doesn't become you. . . . See you later. I'm going over to help with the supper."

She was right and he knew it. He had breached a contract. He had invaded the rights of those who had made it with sole faith in Gunnar Thorkild, scholar, gentleman, respected inheritor of an older tradition than their own. Why had he done it? Wounded pride was no answer. He had already dealt out his own insult to Peter Lorillard. Fear of the votes? That was too flimsy a pretext, with so many and so eloquent voices in favour of compassion. The real reason lay much deeper, and was much more shameful. The history of the *alii*, the high ones, was a seductive legend. The *mana* which they transmitted to him was a gift as dangerous as the Midas touch or the godlike empery of the Caesars. It tempted, if not to tyranny, at least to a taste for homage and the smell of incense. He had repeated the same mistake he had made in his academic career. He had demanded too much credence for too little evidence; too much tolerance for too arrogant a presumption.

Almost immediately, reaction began, and he swung violently from guilt to resentment. Why the devil should he make kowtows to a small group of professional grumblers—Simon Cohen and Yoko, and Peter Lorillard! Why should they have the right, denied to him, of perpetual carping and negation? Well, let Lorillard or Castilo or Cohen try their backsides in the chief's chair. He himself was glad to be out of it! The first smell of cooking wafted across from the fire pit; but tonight he had no appetite either for food or company. He strolled down to the beach, built himself a backrest in the sand and sat staring out across the lagoon, trying, as his grandfather had taught him, to plait himself together again.

This time it was not so easy. Behind him he could

hear, muted by distance, the talk and laughter around the fire. Before him was the big ocean, tossing now with the turbulence of a distant storm, which would make Charlie Kamakau's first passage a nightmare. Had he himself been asked to lay the odds on his own survival in such circumstances, he would have put them at three to one in his favour. He was skilled, sane, never seasick, and mere distance held no terrors for him. Charlie Kamakau, too, was a good sailor; but his experience was on large vessels, not in small island craft; and even for a man, sane and healthy, the solitude of the great sea was a constant threat.

Which brought him, by a round turn, to the vessel which they now must build for themselves. The big craft, like the *Ndrua* of the Fijians, and the old Hawaiian *Wa'a Kaulua*, took, sometimes, years to build. They were capable of very long journeys; but to sail them required more skill and endurance than his own people could command. The old migrants lived on them for long periods; but they were wet, uncomfortable, and in big seas, they rode like roller coasters. Besides, with Charlie Kamakau gone, and Tioto maimed in one hand, their manpower was seriously depleted. Carl Magnusson was a diminishing force, and the casualties among the women—Jenny, Barbara, and Martha now pregnant—were a further handicap. With a small start of surprise, he realized that he was thinking as if he were still chief and arbiter of their destiny. . . . He heard a footfall in the sand behind him. When he turned he saw that it was Yoko Nagamuna. She asked in her little-girl voice:

"Mind if I join you?"

"You're welcome."

She sald down onto the sand beside him. "They're all talking their heads off round the fire. Everybody's so serious . . . blah-blah-blah! I got bored."

"It hasn't been a very cheerful day."

"What's happened to your sense of humour, prof! You always used to be good for a laugh or two."

"I'm out of practice. Say something funny!"

"Do you know the story of the woman who was snatched by the gorilla at the zoo? He pulled her inside the cage, slammed the door and started to undress her. She screamed to her husband: 'What do I do, Harry? What do I do?' Her husband just shrugged and said, 'Tell him you've got a headache!' "

In spite of himself, Thorkild laughed.

"There's another version," said Yoko, straight-faced, "where the woman steps into the cage. A few minutes later she's back, shaking her head. 'No use!' she says. 'Just like my husband. Psychic impotence!' "

"That's very sad." Thorkild chuckled. "I could cry for her."

"Save your tears," said Yoko. "Next week she turned lesbian and lived. happily ever after with a beauty editor."

"The moral being . . . ?"

"I'm in love with Hernan Castillo—and he couldn't care less because he's in love with Ellen Ching and she couldn't care less either, because she's got Franz Harsanyi but she'd rather have me, and I'm not interested."

"That's quite a tangle."

"It's a mess of worms, Professor! Which explains why I am one very bitchy lady."

"It's sad, Yoko; but I'm afraid there's nothing I can do about it."

"You've got your hands full already, haven't you? What with Sally and Jenny and Martha Gilman. . . . Don't you yearn for that nice little bachelor apartment in Honolulu?"

"I haven't had much time to think about it."

"But now you will have. How does it feel to be a private citizen again?"

"You are bitchy!"

"Do you blame me?"

"Yes, I do. You make mischief. When it snaps back and bites you, you make more mischief. That'll scare anyone off—man or gorilla!"

"Thanks for nothing, Professor!"

"Listen, woman! We're all lonely. All scared. . . . Even when you're in love you wake up in the dark and see hobgoblins on the ceiling. Look at that sea! It's boiling! Charlie Kamakau's out there, alone; and I sent him."

"And your Sally's back there at the fire talking some mishmash about 'putting things together again'! Why isn't she here with you?"

"Lay off, Yoko!" Thorkild heaved himself to his feet. "Sally's had a rougher time than any of us; and she's worried as hell because she's almost out of drugs."

"I'm worried about that as well," said Yoko Nagamuna. "Which makes another little item for your logbook. I'm pregnant too. One night on the beach with Simon Cohen . . . and not a very good one at that! So how does that grab you, O wise one?"

"Oh God—I'm sorry!"

"Don't be! I bought it; just don't spit in my eye. I never thought I'd say it to you, but I could use a kind word. . . . Will you walk me down to the end of the beach?"

"Sure."

"I won't keep you away too long."

"It doesn't matter. There's nothing else to do."

"Oh yes, there is. I have a message for you. Because I belong to the opposition, they sent me as a kind of ambassador. They want you to be chief again."

They had kept a place for him at the fire pit. They had baked a small fish and a sweet of *fei* and coconut for the meal he had missed. They had appointed Lorillard to speak for them, but before he did so, Thorkild made his peace:

"I have an apology to make. I behaved badly. I broke the contract we made together. I hope you'll all forgive me."

It was as if he had not spoken. Peter Lorillard said, formally:

"It's clear that most of our problems arise out of personality conflicts. We all agree that we need to separate the conflicting elements. We also agree that we still need a chief as the focus of our unity. So we hope you'll consent to resume, Thorkild."

"I'd like to hear your other proposal first."

"Martha and I, Willy Kuhio and Eva will colonize the terraces and cultivate them. If our health holds good—and Sally will give us a regular checkup—we'll stay there. That leaves yourself, Franz, Hernan Castillo, Briggs and Simon Cohen, five able-bodied men, for the boat-building, with Carl, Tioto and the women for all the rest of the jobs. Young Mark says he would like to stay down here. If we need a rest or a change of scenery we swap jobs. . . . Does that make sense?"

"It seems to, so far."

"Until we learn to hunt or domesticate the pigs, you'll have to supply us with fish. We'll send you down fruit and vegetables. There's one other thing . . . Subject to the general authority of the chief and the tribe, we'd like to—well—do things our own way on the terrace. No offense, but . . ."

Thorkild grinned amiably. "I know! It saves personality problems. When do you want to leave?"

"In the morning. After we've drawn stores and tools."

"Good. It's settled then!"

"So let's drink to a quiet life." Carl Magnusson held up a bottle of liquor. "We've got six quarts left after this. We'll give two to the mountain folk and save the rest for births and funerals."

One thing was now abundantly clear to Thorkild. The beach-side community had the advantage in man-power, but it was now much less stable than before. It was idle to expect that either the men or the women would adjust themselves easily to a situation fraught with so much stress. So, without consulting anyone, he made a risky decision. First he called Simon Cohen and told him bluntly:

"This is truth and consequences, sonny boy! You've got one girl pregnant, and she doesn't want you. Bar-bara's carved up, but she'll recover. I'm not a stud mas-ter mating mares and stallions, but we've got to get some kind of stability into our arrangements. Those scars you've got tell you what happens when that sta-bility is destroyed. So, sixty-four-dollar question: what are you going to do?"

Cohen took it coolly enough. So far as life on the island was concerned, he'd as lief shack with Barbara as anyone else. . . . She was good in bed; she had a sense of humour; and the scars wouldn't show in the dark. . . . Simple Simon was a pragmatist. So, no prob-lems, no complications. . . .

Thorkild hesitated a long time over his next move and then, uneasily, decided to pin his faith to the brusque Chinese common sense of Ellen Ching. She agreed, without hesitation, to preserve his confidence. He told her of his talk with Yoko Nagamuna, of his own fears, and of the arrangement he had concluded with Simon Cohen. He added:

"I'm not setting up as a marriage broker. I'm looking for advice."

Ellen Ching gave him a small, frigid smile, folded her hands in her lap and told him:

"I learned a long time ago that you settle for what you are and what you can have. . . . I've always been a two-way switch. Yoko's always known it, but I'd as soon play girl games with her as with a rattlesnake! Franz Harsanyi and I? Well, he's soft and kind with a head full of dreams—a poet, I guess. He thinks he's in love with me, but that's only because I understand him and we don't fight, and he feels warmer with me than I do with him. If it helps you to have me as his hausfrau, I've no objections—and he'll think he's married the Mona Lisa. . . . If you're wondering why I'm so easy about this you might as well know I'm not the Hakka matriarch you thought I was. I'm scared stiff of children and I'm all sewn up inside so I can't have them."

"Tell me about Hernan Castillo."

"He's cute, isn't he? Small, brown, handsome, courteous, good-humoured. The best of both worlds. . . . But make no mistake, chief. He's pure artist. Solid bronze—totally self-sufficient! You heard him. What you can't use you throw away! Oh boy . . . !"

"What are Yoko's chances with him?"

"She's a tough one herself. With me out of the running, she'll make out fine. So long as Hernan's got his sticks and stones to play with, you could mate him with a hole in a wall and he wouldn't know the difference." She relaxed and gave him a sidelong sardonic smile. "Are you sure you know what you're doing, chief?"

"No! . . . I'm sailing by the seat of my pants."

"Some people might say you were acting like a first-class fascist."

"What's the alternative? Another blowup?"

"Hey-hey! I'm on your side, remember! I like a nice orderly life too, which reminds me—when you've finished police rounds, your own girl could use a little loving care. She's starting to fray at the edges."

"Thanks, Ellen. You're a pal!"

"I also come in season like any other girl. You're on fair notice, chief. Don't leave any loose change lying around. I can still be tempted!"

After which salutary council he went off in search of Jenny. He found her at the water's edge scaling and cleaning fish and laying them out on fresh leaves. Her eyes lit up when she saw him and she made a comic face of disgust.

"I hate this job! All guts and gore!"

"I'd like to talk to you, Jenny."

"You look awfully serious. Have I done something wrong?"

"No . . . but maybe I'm about to make a big mistake. I've made quite a few lately."

"I don't think you have . . . and I said it last night around the fire!"

"Jenny, yesterday was one of the worst days in my life. . . . We were talking about killing a man because he couldn't accommodate to reality. Maybe in the end I have killed him."

"You mustn't blame yourself. You can't."

"To tell you the truth, Jenny, some of the blame lies on poor Charlie himself. He turned away from real life, and ended in a world of nightmare and fantasy."

"I know. . . ."

"And that's what you're doing now, Jenny!"

"I . . . I don't understand."

"Then I'll have to make you understand. You're the

luckiest girl alive. You've got a good man, head over heels in love with you. You love him too; but you won't admit it, because you think you're in love with me. . . . No, don't turn away! You're going to hear this and understand it. I love you, Jenny—but the way a father loves his daughter and wants to protect her and see she gets the best deal in life. But that's it! End quote, period, finish! If you have fantasies about me making love to you, forget 'em! I'd be impotent—not because you're not beautiful or desirable, but because, to me, you're *kapu*: forbidden! Now, there are two choices: take the sweet fruit and eat it; love the man who belongs to you; enjoy the love he's offering you; be glad of the other love that surrounds you. . . . Or climb that cliff, jump off, and let the sharks eat you for dinner! I'll be sorry; we'll all be sorry. But the next day we'll go about our normal business; because we've only got a small life, and we can't spend one more goddam bit of it on you!"

He turned on his heel and left her, squatting in the shallows, sobbing like a child over a broken doll. As he walked into the camp he found Adam Briggs, raking out the first charcoal from the kiln and putting it into baskets. Thorkild tapped him on the shoulder.

"I've just been talking to your girl, on the beach!"

"Did she say anything about me?"

"I didn't give her a chance. I told her she could either marry you or feed herself to the sharks."

"Hell, man!" Briggs was horror-struck. "That's no way to talk to the girl!"

"You know a better one, go try it! I've run out of words!"

Briggs took off like a sprinter from the block. Thorkild shrugged and went over to inspect the mash can. The mixture looked foul, but it was fermenting steadily. It was real grade A jungle juice, potent enough to put a leap on the lame or blow the heads off the unwary.

Sally Anderton was standing, drenched and dishevelled, under the cascade, washing clothes. Thorkild plunged in beside her and clasped her in his arms.

"That's enough, woman! Cease and desist! Chief's orders!"

"Please, Gunnar! Can't you see I'm busy?"

"We're all busy! Lorillard's making like a great pioneer in the jungle. Franz Harsanyi and Ellen Ching are moving house. Adam, I hope, is proposing to Jenny. Castillo's working on the plans he's got to show me this afternoon. And you and I, my love, are going to work at being civil and sweet and sexy with each other!"

"You have been a busy preacher, haven't you? Three shotgun weddings in twenty-four hours. It must be a record. I just hope they stick."

"Even if they don't, it slows things down for a space. . . . Come on, let's see you smile."

"I don't feel like smiling. I'm just goddam fed up, with myself and everyone else! And I don't feel like making love either!

"Did I ask?"

"No, but . . ."

"Easy, sweetheart! Easy!" He lifted her in his arms, carried her out of the pool and set her down on the soft moss of the bank. She lay there, weeping quietly, while he sponged her dry and then pillowed her head in his lap, and soothed her with soft crooning words. . . . "You can't mend the world, Dr. Anderton. You can only try to go on loving it, which is sometimes harder to do than hating. One day I'll take you up to the place where my grandfather, Kaloni, sits with his ancestors and mine. At first sight it's eerie, shocking: old bones in a high place and the seabirds, predatory and indifferent, wheeling over them. . . . Then the meaning comes home to you. Those men up there had encountered all the terrors of the sea: the great storms; the long calms when the water ran out and they must suck the sea dew from rags, or chew the raw flesh of fishes to slake their thirst; the big white shark that leaps from the water to attack an unsuspecting paddler, or a woman trailing her hand in the current; the sickness, and the dying and the bodies thrown overboard in the darkness. . . . But the end, the end you see up there, is peace. They're above the storms, beyond the reach of the highest waves. They see the sun rise and set and the great march of the constellations. The wind is a menace no longer, but music. That's the last thing they know; and the knowing makes the past plain and the future a pillow on which to rest. . . . You can rest too, Sally; and I'll sing you a song for your sleeping.

"Under the pikake tree
    The air is sweet,
    But I cannot taste it.
    The sky is full of flowers,
    But I cannot see them,
    Because my lover's face
    Is there
    And his lips are on my mouth."

EIGHT

and not spoil the big number. They would share the

THE SHIP, SAID HERMAN CASTILLO, MUST BE easy to build, easy to sail. It would be folly to try to emulate the great builders of the Pacific: the Marquesans, the Samoans, the men of Fiji, who used an elaborate joinery, with flanged planks and caulkings of sap, and a variety of curves for stem and stern. The simplest design was that of the *vaka,* the long, trading canoe of Pukapuka, which could be hollowed from a single log, trimmed by a single outrigger and fitted with two masts and sails resembling a modern Bermuda main.

They should build it to carry six, but to be sailed or paddled by four men. The method of building was set down rigidly by Castillo. The larger and the smaller trees would be cut, trimmed and hauled to the beach. The smaller tree would be worked first, into the outrigger so that they might practice their prentice hands and not spoil the big timber. They would shape the exterior hull first, then cut out the interior, using fire to char the core and stone adzes to chip it out afterwards. The outrigger itself would be hollow like the main hull, so they could use it, meanwhile, for fishing the lagoon or the deeps near the coast.

For the sails they could resew the canvas from the ship and resplice the cordage; but they would need also palm fiber and sennit for bindings and lashings, and this must be provided by the women. He himself, Hernan Castillo, would direct the work, and he would now give them some lessons in how to fell a hardwood with a stone adze. You did not hack into it like a Canadian woodsman with his blue-steel axe. You cut two circles around the trunk, one about a foot above the other. You cut them deep as you could go, eating transversely into the wood. Then you changed stroke and cut downwards until you had pared away the intervening mass. Then you continued, transverse, vertical, until you had nibbled away the trunk like a beaver, and it would fall whichever way you chose. . . . There was also an incantation which made for successful work. It said, more or less, "Today, O tree, you are a tree . . . tomorrow we are going to turn you into a man-tree!" There was also a counsel for the women: *"a tata tu i kete"*—the axeman's strength was in his belly and he needed good food to keep him working.

"So now," said Castillo with a monkey grin of triumph, "you start chopping. I'll keep your tools sharp and teach the women what they have to know and celebrate my nuptials with that very persistent lady, Yoko Nagamuna, who has talked me into what passes for matrimony."

The work was slower and harder than they had ever imagined. The stone adzes bruised the wood before they cut it. Their short hafts jarred bone and muscle.

At the end of a day's labour the smaller tree was still standing and the larger one looked as though it would still be there ten years later. The women had made their own discovery: they would need a mountain of thread and fiber. . . . Which prompted a reminder from Carl Magnusson that they still had a great many tomorrows, and Mark Gilman was turning the chips into charcoal and maybe Castillo, the toolmaker, should think about turning some of the scrap metal into other, more serviceable tools.

"I've been thinking about it," Castillo agreed. "We can generate enough heat. We can cast in sand. We need a crucible to melt the metal. Any ideas?"

"Clay," said Gunnar Thorkild. "We found pottery on the terrace."

"No guarantee that it was made on this island."

"The island's volcanic," said Carl Magnusson. "Clay is formed both by weathering and a hydrothermal process. Chances are we'd find some deposits if we looked for them."

"Let's make it a holiday project," said Franz Harsanyi. "We should begin to move around the island; otherwise we'll all get claustrophobia. We should make rest days and begin to enjoy them."

"The boy's got brains!" Molly Kaapu was enthusiastic. "We go visiting, exploring. I keep thinking of them gull eggs up on the cliffs. . . ."

"Clay," said Hernan Castillo stubbornly. "White, red, blue . . ."

"Let's forget work and make some music," said Jenny. "Get your flute, Simon."

"I'm sorry." He was short and irritable. "I promised to sit with Barbara for a while."

"Be patient with her," said Sally quietly. "She's still feverish and fretful."

"For God's sake! I'm not a monster."

"I'm sorry, Simon.

As he hurried away across the compound, Yoko Nagamuna made a large operatic gesture.

"Ah! Sweet mystery of life . . . !"

"Don't knock it, kid!" said Adam Briggs softly. "It's all we've got."

Jenny laid a hand on his arm and asked:

"May I tell them, please?"

"I guess now's as good a time as any."

"Well . . ." She flushed and stammered and then finally got it out. "Adam and I, we've decided we want to get married—I mean really married—and have it registered in the log, or whatever we do that says we mean it and want to stay together always. Can you arrange it for us, chief? It may sound silly, but . . ."

"It's not silly, Jenny," said Carl Magnusson quietly. "It's an important event for us.

"We'll make a feast," said Thorkild. "Invite the others down. When would you like to do it?"

Adam Briggs laughed. "I've been waiting so long for her to say yes, the date hardly matters. But let's make it definite. When the two trees are down and my liquor's fit to drink then we'll do it. One thing I won't stand for is a dry wedding. . . ."

Later, as they walked by the lagoon, where Tioto and Mark were night-fishing from the coracle. Sally smiled in the darkness and mocked him affectionately:

"How does it feel, marrying off your foundling?"

"Are you laughing at me, woman?"

"Crying a little too. This was such a cruel place in the beginning."

"I know."

"And they really are in love, aren't they?"

"Seems so."

"How will you do it? The ceremony, I mean."

"Well, we have a little speech and a prayer and then they exchange vows and we write it in the log and witness it. It shouldn't take more than five minutes. Then we'll have the luau afterwards."

"Gunnar, I was thinking . . ."

"About what?"

"Lorillard and Martha. After all, he says he wants to marry her and she's pregnant and . . ."

"Now wait a minute! Not me! Not this time! If you want to drop that hint you do it yourself!"

"That's just what I was thinking. Molly Kaapu and I are taking the day off tomorrow. We're delivering the fish and the wedding invitation at the same time. Besides, I don't think we'll ever have to raise the question."

"Better you don't!"

"But when I tell them you and I are getting married too . . ."

"What the hell do you mean?"

"Just what I say, darling. The old way may be good enough for you and your grandfather; but not for me, it's the entry in the log and the witnesses and kiss the bride and all the rest of it. . . ."

"Well, I'll be damned!"

"Not now, darling. You'll be saved, in the Christian dispensation! And as chief, you'll be making a proper contribution to public order and decency. Any objections?"

"You'd overrule them anyway."

"At least you're learning, my sweet!"

"So read me the next lesson, Doctor. How do we divorce Peter André Lorillard so that he's free to marry Martha Gilman? Now that she's caught him— for better or worse—I'd hate to see the bastard wriggle off the hook!"

"And I've got a bigger problem for you, Professor."

"Oh, what?"

She pointed out across the starlit water to the two figures in the canoe.

"There's a young boy growing to puberty, with no girls of his own age and his closest companion a very sweet but very gay young man."

"What do you expect me to do about it?" grumbled Thorkild. "Make a woman out of his rib?"

"That might be hard, even for Gunnar Thorkild. The question will be which of us women is going to make him into a man."

Next morning on the way up to the timber stand, Thorkild went in to see Barbara Kamakau. The fever had abated during the night. She had slept more peacefully. Sally had bathed her and dressed the wounds. Thorkild sliced a fresh papaya for her and, as she ate, talked over the events in the camp. She was interested at first, then she became moody and withdrawn. Finally she burst out:

"Chief, you're a kind man. I know you mean well. But you've done a terrible thing."

"What have I done, Barbara?"

"You don't know; how can I tell you? It's Simon. He was here last night. He said you ordered him to shack with me, like I was his wife. He said O.K., he didn't care; there wasn't much good tail around anyway. So I'd do for while he was here. When we got off the island, he'd go his way. I'd go back where I came from. I said I didn't want him that much. I never begged for a man in my life. I wouldn't do it now. . . . He said that's how it was arranged, so to hell with it. I'd do what he wanted, when he wanted it. . . . Charlie used to call me a whore, but I wasn't.

I never went with a man I didn't like. And this one I don't like anymore. He's a pig. . . ."

"Believe me, Barbara, I didn't know. I thought you liked each other! I thought it would help to have him caring for you. I'm sorry. . . . You don't have to worry now. It's finished. He won't bother you anymore."

"You understand, chief. I'm not cursing you, but . . ."

"I understand, Barbara. You just get yourself well."

"I'm well now. Sally says I can get up for a while tomorrow; but how can I walk around, all cut up like this?"

"The girls will give you their dresses. No one will see the scars. You're lucky. Your face is unmarked."

"I know. That was another thing Simon said. Because of me his face is marked up and Tioto's lost the use of one hand. I didn't do it. I didn't want it to happen!"

"They know that. We all know it."

"But where does that leave me? What man's ever going to want me once he sees me stripped?"

"Have you ever been to Suva, Barbara?" He looked as solemn as a preacher at a funeral.

"Suva? No. Why?"

"Well, I'll tell you a secret; and if you tell the doctor, I'm a dead man. In Suva there's a girl called one-eyed Pat Patel. She's half Fijian, quarter Indian and the rest Australian beachcomber. She's got one glass eye wears a black wig because she's bald without it, and she's got a snake tattooed round her middle. She's as ugly as sin and worth a million dollars Australian, all of which she earned in bed!"

"You're making all this up, chief."

"Cross my heart! I don't know whether it's the snake or the wig that does it. See you later."

By the time he reached the timber stand he was

fuming. He positioned himself at the smaller tree where Cohen was working and fell into rhythm with him. When they took their first breath, he said:

"I called in to see Barbara this morning."

"Oh yes?" Cohen's indifference was monumental.

"She was very upset."

"That's the way she was last night."

"She told me what you'd said to her."

"Did she now?" He stood straddle-legged, balancing the axe in his hands, smiling at Thorkild. "Well, she never was very discreet. . . . Besides, Thorkild, when you hold a man up by the ears and drop him in the dreck, what should he do? Sink or swim?"

Thorkild hit him. The blow rolled him over and over down the slide. He got up slowly and climbed back, wiping the blood from his mouth with the back of his hand. He bent to pick up the axe, but Thorkild trod it into the rotted leaves. Cohen looked at him with contempt and loathing.

"All you need now, Thorkild, is jackboots and a bullwhip, and you've got it made! I'm moving out— up to the terrace!"

To which, when he had gone, Franz Harsanyi added a protest of his own:

"I know he's a turd with women; but that was damned ugly. You start with fists. You end with axes and jackknives."

"Let's cut timber," said Adam Briggs dryly. "I'm working out a bride-price!"

"Up there on the mountain"—Molly Kaapu was pounding out a paste of coconut and breadfruit— "they're doing just fine. They've got one hut built and they're halfway finished another. They've found a new spring for fresh water and they've started a taro patch. . . . Willy and Eva, they're happy like lovebirds. You know that old *kapu* place? Well, Eva, she's put up a big bamboo cross and she hangs flowers on it every day. . . . She says it makes her feel easy up there. Martha? She's O.K. Lorillard ain't no ball of fire and he talks like he's writing a Navy report, but he's kind to her and they're rubbing along. They figure they'd like to be legalized and written into the log like the others. . . . And what's this I hear about you and that young Simon?"

"If you know it, Molly, don't ask me."

"So I won't ask you, Kaloni. I'll tell you. And you listen to old Mother Molly because she's been around a lot longer than you. . . . All the time you make the same big mistake!"

"For God's sake, Molly. I know I make mistakes, but . . ."

"You're not hearing me, Kaloni! I said one mistake —one big one. You're still *haphaole*. You don't come together like you did when your grandfather was with us."

"I don't understand."

"Good! So that's where we start. You don't understand what you are and what these people want from you. They don't want you to cut timber, sweeten the girls when they get the curse, run round the island looking for clay pits or whatever. They don't want you mixing in their quarrels. They want you apart and different. That's the way it was in the old days. The chief didn't build boats. He made the feasts that kept the builders working. He didn't make arguments. He settled them when they were brought to him. You don't do that. You got your sticky fingers stirring everywhere. And you make a big, big mess!"

"Molly, we don't have that much manpower!"

"And we don't need it. If there was just you and me, Kaloni, we could live on one hour's work a

day. . . . What are you trying to do? Build a state
capital or something? Who cares?"

"They do!"

"Only because you keep making them care. When
you were in your house back home, you were a
bigger man than you were here. People wanted to see
you, because you knew things, and you didn't make
fights, and you could smile and sing . . . and when you
got all balled up I could straighten you out in ten
minutes. Not anymore! No, sir!"

"So what do I do, Molly?"

"Step back; talk less; do less. . . . Maybe take the
boy with you—because he needs a man to teach him
a man's ways—and see what else we have in this
place. You've got to be a real chief, Kaloni; you've
got to have secrets that everybody needs and nobody
else knows, not even your own woman!"

He knew she was right. He could not, for the life
of him, see what to do about it. All his effort, all his
planning had been dedicated to the dissemination of
knowledge, the sharing of skills, so that in the event
of death or casualty, the skill and the knowledge
would still reside in the community. Now a gossiping
old woman had shown him that he was committed
to a fallacy. The identity and the security of the community depended on the existence and the exercise of
power. Knowledge was an instrument of power. It
must be preserved, but it must be reserved also, an
arcane and sacred deposit in the hands of kings, priests
or commissars. This was the essence of *kapu,* the foundation of respect for established order. The king might
die of the plague or fade gibbering into senility; but
kingship remained inviolate, because none could exercise it without the *mana.* In the country of the blind
the one-eyed man was paramount. After every revolu-

tion they shouted for the genius who knew how to run
the water supply and where the records were buried.

It was a dangerous and tendentious proposition,
but perhaps less dangerous than a defective and confused scholar, waving the banner of democracy over
a lost island. Think about it then—the exploitable
mystery. God? Not here, not with this tribe. For most
of them God was folklore, fantasy, allegory, a riddle
without an answer. Besides, Gunnar Thorkild had no
patent to proclaim redemption, lay on hands, drive
out spirits. . . . But he was a navigator. He dealt in
time, space and motion, dimensions so simple and
yet so complex that common folk abdicated them
to the experts without firing a shot. Ask any average
healthy red-blooded citizen to make an act of faith
in a creating, conserving deity, he would hedge, hes-
itate, qualify and gloss—and might well ask to have
you certified. Ask him, however, to step into an aircraft, a submarine, a space capsule, and he would
cheerfully risk his life, wife, mistress or first-born,
on hearsay testimony that the pilot knew his job!

So why leave them complacent? Make them value
the secret science. Write the theology for them. Make
them reverence the sacred lore: rotational time and
correct universal time and ephemeral time; vectors
of forces and the calculation of linear progression
over a curved surface! Let them see clearly that,
without the magical powers of Gunnar Thorkild, they
might well set out for Papeete and end locked in
ice among the penguins of the South Pole.

The first step was to establish exclusive claim and
deny access to the vulgar. Therefore he collected
from Franz Harsanyi all the books, charts and other
salvage from the wheelhouse of the *Frigate Bird,* and
transferred them to his own hut. His explanation was
accepted without question; while their boat was build-

ing he must reconstruct the mathematics of the voyage and establish the position of the island by solar and sidereal observations. The second step was to attach and train the neophyte, Mark Gilman. So one evening, after supper, he walked the boy down to the beach and told him:

"Mark, I'm going to lay a man's job on you. We're building a boat to get us home. I'm going to teach you, from the beginning, everything, but everything you need to know to get it there."

"Why me, Uncle Gunnar?"

"Because you'll remember, when the others like Adam Briggs or Peter Lorillard forget or get sick or maybe even die. That memory of yours makes you a very important person because you can hold the knowledge of centuries in your brain box."

"What do I have to do?"

"So many thing I can't begin to tell them all at once. We'll work at them every day and sometimes at night. . . . I'll teach you about time. We'll make a clock. I'll show you how to measure speed with a Dutchman's log. We'll make a quadrant like the old sailors used, and I'll show you how to shoot the stars with a coconut. When we're finished, you'll know enough navigation to sail to any port in the world. What we don't have in our books we'll reconstruct for ourselves. . . . Are you willing to try?"

"Sure."

"Good. We'll start tomorrow. . . . Now here's the important part. We don't just have to navigate a boat. We have to navigate people as well: give them confidence, make sure they trust us and obey us in time of crisis. For example, in an aircraft, you don't have passengers rushing up to the cockpit to tell the captain what to do—not even if they're pilots themselves. He doesn't tell them what he's doing either.

His job is private, secret, because he can't waste time spelling out why and wherefore. . . . You and I must be the same. The people will learn to respect us, not only because we know, but because they don't. Is that clear?"

"I think so. . . ."

"Later on, when the boat is nearly finished, we'll begin teaching Adam Briggs. But for the moment, it's just you and me . . . like the magician and his assistant."

"And when I know how the tricks are done, I'll be a magician too."

"That's right!"

"Now I understand what Peter Lorillard meant."

"Oh, what's that?"

"Something he said, while you were down on the beach with Charlie Kamakau. He said you were a great one for pulling rabbits out of hats, but the real master was the rabbit who could wave a wand and make the magician disappear!"

"And that's how good you'd like to be, eh?"

"That's how good I'm going to be, Uncle Gunnar. You wait and see!"

His laugh was limpid as water; but Gunnar Thorkild felt an odd shiver of fear, as if he had heard the wind whispering through the empty mouth of a skull.

The trees were felled, stripped, hauled down the slide and rolled, with Herculean labour, to the building place on the beach. The liquor was made, skimmed, strained through fabric and pronounced by Sally fit—if not exactly advisable—for human consumption. The fire pit was filled with fuel. The huts were garlanded with flowers frangipani, and hibiscus and slipper orchids from the high slopes. Lorillard and Willy Kuhio had delivered the wedding gift from the terrace farm: a young hog trapped and speared in a thicket, and carried down on bamboo poles. The women had vied with each other to produce a variety of exotic confections—a luau worthy of this first festive occasion on the island.

Magnusson, with gravity and irony, had phrased the entries for the log: a bill of divorcement for Peter André Lorillard, who claimed cause but was deprived by misadventure of legal decision; a certificate of marriage for three couples who, having declared their desire and intention to live publicly and honorably as man and wife, were so recognized by the community. He had also transcribed the formula of the vows, and the notes for a short homily which he, as the patriarch of the group, proposed to deliver. It would, as he put it to Thorkild, lay balm to certain recent wounds and offer a hope to the unregenerate. Thorkild himself was a shade less than happy.

"Lorillard doesn't need regneration. He's so damn sanctimonious about the whole business, I want to throw up." He made a mimicry of Lorillard's fruity accent. "They love the life up there. They feel content and neighbourly. It's marvellous the way they grow. And Simon is a tower of strength. . . . I'm sure he is, but he's also a good hater. He wouldn't even shake my hand when he arrived."

"Forget it." Magnusson dismissed the subject with a gesture. "You're removed from all that now. You can pretend it doesn't exist—I'm glad to see you're taking my advice."

"Your advice?"

"Molly's, then." Magnusson grinned like a happy satyr. "I wrote the score; she wrote the words. You, thank God, were bright enough to understand the song. . . . One thing I do understand, Thorkild, is the usage of authority. You can keep an idiot on the throne for half a century provided no one hears him talk, sees him eat or knows what he does in bed!"

"Thanks for the compliment!"

"It's the best advice you've had in your life. Admit it! The awe is building up beautifully. They treat you like an alchemist, with the first lead brick ready for transmutation. That sundial, or whatever it is, is very impressive. Young Mark is a joy to see. I've never seen a kid so absorbed."

"He's an odd one, Carl. He's coming into early puberty. All the signs are there: the highs, the lows, the aggressions. But there's something else. It's a firefly thing: now you see it, now you don't; a kind of furtive mockery, as if he's just lying in ambush, waiting to spring a trap."

"On whom?"

"I don't know."

"He could be jealous of Lorillard, even of the baby Martha's carrying."

"Or Jenny and Adam Briggs."

"I'd never thought of that."

"Or it could be just the first sense of strength—knowing that he can master abstruse ideas quicker than other people and retain them more easily. I guess we all needed some anchor at his age. For me it was my grandfather. For him, perhaps, it's what we're doing together. . . . Anyway, let's round up the victims. Got your speech ready?"

"Graven on my heart," said Magnusson piously. "Pity I shan't live to see it published."

They stood, three couples together, between lighted torches, with Carl Magnusson officiating and the rest of the tribe gathered in front of them. Everyone wore a lei of frangipani blossom. The brides were crowned with flowers. For each couple, Hernan Castillo had made a wedding ring of mother-of-pearl. Magnusson's speech was short but strangely moving.

"My friends, we set out in a spirit of adventure to find this island, which has now become our home. We have dead buried here. Love has been found here, life begotten. There are some who are still making trial of their relationship, others who now wish to affirm it, make it permanent and exclusive by a public act of marriage. We offer them our affections and our good wishes. We pray over them in words we can all say with sincerity because they will go on sharing our life and we theirs. We were all spawned out of a common earth, in which we shall sleep finally together, on which I pray we may learn to live peaceably and generously."

When he had finished he was weeping quietly and without shame—an old weathered man, with the end of his days stark before him. Then he recovered himself and led them through the recitation of the vow and the exchange of rings. Finally, he faced them with a word which was at once a plea and a challenge.

"One man's prayer may be another man's curse. I trust you will all consent to join me in this one: that the Lord of us all, whom we call by so many names, who leads us by different roads to the same end, may look down in mercy on us all. Amen!"

"In the brief hush that followed, Mark Gilman said loudly, "I think it's all shit! I think God's a shit too!"

The next moment he was off and running headlong towards the beach. Martha Gilman hurried after him, but Magnusson drew her back.

"Let him go! I'll bring him home afterwards."

"He's drunk as a fiddler," said Simon Cohen cheerfully. "I saw him sampling the liquor."

"He's a sad little dog," said Ellen Ching. "All alone and baying the moon."

"Let's start the party," said Sally Anderton firmly. "Little dogs always come home to the fire."

Gunnar Thorkild said nothing. What passed or might pass between the sorcerer and his apprentice was no man's business but their own.

It was a very drunken evening. The food put fire in their bellies. The liquor was sweet and easy to drink. There were few veils to shed and—God damn!—after hell and high water, what else was left but eat, drink and be merry and kiss the nearest and cuddle the sleepiest and pick up the pieces in the morning? They sang, they danced, they declaimed, they told long stories that tailed away before the climax. They laughed and cried and stroked and clutched and fell apart and toasted absent friends and staggered down to the beach and back again to the liquor can, and in and out of the huts, to fall, finally exhausted, around the hot stones of the fire pit.

It was good, they said. It was delightful and decorous and delectable, and every other dee in the goddam dictionary, thus to divert themselves. They were brothers and sisters, weren't they? And wives and husbands and lovers, all cast away with no one—not a single, solitary individual—to care whether they were alive or dead! "I remember . . ." she said; and he remembered and they remembered . . . "And for Christ's sake, look at that moon! And is this today, tomorrow or yesterday? Well, who the hell cares? We pay our taxes, don't we? Then why don't they send in the Marines? You know about the Marines, don't you? . . . You can't go to bed yet, Carl! Need any help, Molly? See, that's love for you! That's really love! Hello, Barbara! Oh, excuse me, Ellen! Tioto, I got to tell you, we really felt bad about you and Malo. . . . Let's do that! Let's go, put some flowers on the graves. That's right!

That's what Carl said. We're still here. They're still here. That's nice. I mean it makes you feel right. One good thing about island weddings, you don't have to get up in the morning. Now listen, chief! Don't be like that! We love you. We love Sally too. . . ." On the far edge of the compound, propped against the stake which was the gnomon of the sun clock, the boy sat watching, baleful and contemptuous, until the last reveller had sunk to rest and the first sun showed over the flank of the mountain.

The rest of the camp was still asleep when Thorkild hauled him to his feet, fed him fruit and coconut milk and bustled him down to the beach. They pushed out the small canvas canoe and, with Thorkild paddling, made straight for the channel. All the time Thorkild uttered not a word, and the boy complied in passive silence, as if he were engaged in a silent struggle with a jailer. It was only when they reached the channel, turbulent with the incoming tide, that his decision began to weaken.

Thorkild was still silent. He drove the canoe through the churn of the current and out, relentlessly into the big swells of the deep. The boy was pale now and uneasy, clutching the bamboo strakes, and staring over Thorkild's shoulder at the island receding behind them. Finally, his control snapped and he said:

"Where are you taking me, Uncle Gunnar?"

"Out. . . . How far are we off the reef?"

"I—I don't know."

"It's your business to know." Thorkild was brusque and wintry. "Tell me when you've made a reasonable estimate."

He paddled on, steadily, until the boy said, "I'd say we're about half a mile off."

"More or less?"

"More."

"Good. We'll go out farther."

"But, Uncle Gunnar . . ."

"I'm not your uncle. You're not a child. I'm your chief and your teacher. Now, begin again."

"But, chief, you said this canoe was unsafe."

"It is."

"And we weren't to take it outside the reef."

"I did say that, yes. But I'm the chief. I give you the orders. You obey."

"Why are you staring at me like that?"

"Why are you afraid, Mark?"

"This thing leaks. We're making water."

"What do you do when a boat is making water?"

"Bail it."

"Well. . . ?"

The boy began to bail furiously, splashing the water overside with his palms. Thorkild swung the canoe round and faced inshore, rising and falling with the swells.

The boy stopped bailing for a moment and looked at him.

"What are we waiting for?"

"What do the birds tell you?"

"I haven't seen any birds."

"To your left, far out."

"Oh . . . yes. They're fishing."

"Which way is the shoal running?"

"I don't know."

"We'll wait here until you can tell me."

"I can't watch and bail at the same time."

"Then we stay here and sink, and the sharks which are following that shoal will eat us instead. . . . Unless, of course, it's running the other way, which is what I asked you."

"I can't tell. The light on the water dazzles me."

"Then tell me where to move the boat."

"I don't know. I can't judge."

"This canoe is made of white canvas. From below it looks like the belly of a fish or a man. A hungry shark or a mean one would attack it. Because it's only canvas and bamboo, it would sink instantly. . . . Which way is the shoal running?"

"This way, I think. Yes, this way!"

"Which way do we go?"

"Away from it."

"Frightened fish and hungry sharks swim faster than I can paddle. Which way?"

"I don't know."

"You can see the shark now, look! There he is! Which way do we go?"

"You're the chief! It's your job!"

"You're the navigator. You're the big one who thinks it's all shit! I'm waiting for you to tell me what to do."

"Just . . . get us in, back to the channel. Go straight across the track of the shoal!"

"Thank you. Now start bailing again!"

Halfway back to the channel, he stopped again and handed the paddle to the boy.

"You take us in from here."

"I'm not strong enough. I can just manage it in the lagoon with Tioto."

"I've had a long night. I'm tired. I could be sick. . . . And if you don't get her head round, we're going to sink."

He folded his arms and sat stony-faced while the boy laboured desperately to pull the tiny craft out of a broach and drive it, bow heavy, towards the opening in the reef. Then he goaded him again.

"We're not going to make it, I'm afraid. We're drifting down along the reef. Once we're in those breakers, we've had it. What are you going to do?"

"I can't do any more! I can't. . . ! Please, Uncle Gunnar, please!"

"I'm not your uncle. I'm your chief."

"Please, chief."

"Don't interrupt me. I'm praying. That's all we have left now. Why don't you pray, Mark?"

"I can't. I don't believe it . . ."

"I know. God's a shit. I'm a shit too, aren't I? So's your mother and Peter Lorillard . . . all of us! We look ridiculous and are ridiculous, and you can spit insults at us just because we find a small happy moment in our lives. Fine! You're on your own now. How does it feel?"

"I'm sorry!"

"It isn't enough."

"I'm sorry! I'm sorry! I'm sorry!"

Thorkild took the paddle from his hand and, with swift, strong strokes, turned them out of the current and homeward towards the channel. When they beached the canoe, he hauled the cowering boy out of the water and planted him on the dry sand.

"Look at me, Mark."

"Yes?"

"Yes, what?"

"Yes, chief!"

"What happened out there is between you and me. What happened here is between you and the whole tribe. What are you going to do about it?"

"What do you want me to do, chief?"

"No, Mark. What do you want to do?"

"Run away and hide."

"That's what Charlie Kamakau did."

"I'm not like Charlie."

"Aren't you? You wanted to kill us all last night."

"I didn't mean it, truly!"

"So what will you do?"

"I guess . . . I'll have to apologize."

"Put things together again. . . . Think of it that way. You'll find it easier. One more word!"

"Yes, chief?"

"It was dangerous today. A man never knows enough to cock a snook at the sea, or at God, or the lowest of his creatures. Run along now and find your mother."

They were all awake, dousing their headaches in the lagoon or grumbling through the small tasks of straightening the campsite after the night's festivity. Thorkild drew Lorillard aside and walked him down to the sun clock.

"As you see, we've started remote preparations for the voyage. It'll be a long time yet before the boat is ready, and a while after that before we've trained people to handle her. Still, it's visible progress, and that's good for us all."

"Have you thought about who's going?"

"No. It's much too far ahead; and we don't want people unsettled. How are you faring up there on the mountain?"

"Fine, so far."

"Martha?"

"She keeps well. She gets tired sometimes; but she says the work is good for her. I think she misses the company down here."

"What about Simon Cohen?"

"Fine. He works hard. He makes music for us at night. Sometimes he gets restless and edgy. But that's natural enough, I guess, without a woman."

"He's had two already. Neither wants anything more to do with him."

"So he told me. Your—ah—intervention didn't help, of course."

"I'm—ah—intervening less now."

"I heard that too. That was a good party last night . . . in spite of young Mark's outburst."

"I think you'll find he's apologized by now."

"He has. I heard him. I'm not sure it means very much. He resents me. . . . And Martha worries because he simply doesn't want to know about the baby."

"Give him time. He's just starting to grow up."

"Martha asked him to come back with us. He refused."

"He's better down here. I'm keeping him busy."

"Martha doesn't see it that way."

"How does she see it?"

"I guess she's jealous—of you and Sally, and your hold on the boy. . . . She's jealous of me, too, this morning."

"Oh, why?"

"I was pretty drunk last night."

"Weren't we all?"

"Martha says I was making time with Yoko."

"Were you?"

"I guess—a little. Martha and I haven't . . . well, she's pregnant, she gets tired and . . . You know how it is."

"Seems to me, old buddy"—Thorkild laughed—"it's orchids-and-candy night for you."

"We've got orchids growing out of our ears up there." Lorillard was deep in depression. "And who makes candy in this neck of the woods?"

"Like to make a trade?" Thorkild asked innocently.

"What sort of trade?"

"You talk sense into Cohen. Tell him I want to kiss and be friends and it's a good thing for everyone if we do. . . ."

"And?"

"And I'll find you a candy bar for Martha."

"Well, it's worth a try."

"Wait here." He came back a few minutes later with the gift, a necklace of tiny shells threaded on sailmaker's twine. "Take these! Hernan Castillo made them. I was going to give them to Martha before she left. They'd come better from you. . . . And by the way, this is my last—ah—intervention."

"You're a clever bastard." Lorillard looked at him with wry admiration. "So clever I could spit. But thanks anyway!"

As Lorillard walked away, Tioto came over to the sun clock. He was smiling, but sidelong and wary. He spoke in the old language.

"Kaloni . . ."

"Yes, Tioto?"

"Between us, no lies, eh? You know me, I know you. This is a big matter."

"Tell me then and let me judge."

"Last night, before the luau, the boy said dirty things."

"He did."

"He sat all night, watching us, like a dog in a bad temper."

"Yes."

"I watched him too. Later I tried to make him go to bed and rest. He would not do it."

"You tried."

"But that is not the big matter. During the eating and the drinking there was much talk: big talk, small talk, love talk. I made some talk myself, but I listened too. I heard Hernan Castillo say about the boy, 'The poor little devil, he's lonely.' Then the other one, Harsanyi, said, 'He's just going into the dark tunnel. He'll come out of it in time.' Then Yoko, she laughed and said, 'He won't if he hangs around Tioto!' "

"And that's the big matter, Tioto?"

"That's it, Kaloni. I say it now, once only. You hear it and believe it. I see what you do with this boy. I see why you do it. You're a chief and a navigator. You prepare him for the *mana*. So, to me, the boy is *kapu*. No way can I love him or touch him. It would be as if I lay with my own mother. You know that."

"I know it, Tioto."

"Then you make others know it, eh? It is hard enough to be alone. It is too much to be insulted, when there is no other house that will receive me."

"You will not be insulted. The words of last night you will forget. They were like spray tossed up on the cliff. But today's words and tomorrow's—for those they will answer to me."

"I am a lonely man, Kaloni. Last night I went in to Barbara Kamakau. Not to do anything. Just to talk. She was gentle to me. Afterwards I went down to the beach and slept by Malo's grave. It was he who told me to talk to you."

"You're a good man, Tioto."

"Ai-ee! The man plants banana for his family; the fruit rat eats it; the man kills the fruit rat and roasts it. . . . Good, bad, who knows? The old ones understood better than we do, but they have been dead a long time."

The upland party had decided to remain another twenty-four hours in the camp, to sleep off the effects of the party and fish in the cool of the evening. It was a drowsy, desultory day, and Thorkild spent most of it by the cascade with Sally, bathing, dozing, chatting in disconnected fashion about the night's events. Thorkild was inclined to be casual and dismissive about the whole affair. Sally took a more clinical view.

". . . That liquor was very potent. Our tolerance for

alcohol was lowered; and of course there were lots of pent-up emotions waiting to be released. Apart from minor damage to our livers, it probably did us all good —like the old Saturnalia, when everyone was let off the leash and even the slaves were manumitted for the festival. We've got three newly married couples, which stabilizes the community. Good words were said —and a few bad ones which were better out anyway. All in all, a useful experience. It might pay us to repeat it at discreet intervals. . . . How does it feel to be married, Mr. Gunnar Thorkild?"

"No different. I've always felt married to you."

"That's nice to hear."

"Did you talk to Martha?"

"At length, dear husband—at great length! She misses the life down here. She doesn't like sex anymore—at least not with Peter Lorillard. She blames you for her exile; I'm afraid I was rather terse about that. And what she didn't say, but I could hear plain as a police whistle, was that she feels she's made a bad bargain with a dull man!"

"I'm afraid she always makes 'em! She wants what we don't have—a perfect world."

"Mine's as near perfect as I want."

He was just bending to kiss her when Simon Cohen, glum-faced and faintly truculent, marched into the clearing. He made a mumbled apology to Sally and then the flat announcement:

"I hear you wanted to talk to me, Thorkild."

Sally scrambled to her feet. "I'll leave you."

"There's no need," said Simon Cohen. "It might help if you stayed."

"Very well."

She sat down again. Cohen settled himself on the bank beside them. Thorkild said quietly.

"Simon, we were good friends once."

"I know." Cohen was bitter. "That's why we're here."

"Can we start again?"

"You mess me up with a woman. You damn near break my jaw. You rig the social situation so that there's no place left for me. . . . You tell me where we start, Professor!"

"Please!" Sally Anderton laid a restraining hand on his arm. "Before we go any further, can I say something?"

"Go ahead."

"In the situation we have now, where we're stuck away at the far end of nowhere, what are you prepared to settle for? I'm not talking about you and Gunnar here. That's men's pidgin and I've no part in it. I'm talking about sex, companionship, love—or even celibacy, if that's what you want."

"That's what I've got," said Cohen grimly. "And I don't like it one little bit."

"But you fouled up your own situation with Barbara."

"I didn't. Your husband did. If he'd just kept his beak out of it, we'd have made sense in the end. But no! He wanted everything neat, tidy and tied with pink ribbon. All right! So I was dumb too! I insulted the girl. I said all the wrong things. No, not all; because I was trying to say honestly and clearly that if we ever got off this onion patch, I'd be back to square one, a good little Jewish boy who wanted to marry a good little Jewish girl, in synagogue, with all the trimmings. You may laugh, but that's what I do want!"

"We're not laughing, Simon." Sally was very subdued. "We're bleeding. For you and ourselves. And for Yoko, who's carrying your child." . .

"So I fouled that up too. I know it. But Yoko's finished with me. She told me so herself, last night."

"Which leaves Barbara, doesn't it? She's alone too, remember, and hurt, inside and out. I'm not saying you should get together. It may be the last thing either of you wants—or the cruellest thing you could do to each other. But at least you should restore the decencies between you. She can't make the first moves. She doesn't even know the words. If it'll help, I'll talk to her first."

"No, thanks! A matchmaker I need like another smack on the jaw!"

"If it helps," said Gunnar Thorkild, "you can take a smack at mine."

"I'd probably break my hand, and I need that to make music. See you later."

"That," said Sally Anderton judicially, "is one very screwed-up young man."

"I knew his mother," mussed Thorkild. "A most formidable lady who once invited me to bed. His father was a concert violinist who made off with his manager's daughter. Not the best luggage for this kind of travel."

"Time to dump it then." Sally was sick of the whole argument. "Because no one else is going to carry it. Come on, my sweet, let's go join the world!"

By nightfall they were all agreed on one proposition: they were dead and ready to be buried. They moved off like homing animals to their earths. Before the moon rose, the camp was silent. Only Thorkild was wakeful, standing on a stool at the entrance to the hut fixing an intricate contraption of string and bamboo tubes.

Sally asked sleepily, "Gunnar, what are you doing?"

He tapped the bamboo and it gave out a thin, sweet carillon. "Japanese wind bells. I made them for your wedding present. There's a poem about them.

"So long as the wind blows
There will be a love-song
In my house."

"Thank you. Tell me the poem again—in the morning."

"Go to sleep, Sally."

"What about you?"

"Soon. . . . Good night, Mrs. Thorkild."

He drew the covers over her and went out, sniffing the air, heaving with sea spray and fire smoke, and the cloying vapour of the jungle. There was a figure standing by the gnomon. He walked down to see who it was.

Magnusson hailed him softly. "Thorkild? It's me, Carl."

"Anything the matter?"

"Nothing. I don't sleep very well. . . . I'd love a good cigar."

"Sorry, we're fresh out."

"Beautiful, isn't it?"

"Beautiful."

"Would you believe it? Finally, I think I'm a happy man."

"I'm glad, Carl."

"There's a fat old woman in the bed next to mine. She snores and farts all night and in the morning she kisses me awake and I love her. . . . Are you happy, Thorkild?"

"I'm getting there, Carl."

"Lend me your arm. I'd like to go down to the beach."

They settled themselves just above the tideline. Thorkild began shredding a palm leaf, while Magnus-

son tossed coral fragments into the water and talked
in rambling monologue.

". . . I've been looking for a word all day. Now I've
found it. It's what I've come to finally: tranquillity. . . .
I drank too much last night. I felt foul this morning.
But under it all, I was tranquil. . . . There's something
I want to tell you, but you must promise to keep it a
secret. I've lost the sight of one eye—the left one. I
know what happened. . . . a blood vessel burst, back
there somewhere. Don't try to look shocked! You and
I are way beyond hypocrisies. It's a kind of admonition, I'd say. I've seen enough. It's time I started looking inward and making some judgments. . . . I'd like
to ask you a favour."

"Anything."

"How do you figure the account between you and
me?" . .

"I still owe you, Carl."

"Then I want to claim the debt. . . . Now listen
and don't interrupt. One day, soon—I'll tell you when
—I want you to take me up to the high place where
your grandfather is."

"Carl, it's a hell of a climb!"

"So we do it the easy way. We can stay overnight
on the terrace with Willy and Eva. But I want to go
there, Gunnar!"

"I'll take you."

"And I want you to leave me there."

"No!"

"Yes!"

"Carl, listen to me!"

"You listen to me! Your grandfather was older than
I am. I saw you lower him over the side of the *Frigate
Bird*. I saw him sail off, with all his manhood intact,
to meet his ancestors in the high place. I wanted to go
with him. I pleaded to be taken, remember? I couldn't

imagine, and I still can't, any better way for a man to meet his end and make the last debate with his Maker. I don't want to die here, in bed, like a vegetable, one sense failing after the other, while the women mourn around me and the whole tribe waits for it to be over, so they can go about their own business again. . . . I'm a proud man, Thorkild. Don't make me plead!"

"Carl, that's the last thing I want to do. But will you hear me—just for one moment?"

"Make it short then." . .

"Okay. Here it is. You're a big man and a lonely man. I promised myself that, when your time came, I'd be there, like a son offering the pieties, holding your hands, closing your eyes, kissing you good-bye."

"You think I didn't know that? You think I don't want it? More than most I need the pieties. But do them my way, eh, son?"

"Carl, it's so lonely up there."

"Was your grandfather lonely?"

"I don't know."

"I promise you he wasn't. Look, I've been an adventurer all my life. I won. I lost. I went out hunting again—women, money, power, everything! Not because I needed them, but because always there was one more mountain, one more river and behind them all, the light—a will-o'-the-wisp maybe, but still a light to follow. It's there, up on the high place; and you're going to take me to it!"

"I wish Flanagan were here," said Thorkild with sublime irrelevance.

"Why Flanagan?"

"Because he told me this would happen." He laughed, foolishly, at the recollection. "He said one day you'd climb on my back like the old man of the sea and I'd beg and beg to get you off."

"Strange man, Flanagan," said Carl Magnusson absently. "He told me something different. He said I could ride you to hell but I'd never break your back. . . . Well? What's the answer?"

"I take you and I leave you. And may God have mercy on my stupid soul."

"Amen," said Carl Magnusson. "Take me home to bed."

The departure of the uplanders made a curious impression on everyone. They were not going far. The track to the terrace was now a well-beaten thoroughfare. The food carriers made the journey every couple of days, to take up fresh fish and bring down fruits and vegetables. It was rather that, for the first time since their arrival on the island, they had achieved a sense of family, of tribe, of intimate mutuality. Tools were left to be repaired. There were new ones to be taken back. Concerns had been expressed. A currency of kisses and embraces, of arguments and issues, had been established. Just before they left, Simon Cohen came to see Thorkild and informed him in his usual graceless fashion:

"I spoke to Barbara, told her I was sorry and asked whether she'd join me on the mountain. She said she'd wait till she was better, and then she'd think about it. Also she'd have to ask the chief."

"She can go or stay, just as she pleases."

"If she asks your advice, what will you say?"

"Nothing. She has to decide for herself. What about you and me?"

"The same. Nothing. We don't have to like each other to get along."

"True. You're welcome down here anytime."

"Well, that's it, I guess. Aloha!"

"Aloha!"

Martha Gilman, too, came to bid him good-bye and make a kind of peace.

"I see what you're doing with Mark. I'm sure it's good for him; but he's just a little boy and he still needs some mothering."

"He gets it, Martha." Thorkild was careful with her. "Molly Kaapu spoils him and Jenny's always making a fuss over him and Sally keeps an eye on his health. Don't worry. Enjoy your own life."

"I'm trying, believe me."

"Don't try too hard."

"Gunnar, I want to be down here when the baby comes."

"Of course."

"I know Peter won't like it, but . . ."

"He'll come to it. Relax, woman."

"I need you around to teach me. . . . We had good days, didn't we?"

"Because we put good things into them."

"Kiss me?"

"We'll always be kissing cousins, Martha. Take care now! Aloha!"

As he stood waving them up the hill, Adam Briggs was beside him. It was he who pronounced the simple, haunting epilogue:

"There were times, chief, when I thought we'd tear ourselves to pieces like cats in a bag. Now we're human folk again. It's not the new Jerusalem, but we might—we just might—start building it."

NINE

THEY HAD GAINED SOMETHING; THEY HAD LOST something: the sense of urgency, the unspoken desperation, that had driven them, both to effort and to conflict, during their first weeks of sojourn on the island. They were no longer plagued by monotony, understanding now that the slow rhythm of their days, like the rhythm of tide and surf, of sun and rain shower, was more satisfying and more productive than the short frenetic bursts of energy by which they had worn out so much of their old lives.

The boat could not be made with hacking and slashing. It must grow slowly under their patient hands, as the original timber had grown in the forest. The best fish came in with the tide. They must wait for low water to garner the reef. The women, too, imposed their own, instinctive demand for domesticity and order. Two of them were breeding. Others hope to breed. They wanted no wild excursions or exuberant plans.

Emotions, too, became shallower and more subdued, since there was nothing to stimulate yearning and few objects to satisfy it. The married had, perforce, to be satisfied with their choice; and if the unmarried chose —as it seemed they sometimes did—to play other games, it had small consequences in the life of the community.

There was a slow, but perceptible, flush of decoration in the camp. People collected shells and coral branches and pieces of driftwood. Ellen Ching began to bring down orchids and hibiscus and ginger flowers, to plant in baskets and in pockets dug out of the sand and filled with mulch and earth. Yoko Nagamuna made cowrie necklaces and bracelets. Sally and Molly and Barbara were beating pieces of tapa bark and trying out vegetable dyes to print them afterwards. Tioto had made a bamboo raft which could be poled around the reef. Franz Harsanyi was scribbling furiously on the flyleaves and margins of their books and was darkly secretive about what he wrote.

Thorkild, for his part, was constantly busy with the education of Mark Gilman. There was a space reserved for them near the sun clock, where they had set up a pendulum and laid out a large square of land, swept smooth every morning, on which they drew diagrams and worked out problems of trigonometry and navigation. For optics, Hernan Castillo had made, to Thorkild's design, a quadrant which involved sighting through an auger hole across the surface of water in a coconut shell and sliding a pointer across a fixed scale.

The boy drank in knowledge avidly. He would repeat a whole series of procedures and calculations without a slur or a mistake. He had an almost demonic urge to excel; and when, as he sometimes did, he caught Thorkild out in an error of calculation, he would whoop with joy and shout it to any who would listen around the camp. For the rest, he remained wary and secretive, lapsing into silence on any question that touched his private thoughts or his social relationships. With the women he was alternately shy and cocky. When Ellen Ching ducked him in the water for some impertinence, he sulked away from her for days afterwards. When Jenny was alone, he sidled close to her; but as soon as Adam Briggs came near, he scuttled away, furtive as a field mouse.

The only one with whom he was prepared to unbend was Carl Magnusson. He would walk with him, deep in colloquy, on the beach. Sometimes, when the old man was low and disinclined for company, he would eat with him outside his hut; but never once did he hint at the subject of their talks. Thorkild insisted that, every two weeks at least, he must join the messengers of the terrace and visit his mother. Always he returned, silent and resentful, full of small spites which Thorkild affected not to notice. It was hard enough for the boy to be deprived of the companionship of his peers. It was too much to expect him to be more perfect than his elders.

One day, about six weeks after the luau, Barbara Kamakau announced that she was ready to join Simon Cohen on the mountain. She would go up with the messengers, talk to him, and if he were still of the same mind, she would stay. She summed it up with plaintive dignity:

"It's no great romance, chief; I know that. But it's better than being alone. I wish I had more brains, so I could talk about the things that interest him. But I know how to keep him happy in bed, so I guess it balances out. If he gets tired of me, I'll come back to the beach. Only one thing worries me. I don't want to finish on the waterfront in Honolulu with a baby that hasn't got a father."

"Whatever happens," Sally Anderton assured her, "the chief and I will see that you're cared for. That's a promise, Barbara."

"I believe it. I don't say things very well, but if ever you need me I'll come running. . . . Well, here we go, up the mountain. I just hope Charlie doesn't come back to haunt me."

"How could he? He's probably sitting in a bar in Honolulu right now."

"No, he isn't. That much I know."

"How can you know it, Barbara?"

"Nobody's come to find us, have they? Charlie hated me, but not the rest of you. He loved Mr. Magnusson. No, he's dead!"

"Then forget him!"

"Yes. That's best. Wish me luck."

When she had gone, dragging and uncertain, to join the messengers, Sally turned to Thorkild.

"What do you really think happened to Charlie?"

"I'll read you the odds, sweetheart. Even money he's dead. Long money he's landed crazy on some piddling atoll, and is trying to make some French official understand who he is and where he came from. Longest odds of all, he's home in Honolulu and the Navy's scouring the seas to rescue us."

"And you live with that every day?"

"No!" He rejected the thought utterly. "Understand me, Sally. I weigh the odds. I decide. Then I forget it, because I can't afford to think back. Even you—and God knows, I love you so much my heart breaks—I toss into the balance and weigh with the rest of them. Lorillard taught me that. Triage: save whom you can and forget the rest. It was Flanagan's proposition too: do the best you can for the most and let God make up the balance sheet."

"Don't talk like that. It frightens me."

"The hell it does! You know! What did you tell me when Jenny's baby was born? Bury it! The child's dead. We have to live tomorrow. So mop up the blood and be done with it!"

"And you, my husband?"

"I bury the dead and solace the living—and die the little death with my woman each night. You wanted to mate with the high one. That's what it means!"

"Tell me you love me."

"I love you. Heart of my heart, I love you!"

Hernan Castillo, offspring of Spanish conquistadores and Malay princesses, and Filipino beer barons and soft ladies with puffed sleeves and private pews in Manila Cathedral, had problems of his own. Not great problems, he added, smiling, not immediate ones, but problems nonetheless. It was like this: here he was shacked up with a woman who was carrying another man's child; he didn't mind that; she was comfortable, useful and grateful—something of a bitch, sure, but, you know, grateful. Here he was, building a boat which he had designed to take them back to civilization. No dispute so far? None at all. Good! Now, if the boat came out of his head, he figured he had the right to sail on it. Yes or no?

Yes and no. Gunnar Thorkild toyed reluctantly with this new jesuitical logic. The boat was being built by many hands. Even the women had claims on it. But suppose—just suppose—the designer's claim were paramount, and he were one of the first to sail. What then?

Then, said Hernan Castillo, scion of diverse matings, another question arose. He wanted no other claim

filed against him—like paternity suits and maintenance
for another man's love-child. Now, sure, it was all a
long way off. But he was building this goddam boat,
because he knew it would goddam sail—and tomorrow night be a year away, but it would come and he'd
like some kind of insurance policy. His first girl friend
had been a Japanese and they were sweet as honey;
but they spun webs around a man, and if the webs
didn't hold, they'd run amok with a carving knife to
cut off his balls, or they'd stick their heads in a gas
oven, and when they were pulled out, make a de-
nunciation to the police. So—with fair notice—would
the chief think about it and advise him how to handle
an awkward affair?

The chief would think about it. But the chief suggested, wearily, that the decision ought to be deferred,
at least until the child was born. All tribal matters
were recorded in the log. A ship's log was good evidence in civil or criminal suit. But for Christ's sake,
man, don't start rocking the boat before we've even
built it! Of course not! Hernan Castillo was as mag-
nanimous as a grandee. So long as the position was
clear, he was happy to trust to the wisdom of the
chief. . . . And by the way, if they wanted him to cast
metal, he still needed a crucible. Perhaps someone,
soon, might go looking for a clay dig?

When he had gone, bounding like a rubber ball
across the compound, Thorkild was shaken with laughter. There was no way you could win, no way they
could let you win. They were like moles under a cro-
quet lawn: as soon as you had flattened one mound
they threw up another. It was the nature of the beast.
They weren't malicious. They demanded attention for
their singular needs and their singular merits and tears
for their Job-like miseries. Give them paradise today
and they would still dream themselves into hell, out of
sheer boredom.

What amused him most was how little Castillo understood what he was asking. He had designed the boat. He was happy to build it. But in fact he had never in his life sailed a native craft on a big ocean. Since he had come to the island, he had never been outside the reef. It would be interesting to see what happened when he went out on the first sea trials; for Thorkild was resolved that every man and woman on the island must go out, before the crew was chosen for the voyage. They must go, not for a pleasure cruise round the island, but far offshore, fishing and cruising by day and night, until they were as near to sea creatures as he could make them. He could not afford to risk a year's labour, a seaworthy craft and six lives and all hope of rescue on untrained landlubbers. Later, as they fished together in the lagoon, he developed the thought for Adam Briggs:

". . . I propose to train three skippers: Lorillard, Willy Kuhio and you, Adam. The boy will work as navigator with each of you. I'll work you and the boat like an orchestra until the harmony's as perfect as we can make it. Then I'll make the choice."

Briggs seemed reluctant to accept the idea. He pondered over it for a moment and then said:

"But I thought you'd lead the expedition, chief."

"No, Adam. I thought about it a long time and decided against it. It's a question of morale—and if you like, insurance. The advance party will be going home with a very good chance of making a safe landfall. The rest will be left wondering and hoping. They'll need a strong hand to hold them together. If we lose the advance party, we have to start again from the beginning, with less manpower and much lower spirits. I'm better equipped to handle that problem than anybody else. . . . How are things with you and Jenny?"

"Great! Just great! There's so much love in that girl; it just bubbles out like spring water. . . . I'll tell you a truth: I don't ever want to go home. Neither does Jenny. . . . So put me on record, chief. I'll train with you. I'll help train the others. But I'm not leaving this island."

"That's a big decision, Adam."

"You think so?" He was suddenly urgent and eloquent. "What's back there that we need so much? We eat well and we sleep safe and we wake to smiling faces—and everywhere we turn there's something beautiful: the fish, the birds, the sunset. Man, we're liberated! Why should we put chains on ourselves again? I keep saying this to Franz and Castillo as we work. The only good thing about the boat is that it opens the big sea to us, gives us choice. But for Jenny and me the choice is made. . . . What about you, chief?"

"I want to stay too, but . . ."

"But what?"

"I have to wait and see. I'm responsible for a lot of people."

"You're a glutton for grief, aren't you? Have you ever really thought how far you are—or can be—responsible?"

"I have. And the answer's plain. I'm responsible right down the line. And I've got to say this, Adam —even though it may never happen—if I send you, you go!"

"I admire you, chief," said Adam Briggs softly. "Jenny loves you. I . . . I love you too, I guess. You're as close to me as a jungle buddy . . . but don't make me fight you!"

"Ever play poker, Adam?"

"Often."

"High stakes?"

"In the Army, sometimes."

"So you know, after you've bought, you bet the

cards in your hand, because there's no more to come."

"Or you fold and don't bet at all."

"Would you like to bet now?"

"On what?"

"A blood match. Winner takes all. Briggs versus Thorkild."

"Hell, chief! You know I didn't mean that!"

"Neither did I," said Gunnar Thorkild. "So let's not even dream about it. Let's live one day at a time."

It was easy to say; much, much harder to accomplish than subsistence itself. It raised the perennial problem of the discontinuity of experience within the tribe itself. There was no common faith, no common past. There was no single frame that could contain their diverse hopes and fears. No matter how closely they were confined by geography, how stringently bound by the monotony of their daily round, there was still no tribal dream to make them one. Even the patent of the chief could be withdrawn at will, by vote or by cabal. As they fished, drifting slowly along the inner fringe of the reef, he tried to explain it to Adam Briggs who listened patiently and then made his own point.

". . . No way you can make it different, chief. Maybe if we live here two, three generations, our grandchildren or our great-grandchildren will have that dream you talk about: all the legends and the stories and the attitudes linked together and joining past and present. But we're stuck with the luggage we've got, and we'll hang on to it until the last label peels off and we don't really remember why we kept it. . . . Hey! Look at that big crayfish! There, in the crevice!"

"Can you reach him?"

"No. I'll go overside. It's shallow here. I can walk up to him."

"Watch your feet. That coral's sharp."

"I'll watch it. Hang out now. I'm going over."

While Thorkild balanced the canoe, Briggs rolled himself over the side, swam a few strokes to bring himself into the shallows at the base of the reef, then stood up and began a slow, cautious approach to the big cray. He was within a hand's reach when he screamed and fell back, thrashing helplessly. There was no way to haul him inboard again. Thorkild capsized himself into the water and tried to take hold of him. He was obviously in agony and out of control and Thorkild had to hit him and half drown him before he could roll him on his back and swim with him to the shallows. Then he laid him on the sand and examined his footsoles. On the left foot there was a line of punctures, extending from the ball to the heel. Briggs began to scream again, writhing and twitching on the sand. Thorkild heaved him onto his shoulders and hurried, stumbling, to the camp. When the others crowded about him, he shouted them away.

"Call Sally! Franz, Tioto, get the canoe . . . otherwise we'll lose it! One of you get some whiskey from Carl."

He laid Briggs down on his own bed and poured liquor down his throat until he gagged and thrust it away. Then he showed the sting marks to Sally and to Jenny.

"See those! Stone-fish! The poison induces high pain, spasm and fever."

"What's the antidote?"

"None. Treat him for shock if you can. Dose him for pain if you've got anything. Then wait."

"For what?"

"He'll die quickly. If he lives he could be sick for weeks."

Jenny screamed. Thorkild slapped her hard and thrust her out of the hut into the arms of Molly Kaapu.

"Get her away from here! Get everyone away! I'll be out to talk to you later!"

He turned back to Sally, who was listening to Briggs' heartbeat and taking his pulse. He was groaning and shivering, and when the pain took him, he gave a high, wailing scream—ee-ee-ee!—and his face contorted into a rictus of agony. Sally turned away and began rummaging through the medicine chest. When she straightened up there was despair in her eyes.

"Nothing worth a damn. Burn salve, Carl's prescriptions, tinea ointment, iodine, aspirin and purgatives!"

"Try praying," said Thorkild bleakly. "I'd better go talk to the others. I'll be back in a minute."

He assembled them round the fire pit and told them what had happened. He continued with a brief, harsh lecture.

". . . We talked before about the danger of going barefoot round the reef. We've all got careless, me included. Now this happens. So for Christ's sake, let's learn! At least you can make matting soles and tie them on your feet. Let me tell you about the stonefish. . . . He's an ugly bastard, brown and grey, so he's hard to see against the sand. He's covered with warts and slime. He's got a round mouth, green inside, and thirteen spikes on his back, all poisonous. If you see him, don't touch him—and tread warily wherever you are. Adam's very sick, but he's strong. We hope for the best. . . . Oh, and we'll take turns to watch him at night. That's all." He put his arm around Jenny and drew her away from the group. "I'm sorry. I didn't mean to hurt you."

"I needed it, chief. Can I go to him now?"

"Hold tight, kid! It's going to be a rough ride."

It was rough and it was long. The first night the men had literally to wrestle to hold him on the bed.

Then the fever took him, so high at times that they rolled him in blankets and kept dousing him with water from the cascade. His foot swelled like a melon and the poison crept up the shank, and he wept helplessly at the throbbing of it. At Ellen Ching's suggestion they churned up pepper root and made kava and used it for an opiate to give him a brief tranquillity. One long, grim day, Sally debated whether or not to amputate, and decided finally that the shock of surgery without anaesthetic would certainly kill him. That same night, distraught and desperate, she asked Thorkild and Jenny whether, if gangrene set in, she would be justified in putting Adam out of his misery. It was Jenny who decided the issue. She took them both by the hand and led them to the somber little group assembled round the fire pit and said:

"We've been wondering whether it's right to kill Adam. He's my man and I don't want to see him suffer anymore. So I'm going to ask you all to do one thing for me. It may mean nothing—but it may be the most important thing of all, and we've neglected it. I want you to pray with me. Even if you don't believe, please, just say the words with me. In case you don't know the words, I'll say them and you repeat them. . . . Please, oh please. . . !"

Her voice cracked and she stood there weeping helplessly until Thorkild rose and held her and began: " 'Our Father which art in heaven . . .' "

" 'Our Father which art in heaven . . .' " The chorus was ragged at first, then it grew stronger, rising on the wind, rolling out over the surf beat. . . . " 'And lead us not into temptation, but deliver us from evil, for Thine is the kingdom, the power and the glory for ever and ever. Amen.' "

"Thank you," said Jenny, brokenly. "Thank you from both of us."

"I think we all needed it," said Franz Harsanyi softly.

They were so absorbed in the emotion of the moment that no one missed Mark Gilman. He had slipped away, down to the beach. He was tossing coral pebbles into the lagoon and chanting, over and over, a burial shout from the Low Islands, which Simon Cohen had taught him.

> "Swing the King high,
> Close to the sun,
> Swing the King low,
> Close to the ground,
> Then toss him into the grave!"

"I kept remembering the Bible." Adam Briggs lay weak and placid in the deep shadows of the hut. "When I was burning up I thought any moment I'd be hauled away, like Elijah, in a chariot of fire. When I was cold I thought I was Jonah floundering in the deep sea, waiting for the whale to swallow me. You know what I feel like now, chief?"

"No idea, Adam."

"Like Lazarus, when he heard the big voice telling him to come out into the sun, and he couldn't walk because he was tied up in the graveclothes. Then, all of a sudden, he's out; and there's the world, new and shining, as though he's never seen it before, and he has to start learning it from the beginning. . . ."

"You were very lucky!"

"I know it; and I'm so grateful I'd like to sing myself out of this hut with psalms and canticles. . . ! How long before I can get out, chief?"

"A couple of days, Sally says. And then you take it very easy. That foot won't heal for weeks yet. You're so thin you're a candidate for the bone yard."

"I know. I can touch the bones with my fingers. Chief. . . ?"

"What?"

"Jenny said you prayed for me; you all prayed."

"We did."

"Now that's a wonderful thing, straight from the heart! People don't show their hearts very often. When I get well again, I'm going to make a new can of mash, and gather me fruits and catch me fish and call everyone to a luau where Adam and Jenny Briggs say thank you. And I'm going to find me a tree and fell it and haul it down and make me a little boat and give it to everyone, and say this is a boat made by the man you brought back from the dead."

"Adam, you don't have to do those things."

"I want to do them, chief."

"Fine! But not yet awhile, eh?"

"One day, soon. Something else I learned, chief . . ."

"What?"

"You were right when you said to live one day at a time. Sometimes it's one hour, one minute. You're a wise man!"

"You talk too much. Get some sleep."

"Yes, sir! No argument from Adam Lazarus Briggs!"

Outside, in the lowering light of a stormy afternoon, Ellen Ching was waiting for him. She took his arm and walked him over to the cascade and made him sit down and talked to him in her crisp, direct style.

"Chief, I don't bother you much."

"No, you don't, Ellen."

"I run my house and mind my own business, right?"

"You do."

"I don't panic. I don't rock the boat."

"Check!"

"I'm mixed up, but not screwed up."

"Check again!"

"So, when I talk to you, I want you to take me very seriously."

"I do. I will."

"Chief, you've got big trouble in a small package—Mark Gilman. No, don't say anything. Just listen. This is one frightening child. He's got brains for three people. He's—what?—rising twelve, but he looks fifteen and already he's loaded for bear and looking for it. That's one part of the problem, and, if you'll pardon the expression, it's the part that can be handled by me or Yoko, or even Jenny. It's the other part that worries me. Now, you know, one way and another, he gets a lot of care, and from Jenny and Molly and Sally, a lot of loving. Yet he's so full of hate, the loving doesn't even touch him. He could kill somebody one day. You'd better believe that!"

"Whom does he hate, Ellen?"

"Well, let me tell you what's happened, then you try to sort it out. . . . Now, this isn't hearsay. It's what I've seen and heard myself. You know how we all swim naked, alone or together. It's a normal thing. No surprises. It's like a drink of water. Now, several times, when I've been alone, he's stood off and watched me, not curious, not lecherous, just cold and contemptuous. Each time he's said the same thing: 'You'll make a beautiful corpse. Miss Ching!' I know, it's a lousy line, straight out of a B movie; but he's said it—said it and walked away."

"Anything else?"

"Oh yes. I didn't notice this for a while, but then I caught the pattern and watched it. Every night while Adam Briggs was very sick—remember we had someone with him all the time—Mark would walk down to the sun clock, stand against the pole—what do you call it? . . ."

"The gnomon."

"That's right. He'd stand against it, face Adam's hut, and spread out his arms, the way you've taught him to measure star angles. Then he'd recite something in Polynesian dialect. It sounded like: *Kai yoki yoki io.* I asked Franz Harsanyi what it meant and he said it was a death chant for a king. It says . . ."

"I know what it says. Go on."

"Well, after that he'd wait around for Jenny, and either go down to the beach with her or sit in her hut, talking till all hours. I listened one night, and I heard him say:

"Jenny, you're mine really. The chief gave you to me. I'm just lending you out until I'm ready."

"And what did Jenny say?"

"Oh hell! All the sweet things a big girl says to a little boy who thinks he's in love. She's milk and honey, chief. You know that. She wouldn't know a psychopath from a hole in the ground. While he was carving her up, she'd want to believe he was writing his autograph round her navel!"

"Strong words, Ellen!"

"Too strong; but I'm still anxious."

"How do the others feel?"

"They agree he's kooky. . . . They put it down to puberty, loneliness, mixed up family, lack of peer companionship, this, that and the kitchen sink! But if the boy's sick or unhappy, something has to be done about it." She gave him that cool, placid Kwan Yin smile. "And that means you, chief, I'm afraid."

"I'll watch him for a while."

"By the way, chief, people should say it; but they rarely do. We prize what you and Sally do."

"Thanks, Ellen."

"Old Chinese saying, chief: any fool can boil rice; for moon cakes you need a sober cook."

It was a pretty compliment, but it helped not at all to interpret the problems of a highly intelligent child, isolated in an adult world. He could not say it, but he had also to be wary of the testimony of a woman who feared children and was admittedly ambivalent in her attitude to the male gender. Her concern was genuine. He had to be very reserved about her observations and her diagnosis. So he sought out Carl Magnusson and told him of the conversation. The old man was troubled.

". . . The odder they think he is, the odder he'll get. The kid's got antennae like a butterfly. He reads your thoughts before you've even found the words for them, then he tells you what he thinks will raise him in your esteem. Kooky? That's a bastard word that means anything and nothing. . . . Let me tell you what I know. All his props have been knocked away. He knows how his father died; his mother's married Lorillard, whom he despises; she's carrying a child whom he sees, even now, as a usurper. You gave him Jenny, whom he loves. Adam Briggs took her away. Which leaves you, his uncle Gunnar, who, he hoped, would marry his mother and become a father to him. You rejected that role and assumed another—teacher and chief. So now he can't seduce you and he can't dominate you. What's the poor little coot got left? Just the knowledge you're pumping into him, which he sees as an ultimate source of power, authority, identity—call it what you will. . . . Dammit, Thorkild, he hasn't even got a pet to spend love on! He's being hauled by his ears into adulthood. His feet are off the ground and he's dangling in mid-air. The hell is that he understands it—or says he does!—but he doesn't know what to do about it. . . . I'm afraid we don't either. If we joke, we insult him. If we're tender, we demean him. He's excluded from our crises and from our celebrations. No wonder he's got fantasies of hate and killing. . . . Oh yes, I do believe he's got them! I wish I knew how to purge them out."

"I don't know either, Carl. . . . You see, the structure of the tribe is still defective. We've got the old, the mature, the young—but he's the only child, and before the babies are grown he'll be a man. That's why I'm training him, so that he can be among the first to leave the island. Meantime, the wounds become deeper, the alienation more complete."

"We're great doctors, Thorkild. We know all the diseases—and have no cure for any! I wonder . . ."

"What, Carl?"

"I was just thinking. Years ago, when I was cruising the Greek Isles, I went to Cos, the island which was sacred to Aesculapius the Healer. In antique times there was a great hospital there which was famous for its treatment of mental disorders. Patients came from all over the Mediterranean. They were lodged in the hospital, which was, in fact, a temple, and treated by the priests. The treatment always interested me, because, in a sense, it is still valid today. . . . There's a point to this, Thorkild, so be patient with me, eh?"

"Go on, Carl!"

"Where was I? Oh yes, the treatment. The patients were housed in rooms overlooking the sea, open to the cooling winds. They were cosseted by slaves, charmed with music, sedated with opiates. They drank, daily, from the sacred spring. All this was prelude, preparation. The cure was accomplished by what was called 'the experience of the god.' So far as we can gather, the patient was taken, blindfolded, to the inner shrine, deafened by loud noises, terrified by long silence, shocked by some voice which proclaimed a divine presence. That was the essence of it apparently: shock treatment, after which the patient was led back to his quarters, exhausted but serene, to convalesce in comfort and pleasure in sight of the sea. . . ."

Thorkild smiled. He had never heard Magnusson so eloquent on so arcane a subject. Magnusson continued:

"As with all legendary skills, there are no statistics of cure or failure; but the principle still holds good in modern therapy. It might hold good for Mark Gilman."

"If we had the priesthood and the temple, and the faith on which they were founded."

"The boy has faith," said Magnusson firmly. "He denies it, because most of his household gods have failed him. Your role has changed, but you haven't failed him yet."

"And the rest of it? The priesthood, the temple?"

"You're the priest. Even to the rest of us, you've assumed a sacred character. . . . Why you and no other, I don't know. But the mystery is there, visible."

"Don't make jokes like that, Carl!"

"I'm not joking. I'm saying that, if you prepared him for it—and you're the only one who could—the boy might benefit from the experience of the god. You needn't think of it as a cure, but as a rite of passage, that makes him at one stride the man he wants to be."

"You'd better spell it, Carl—slow and clear, eh?"

"I'm thinking," said Carl Magnusson, "that, when you take me up to the high place, you take the boy too!"

"God Almighty!" Thorkild's voice was a hoarse whisper. "You can't mean it! You can't!"

He brooded on it for days. He lay sleepless at night,

pondering the enormity of the act which Magnusson had proposed to him: the deliberate manipulation of an adolescent mind, to open it to reality and make the reality tolerable. The risks were all too evident, the prognosis doubtful. And yet . . . and yet . . . Every society, religious or secular, had its rituals of passage and initiation, baptism, bar mitzvah, ceremonies of mutilation and of purification, rites of knowing and enduring. He remembered his own night in the sacred place on Hiva Oa, when he waited for the *mana* to enter into him. It was the memory of the calm and the quiet joy which came afterwards which decided him to commit to the risk.

The decision once made, he must consider how to prepare the boy, and, indeed, the whole group, for an event of social and psychic significance. There could be no false note in it, no hint of conspiracy, no taint of theater, no possibility of a comic slip which would, an instant afterwards, precipitate a tragedy. His own performance must be impeccable, inspired; and—a new, strange fear beset him—after it, he too would be forever changed, because he could never belie or gainsay the priestly character he must assume as arbiter of life, death and spiritual affairs.

There was another terror in the thought. Now he was not merely an inheritor, a chronicler, an interpreter. He must, himself, become a maker of images and legends and magical rites full of potency. Magnusson alone would be privy to his secret. But when Magnusson died there would be no one—ever again—to whom he could unburden himself; because even Sally would consent to the magic, and having consented, would lie forever under its thrall.

It was not all illusion. The reality was mysterious enough: an old man would announce the hour of this encounter with death and walk out to keep it. A boy, sick with the strange malady of youth, must be healed at one stroke into manhood. The tribe must acknowledge, with piety and with gravity, a death and a resurrection.

So, enough of argument! For priest and patient both, the long prelude must begin.

It was late, long after midnight. Thorkild and the boy had sat for hours, observing the transit of the dog star across the northward heaven. The boy was rocking with fatigue; but he refused to go to bed because, he said, his mind kept whirling round and round, and he hated to lie, alone and wakeful, in the dark. They walked back to the fire pit. Thorkild raked the hot coals together and began baking a small fish from the evening's catch. The boy sat silent, munching a banana, staring into the red heart of the fire. Thorkild said:

"You did well tonight."

"I always do well with stars."

"It's different at sea. You have to contend with the motion."

"I know. I'll learn."

"Mark, we have things to talk about."

"If it's about growing up and sex and all that stuff, forget it, chief! I know it all."

"I'm sure you do."

"If it's about my mother, I don't want to discuss it."

"It isn't."

"Have I been rude to someone?"

"If you have, I don't know about it."

"Well . . . I'm listening, chief."

"Before I start, I must have a promise from you—a man's promise."

"I can't give that."

"Why?"

"Because I'm not a man. I'm a little boy. That's what everyone tells me. That's the way everyone treats me."

"Not I."

"Well, maybe not quite the same; but you're still the teacher and the chief. I'm the junior-grade student."

"And when you're twice your age, you'll still be learning and there'll always be a high man somewhere over you."

"If this is another lecture, chief, I'm tried."

"It's not a lecture. I asked you to keep a secret."

"No. You asked me for a man's promise. I said I couldn't give it."

"What promise can you give?"

"Mine—just mine! Cross my heart, spit in the fire, strike me dead! Good enough?"

"No. Not good enough!"

"What do you want, chief?"

Thorkild did not answer him. He bent and raked the coals away from the leaf-wrapped package, lifted it out with a pair of sticks and laid it on the sand between them. He said:

"We'll have to let it cool. Why don't you cool down too, Mark?"

"I'm cold."

"Mark, who are you?"

"I'm me—Mark Gilman."

"That's your name. I asked who you are."

"I'm me. What you see. The one who's talking to you."

"Mark, I look at you, and I don't believe what I see. I know how old you are and I know you're older. I hear the words and I know they mean something different. You tell me what you feel, and it's a fairy tale! Level with me, Mark!"

"Why should I?"

"Because I need you—the real you."

"You don't need anybody."

"Do you like Mr. Magnusson?"

"You know I do."

"He's going to die, Mark."

"Everybody dies. What's different with him?"

"Not much. It will happen soon; that's all."

"How soon?"

"Have some fish. It's good. I like the way the skin comes off with the leaves, don't you?"

"Why don't you talk to me properly?"

"Because you don't want it. I talk of a man dying and you play games. You bore me. Go to bed!"

"I'm sorry."

"Sorry, what?"

"Chief."

"So Carl Magnusson is going to die; and you ask me, what's different?"

"I didn't mean that."

"What did you mean?"

"I mean, people use dying for an excuse. . . . Like my mother . . . 'Your poor father's dead. Now there's only the two of us. We must care for each other, Mark.' Or Jenny: 'My Adam could die, Mark. How dare you be so cruel.' Like that's shit, man!"

"So, go to bed."

"I want to know about Mr. Magnusson."

"Ask him yourself."

"Please, chief!"

"He's going to die. Already he's half blind. He lies awake at night and hears death walking outside the door. He's told me that, because I'm his friend, and my grandfather was his friend. But he doesn't want to die here, with people crying round his bed. He wants me to take him up to the high place, where my grandfather is, so that he can die up there, among the great men of the past. And I'm going to take him and leave him. . . . The secret is, he asked for you to go with him—because he loves you and he sees what I can't see: a man called Mark Gilman."

"I'll go. I want to go!"

"How can you, after what you've just said?"

"I wasn't talking about him."

"All the dead look alike, Mark—and the same flowers grow over them all. Problem is, a man's last hours belong only to him. No one has the right to intrude with complaints or excuses or fears or hates. Those who will be left behind must be able to give him friendship and peace and an unselfish prayer. If you can't do that, don't come."

"Why doesn't he want the others? Willy and Adam and . . ."

"I don't know."

"Is he going to kill himself?"

"No. Did you think he would?"

"My father did."

"Not the way I heard it, Mark."

"Oh yes! That's what the lecturers said at school. Heroin addiction is suicide, slower than most, but equally sure."

"Let me ask you something, Mark. It's about Charlie Kamakau."

"What about him?"

"Some of our people voted to kill him. You voted against it. Why?"

"Because killing him was pointless. Death doesn't change things. It just stops them."

"Then why did you wish death on Adam Briggs?"

"I didn't. I . . ."

An instant later he would have been up and away,

but Thorkild clamped an iron hand on his shoulder and held him.

"Let me go!"

"Be quiet! You wished Adam dead because you want his woman. . . . That's a man's thought. You wish Lorillard dead, and the child your mother is carrying, because you want your mother only for yourself. . . . That's a child's thought. Both are destructive; because, as you said yourself, death only stops things. It wouldn't change Jenny's love for Adam, or your mother's desire to bear another child. . . . You're lonely, living in a dark room, trying to change from boy to man, as the caterpillar changes into a moth. You want to get out. You can. The key's in your hand; but you're turning it the wrong way, locking yourself inside with your fears and your griefs and your hates. . . . Mark, a strange and solemn thing is happening. Inside that hut over there is a man—a real *Kāne,* full of courage and dignity. He knows he's going to die. He's asking his friends to link arms with him and walk him up the last miles to his resting place. You're one of those friends. I'm the other. The journey's long. The place, when you come to it first, is frightening; but there is peace there for Carl Magnusson. For me there is the company of my great ancestors. For you, Mark, there is something else—the thing that will make you, once and for all, a man."

The boy was still now, staring across the compound at the dark doorway of Magnusson's hut. In a small, unsteady voice, he said:

"I want to come, but I'm afraid."

"I was afraid, Mark, when I went up to find my grandfather. Magnusson is afraid too; but here's going, just the same."

"What is this—this thing up there?"

"I can't describe it to you, Mark. There are no words for it. . . . Tell me, do you remember your Bible?"

"Some, yes."

"Remember the story of Moses going up the mountain to receive the law from God. . . . When he came down, the people couldn't look upon his face because it was so bright and shining, with the glory and the terror he'd witnessed?"

"Yes, I remember."

"Well, where you are going—if you go—there is a terror and a glory too. There will be a moment when it will seem unbearable. . . . But I promise you this: when that moment passes, and you walk down to the terrace and the beach, you won't have to say anything or prove anything anymore. People will look at you and know that Mark Gilman is a man."

"Will you be with me, all the time?"

"It's a sacred place. I'm its guardian. I must be there."

"I'll come."

"Then you should tell Carl Magnusson yourself in the morning. . . . And remember, until he is ready to announce it, this is a secret between the three of us."

"Yes, a secret."

"We should go to bed now."

"Please—one question."

"Yes, Mark?"

"What would happen if I didn't go?"

Thorkild turned the question over and over, groping for the words to answer it. Finally he found them.

"Nothing would happen, Mark. You would remain, as you are now, searching, confused, at odds with yourself and everyone else. You would grow in time to a man's age and a man's estate. But always, for the rest of your life, you would be haunted by the feeling that you had mislaid a part of yourself, the part that you would have found on the mountain. . . . That's what would have happened to me if it hadn't been for my grandfather. Even so, it took me more than half a lifetime to find what I had missed."

"Thank you for telling me, chief."

"Thank you for listening. . . . Cover the fire before you leave it. Good night, Mark."

The smaller canoe, which would later become the outrigger of the larger craft, was finished at last. It was long and narrow; so they balanced it with another and smaller outrigger cut from a sapling and lashed to thick poles of bamboo. They stepped a mast and made a small matting sail and spent a week cruising it round the lagoon, testing the balance before committing it to the big sea outside.

Because it was a new, tangible triumph, a lift to their hopes and hearts, Thorkild commanded a big luau to celebrate it. A fresh batch of liquor was brewing, the terrace folk were invited down to spend a day's fishing and a night's feasting, and watch the first deep-sea trial of the new vessel. Adam Briggs was bitterly disappointed because he was still hampered by his injured foot, and must content himself with being a passenger inside the lagoon. Mark Gilman was elated because Thorkild had pronounced that this should be the first test of his skill as a navigator. Carl Magnusson limped about the camp, exhorting all and sundry to make this a day and a night to remember; because —hell and blazes!—to build a ship was a proud thing and he had launched several in his time, but none so beautiful at this one!

The terrace folk came down laden with gifts—fruit, taro and pig meat—and the news that they had now penned a sow and a boar in a bamboo stockade and the sow would soon have a litter. Willy and Eva

Kuhio were placid and cheerful as ever. Willy was as happy with the boat as though he had built it with his own hands. Simon Cohen was a surprise. He had put on weight and acquired a sense of humour, and had brought down new instruments, a pair of pigskin drums, a set of panpipes and a curious one-stringed instrument from which he managed to scrape out a passable tune. Barbara was full of chatter and eager for gossip. Martha Gilman, thickening now and tired after the walk, was content to sit in the shade and let the activity flow round her. She was delighted at Mark's enthusiasm and the new, if still uneasy, freedom of his approaches to her. Peter Lorillard looked unwell. He had lost weight. His skin was pasty, his eyes, red and sunken. He had had a cold and a sore throat —nothing much; but yes, he would be glad if Sally could examine him before he went back.

The weather was kind to them. The sky was clear, the wind fair and steady, the sea comfortable. In the morning they sailed the lagoon in threes and fours, so that everyone who wished could try the new boat. At midday they ate a light meal and then Thorkild announced the big sea trial. Willy Kuhio, Hernan Castillo, Tioto and Mark Gilman would take the boat out through the channel and make a course which he had laid—two hours out, two hours back. Mark Gilman would navigate. The others would handle the sail and the paddles. They would be back just before sunset when the turn of the tide would carry them home past the sentinel rock.

Martha Gilman paled visibly as she saw them push out and head for the break in the reef. Thorkild patted her shoulders and admonished her:

"He has to do it, Martha. Don't try to hold him."

"You're a hard man, Gunnar."

"I'm also a good teacher. Trust me. Trust the boy too."

He broke off and stood watching, nodding his satisfaction as they cleared the channel and headed out, reaching across the wind, picking up speed as they cleared the last bluff.

Peter Lorillard gave a whistle of surprise. "My God, she's fast!"

"Twelve—fifteen knots." Thorkild grinned. "Not bad for amateur builders, eh?"

"How long's your course?"

"About forty miles."

"And you think the boy can handle it, first time out?"

"I'm sure of it. . . . Listen, Peter, if you're not feeling well, why don't you bring Martha down here to the beach for a spell. I can send Franz Harsanyi and Ellen Ching up to take your place."

"No, thanks. I prefer my own bailiwick."

"The neighbours are friendly," said Martha Gilman, acidly. "That helps, of course!"

"For God's sake, Martha! Must you?"

"Excuse me," said Thorkild hastily. "I've got to talk to Sally."

He found her, sitting in a shady spot on the beach, talking with Eva Kuhio. He sat down with them and was immediately drawn into their talk.

"Eva was telling me," said Sally, "that Peter and Martha are quarrelling a lot. Peter hasn't been well—one look at him and I'm already worried. Martha nags him out of the house and then wonders why he spends so much time with Simon and Barbara."

"They don't mean harm," Eva hastened to explain. "They're jokey people, you know. He likes to talk sexy. She likes to play sexy, and there's no problem for Willy and me. Peter Lorillard likes a joke too, and he's always been free with his hands; again, what's the harm? But Martha always makes a big mouthful of it. . . . If she'd laugh and relax, he'd like better to be with her. Still, maybe when the baby comes . . ."

"I suggested they both come down here for a while," said Thorkild. "Lorillard wouldn't hear of it."

"And I don't blame him." Eva was stout in her defense. "He loves it up there, like we do. He's planting and grubbing and opening up new ground, and collecting orchids, and now this pig-breeding. When I look out and see him and my Willy and that Simon talking away and laughing and singing, I start singing too. . . . But not Martha! If the moon was all gold and you gave her a slice of it she'd still be unhappy."

"Why don't we invite her down by herself?" asked Sally. "Just for a week or so."

"No!" Thorkild was harsh. "I don't want her down here until . . ."

"Until what?"

"Until I've made some more progress with Mark. I'm just getting him licked into shape, and the last thing I need is a mother clucking round him at every step."

"Calm down, my love! It was just a suggestion."

"The chief's right. Sally." Eva was placid as the earth-mother. "You mend the things you can and let time take care of the rest. That's what I like about Barbara. If today's good she's glad. If it's not, tomorrow is just round the corner. Sad to say, Charlie never knew how to handle her."

"And Cohen does?"

"Well . . . I think it's the other way round. Except he doesn't see it. I'm beginning to like him now; and it's good to have the music at night. . . ."

"I think you and Willy make some of it, Eva."

"There's music down here too," said Sally with quiet

pride. "I'm beginning to hear the harmonies. . . . Oh, I almost forgot. Carl wants to see you, darling. He's resting in his hut. I told him I'd send you along later."

"Anything wrong?"

"I don't think so. Something to do with the luau tonight."

"Fine. I'll trot over and talk to him. . . . See you girls later."

"Gunnar, are you sure they can handle that boat?"

"If they can't, my love, I'll personally feed them, member by member, to the sharks."

"Listen to him!" Eva Kuhio laughed. "You'd think he was like the old ones: lord of life and death. Don't you worry, Sally, my man will bring 'em home."

Carl Magnusson was lying on his bed. Molly Kaapu was sitting beside him, fanning his face and grumbling at his perversity.

". . . Will you look at him! This stupid old *lōlō* thinks he's twenty again! All morning he was trotting about, husking coconuts, chopping fire sticks. Now look at him! Flat on his back and grey as a goose!"

"Woman! You talk too much!"

"Okay! So I let the chief talk to you. Maybe he can beat some sense into that thick *haole* skull!"

She waddled out, a vast mountain of indignation. Thorkild sat down on the stool and picked up the fan.

"You wanted to see me, Carl?"

"Yes. The luau tonight . . ."

"What about it?"

"With everyone together and the boat launched, I think it's a good time to speak my farewells. In the morning you'll take me up the mountain."

"Carl, are you sure?"

"I'm sure. And this would be the right time for the boy, too."

"We'll leave at sunrise."

"No, we'll go straight from the *luau*. The track's clear enough to follow at night. We'll rest on the terrace and push on from there at sunrise. No arguments, Thorkild. I want a clean exit, with a full belly and flowers round my neck."

"What can I say, Carl?"

"Nothing. Save it for the supper. Then say it loud and clear, so they'll remember it for a lifetime. . . . For the rest, keep Molly out of my hair; and wake me when you see the boat coming. I want to be on the beach to welcome young Mark."

An hour before sunset, they were all on the beach, waiting for the first sight of the home-coming craft. An hour after, they were still there with torches lit and a beacon fire blazing to lead the voyagers in through the narrow passage, turbulent now with the tide rush. They were garlanded, because Thorkild had so commanded. The pit was stoked with coals. The meat was roasting. Anxious voices were raised, but Thorkild silenced them with a shout. This is the way of the sea. They had best get used to it. They could sing if they wanted, but murmur and complain, no! They began to sing, raggedly at first and then in stronger chorus until Thorkild silenced them again.

"I see them!"

"Where?"

"There; as they ride on top of the roller, the sail blacks out the stars."

"I've got 'em," said Lorillard.

"And I," called Franz Harsanyi.

Then they were silent again, a long time, watching the tiny craft surfing the near rollers, clawing its way up towards the tricky entrance.

"He's too far down," muttered Lorillard.

"He's just right," said Thorkild. "If he can hold that course, the swell will steer him in."

They slipped off it, they clawed back onto it and held and held until the last moment, when they dropped sail and paddled like demons, through the tide-rip, with the boy shouting crazily over their heads:

"We made it! Oh, you beautiful bastards! We made it!"

A great shout went up as they drove the canoe straight onto the sand; but Thorkild held the tribe back and walked down alone to meet the boy. He asked coldly:

"What kept you?"

"We lost the wind, chief," said Mark Gilman respectfully. "We had to paddle for two hours to find it again."

"Did you follow the course I laid?"

"No, chief. I changed it to find the wind."

"He's a good navigator, chief," said Willy Kuhio. "I'll sail with him anytime."

"Me, too," said Tioto. "In the dark and on that sea; he brought us home right on the nose."

"Something important, chief."

"Yes, Mark?"

"That beacon fire's too far to the left. It's dangerous. We'll have to get it exact."

"We'll do that, Mr. Gilman." He lifted the garland from his own neck and placed it on the boy. "Good work! You've earned your feast."

He put his arm around the boy's shoulder and led him up the beach, and the people stood aside to let them pass and settle themselves, first, at the fire pit.

TEN

THIS FEAST, THEY ALL AGREED, WAS DIFFERENT from the other. The food was better, for one thing; the liquor was two notches above the first fire-water. The company had improved too; more educated, more in tune with the times, which also were better because the land was yielding its fruits and the sea was now a measurable risk, and, come to think of it, for a mixed bag of nobodies, they hadn't done too badly on Thorkild's Island. . . . That's right, chief! That's what it was: Thorkild's Island—god-forgotten, man-forgotten in the ever-loving middle of nowhere!

At which high and clamourous point, Franz Harsanyi asserted himself. He wanted to deliver, declaim and specify that if you didn't have a Hungarian, you didn't have a script; and without a script you could not impose a form on the material, the magma, the incandescent—see, he wasn't drunk!—the incandescent lava of their lives. He, Franz Harsanyi, was Hungarian. He spoke, wrote, lived and breathed American, because his own language was unintelligible. He had learned Polynesian because what the American language expressed was an obscenity, from which they should all thank God to have escaped.

To celebrate that escape he, Franz Harsanyi, son of the puszta, had begun to write a poem, an epic, a saga of the castaways from the *Frigate Bird*. This saga he was about to recite, and would continue from feast to feast. Objections? None. He now sought the permission of the chief to present his humble—no, by Christ!—his noble work. Thank you, chief. With gratitude and good heart he would now begin. And if his colleague, Simon Cohen, cared to embellish the text with melody and rhythm, he would welcome it. If the people, the profane but beloved vulgus, would care to repeat the choruses, he would be happy to hear them.

> "Praise God,
>   Brothers and sisters,
>   Wives, sons and lovers! . . .
>   Once upon a time,
>   Long out of our time,
>   There was a man,
>   Who had a dream.
>   Men who have dreams
>   Are mad and dangerous.
>   They deny the great truths
>   Of news at twelve,
>   And commentary at one
>   And blah-blah-blah
>   And cornflake ads
>   And colonels chomping chicken,
>   Licking their fingers afterwards,

Because
To lick a sticky finger
Is already paradise!
Are you with me, brothers and sisters?
Brother, we're with you!
This man—professor yet!—
Haphaole nobody,
Said 'Come with me!
Come sail away
And find this nowhere island.'
So we sailed.
He didn't even own
The ship we sailed in;
Wrecked it, nonetheless,
And dumped us here,
On Thorkild's Island.
Castaways together.
O God, help us,
Brothers all and sisters all!
He mated us,
Berated us,
Put us together.
Pulled us apart,
Fought us,
Besought us,
Hammered and clamoured
And generally fraught us
And finally brought us—
To love and to cherish
—You like it or perish!—
This granular speck,
This great lump of dreck,
Dredged up from the drink,
The bottomless sink,
Now let's be specific
Of the goddam Pacific. . . .

And nobody knows that we're here!
God rot Gunnar Thorkild!"

There was more, pages more, he protested. But they dragged him down, and gagged him with a banana, and promised that they would hear him again—but not yet, Hungarian scribbler, not yet! Music they would have; and Simon Cohen played while they sang and danced. Then, when the songs had tailed away, Carl Magnusson rose painfully to his feet. Molly Kaapu held out her hand to steady him. He drew her up to stand beside him. Then he began:

"I liked Franz Harsanyi's poem. I once put twenty thousand dollars in a musical by a Hungarian. I lost the lot; but I had a wonderful time with his girl friend who came from Bolivia! I'm sure Franz is a better writer and a better lover than he was!" He let them laugh awhile and then hushed them with a gesture. "My dear friends—and you, Molly, who are much more than a friend to me—I beg you to hear me out. I'm leaving you tonight. My friends, Gunnar Thorkild and Mr. Mark Gilman, are going to walk me out of here. We're going to rest in your house, Willy, if you'll allow us. At sunrise, we're going up to the high place where Kaloni Kienga and his ancestors sit, looking out at the sea. I'm going to stay there and sleep quietly with great men until judgment day—whatever and wherever that may be. Before I go, I want to embrace each one of you, and tell you that because of you, because of the things we have done together, I go a happy man. . . . Nothing in my life pleases me so much as this moment. Nothing you can do or say will give me so much joy as a last kiss, a last handshake—and no words at all. I am proud that it was my *Frigate Bird* that brought us here. I am proud that Mark Gilman, who came a child, is now almost a man. I am honoured that Gunnar Thorkild, who once came to me for help, is now my chief and will walk with me on this last journey. He will speak to you now. Then, I beg you, let us go quickly and quietly."

They were all silent, caught in a syncope of grief and foreboding. Gunnar Thorkild rose in his place. It was the moment he had dreaded, the exalted, open moment when, with the right word, he could bind them to him forever and with the wrong one lose them utterly. He closed his eyes, gathering himself, a blind man stepping out into blackness. Then he flung out his arms in a hieratic gesture and his voice rolled out, solemn and sonorous over the assembly:

"Carl Magnusson, our friend, is about to leave us. He wants no tears, no eulogy. We will respect his wishes. Like my grandfather and all the others on the high place, he passes out of our lives and into our common memory. I could not prepare you for this, because he had charged me to hold it secret until the final moment. Neither could I prepare you for another moment, another passing, which is now upon us. . . . Stand up, Mark Gilman!"

The boy rose, slowly, and stood rigid before them, the light of the torches and the pit shining on his naked breast and shoulders.

"Look well at this boy! You will never see him again; because, when he comes back to you, he will be a man. You men will receive him into your fellowship. You women will acknowledge him, treat with him as you do with other men. Today, you saw him go out in a frail boat, to meet the great sea. You saw him bring it home, with its crew, safe through a dangerous passage. Tonight he goes out with me and with Carl Magnusson to the encounter that will make him a man. He will see life. He will see death. He will hear and he will recognize that which we call the voice of God—the rumbling at the deep foundation of all things. He is afraid now; but when he returns he will be at peace. You will wait for him here, all of you, and you will receive him with joy and with respect. This is the nature of life, my friends; a man —a great man—leaves us; a young man comes to us, with the seeds of greatness in him. . . . Now, it is time to go!"

On the way to the terrace they spoke little. Carl Magnusson pressed on, eager and breathless, as though afraid that death might escape him before he recognized it. When Thorkild remonstrated the old man rebuffed him angrily. He knew his own heartbeat and the sound of the hammer in his skull; he would not waste himself on argument. By the time they reached Willy Kuhio's hut he was tottering with exhaustion. When they laid him on the bed he collapsed silently into a deep sleep. Thorkild sat with him until his pulse steadied and his breathing became more regular, then he walked outside to join Mark Gilman.

The air was damp and heavy with scent of *pikake* and ginger flowers. The moonlight lay silver on the rows of plantation trees, sugarcane. banana, papaya, and on the beds of wild pineapple and pepper plant and husk-tomatoes. In the shadows they could hear the grunting and scuffing of the penned animals, and the stirring of night birds in the jungle.

The boy said, "My mother was crying when I left. I didn't know what to say to her."

"All mothers cry when their children grow up. She'll get over it."

"Peter Lorillard isn't so bad, is he?"

"No. . . . He's done a good job up here."

"He said he was sorry we weren't staying in his house."

"People change."

"You've changed too."

"Have I?"

"Tonight, when you were making your speech, it was as if you were another man, older and bigger. Even your voice was different. The people were afraid of you. They drew back as you passed. They kept looking at you, behind your back. I thought about the story you told: Moses coming down from the mountain."

"Let's talk about you. How did it feel out there today?"

"Oh, brother! At first I was so scared I wanted to jump overboard and swim home. Even the sharks seemed less dangerous than what I was doing. Then, suddenly, it was like switching on a light. I knew what to do. I knew that I knew. That was the big thing: I knew that I knew. After that everything was easy— even coming through the channel! . . . Oh, I meant to say thank you. I was excited. I forgot."

"I understood."

"Chief?"

"Yes?"

"When you said I would hear the voice of God, what did you mean?"

"Just what I said."

"Have you heard it?"

"Yes."

"Do you still hear it? For instance, when you were speaking tonight, were you hearing it then?"

"Listen a moment, Mark. . . . Tell me what you hear now."

"The birds, the pigs . . . the wind, blowing in the trees."

"Is it the wind you hear, or the trees?"

"I don't know. Both, I suppose."

"I don't know either, Mark. . . . And that's the terror of the high place, and the high man. Is it God he hears or the echo of his own mad shouting? There is a moment when he knows and he knows that he knows, as you did today. There are all the other moments when he does not know—but he still must speak and still must act, and bear the consequence until he dies. . . . When I sent you out this morning, I knew it was a risk—a big one. Suppose you hadn't made the channel and piled up on the reef. I would have been answerable to all the people for all your lives. What was I when I sent you out, Mark? A vain teacher, showing off a star pupil—or a wise chief leading a son of the tribe to manhood?"

"I never thought of that."

"You will now, Mark. . . . Let's get some sleep. It's only a few hours to sunrise."

The walk to the crater rim was a long, slow purgatory. Magnusson's strength was failing, fast. Every hundred paces they had to stop and rest him—while he gulped down the thin air of the summit, and battled to control the spasms of coughing that threatened to tear him apart. More than once, Thorkild offered to carry him; but he refused. He would walk, every goddam step! He would die—by Christ!—on his own two feet. When they came to the mouth of the tunnel, Thorkild propped him against the rock wall and gave him a mouthful of water from the gourd. He gagged and spat it out, then leaned back, trembling and gasping. Thorkild urged him desperately to hold on. Magnusson gave him a pale, twisted grin.

"Don't . . . don't kiss me off yet, Thorkild."

They put his arms around their shoulders, heaved him off the rockface and half dragged, half carried him down the tunnel to the platform of the navigators.

When the sunlight hit him he screamed in pure terror. He was blind—blind! They held him, rocking and writhing, between them until he was calm again. They set him on his feet and let him stand, alone.

Thorkild said softly, "You're not blind, Carl. Open your eyes. Look!"

For a long moment, he stood there gazing out on the blazing immensity of sea and sky and the seabirds wheeling through it. Then it was as if a new life took possession of his aged body. He threw out his arms in a gesture of total embrace. He tossed back his white mane and shouted:

"God! It's beautiful! So beautiful!"

They caught him as he crumpled and carried him along the ledge, and sat him, cross-legged, upon the stone beside the skeleton of Kaloni Kienga the Navigator. Thorkild closed the dead eyes, folded the slack hands and stepped back. Mark Gilman stood transfixed, staring at the dead man on his pedestal. Thorkild drew him forward, lifted his hand and laid it on Magnusson's cheek.

"That's it, Mark. . . . That's death."

The boy said nothing. He turned away and stood a long time staring out over the steep fall of the land, to the sun-drenched sea, and the empty sky beyond. Then, in a voice that was scarcely a whisper, he said:

"I hear it! I do hear it! . . ."

"What do you hear?"

"The voice . . . from the deep foundations."

"Are you sure?"

"Yes. It's so beautiful. Yes . . . I'm sure."

"Are you ready to go back?"

"I'm ready."

They walked side by side along the row of long-dead navigators. When they came to the last platform with its pile of yellowed bones, Thorkild stopped, picked up the weathered paddle and held it out to Mark Gilman.

"Here! This is for you."

"What is it?"

"The paddle with which he made his last journey. . . . The symbol is that of the sea god Kanaloa. Stick it in the sand outside your hut. It will remind you of what you are and what has happened to you today."

"But I can't. . . . It belongs to him!"

"Take it! His journey is over; yours is just beginning."

Their homecoming was an anticlimax. The seaboard folk were busy about their own concerns. The uplanders were anxious to be gone. The impact of the night's drama had dissipated itelf. All the obits for Carl Magnusson had been spoken. Molly Kaapu had been comforted with tears and embraces. The decencies being thus disposed of, they must close ranks and begin again the consoling humdrum round of existence.

Mark Gilman planted the paddle outside his hut and then went out fishing with Tioto. Thorkild gave a brief dispassionate account of the last hours of Carl Magnusson, said good-bye to the guests, wrote his log and retired gratefully for an afternoon's sleep. Just before sunset, Sally woke him and they went down, together, to swim in the lagoon.

She was tired of people, she told him, weary of their pinprick demands, their incessant, plaguing problems. She was sick of being eaten up and seeing him eaten up by hungry piranhas. So, please, tonight they would eat alone; they would drink some of the whiskey Carl had left; they would get a little drunk, go to bed early and make love and never once talk about anybody but themselves. To all of which Gunnar Thorkild said yea, amen, and if he could whistle her away for a week by herself, he would be the happiest man alive.

He made a big ceremony of their solitude. Ten yards from the hut, he printed a large sign in sand: "Do Not Disturb!" He built a fireplace of stones outside the door, commandeered half a bottle of whiskey, two fish and a basket of fruit from the common stock, set out stools and a bamboo bench, and proceeded to prepare the meal himself. One or two hardy spirits wandered by, hoping for a chat, but he hunted them away. Couldn't they read? For once, just once, he'd like to be left alone to entertain his wife.

The exercise, however, proved more difficult than he expected. Sally was more low-spirited than he had ever known her to be. She ate little. She had lost her taste for liquor. She laughed at one joke and lost interest in the rest. She was too tired to stay up, too restless to go to bed. She would like to make love, but later. She was sorry to be bitchy, but she couldn't help it. No, it wasn't the curse, and it wasn't her fault and it wasn't his and—oh hell!—it was all such a bloody, tearful, useless mess! Then the dam burst and it all spilled out.

". . . I feel so helpless; that's all! I spent half my life training for medicine, and now what can I do? Nothing. I'm—I'm just a barber-surgeon, cupping and bleeding! I can't even lay on hands, or minister to the mind diseased like you did last night. . . . Oh, love! Don't try to con me! I knew what you were doing. I knew why. I thought it was the greatest performance I'd ever seen in my life; and I was ten times more jealous than if you'd hauled a woman away from the fire and laid her in front of my eyes! You don't even know how to empty a bedpan, but you're the healer, not me! Can you imagine how that feels?"

"And what, my sweet, brought all this on?"

"What does it matter?"

"I want to know."

"Peter Lorillard. I examined him this afternoon. His throat's raw with what looks like streptococcal infection. His lymph nodes are enlarged and he's got a lump the size of a pigeon's egg in his groin."

"Which means what? Filariasis?"

"It could. But there's no way I can prove it without blood tests. Even if I could, it wouldn't make any difference because I've got no drugs to treat him with. It might also mean that he's got glandular fever, or quite possibly cancer."

"So what did you tell him?"

"Oldest lie in the book. I substituted the symptom for the disease. He's got swollen glands. I told him they'd probably clear up quickly."

"You really have had a bad day at the office."

"Don't laugh at me. I'll start crying again."

"I'm not laughing. Come on, lover. I'll take you to bed."

"I haven't even asked you about Carl or what happened up there."

"It'll keep. Come to bed."

"Please! Be patient with me tonight. I'm rather fragile."

"Your command is my pleasure, madam!"

Afterwards, even that small joke turned sour. As he was caressing her breasts, his fingers encountered a hard lump. She moved his hand to another spot. He would not be put off. He asked:

"Is this something new?"

"Yes. It's nothing. A blocked duct probably."

"And possibly?"

"All right! Possibly! What difference does it make? If it gets better, fine!"

"If it doesn't?"

"At my age, and without surgery, it means a quick development of secondaries and a negative prognosis. . . . And before it gets too bad, you, my dear lover, are going to walk me up that mountain and very quietly put me to sleep the way I showed you! . . . And if you weaken on me I'll walk myself up and toss myself off the highest cliff I can find! Is that clear?"

"How long have you had this?"

"Three weeks, a month."

"Is it operable?"

"Either way, yes. But who's going to operate? You?"

"The best surgeon in the best hospital. I'm going to get you home, if it's the last goddam thing I do."

"Oh, my love, don't torment yourself. My way's much easier—less messy too. I wish you hadn't found out."

"I'm sorry you didn't tell me sooner."

"It wouldn't have made a scrap of difference. We'll talk no more about it. Just hold me. Give me good dreams."

When she lapsed finally into sleep, he eased himself away from her and went outside. The night was full of stars, low and tempting as fruit on a tree— dead sea fruit, dust and ashes in the mouth. He walked over to the spot where the great log was being slowly shaped and hollowed. Hernan Castillo stood leaning against it, chatting with Franz Harsanyi. Thorkild asked him casually enough:

"How long do you give it now, Hernan?"

"Six months at least. Possibly more."

"What? With everyone working?"

"It's not the man power—or the woman power,

chief. We've got plenty of hands, but not enough effective tools to put in 'em. Stone axes don't last like steel. The handles break; the bindings come off. Then I have to stop work and repair them. The two steel ones we have must be constantly honed. . . . I've tried teaching Franz and some of the others how to make stone heads and blades, but they haven't the knack. There's another thing too. We've established a good rhythm now. If you break it you'll find the work will go slower and not faster."

"I guess it will at that."

"What's the hurry, anyway? We've got a perfectly serviceable craft out there. Why rush the big one and botch it?"

"No rush, Hernan. It was just cracker-barrel chat. . . . Franz, I didn't have time last night to compliment you on your epic."

"Thanks. It's crazy. But it passes the time."

"When we get home I'll guarantee to find you a publisher!"

"That's a nice safe promise," said Harsanyi with a laugh. "It leaves all your options open."

"Yes, doesn't it? . . . Have you fellows handled the new boat yet?"

"Just round the lagoon. Why?"

"I'll have to start training you, soon, for the big water."

"Don't bust a gut over it, chief," said Hernan Castillo. "I can't wait."

"The longer the better," said Franz Harsanyi. "After seeing young Gilman's performance, I abdicated!"

"From this, nobody abdicates," said Thorkild flatly. "I'll be breathing down your neck in a few days."

He left them groaning a duet of protest and walked over to the fire pit where Molly Kaapu sat alone, warming herself at the embers, swaying and crooning an old lament. He sat down beside her, took her big, work-hardened hand in his own, and began to talk to her in the old language.

"You miss him. Molly?"

"I miss him, Kaloni."

"Something you should know, Molly. You made him very happy."

"He said that?"

"He said more. He said he loved you."

"Ai-ee! That breaks my heart, Kaloni. . . . Why did he go like that? Why didn't he stay with me?"

"Because he wanted you to remember him as a man—a high man! He didn't want to be an old man, turning into a child again."

"I'm a lonely old woman, Kaloni. Who needs Mother Molly now that he's gone?"

"I need you."

"You have your own woman."

"Molly, I've got a shark on my tail."

"You want to tell me why?"

"Not now. Tomorrow, maybe—or the next day. I need to think."

"Kaloni, when you got a shark on your tail, you got no time to think. You hit the first big wave and ride it into the beach. You hear me?"

"I hear you, Molly. . . . Thanks!"

"Kaloni."

"Yes?"

"You miss the wave; you have to turn and punch the shark on the nose. No other way."

"And what if he bites my arm off?"

"Stick your head in his mouth. He'll break all his teeth on it, eh?"

"And to hell with you too, Molly Kaapu! Come on, you can't sit here all night! I'll walk you back to the hut."

In the morning, early, while Sally was still sleeping, he left the camp and walked up the jungle trail to the terrace. When he got there he found Lorillard already at work, slashing out a new clearing on the far side of the plantation. Lorillard was surprised to see him.

"You're a rare visitor, Thorkild. Something wrong?"

"Yes. I need to talk to you. I'd rather the others didn't know about this for a while."

Lorillard led him out of the clearing, into the jungle fringe.

"We're private enough here. What's the problem?"

"Before I start, let me say something. You and I have always been at odds, Peter. I'm begging you now to forget all the past and help me if you can. Will you do that?"

"I'll try."

"Here it is, then. Sally examined you yesterday. She gave you a bland diagnosis, because she's helpless to do anything for you. It's her opinion you may have filariasis—or as a long shot, something more serious."

Lorillard nodded and gave him a thin smile. "I guessed as much."

"There's more. Sally has a lump on her breast which could be a malignancy."

"Oh God, I'm sorry."

"Now that's two people in urgent need of medical attention."

"Which they can't get. So they're forced to endure what can't be cured."

"I'm afraid it isn't that simple—at least for Sally. If it turns out that she has a malignancy, she's asked me to kill her!"

"I'm not surprised." Lorillard was very calm about it. "I'd probably do the same thing. To me it seems normal and logical; if the patient suffers unbelievable pain without any hope of relief, how can you refuse the mercy of death? If there is no case against you at law—and here there certainly isn't—how can you possibly reject the plea? This is one of those situations where conventional morality has no reference, and there's certainly no room left for hypocrisy. I'm sorry if that sounds cold-blooded; but I've been toying with the same thought as Sally."

"I understand. From a personal point of view, I'm in no position to argue the proposition. From the point of view of this small society of ours, it raises some frightening consequences. Everyone who falls terminally ill claims the same right of release from suffering. The rest are all doomed to become, at some future time, executioners."

"Or executioners of a filial or social duty. . . . You're the traditionalist, Thorkild. I never thought to find you so squeamish."

"I'd like to avoid the issue if I could."

"No doubt. But we patients may be denied that luxury."

"Which is the point I came to discuss. If there were a chance, a reasonable chance, to get you and Sally back to civilization for diagnosis and treatment, would you take it?"

"Naturally. . . . But the chance diminishes with every day. The big boat can't be finished for months yet."

"I'm thinking of the little one."

"Jesus Christ!"

"No, wait! You think about it for a while. You're a seaman. You've been through survival training. You know that, with sane and experienced people, the odds in favour of survival are pretty good. That craft is fast and it's seaworthy. We've got a fairly accurate fix on our present position. We're at most five hundred miles from the nearest inhabited soil—east or west. Say you make a hundred and fifty miles a day—no, put it at the very lowest, a hundred. That's a five-day journey at most. And once you're up among the atolls you're home free. The boat's not too roomy but can carry food and water sufficient for four people. It's not really such a stupendous undertaking. . . . If you're fit enough to work like a dog up here, you're fit enough for a week's sailing. So is Sally. If I gave you Mark, who is a good navigator, and light to carry, and one more man, I think you'd have a much better than even chance. Once you got anywhere within shouting distance of a radio station you'd have the whole goddam Navy steaming out to pick you up."

"And if we don't make it. . . ?"

"Then you and Sally wouldn't be that much worse off. And we'd lose two men, who would have accepted the risk anyway."

"What about the rest?"

"They'd still be here, living, building the big boat."

"And who would be the other man?"

"There's a choice. Willy Kuhio, Adam Briggs, Tioto or myself. The rest you can forget. They lack the training and the sea sense for this kind of job."

"Strike out Tioto. He's good and he's willing; but he's handicapped."

"That leaves three."

"Two," said Lorillard with sober conviction. "The others would kill us before they'd let you go."

"I'm prepared to put it up to them, if you'll buy the general idea."

"What have I got to lose? I'll buy it. I wonder if you'll be able to sell the others. Have you spoken to anyone else?"

"No. You were the first. I'd like you to keep it to yourself until I give the word."

"Of course. I'll give you a warning though. You take away two men, the women are going to have something

to say about it; and with the doctor gone, and two
babies on the way, they're going to say more."

"Molly Kaapu's a passable midwife."

"I didn't say there weren't answers. I was just preparing you for the questions. You realize that you'll
have to come to an open debate on this."

"Yes."

"In that case, let's get our debate over now. If we
do mount this—this expedition, who commands it?"

"If I go, I command it."

"If you don't?"

"Then you're the natural choice."

"And you'd support me?"

"Man, I'll be putting three lives in your hands. My
wife's among them!"

Lorillard held out his hand. There was in his voice
a note of regret and reluctant admiration.

"A pity we didn't learn to trust each other sooner.
Still, that's water over the dam! I'll come down any
time you need me. I wish you luck. You may have
a bigger battle than you expect. . . ."

His first and his longest battle was with Sally herself. It went on for two days and a night of tears, angers, endearments, arguments, counter arguments and
finally outright rebellion. She would not go. They could
carry her to the boat by main force; she would leap
overboard rather than submit to this ignominious dis-
missal, this useless risk of four lives. There was no
proof, no way to prove yet, that the growth was ma-
lignant. Lorillard was obviously ill—yes. He has chosen
to go. Fine! He was a free agent, which was exactly
what she, herself, demanded to be. And what about
her duty to the community? There were two women
coming to term, who would need all the skill she commanded. There would be infants to be nursed through
the first dangerous months. More! How could she ex-

pect other married women to risk their husbands' lives on her single behalf? The whole idea was monstrous. She would not entertain it an instant longer.

Was it more monstrous—Thorkild brought her back, time and again, to the wintry argument—was it more unthinkable than to ask a lover, a husband, to contemplate for months on end an execution in cold blood, knowing all the while that a chance of salvation and cure had been thrown away? Which would she rather share with the group: the risks of an escape, or the long-drawn horror of a painful dissolution, that all would read as the paradigm of their own end? . . . Dilemma? Sure, there was dilemma; and every single man and woman was impaled on the horns. If someone didn't pull them off, they would all bleed to death. . . .

There was one more solution, simple and trenchant. He, Gunnar Thorkild, would take the boat and sail, single-handed, to Tubuai or the Austral Islands. This would put only one man at risk; and, for the grandson of Kaloni Kienga, the risk would be minimal. This, too, she rejected out of hand. It would leave the tribe without a head. Small as it was, it would disintegrate quickly into warring cells, because there was no one else strong enough to hold them together. He should not, he must not, discount the importance of his moral power, which was, in part, his own creation and, in part, an endowment from the people themselves. The moment he left, they would believe themselves betrayed. If he failed in his mission this anger would be turned on those who had caused it to be undertaken: Lorillard and herself. So, impasse again. Thorkild felt like a man drowning in a bath of feathers. He strode away in search of Adam Briggs.

Briggs, normally warm and forthcoming in discussion, declined this one altogether. When Thorkild pressed to know why, he explained with deliberate care:

". . . This is Charlie Kamakau all over again, except this time it's much more complicated. Everyone has a special case to plead. Let's start with something very simple: the boat. We all built it, we all own it. We use it for fishing, on which our food supply depends. If we give it up for a mercy mission, which may or may not succeed, our economy's at risk again. . . . Now, understand; this isn't me, Adam Briggs, talking. This is the argument you'll get—and it makes sense! Let's go further. After a lot of trouble and blood, you've finally got a community that's balanced off and settled down. That doesn't mean that everyone's whistling "Moonlight and Roses"; but they're settled and rubbing along. You pull two men out, and, if they don't come back, you've got two extra women. More trouble and more problems! . . . But—and this sounds rougher than I mean it to be—if Sally dies and Lorillard dies, there's grief and loss, but still a balance. Now let's talk about you. Deep down inside, we all know you're the man who got us together and brought us here. If things go wrong, we've always got someone to blame . . . you! On the other hand, you've done great things—like Franz Harsanyi said in his poem, hammered us and bullied us and held us together like a lynch pin holds a wheel. Pull out the lynch pin and we spin into madness. It'd be like the Pope marrying a nun! I was brought up in that kind of madness, chief. If you couldn't blame it on the blacks, you'd pin it on the Jews or the Catholics. . . . It's the scapegoat principle; and the theory is that your back's broad enough to carry us all. . . ." He broke off and gave a small, embarrassed laugh. "And after all that, will you still believe I bleed for Sally and you; and I'm sure as hell glad I don't have to decide the issue."

"So who does decide it?"

"The votes, I guess."

"Or I do?"

Briggs looked at him and shook his head mournfully from side to side. "No, chief. Don't ever try it! This time you lay out all the cards face up, and let the people decide."

"Sally's my wife!"

"And you're our chief."

"And I have to plead for Sally's life?"

"I hope not, chief. But if they force you to it, the pleading had better be mighty eloquent."

"And what about you, Adam?"

"I've got a wife too, chief. And I'm not about to put her to the vote."

"You mightn't have a wife, if Sally hadn't been here to help her."

"And you, chief, and the other woman! I don't forget any of that. I just say that today's a new day and I can't bet on tomorrow because the horses aren't posted yet."

"Well, that says it! . . . How's the foot?"

"Almost better, thanks."

"That makes it easier then."

"Makes what easier?"

"To ask you to nurse Sally when she gets sick, and knock her off when she can't take any more."

"You son of a bitch!"

"It's the name of the game, isn't it? All dogs together in a dog's world. . . . See you around, Mr. Briggs!"

Never in his life had he felt so resentful or so solitary. He went down to the beach, pushed out the boat, hoisted the sail and took it racing up and down the lagoon, in a frenzy of frustration and anger. He skirted the reef dangerously, slalomed through the coral heads, swung close inshore so that his bottom was inches off the sand, then out again, shouting and cursing at the top of his voice. A small group gathered on the beach to watch his antics. He ignored them. They would still be there, applauding the butchery, when Sally came to die and Lorillard and anyone else who could not tolerate the obscenity of the universe.

Carl Magnusson, you old pirate, I wish I were up there with you, looking down, like the Guatama himself, on this spinning wheel of creation. I wish I could talk to you now, Carl! I wish I could know what you know, see it plain, read it, calm and simple as a petroglyph . . . dancing figures on black volcanic stone. I'm going home, Carl. I'm beaching this thing and going home, but what do I do when I get there? Carl, I searched all my life for this place. You helped me find it. I knew, the moment I saw it, breached the magic portal, it was my place. Now they've defiled it for me. What do I do?

His anger spent at last, he beached the boat and walked up to the cascade to refresh himself. He found Yoko Nagamuna kneeling by the spring, washing taro tubers in preparation for the evening meal. She was swollen now and moved awkwardly, like a comical doll. Thorkild walked into the pool and began helping her wash the vegetables. He asked:

"How are you feeling, Yoko?"

"No bad. The baby's moving a lot. I'm retaining too much fluid, Sally says; but otherwise I'm O.K. . . . . I'll be glad when it's over."

"Hernan is treating you well?"

"Oh, sure, he treats everything well—sticks, stones, people. He just doesn't get excited about anything. Sometimes I could scream. He's as methodical as a clock. All I hear is the ticking. Sometimes I wish he'd beat me or shout at me just to break the monotony!"

"Don't knock the placid life, sweetheart! It's got a lot to recommend it."

"What's this I hear about Sally?"

"What did you hear?'

She gave him her old, mischief-maker smile. "No way to keep secrets in this place, chief. I heard Jenny and Adam quarrelling in their hut. Naturally I listened. That's how I knew about Sally and what you want to do. You've got problems! Seems we may all have a problem."

"So let's talk about your part of it, Yoko. . . . What do you think I should do?"

She laughed in his face. "Oh no, chief! Not that way! You come clean with me first! Are you canvassing votes, asking for advice, or counting heads?"

"Frankly, my little geisha, I'd like to break a few heads!"

"Mine too?"

"You know I never hit pregnant women or men with spectacles. . . . I'll rephrase the question. Two people need urgent medical attention. We want to get off the island. I want to mount an escape mission that involves risking their lives and two others, but which has a reasonable chance of success. Would you agree to it or not?"

"So you're counting heads and canvassing votes."

"If you like."

"Will you go or not?"

"Either way."

"If you go, I say no. If you stay, I'll vote for the mission."

"And I didn't think you cared!"

"I care for me, chief. Just me! . . . If you're around I'll know there's someone who will spare me half a thought sometimes. If you're not, then I'm just a little Nisei girl with a baby she doesn't want and a protector who'll dump her the first chance he gets. Also, if your wife's gone, there'll be a little more of you to share among the rest of us. . . . That's my answer."

"Anything to add to it?"

She gave him a sidelong conspirator's look. "I watched you out on the lagoon. You were like a crazy man. The others saw it too. They were worried you'd break the boat. I wasn't. I just wondered what put the burr under your tail. . . . Want to tell it to your little geisha? Or do you think I'd make mischief out of that too?"

"Would you, Yoko?"

"For what?" She tapped her swollen belly. "I've got all the mischief I can handle in there. What's bothering you, chief?"

He hoisted himself out of the pool and sat down on the bank beside her.

"Two things, Yoko. Sally refuses to go; and even if I managed to persuade her, I'm still in a jam. There are only three men I can count on to sail the boat with Lorillard: myself, Willy Kuhio, Adam Briggs. The fairest way to make the choice would be by drawing lots. Now, if I can't go, that leaves two. And this morning Adam made it clear he wanted no part of it. I can't understand why. I've always been closer to him than any of the other men, and he'd always told me the one thing he wanted to be was a great navigator. . . . This morning, though, he was like a stranger. At the end there were hard words, harder still to unsay. . . ."

"And you don't know why?"

"No. Do you?"

"You may not believe me." She was hesitant and subdued. "Then you'll think I'm making more trouble. . . . And I'm not, because I'm so damn tired, and I'm scared of having this baby, and I'm lonely because Hernan doesn't care, and even if I deserve it, that's hard to take now. . . ."

She began to weep, in an odd, whimpering way, like a hurt puppy. Thorkild reached out to touch her. She drew away.

"Don't do that, please! I'm messy and ugly and I don't want pity or kindness. I know I'm a bitch. I always have been. But now I'd like a little loving for a change. . . . Even Ellen's kind of loving would do!"

"Let's share the crumbs!" said Thorkild, with a grin. "Dry your eyes, geisha girl! Tell me how I fouled up with Adam."

"He feels you're a threat to him."

"For Pete's sake, why?"

"Oh dear! It's all so complicated—so goddamn silly. And yet it's not his fault. . . ."

"Go on!"

"Well, in the first place, he knew you were Jenny's big love. So long as you were there, he could get nowhere. You stepped back. It was like handing her to him on a plate. At first he was so much in love with her it didn't matter. Now he's had time to brood on it. Next, you started training young Mark Gilman, pushing Adam into second place. You'd promised, remember, to make him a great sailor like yourself. . . ."

"How do you know all this, Yoko?"

"I told you. I heard the argument. Some of it was ugly. There's something else too. When your grandfather was on board the *Frigate Bird*, he made some kind of prophecy that, one day, Jenny would bear a chief's son!"

"My God! I'd forgotten that."

"Jenny hasn't. Whether she believed it or not, it became a sort of party piece with her, like a schoolgirl's first visit to a fortune-teller: the tall dark man in her life and all that. At first she and Adam made a joke of it; but the joke's worn thin. So, today, when you talked to Adam and he saw that he might be chosen to go, and that Jenny would be left here on the island, and that you'd be without your wife . . . You see it all adds up, doesn't it?"

"To a bloody, stupid mess."

"And you can't, you mustn't try to clear it up," said Yoko Nagamuna. "Just leave it there and hope it will go away. But for everyone's sake you had to know. . . . And believe me, please! That's not mischief."

"I believe. Let's bury that one, shall we?"

"That's the trouble, chief. You can't bury anything. You plant it and it springs up one fine day—like armed men, or the trees that eat the temple. It's a hard lesson; I'm afraid I learned it too late in the day."

"You've taught me something," said Gunnar Thorkild quietly.

"What's that?"

"Some geisha look better without the wig and the war paint. . . . Thanks!"

There was another blow coming. The air was too still. To the east, the clouds were piling into a black solid front. Already the sea was rising and the seabirds flying home to their crannies on the high crater. It was the season, now, when the big ones built up: hurricanes that swept along Capricorn, clear to the coast of Queensland. There was no time now for arguments and recriminations. This was elemental danger. They had to secure themselves against it.

Thorkild hurried, shouting, about the camp. The boat, the canvas canoe and the raft must be hauled right to the upper edge of the camp. All tools and utensils must be stowed in the store hut. The hot coals from the fire pit should be collected in a pierced tin can and carried with dry firewood to a deep cranny in the rockface. Food and drink should be collected for use during the storm. They would all shelter in the huts under the lee of the cliff, away from falling coconuts that would split their skulls, or trees that a great wind could uproot like match sticks. If the huts went, they would take to the jungle and shelter with the folk on the terrace. Move, everybody! Move!

There was darkness first, as if a black pall had been laid over the land. Out of the darkness came lightning—great, jagged tongues licking down from the sky—and, an instant after, deafening thunderclaps whose echoes rolled over them like avenging chariots. Then the rain came, torrents of it, lashed and swept by the hurricane wind that spiralled around the solitary cone-shaped island in the middle of an empty sea.

The noise was deafening, the thunder, the relentless slam of the rain, the banshee howl of the wind, the pounding of the surf and the surge of the wash over the tidemark and into the compound itself. Tall palms were uprooted bodily. Others were snapped clean in two. The unsheltered hut collapsed like card houses, their thatch torn off, their walls shredded. Those under the lee of the cliff fared a little better. Their frames held; but the roofs sagged and leaked and their matting walls were breached, drenching the occupants with icy water. The track to the terraces became a muddy torrent, scouring through the camp, littering it with jungle debris. The only thing that held firm was the great log which was to be their boat; but they watched anxiously hour after hour as the sea wash and the mountain torrents surged around it.

Long after nightfall the storm was still raging, as if it were anchored forever like Prometheus to the mountain. There was no lightning now, only the incessant wail of the wind and the beat of the rain, and the ominous surge of the sea. The huts were awash. They could not light fires or torches. They ate what they could hold down, and voided themselves in corners, and then huddled together for comfort against the whirling nightmare.

Then, slowly, the nightmare passed. The wind dropped; the rain ceased; and the moon showed pale and grim through the ragged curtain of clouds. They walked out, shin-deep in water to survey the damage. The big log was still there. The canoe was awash, but intact. For the rest it was like the abomination of desolation. The storehouse had collapsed and water was pouring through the ruins. Five huts had been totally destroyed. Their taro patch was a quagmire; and half the precious coconut trees had been uprooted or snapped. The whole beach was a welter of white foam. The compound was a swamp, covered with nameless refuse.

For a while no one said anything. Some of the women were weeping quietly. The men were too stunned even to curse. They waited for Thorkild to give them a lead. He was nowhere to be seen. It was as if he had been whirled away by the wind or swallowed by the sea. A few moments later they saw him, crawling like some bedraggled animal, from under the wreckage of the store hut. He was carrying two bottles of bourbon, the last of Magnusson's stock, and a small can of diesel. He announced calmly:

"First we have a drink. Then you girls bail out the hollow in the big canoe. We'll use that for the fire pit. Bring down the coals and the firewood from the rock. Scrape up what food is left and we'll make something warm. Jump to it now! We start work at first light."

The clear, bright dawn made a mockery of the ruin that surrounded them; but Thorkild gave them no time

to bewail their misfortune. He sent Mark Gilman up
the mountain to see how the terrace folk had fared
and to solicit their help if they could spare it. Then he
harried his abject tribe like a slave driver. The standing huts must be drained, swept, thatched and walled.
The stores must be salvaged, dried, restacked and
placed under temporary cover. The compound must
be cleared of litter, the fire pit emptied and refuelled.
Fallen coconuts must be collected and stacked. The
canoe and the raft must be checked for damage and
damaged lashings renewed. The ruined huts should
be demolished. The logs of the fallen palms would
be useful. They should be sized and stacked. Later
they could be used to frame a stouter building. . . .
Someone should check the fish traps to see if any had
survived. Later, when the lagoon calmed down, they
should fish for their supper. . . . He would brook no
grumbling or complaints. The means of life were still
to hand. Worse things happened in earthquakes and
forest fires.

At midday, Mark Gilman came back with Willy
Kuhio and Simon Cohen. They brought meat, fresh
fruit and news. On the plateau they had fared better. The mountain walls had sheltered them from the
main force of the wind. The houses had held, although the roofs had leaked badly. The main damage
was to the garden plots themselves, where newly
opened topsoil had been washed away. Lorillard was
working now, with the women, to replace the lost soil
and stake up the young plants. Willy and Simon would
stay down as long as they were needed. The early inhabitants must have known something, settling up
there instead of on the beach. By nightfall the site
was habitable again, although they would have to
share sleeping quarters until the new huts were built.

"And this time," said Thorkild grimly, "we'll plan

and build for permanence. It's clear we're going to be here for a long time yet."

"But I thought . . ." Jenny blurted out the words and then stopped in mid-sentence. The others sat silent, attentive only to their food.

"Yes, Jenny?"

"Nothing."

"As I was saying," Thorkild went on calmly, "we'll need to build more comfortably and permanently. The big boat will take a long time to finish. I did discuss with some of you—and it is clear that they have discussed it with others—the possibility of sending out the small boat, with a picked crew, to get our sick people back to civilization and send a rescue party for the rest of us. This project obviously does not recommend itself to you. My wife, for example, may be seriously ill; but she simply refuses to go, because she feels the community needs her, and she cannot take the responsibility for breaking up family groups. This is her decision. I disagree with it. I cannot change it. Peter Lorillard also is failing; but without facilities neither an adequate diagnosis nor adequate treatment can be offered to him. He would be prepared to risk a rescue bid, but he would in no way insist on it. I, too, would be prepared to risk it, even single-handed; but it has been made clear to me that the community has claims on me which it is not prepared to waive. So that question is closed, and we are back to our normal life here. . . ." No one spoke. He went on in the same detached fashion. "I'd suggest we floor the houses this time, frame them more strongly, make gable roofs with thicker thatch and provide more space for family groups. If it finally appears that Peter Lorillard is suffering from filariasis, which is a parasitic disease carried by mosquitoes, then I am going to insist that we make different arrangements for farming the terrace. We'll take short turns working up there, and then retire to the shore where the sea breezes keep the mosquitoes away. . . ."

"May I ask a question, chief?" It was Ellen Ching who spoke, crisp and detached as always.

"Certainly."

"It's for your wife. Sally, what is the prognosis for a case of filariasis?"

"Prolonged exposure and continued deposit of the parasites cause permanent blocking of lymph glands and ultimately the swollen condition which is called elephantiasis. The patient becomes permanently debilitated and disabled."

"And in the case of cancer of the breast?"

"Without mastectomy and postoperative treatment, death."

"Thank you. A question for you, chief. What are the chances of a small boat with a skilled crew making a safe arrival?"

"With a skilled crew, much better than fifty-fifty."

"Thank you. That's all I wanted to know."

"Since we're not all present," said Gunnar Thorkild firmly, "I don't think we should discuss that question any further."

"I agree." Ellen Ching was precise and persistent. "But we do have a council appointed to represent our views to the chief and offer him advice. I think it's time the council started doing its job. . . . In these circumstances it's shameful to expect one man to carry the can for all of us."

"We've lost one member," Briggs reminded them. "Charlie Kamakau."

"We'll co-opt another," said Ellen Ching. "And since all this can only embarrass Sally and the chief, I suggest we defer it until tomorrow. I'll go up to the terrace and talk with Peter Lorillard and Martha. Then we'll arrange a full meeting. Agreed?"

"Hold it!" Thorkild scrambled slowly to his feet. "Boys and girls, one and all. Let me tell you something. I'm tired! I've nursed your sick and buried your dead and showed you how to catch fish, build houses, eat, sleep and swing your partners. And now I'm so damn tired, you could stop the world and toss me off and I wouldn't give a hoot in hell. So now, if you don't mind, I'm going to take a walk with my wife."

He pulled Sally to her feet and left them, shocked and gape-mouthed, staring at each other across the fire pit.

They walked down to the far end of the beach, picking their way cautiously over fallen trees and torn palm fronds and tangled roots and all the detritus of the storm. They found a dry rock and perched themselves on it, looking out over the waste of white water to the scatter of stars and galaxies. Sally said lighty;

"How long did you work on your speech, Professor?"

"No time at all. It came straight from the heart."

"It sounded to me like another of your political pieces. . . ."

"It was a long night and a long day; and I'm human too."

"Then why did you have to bring me into the argument?"

"Because, like it or not, you're a large part of the argument."

"It wasn't fair."

"So you tell me what's fair, sweetheart! They'll sleep dry and fed tonight because I drove 'em. They'll talk their heads off because I made sure they'd have leisure to do it, while I'm too damned tired even to spit."

"Gunnar?"

"What?"

"That storm . . ."

"Yes?"

"If we'd been out at sea, you and I, in the small boat, would we have survived?"

"We could have, yes."

"If it had been Willy or Peter instead of you?"

"Yes, again."

"Can you imagine what it must have been like out there tonight?"

"I know what it was like. I've been there, more than once."

"And you'd still want me to go?"

"Want it? No. Send you, yes. Because you'd still have a chance, a ticket in the lottery. Stay here and you've got no hope, no chance at all."

"But I've still got some life with you."

"And death at my hands afterwards."

"Is that what you're afraid of, Gunnar? Would you rather it were the sea that sent me off than you, my lover, my husband? Would that be easier for you?"

"No. One way I'd know you had left, loving me. The other even if you survived and were cured, I'd never be sure. You might hate me for the rest of my days; but still . . ."

"What?"

"If you were alive and well, I think I could bear it."

"You were such a light man once. I loved you that way. Now I hardly seem to know you."

"Because I care so much?"

"Because you care too much. None of us is that precious."

"You are, to me."

"But suppose I want the other way, the easy, quiet way, the pinprick while I sleep and the long, quiet darkness. What then? You gave Carl what he wanted. Would you refuse it to me?"

"You refused it to Charlie Kamakau. You said, and I remember it very clearly, 'I won't do it because I swore to cure, not to harm.' "

"That was Charlie's life. This is mine. I dispose of it as I wish."

"No, you're asking me to dispose of it."

"Because, don't you see, we're one person. . . . It may never happen. All I want to know is that if it does, we're agreed. Then I can live quietly and happily —very happily, my love! Gunnar, why are you fighting me so hard on this point?"

"First, because you're excluding all other possibilities, and I think that's wrong."

"But if I choose to do that?"

"Then we're two people again, not one. Second reason: what you're asking me to do has consequences for everyone else. Long consequences. I can't measure them all, but I can't commit to them as lightly as you think."

"I don't care about other people. It's me! My life! My body that suffers!"

"And when you are gone, my sweet—however you go—I am still here, people are still here, and the law and custom they live by still obtains. Look! If there is no other way of sparing you intolerable suffering, then, for me and for them, a different situation exists. The essence of the act hasn't changed, but the circumstances and the consequences have. The decision is ad hoc, made under extremity. This way it's a clear collusion; it's precedent; it says, 'Yes, a killing is arranged. Other killings can be arranged.' Don't you see the enormity of that?"

"All I can see . . ." Her voice was like a winter wind, cold and distant. "I've asked you to promise me an act of love, if and when I need it. You've refused."

"I've offered you a chance of life. You've refused it. You make death a test of love!"

"And you've failed the test. Good night, Gunnar."

"I'll walk you back—otherwise you'll break a leg."

"I'd like to sleep alone tonight."

"Sorry, I can't oblige you." Even in this extremity, he found still a hint of humour. "We've twelve people in four huts. You'll have the women for company."

As they passed the fire pit he fell back to say good night to Molly Kaapu, who was still there chatting to Ellen Ching and Franz Harsanyi. Molly gave him a long, searching look and asked, in the old language:

"That shark still chasing you, Kaloni?"

"It's just bitten my arm off, Molly."

Franz Harsanyi, the linguist, thought it was a joke and capped it with another.

"So long as it didn't get your *hua hua* you're in good shape, chief!"

"We saved some whiskey for you," said Ellen Ching. "You look as though you need it!'

ELEVEN

EARLY THE NEXT MORNING ELLEN CHING WENT up, alone, to the terrace to speak with Lorillard and Martha Gilman and arrange for a meeting of the council. She hoped that they would agree to co-opt Willy Kuhio, so that the members would then comprise two women, Martha and Ellen, and three men, Franz, Adam Briggs and Willy. Thorkild made no comment on the proposal. He was determined that, henceforth, he would force them, by silence, to propose solutions for their own problems, leaving him free to dispose of matters in dispute and then only at their common instance.

Now that he had felt the full burden of command, seen all the strategies by which even friends and lovers sought to evade responsibility and reduce their personal risks at the expense of others, he was deeply disillusioned. He remembered vividly, as if it were yester-

day, Flanagan sitting in his wheelchair, shaking as if
with the ague and thrusting the truth at him. ". . . The
mana will come; but you'll suffer for it. People will
lean on you and you will fall under their weight. They
will lift you up and you will try to flee them, but they
will not let you escape. What you do then, God only
knows. And you'll die begging Him to tell you; or
you'll live, begging Him to die, because the burden is
intolerable. . . ."

Flanagan's prediction was fulfilled. The *mana* was
not enough. The burden was intolerable. They would
never, never let him escape it. But in one important
particular, Flanagan was wrong. Gunnar Thorkild had
no God to call on; the people, with the exception of
Willy and Eva, had none either. They relied, as he did,
on a tangle of traditions, legends, unexamined moralities, vague ethics, gut religion and confused philoso-
phies. He himself had invoked them all and found
them crumbled to powder in his hand, like cerecloths
from an ancient tomb.

This was the real root of his quarrel with Sally. He
had no certain standing ground to share with her, no
authority to invoke, no interest that could, demonstra-
bly, transcend her own, no dream, dogma or example
that would give meaning to her suffering. He had failed
her. He would in the end fail them all. He was an
empty man. His island paradise was exactly what
Franz Harsanyi had called it—a piece of dreck, fished
up from the ocean floor.

While the others were erecting the new store hut,
he worked alone, squaring off fallen palm trunks, grading and stacking them for use as beams and pillars for
new dwelling places. This time, he thought, with bitter humour, there should be a chief's house, separate
from the rest, more imposing, so that the emptiness
that dwelt in it might be less evident. There should be

a platform in front, from which comands and edicts could be proclaimed, and judgment made to sound more pompous. He might even go back to ceremonial costume, a cloak and headdress of bird feathers, a breastplate of shells. . . . As he toyed with these sardonic fantasies, Mark Gilman came calling in triumph:

"I found it, chief! I found it!"

"What did you find, Mark?"

"My paddle. . . . I thought it had been washed away, but I found it over there."

"I'm glad. That's a good omen!"

"Chief . . ."

"What?"

"Last night, all through the storm, I kept asking myself what I would have done if I'd been caught outside in the open sea."

"And?"

"I worked it out. The boat would still float. Even if it's full of water, with people in it, it doesn't sink. So, as long as you could stay with it, keep it from capsizing or turning turtle, you'd still survive, wouldn't you?"

"Sure. A craft like that is buoyant as a cork. It's made for surfing the big rollers. In a confused sea, of course, you've got to keep working, paddling to keep her head up. If it's a long blow you have to rest two and work two—although there's precious little rest for anyone."

"That's what I was getting to: the ones that are resting. If we had lashings or kick straps or something to hold them steady while they rested, would that make sense?"

"It could, yes. Got any ideas?"

"Some. I thought I'd ask you first."

"Go to it, then. See what you can work out."

"Are we . . . are we really going to try for it, chief?"

"I don't know, Mark. I'm waiting for the council to decide."

"Peter wants to try. My mother agrees with him. I'd like to go too."

"That's all up to the council, Mark."

"Why are you leaving it to them? You never did before. You're still the chief, aren't you?"

"Yes. I'm still the chief."

"Then why. . . ?"

"Sit down, Mark."

They sat together on the fallen trunk and Thorkild laid out his answer, phrase by uncertain phrase.

"It isn't easy to explain, Mark. Remember what I told you on the way to the high place. A chief has to act, even though he's not sure he's doing the right thing. . . . Well, so far, that's what I've done. I've made mistakes; but the consequences haven't been too disastrous. . . . However, this decision is the biggest yet. Lives are involved; big risks. I'm tired. I'm confused—less certain of myself than I've ever been in my life. I want help. I need advice. It's the council's job to give it to me." He gave a small, unsteady laugh and rumpled the boy's hair. "I guess I need a bit more than that."

"What, chief?"

"The impossible, I'm afraid. Thunder and lightning and a voice out of the cloud saying, 'This is the law! This is right! Do it and you are saved!' Even a human voice would help. . . . Yes, I'd settle for one human voice that said, 'Believe and go forward.' Unfortunately people don't act like that. They want signs and wonders and the right to kill the wonder-worker when he fails them."

"That's not fair!"

"It's life, Mark."

"Why is Sally angry with you? She is, I can see it."

"That's our business, Mark."

"So you've got no one."

"Let's say I'm sailing single-handed for a while. Sometimes that's necessary. Your mother had to do it for a long time. Never forget those old men on the mountain, Mark. They had to earn that place: the peace, the silence, the splendour. . . . Run along now. They need help back there."

"Not yet!" He stood up, set and stubborn, challenging Thorkild. "You told me I'd earned my place as a man."

"You have."

"Then I have a right to speak and be heard."

"The same as anyone else."

"Thanks. That's all I wanted to know."

"Mark?"

"Yes?"

"Think well before you speak."

"I don't have to think. I heard the voice. I know what it meant. I'll get back to work."

He strode off, holding the paddle before him like a banner. Thorkild stared after him, frowning. The boy was strange seed. He had had strange nurture. How would he spring up—a fighter, armed and dangerous, or a twisted tree that twined its roots about the foundations of the temple and, in the end, toppled it to ruin?

A short time after the boy had left, Jenny came, bringing fresh food and coconut milk for his midday meal. Everyone was eating on the run, she said. They wanted to have the store hut finished by nightfall. Ellen Ching was back. Willy Kuhio had been co-opted to the council, which would meet tomorrow on the terrace, so as not to interrupt the work of reconstructing. The councillors would stay the night on the mountain and return on the following day to convey their recommendations to the chief and hold a full tribal meeting afterwards. They wanted to do things very formally this time. There were deep divisions of opinion. They wanted all to have the opportunity to represent their private views. . . . If Thorkild didn't mind, she'd sit and share the meal with him. She'd brought enough for two. She'd like to talk to him, seriously. Why not? Everyone else did.

"I know, prof. . . . They talk so much I could scream."

"It's the tribal way, girl. Small island. Small people . . . every subject is talked dry."

"Even so! I was damned glad you sounded off last night. You were dead on your feet; but nobody seemed to notice."

"Relax, kid!"

"Don't call me kid! I'm a married woman, remember?"

"I'm sorry. I keep thinking of the little girl I picked off Sunset Beach."

"I'm trying to forget her."

"What did you want to talk about?"

"Adam and me."

"No!"

"Adam and you, then. He told me what happened. We had a blazing row about it."

"I heard."

"Everybody heard. That's why you've got this crisis on your hands. Anyway, he said there was no way he'd go on this expedition. He was just married. He wanted to stay on the island. I told him that, if he didn't at least put his name up, I'd never respect him again."

"I'm sorry you did that, Jenny."

"So was I, afterwards."

"Did you tell him so?"

"Yes. But he was all closed up, has been ever since."

"You challenged his manhood."

"Didn't you?"

"No. He and I disagreed about how much he owed the group and how much he owed to you and to himself."

"That's the argument you had with Sally, isn't it? . . . Oh, don't look so surprised! That's all over the camp too. I heard Molly Kaapu arguing with Sally, both shouting at each other. . . . It's a good thing you're out of the way. Where's it all going to end? Nothing can ever be the same after this—for any of us!"

"Jenny, you know about putting things together again. You must do that with Adam."

"I've tried."

"Try again, harder and for as long as it takes."

"He won't listen. He says . . ."

"Says what, Jenny?"

"He says there's a ghost in our bed."

"There's a ghost in everyone's bed, Jenny. Mostly they're dreams we've cherished too long, hopes we've remembered. Follies we'd like to have enjoyed. Only loving will chase them out."

"It takes two to make a loving."

"Never believe it. . . . Always there's the giver and the taker . . . which is why millionaires marry B girls and the B girls become patrons of starveling poets."

"You're crazy, prof!"

"Nutty as a fruitcake, girl. Thanks for lunch. I've got work to do."

By noon the next day the councillors were back, bringing with them the rest of the terrace folk: Lorillard, Martha Gilman, Barbara Kamakau and Eva

Kuhio. Lorillard strolled down to the beach with Thorkild. He was uneasy and dispirited.

". . . We talked very late last night, and again for an hour this morning. It was a rough-and-tumble debate; and there were some pretty bitter exchanges. I'm still not sure how we should handle things today. Strictly speaking, I suppose, the council should inform you of its resolutions and then you open them for discussion in the full assembly. On the other hand, because people are sensitive and discouraged just now, we want to avoid suspicion of secret dealing—especially where you're concerned."

"The simplest way"—Thorkild was firm about it —"is to have a full assembly. The spokesman for the council puts its views publicly to me and to the group. Then we throw the discussion open, as we did before."

"That's fine." Lorillard hesitated. "But frankly, Thorkild, we're worried about you. You've been under strain. You're personally involved, because of Sally. We don't want another blowup, like the one we had over Charlie Kamakau."

"There'll be no fireworks," said Thorkild quietly.

"I have to warn you, Sally will be dragged into the argument."

"Then she'll answer for herself."

"As bad as that?"

"I'm afraid so."

"In that case, I'd better tell you . . ."

"Don't tell me anything." Thorkild cut him off abruptly. "Let's play it straight down the line."

"One more word. This isn't a war game. They'll be using live ammunition."

"So be it," said Gunnar Thorkild heavily. "Let's get started."

It was a somber group that gathered on the compound. Thorkild and Molly Kaapu sat together, with

Lorillard and the members of the council opposite them and the rest of the tribe ranged on either side. Simply, and without rhetoric, Thorkild opened the meeting and called Lorillard to address it. Lorillard said:

"I am asked to act as spokesman for the council which you elected. The chief has asked that we report to him and to you at the same time. He has not heard—in fact he has refused to hear—any of the things I am about to tell you now. I hope that is clear to everyone. . . . Now, I want to call to you the principles by which we agreed to live on this island: our labour and the fruits of our labour would be a common trust for a common good; decisions made by the chief after consultation with his councillors or with the full assembly would be binding on us all; we agreed to obey them and . . ." He paused a moment to emphasize the point. ". . . and we agreed to enforce obedience on one another. Do you agree with that summary?"

They agreed. The formality pleased them. It made them feel safe and important. They were the final arbiters of tribal destiny. Lorillard went on:

"Now, at a critical moment in our lives, we have to interpret those principles, apply them to very special circumstances. We have to do justice, the best for the most. Now, because I do not wish even to appear to plead a case, I am handing over at this point to Ellen Ching. . . ."

She rose to face them, cool and formidable.

"We have two people who may be very seriously ill, and to whom we can offer no hope of treatment. The suggestion is that we send them out in our small boat with two other crew, so that they can sail to the nearest inhabited island and send back a rescue party. We've discussed this proposal in council and we recommend it to the chief and to you. There is, however, a problem. Peter Lorillard is ready to go. Sally refuses. We, the council, say that Sally must be forced to go— for her own good and the good of the rest of us. Another matter: there is disagreement on who should make up the rest of the crew and how they should be chosen. Franz Harsanyi will talk to you about this. . . ."

Franz was less formal but far more emphatic.

". . . Here's the problem. Sally refuses to go. She says she's got a right to dispose of her own self. We say, if she stays, it's not for her good or ours; and she, like the rest of us, agreed that obedience should be enforced. Next: who's the crew? We've got Lorillard, who's a good sailor, Mark Gilman, who's a good navigator, Willy Kuhio, Adam Briggs and the chief himself. The chief's ready to go single-handed. Some of us think he's more needed here. Willy and Adam are married. They're naturally concerned for their wives, if anything happens to them. Adam doesn't want to go. He'd be happy to end his days in this place. . . . On the other hand, he made the same promise as we all did—common labour for a common good. . . . Now that's as honest as I can make it. That's as far as the council could get. We agree with the first principles. We want the project to work. How do we make it work so that it's fair to everyone? From here on, we'd like to hear your opinions."

Mark Gilman stood in his place. "May I be heard, please, chief?"

"You may."

He stood for a long moment in silence, surveying them with so plain a contempt that it shocked them all. Then he began to speak, vividly, passionately, like some young Baptist with the dust of the desert still on him.

". . . Last night, while you all slept, I went up to the high place. I sat among the dead men, watching

the stars. I saw the sun rise this morning. There is a
voice that speaks up there. The chief has heard it. So
have I. I heard it again last night and again at sunrise. It told me about every one of you. It told me to
speak to you all and tell you the terrible things you
are doing to each other. You began so well. You were
kind. You worked together. You shared the things
you grew and the fish you caught. You laughed and
you sang and you put flowers on the graves. . . . Even
when you were angry you made peace afterwards.
Now look at you! Your faces are like stone. Even the
skulls of the dead men are not so frightening. You,
Mother! Your husband is sick, and I never see you
smile at him or say a kind word. You, Adam Briggs!
You were once a friend to the chief and to his grandfather, Kaloni. Now you're too angry to look at him
because you're afraid he may be the ghost in your
bed. Oh yes, I know about the ghost! I went up where
ghosts should be; and there are none—only the voice.
You, Sally? You are not afraid of dying. Oh no! You're
afraid of the sea, and you would rather ask your
man to kill you than risk yourself in a small boat on
the great water. . . . You do evil—all of you. You
spread it like a sickness to everyone else. You wanted
to meet today not to put things together, but to pull
them to pieces, make a pile of rubbish and then command the chief to take it away for you. . . . You want
everything for nothing. You want to stay, you want
to go. But each of you wants the next one to pay the
price. . . . I look at you and I'm afraid, because I see
death in your eyes. But the voice told me . . . the
voice . . ."

He gave a high choking cry and crumpled in the
sand, writhing and moaning. Thorkild went to him,
picked him up and carried him across the compound

to his own hut. Sally and Martha hurried after him; he ordered them back.

"Tell Lorillard to take the chair and finish the meeting."

"But Mark's sick." It was Martha's anguished cry.

"No! We're the sick ones. He's cured."

A long time afterwards, when the boy was sleeping quietly, Thorkild went back to the compound. They were still seated as he had left them, eyes downcast, murmuring quietly among themselves. They fell silent at his approach. Then, when he was seated, Adam Briggs said respectfully:

"Chief, our people ask me to put certain questions to you."

"Go ahead."

"Did you send Mark Gilman to the high place?"

"No."

"Did you know he was going?"

"No. Had I known, I should have forbidden it."

"Did you know that he intended to speak at this meeting?"

"Yes."

"Did you suggest what he should say or coach him in any fashion?"

"No."

"What, then, in your view, prompted his words?"

"My view can have no relevance at this time."

"We would, nevertheless, be grateful if you would express it."

"I think," said Thorkild deliberately, "I think he may have had what the old Greek healers used to call the experience of God. I have no words to express it more clearly, and none at all to explain it."

"You believe that he heard what he called the voice?"

"I believe that he believes he heard it."

"Thank you, chief. I can now tell you that decisions have been taken and we should like you to ratify them. We will send the small boat. Sally and Peter will go. I'll be crewman. We'd like Mark Gillman as navigator."

"And you are all agreed?"

"Seems we couldn't do anything else," said Eva Kuhio. "We heard truth today from that small one— like one of the prophets shouting over the land of Israel."

"There are other matters." Lorillard took the weight off her words. "We'll need training."

"We'll begin it tomorrow," said Thorkild. "I'll work with the men, each morning and also after dark. I'll have you ready in a week."

"If we don't make it," said Adam Briggs carefully, "there will be two wives and a child to be cared for."

"They'll be cherished," said Thorkild. "And when we, at some later stage, finish the big boat and go home, they'll be cared for. I have funds. I will have my interest on the publication of this voyage. Those proceeds will be reserved for the womenfolk and the children. Anything else?"

"My boy," asked Martha Gilman. "Is he . . . is he all right?"

"Yes. But you shouldn't speak to him about what happened. None of you should."

"Can you explain why?" There was a hint of malice in Simon Cohen's question.

"Put it this way," Thorkild answered him without hesitation. "You're a musician. Whom do you ask to explain the music—the flute or the man who blows it?"

When the evening meal was over he walked with Sally to the cascade and they sat dangling their feet in the cool moonlit water. Sally was still distant and

constrained, but at least no longer hostile. Their talk
was halting and shy, as if they had just met after a
long sojourn apart. Finally she told him:

"Gunnar, I've got a confession to make."

"Forget it, sweetheart."

"No. I must tell you. Those questions Adam Briggs
put to you . . . It was I who prompted them."

"The important thing is whether you believed the
answers."

"Yes. But they didn't tell me anything."

"They told all I know. Mark went to the high place
without my knowledge. He came back and made that
extraordinary speech."

"Which was your speech really, my love. All the
things I've ever heard you say, about the old ways,
the good ways . . . and how we spoil them."

"I didn't prompt him."

"No—but you've been educating him, conditioning
him for weeks and months. Your print is on him now
—for always." She gave a little shrug of defeat. "Not
that it matters. The magic worked. God spoke through
the child. The high chief was vindicated and restored
to power."

"Do you really believe that's what I tried to do?"

"It's what happened; and it's what you wanted to
happen."

"Then why did you decide to go?"

"Because I was moved and convinced. . . . That's
the real mystery, isn't it? Tell me something, Gunnar."

"What?"

"If and when we get through, if and when you're
taken off the island, what about us?"

"On my part, my love, there's no question. We're
married. I love you. . . . We go on together."

"Where?"

"You name it. I'll be there."

"You could find me disfigured—and still sick."

"Then I'll care for you."

"You still don't see it, do you?"

"All I see is that I love you, Sally."

"But not enough to give me what I wanted! . . . What you thought I needed, yes! What you thought was right, yes! You broke me to that. Not with malice, with love! But you broke me, just the same."

"And now you hate me."

"I wish I could. I love you, Gunnar, but if I stayed with you now, I'd be fighting you for the rest of my days."

"Is this what happened with Magnusson?"

"What do you mean?"

"You love the high man—until you find you can't bend him."

"Put it that way, yes!"

"I'm sorry you were disappointed."

"You can hate me now."

"No. I'm too grateful for the good times."

"That's my Gunnar! The wind comes and the house blows down. You grin and start building again, and again. . . ."

"What else is there to do?"

"What else indeed! . . . Don't come with me! I'd like to be alone for a while."

Casual, yet watchful as loungers on an alley corner, the men were waiting for him by the big canoe. Hernan Castillo was trying out a new adze, the others watching as he hacked steadily into the belly of the hardwood log. He looked up as Thorkild approached and tossed him the tool.

"Take a look at that blade, chief. Best I've done so far."

Thorkild examined it with elaborate care and tested it on the bow of the canoe.

"Good! How long did that take?"

"About three weeks. . . . Probably the last one I'll make, eh, chief?"

An instant before he spoke, Thorkild saw the snare. He forced a smile and said:

"A month or two from now, it'll be worth a thousand dollars in Honolulu."

"I'll be rich." Castillo laughed. "How many of these damn things have I made?"

"Small reminder." It was easier to smile now. "In the contract, all artifacts came under the head of exploitable material. Profits therefore belong to the expedition organizers."

"What about this baby?" Simon Cohen slapped the hull with his hand. "I've spent so much sweat on her. I kind of hate to leave her."

"Why leave her?" asked Franz Harsanyi. "Heyerdahl shipped a whole raft back to Oslo for a museum piece."

"Hard to believe," said Tioto. "We could be home so soon. Eva Kuhio was right. It's the bad things that make you reach out for the better ones. If our people hadn't fallen sick we'd have been content to wait here until this big baby was finished."

Adam Briggs, who had been standing apart, moved into the talk. "How's the boy, chief?"

"He's fine."

"I hope so. If he's navigator, we're going to have to rely on his memory and his figuring."

"You'll see him tested every day while we're training. And you'll have Peter Lorillard for a backup. You'll find that navigation isn't the biggest problem; it's the boat-handling and the care you take of yourselves."

"Sally's still hating the whole idea."

"Once she's at sea, and committed with the rest of you, she'll measure up to the need."

"I know; but it'll be a rough ride for her."

"It'll be rough for all of us." The snare was visible again. "You'll be logging progress every day. We'll just be waiting."

"I bought the package, chief," said Adam Briggs with thin humour. "You don't have to sell it anymore."

"Don't push me, Mr. Briggs!" Thorkild was filled with a sudden, cold anger. "You bought a package which means hope for everyone—you included."

"We take the risk, chief." Briggs was very calm. "You get the hope."

"Do you want to pull out?"

"No."

"Then shut up, Adam! When my wife leaves with you, she's sailing out of my life; because I've forced her to take a chance for her own survival. So, if we're talking prices, don't forget I'm picking up my share of the tab."

"I didn't know."

"You do now." He faced them, a tight, hard man, bayed at last into a corner from which he must fight his way out. "You all know it! You want my job? Come, take it. You think you can do it better; you're welcome to try, any time! There's just so much of Gunnar Thorkild to spend and I've spent it all. You don't like what Daddy bought you? Too bad! Go earn your own dollars and buy your own hamburgers. But you hear me now, because it's the last time I'll say it. So long as you live on Thorkild's Island, you keep your goddam mouths shut and do as you're goddam told! . . . See you at sunrise for sea trials, Mr. Briggs!"

He turned on his heel and left them. Simon Cohen gave a long whistle of surprise.

"Well! How about that? You prick us and we do bleed. . . . My God, how we bleed!"

Adam Briggs rounded on him savagely. "One more word from you, boy, and I'll break your neck. That's a bigger man than you'll ever be in a million years."

"He wants to be dictator."

"You've got it wrong," said Franz Harsanyi. "That's what we want. We're just not honest enough to admit it."

Every morning at sunrise, every night at sunset, fair sea or foul, he took them out, working them until they could read every shift of the wind, anticipate every quirk of the small craft. He studied their motions as they paddled, taught them the rhythm of work and rest, the trick of relieving themselves from a tiny moving craft, and how to catch fish and save them from the predators that came snapping after the catch. He showed them how to stow food and conserve water and refill their gourds from the rain showers.

Several times, with bullying and cajoling, he forced Sally to go out, to accustom her to the motion and to the panic solitude of the big sea. Always at the back of his mind was the hope that, once the enterprise had become measurable in her mind, once the immensity of sea space and sky had lost its terror, she would relent and turn to him again. But before the week was out, the hope had faded and he resigned himself to his winter solitude.

Finally, when he judged them as ready as they would ever be, he ordered every lashing and fixing on the boat renewed and tested, new tackle to be prepared, food, fresh and dry, to be made ready, and water gourds filled and sealed. He made his last entries in the log of the *Frigate Bird,* sewed it into a piece of canvas, wrapped it again in matting, sealed the matting with sap from the breadfruit tree, and consigned it to the care of Peter Lorillard. It was, as Lorillard remarked, like handing over the proceedings of a lifetime, the tablets of a people forgotten by history.

Then, moved by an impulse of primitive piety, he suggested that the voyagers might like to go up with him to the high place. Sally refused. Lorillard declined with an apology. He wanted to save his strength. Adam Briggs said with a smile:

"No, thanks, chief. That's your past, not mine. . . . I hope you understand."

"I do."

"Talk to me a minute?"

"Sure."

"You and I, we got away from each other somehow. I'd like us to be friends again."

"So would I. . . ."

"I want to thank you for what you've taught me. You'll never know what it means to a man whose ancestors came over in the holds of slave ships, whose boyhood was spent in a shantytown. . . . I'm sorry about you and Sally."

"No way to mend it, Adam."

"We'll get her home safe."

"I know you will."

"If we don't . . ."

"Never think it."

"Let's not kid each other, chief. I know the odds are good; but the risks are big. So, if we don't make it, look after my Jenny. . . . I mean, I know you'll look after everyone, but for her, a special care, eh? I don't want her drifting about, like she did in the old days, belonging to no one."

"I understand."

"I guess you do." He gave a small embarrassed laugh. "It's funny. Last night we were talking about you. Jenny said you were like old Father Noah, with all his family in the ark. . . . We were the birds he was sending out to find dry land again. I didn't like to mention that it was the raven that didn't come back. . . . Tell me something, chief."

"What?"

"Suppose it all works out fine, and a few weeks from now the Navy is standing out there off the reef. . . . Will you be glad or sad?"

"I'll be glad."

"And you wouldn't want to stay here?"

"No."

"Because of Sally?"

"Partly. . . . Partly because of what I've learned in these last few months. I don't have any land hunger. So possession, privacy, dominion, for their own sake, don't interest me. The past, the history, the legends— those things, yes. They represented a part of my identity, which I had to grasp and hold, otherwise I'd be incomplete all my life. Well, I've got it now. I've lived it from the beginning to the end, which is up there on the high place. The rest: the struggle to survive, organize, hold together . . . that was a challenge we met, a triumph for which we've paid quite dearly. We've had a lot of casualties. None of us will ever be quite the same again. . . . But we've discovered one big truth. The earthly paradise is our oldest and biggest illusion. Even if it existed, we'd foul it up. However low the fruit hangs, we'll always cry for the one that's out of reach. . . . So make a good passage, Mr. Briggs. I'm ready to go home and snuff the incense of praise and take the Chair and tenure. Amen!"

Peter André Lorillard made another kind of valediction. He caught fish in the lagoon. He made a fire on the beach and asked Thorkild to join him and Martha and Mark in a private meal together. They were a kind of family, he said, with an oddly touching simplicity, closer now, perhaps, than they had ever been. Now that he and Mark had worked together, they respected each other. Mark was, in fact, a better navigator than he himself had ever been. They were a good team—he stumbled over the trite collegiate phrases—a good team with a good chance at the finals. They'd had a good coach too. . . . He relaxed a little then and went on:

". . . When we get back, I'll be required to make a full report to the Navy, and of course the press will be shouting for the story. I want you to know, Thorkild, you'll have nothing but good words from me. It's little enough, God knows! It's all I've got to offer. I'm something of a straw man, as you knew from the beginning —as Martha here has found to her cost."

"Stop it, Peter!" Martha was embarrassed for him. "You write yourself down all the time! You're not fair to either of us!"

"Let me tell you what I see," said Thorkild. "A man who slaved his guts out on a hillside to feed a tribe; a sick man who's about to embark on a rescue mission with his own life at risk. If there was a straw man, he was burned a long while ago."

Lorillard was silent for a moment, then he said gravely, "We're all faced with the risk. So I can say this plainly: If anything happens to me, Martha will be left as she was before, with a child to bring up alone. . . ."

"If anything happens to you"—Thorkild gave him a crooked, sidelong grin—"Martha and the child won't be alone. They'll be here with the rest of us for a long time."

"How long, chief?" asked Mark Gilman.

"Hard to say, Mark. When you go, we've lost three men and a woman. If we were stuck here, we'd still have to feed ourselves. It would take much longer to finish the big boat. . . . I haven't made too much of this with the others; but in my own mind, I've had to face it."

"I simply refuse to think about it," said Martha firmly. "We'll be home in a few weeks. I'll have my baby in hospital. Mark will be back at school. Peter will get his divorce, and ask for a posting to Honolulu. It's all settled and it's going to happen!"

"You shouldn't talk like that, Mother." Mark Gilman frowned unhappily. "You can't make things happen. You just float with them. That's what the chief says: don't fight the wind, use it. The voice says it too: open yourself and let me be heard. . . . You want to arrange everything and everybody. That's what makes you unhappy. . . ."

"How you do go on! I keep telling you, I'm not unhappy."

"But you do push things," said Lorillard mildly. "You push yourself and other people."

"Maybe Gunnar here can cure me when you've gone."

"Gunnar here has made a big decision, Mrs. Lorillard, and everyone's on notice about it. Henceforth, now and as long as we're on the island, it's work, eat, sleep, drink and be as merry as we can—but there'll be no arguments."

"Come the revolution," said Martha tartly, "you'll all eat strawberries—and God help you if you don't like them!"

"Not future tense, Mrs. Lorillard. Present. The revolution's here. It's happened."

"I'm glad I'm leaving," said Lorillard with a laugh.

"That's the way a chief should be." Mark Gilman proclaimed it like an oracle. "That's what the voice said: a low man makes a low people; only a high one is worthy of the *mana!*"

Before Thorkild went to bed that night he asked Sally to walk down to the beach with him. She was reluctant at first, but he persuaded her with the plea that it would spare them both a last public farewell in the presence of the tribe. They sat together on the sand, tossing coral pebbles, as if ridding themselves of the last scraps and shards of their past. Sally asked:

"When we get back . . . do you want me to deliver any messages?"

"A few. Call in and see Molly Kaapu's daughter. Let her know her mother's safe."

"She's already asked me to do that."

"Magnusson's lawyers and insurers will want evidence of the loss of the *Frigate Bird*. The log should be handed to them. I imagine you'll see Magnusson's widow. Tell her I'll call on her when I get back. . . . Then there are the relatives of the dead ones. . . ."

"Gunnar! This is Sally, remember? I'm a very efficient lady. Between me and Lorillard we'll handle the formalities. I was talking about personal things."

"Oh! Well, I would love you to see old Flanagan. Spend a little time with him. He'll want to know everything. You'll like him. . . . Then call James Neal Anderson. Tell him I'm coming back to clear my scholarly name, claim tenure and the chair and generally disrupt the campus! . . . That's all the folk that matter, I guess. The rest can wait until I get back."

"Time was when you wanted to stay here the rest of your life."

"Time was . . ."

"What will you do when I'm gone . . . for a woman, I mean?"

"I haven't thought of it."

"I don't believe it—not Gunnar Thorkild!"

"I don't believe it myself, but it happens to be true. I went over the moon for you, Sally. I haven't landed yet. If you need me, I'll come—anywhere, anytime. If you don't, well . . . In any case, we'll have to have a big reunion dinner when we all get back. Oh, one more thing. Our marriage is entered in the log. Check your lawyer for legal complications. I'll cooperate in whatever steps are necessary to leave you free."

"And yourself too."

"You're in my blood. I'll never be free of you. I never wanted to be anyway."

"You're a fool, my love."

"I know."

"But I wish you all the best."

"And I you. Kiss me good-bye?"

They kissed and there was sweetness in it and tenderness; but all the passion was gone, blown away on the night wind. As they walked back, hand in hand, along the beach, they saw Mark Gilman sitting on the canoe. They called to him but he did not hear. They went over to him. His eyes were closed; he was swaying from side to side, chanting as if to a drumbeat, in the old Marquesan tongue.

"The sea is empty;
    The sun shines;
But there is no one to see it.
    The fish leap;
But there is no one to catch them.

At night the stars look down
  On an empty ocean."

"What is he singing?" Sally asked in a whisper.
"I don't know. I've never heard it before."

He was lying; because he dared not tell her it was
one of the oldest chants known in the islands: a
mourning for sailors who would never come to landfall.

Their departure was as brusque as he could make
it. He wanted the voyagers calm for their outgoing.
Those who were left he must hold steady and optimis-
tic during the waiting period. So he made a great
show of efficiency and of confidence. Check the stores.
Check the rigging. Take a last run through the sailing
directions. Make the farewells brief: no speeches,
but a swift and hopeful envoi. The tribe watched,
cheering and waving, as they paddled across the lagoon, through the churn of the channel water, and out
past the point where the wind would catch them and
send them scurrying northwards. They lingered until
the tiny craft was no more than a black speck on the
horizon. Then they fell silent and turned back to camp,
the women weeping a little, the men talking in low,
strained voices. At the fire pit Thorkild was waiting
for them. He was no longer brusque, but grave and
concerned for their obvious misery.

". . . They're gone and their chances are
good. They're heading for the Austral and Tubuai
archipelagoes, which are the nearest land to us and
where there is an agent from the French Administration in Papeete. . . . The weather looks good. Even if
they do only a hundred miles a day—and they could
do much more—they'll make the islands in a week.
You must not entertain unfounded hopes or unneces-

sary fears. Remember that these islands are scattered and communications are not the best; so we must allow ample time for them to make contact with a French agent, who must then make a report to the Administrator of Colonies in Papeete. Once that is done, you may be sure that prompt measures will be taken to send a rescue party. . . ."

Ellen Ching cut into his talk:

"Chief, if it's our morale you're worried about, let me tell you we've weighed the risks as well as you have. We've also come to certain conclusions."

"Who is 'we,' Ellen?"

"All of us."

"Then," said Thorkild amiably, "I'd like to hear the conclusions."

"In the first place"—her exposition was dry and precise—"we all believe that it is necessary to set some term to our hopes."

Thorkild gave her a long, puzzled look. "I'm not sure I understand."

"It's very simple. At some point we will be forced to decide whether we are transients or permanent residents in this place. That decision will change radically our attitude to life on the island. It will also change certain of our personal relationships."

Thorkild chewed on the thought for a moment and then nodded agreement.

"I'll be frank with you. It helps that you have faced the issue. I believe, I have always believed, that our hope of rescue is well founded. It is good, however, that you understand we may, one day, have to abandon it."

"We've gone further than that, chief." Hernan Castillo took up the argument. "We think certain arrangements should be changed now. The community is much smaller. Everyone should come down and live here on the beach. The terrace is planted. There is no need for anyone to live there now. It's a lonely place, and it has proved unhealthy."

"I agree," said Eva Kuhio. "Martha shouldn't stay there anyway. Willy and I are well; so are Barbara and Simon; but the longer we stay, the bigger the danger of infection."

"We can send up forage and work parties." Simon Cohen set down the plain facts. "We can bring the pigs down here. Then we can push ahead to finish the beach houses. When those are done, we can concentrate all our energies on the big boat."

"Which brings us," said Ellen Ching, "to the question of our social arrangements. We women have certain views. We want to represent them to you and to the other men."

"Why now?" asked Thorkild. "Why not leave it until we have reached the point of no return?"

"Because some of us have already reached that point. Yoko and Martha are both going to have their babies within the next two months. At any time during those two months Barbara could fall pregnant and be left the same way, an unmarried woman with a fatherless child. . . . That, I think you will all agree, is an unfair situation. Now let's look at what happens if we are not rescued. . . . And while we are looking, let's all be as honest as we can. We are seven women. Molly Kaapu is aging. Martha would then be a widow with a child. Jenny would also be a widow. Yoko would have a child whose father she has rejected. There is Eva, who is married and whose husband is with her. There is Barbara, who has a temporary union with Simon. Finally there is myself, and I have never made any secret of the fact that I can be equally interested in man or woman. On the other side there are you six men. Willy Kuhio is married. Tioto is like myself. The rest of you are free. . . . Now—let's face it, dear friends and darling people!—that's a very unstable mixture. We have to be sure it doesn't become destructive. Question: how do we do it?"

There was a long silence. The women sat blank-faced and unsmiling. The men looked at each other and exchanged embarrassed grins. Finally Thorkild said slowly:

"I'll make the first contribution. There's no way I'll play marriage broker again."

Willy Kuhio spoke, firmly and definitely:

"No way I change. My Eva and I will stay together. That's right, isn't it, Eva?"

"Maybe," said Eva doubtfully. "Maybe it's what we like and what we want. Maybe it can't work that way anymore."

As Willy frowned and stammered, Thorkild interposed, "You said, Ellen, that the women have discussed this. Have you come to any decision?"

"We have," said Ellen Ching. "Martha will give it to you."

There was a long silence while they waited for her to speak. Finally, in an arid monotone, she informed them.

"I have been asked to say this because I have dedicated a son and a husband to the venture on which our hope of safety depends. Jenny has an equal right because she too has sent out a husband. So her voice speaks with mine. Here is the simple fact. All hope for the future of this community depends on us women. If we refuse to breed, if we refuse to care for the two children who will soon be born, this community will die out. If, on the other hand, we are prepared to bear children, then we have a right to demand from our menfolk not simply protection and care, but love as well; because without love we become simply chattels, and that would be a despair—too much to carry for a lifetime. It would be a foolish thing to talk, now, of falling in love and all the quaint, pleasant things in storybooks. That kind of love is beyond us. We know each other too well. We have no surprises left for each other. . . . But we do have bonds, bonds that were forged by danger and by the deaths we have seen and by the efforts we have made together just to survive. We women are agreed that we cannot chop and change between this man and another all our lives. However we arrange it, we need permanence, protection and the kind of affection we have talked about. We are not objects. We are persons. You men are not simply seed-bearers, you too are persons who need a private and personal life. . . . So this is what we have decided. We will cancel out all the unions that now exist. We will withdraw ourselves into our own women's community here on the beach. You men, too, will withdraw from us and live in your own group. Molly Kaapu will be the head of our family. From that moment we shall be free to give ourselves or withhold ourselves from any man who wishes to join himself with us. We shall be free to set the terms of any union which is offered to us. You men will be free to offer or withhold yourselves and, similarly, to accept or reject our terms. We believe that, out of this, there should come permanent pairing and the kind of stability we agree we all need. . . . That's our side of it. Now we would like to hear yours. If you want to think about it and talk about it, take your time. We're in no hurry. Our first need is to protect those who are still vulnerable."

"It's a goddam madness!" said Simon Cohen. "It's like setting up the house of all nations, and asking us to take our pick of the girls."

"You had your pick," said Yoko Nagamuna acidly. "You just can't make up your mind."

"You can't blame him," said Franz Harsanyi mildly. "None of us—and only a few of you women—contemplated the permanence we face now."

"And we still don't face it," Hernan Castillo reminded them. "We still have two, three months before we are forced to decide."

"In which case," said Jenny, "it makes sense for us to withdraw ourselves. I'm certain I don't want to fall pregnant again. I'm sure Barbara doesn't. From this point the risk is all ours."

"It sounds like blackmail to me," said Simon Cohen.

"It's only blackmail," said Hernan Castillo in his detached fashion, "if you're threatened in your own property. None of us, except Willy, have any rights in our women. . . . It seems to me there's a lot to talk about and nothing to fight about."

"I agree," said Gunnar Thorkild. "The women have made their point. If we do stay here, we do depend on them for survival and continuity. I say we go along with it. When do you want to start this arrangement?"

"Now, chief," said Molly Kaapu. "Right now."

"In that case," said Thorkild heavily, "there's work to do to get the houses ready. Let's go to it. . . ."

That night, while the others were busy around the fire pit, preparing the evening meal, gossiping and grumbling about this new and arbitrary change in their lives, Thorkild walked down to the beach with Molly Kaapu. Molly wheezed and chuckled with amusement.

"So what happens when the mule won't drink, Kaloni? You let him go thirsty awhile. That Simon Cohen, he's the bright one. He sees what it means."

"Who started all this?" asked Thorkild moodily.

"I did," said Molly Kaapu. "I got the thought—the others had the words."

"I hope you've got better thoughts, Molly. And simpler words too. Sure, it would be great if everyone paired off and lived happily ever after, but they won't. What happens when the man wants one woman and she doesn't want him? One of them has got to settle for second-best."

"And some," said Molly Kaapu, "some like me have to settle down with no one at all. That's how it always comes out in the end."

"It's not the end I'm thinking of." Thorkild picked up a piece of driftwood and sent it flying out across the water. "It's the beginning. Who makes the first step?"

"You do, Kaloni," said Molly Kaapu placidly. "You do."

Thorkild stared at her in angry amazement. "What do you mean?"

"You're alone now, Kaloni. What are you going to do? Stay alone all your life? You're not made like that; and it wouldn't be good for the rest of us. So, sooner or later, you have to find yourself a wife. If you wait for the others it's you who gets second-best. I don't want to see that happen. The others don't, either. They need you strong and contented and happy."

"So that's the meaning of this bloody little comedy! . . . A matchmaking for the chief."

"That's my idea." Molly Kaapu shrugged. "The others are thinking of themselves."

"Tell me what the women are thinking," said Gunnar Thorkild.

"That takes a little saying, Kaloni. Ellen Ching, she's happy with her Franz—as happy as she would be with any man. Perhaps in the end they stay together.

Simon and Barbara? That would work, too, if he would say just once, 'Okay, you're my woman.' Barbara doesn't ask much, but she wants more than just to be a toy he can pick up and put down when he is tired of playing. Hernan and Yoko? She's the problem. She wants more than he can give. He is content because most of his life is lived in his head and in his hands. If you wanted, you could have Yoko."

"No way in the world," said Thorkild wryly. "I want a quiet life, with a loving woman."

"So you see," said Molly triumphantly. "You know what you want. Which one is it?"

"Martha Gilman will need to be protected."

"That's your conscience talking," said Molly tartly. "Not your heart. Not your head either. Why didn't you marry Martha before?"

"You know as well as I do, Molly. Things never came together for us."

"What makes you think they come together now? I watch Martha. When she wants to talk with a man she talks with Tioto. When she wants a woman for company, it's Ellen Ching. What does that tell you?"

"I'm damned if I know."

"Then I tell you, Kaloni. Always she wants to be the one on top. She wants a man who's not quite a man. She wants a woman who's not quite a woman. That way, she stays a little bit unhappy all her life. She doesn't want more children. Believe me, this is the last. . . . Do you want children, Kaloni? Do you want sons in your house?"

"I did once, Molly."

"And you want them still! You want one to sit in your place when you are gone, to whom the *mana* will pass, as it passed from your grandfather to you. You owe us that, Kaloni. You owe it to the children after us. Think about it. Think hard about it. You don't belong to yourself anymore. You put four lives out there on the big water. If there are none to take their place, then I tell you, Kaloni, you have betrayed them; you have betrayed us. . . ."

In their new bachelor lodgings the men were angry. They had not only been rejected, they had been made to feel ridiculous and inadequate. They were men, weren't they? They weren't just stallions to be led out to stud. If the women didn't want to breed, to hell with it. Better they didn't, because then there would be fewer mouths to feed. All this talk of continuity and carrying on the tribe . . . who cared? Once the big boat was built, they would all be off the island. Besides, what was being offered? None of the merchandise was fresh. Comfort in bed carried a mighty high price tag. Gunnar Thorkild let them rant on until they ran out of words, then he reminded them soberly:

"Isn't it time we threw our excess luggage overboard? None of the ideas or systems we brought with us has much relevance anymore. All we've got is ourselves, the sea and the land. We've got to fish the sea and work the land. When we get too old to do it, what happens? We sit on the beach and die. . . . Unless there is someone else to put the food in our mouths. That's the real meaning of continuity. The women know it better than we do. They know that its promise resides in them and not in us. It doesn't help us to deny a simple fact of life."

"It's easy for you to talk," said Simon Cohen bitterly. "You're the big man. You've only got to shake the tree and the best apples fall into your lap."

"So you pick first, Mr. Cohen! But remember, the apple you get is the apple you eat."

"And that goes for the women too," said Hernan Castillo quietly. "None of us is any great bargain."

"We could make a lottery." Tioto giggled. "We put all the names in a shell and let the women pick them. Maybe that way I end up with Ellen Ching and the chief ends with Molly Kaapu."

"Which might be a very comfortable solution," said Thorkild with a grin. Then, serious again, he went on. "Now that you've got the gripes out of your system, what are you going to do?"

"What do you suggest, chief?" asked Franz Harsanyi.

"Old island custom," said Gunnar Thorkild. "You spread your mat outside the woman's house and sleep there every night until she invites you in."

"And where will you put your mat, chief?" It was Tioto who asked the question.

"I wait," said Gunnar Thorkild. "I defer to you other anxious fellows."

"Not good enough!" said Simon Cohen. "So long as you're in the market, the rest of us are out of it. You spread your mat, Thorkild, we'll take the leavings."

It was Hernan Castillo who had the last word. He turned to Simon Cohen and faced him with a question.

"When Yoko has her baby, Simon, who's going to be there holding her hand—you or me?"

A month passed, and another, in a monotonous rhythm of wind and surf and sunlight and rainsquall. Food was gathered, distributed, eaten; food was gathered again. The sow littered and there was meat aplenty and bellyaches afterward. The new houses were built. They made liquor to lift their courage, and talk—interminable talk—about the voyagers in their little boat.

They had perished at sea. They were wrecked on some tiny atoll and must make their way to another and another before they came to civilization. They had lost the bearings of the island and were trying to work them out again. They were snarled in red tape, arguing with faceless officials in nameless places. . . . Slowly, the arguments were dropped, one by one. Slowly, the sickness of deferred hope passed into a low fever of regret—a regret no longer poignant, but simply familiar, like an old infection that came back when the weather changed.

The sickness showed itself in strange ways. Martha Gilman began to cultivate the company of Hernan Castillo, to whom she poured out every day her fears for her son's safety while Castillo soothed her with long, matter-of-fact recitals of incredible sea rescues and tales of survival. Simon Cohen, tentatively at first, and then with a fanatic persistence, pursued Yoko Nagamuna. He wanted to be the father of his own child. He wanted to make amends for his casual infidelity. He could love her. He did love her. He would stand with her now and always. Yoko, for her part, treated him with a refinement of malice. He was the last man in the world whom she would wish to have as her husband. When the child grew up she would teach it to hate him. She could not bear the thought of sleeping and living with a man who knew only to satisfy himself but not his woman. Their high, screaming arguments became at first an entertainment, and then a nightly irritation to the camp. In the end, Cohen literally spread a mat outside the door of her hut, so that he was there when she went to bed and still there when she walked to the beach every morning. Jenny, obsessed with guilts about Adam Briggs, sought every moment to be with Thorkild; and, when he was not there, she turned to Ellen Ching, who courted her with a grave gentleness, to which, more than once, she seemed ready to succumb. Willy Kuhio and Eva quarrelled for a while and then began to separate themselves from the rest of the community. They worked together. They went fishing together. Sometimes they slept together on the beach before returning separately to their own quarters. Eva Kuhio begged that at least a few would join her in a nightly prayer of intercession for the lost ones. Sometimes Thorkild and Molly Kaapu would join her. Sometimes Franz and Martha Gilman and Tioto. Molly, herself, began to suffer from recurrent fits of depression, snapping at Thorkild, and then forcing Franz Harsanyi to lament with her over the mess and disruption of their lives.

For Thorkild it was a ravaging time. He was plagued with guilts about Sally Anderton and the others. He became solitary and morose. His sexual drive seemed to have deserted him. When this woman, or that, came to him with smiles or plaintive tears, he rejected her. When Molly Kaapu blamed him for his indecision, he snapped at her brutally. When she insisted that only he could end their misery, he was adamant that they would wait out the terms that had been set. They must never be able to accuse him of the ultimate tyranny, that he had robbed them of their illusions. To which Molly had always the same answer: He should let them dream, yes; but he should not force them to endure his own nightmares.

Then, slowly, new couplings began to be made. Barbara Kamakau was seen often in the company of Franz Harsanyi. Martha Gilman, heavy now and near her time, would sit for long hours watching Hernan Castillo as he worked on the boat. The quarrels between Yoko Nagamuna and Simon Cohen subsided into a continuous low bickering which, as Tioto said, laughing, at least kept them occupied and let other people get a night's sleep. Came the day when Ellen

Ching accosted Thorkild at the cascade and challenged him abruptly.

"Chief, I want to talk to you!"

"About what?"

"Either you're a very clever man, chief, or a very stupid one. I can't make up my mind."

"Have it both ways," said Thorkild briefly. "I don't know myself. What's the problem?"

"You're blind if you don't see it. People are pairing. Martha with Hernan, Franz with Barbara. Even Yoko and Simon are settling into an armed truce."

"I'm glad to hear it, Ellen. . . . So, I repeat, what's the problem?"

"Three people, chief. You, me and Jenny. . . . Tioto's out of it. He always will be."

"And I'm to choose between you and Jenny?"

"In a way, yes."

"In what way, Ellen?"

She gave him that slow, sidelong smile and told him:

"You'd be too much for me, chief. I'd be too little for you. If you don't want Jenny, I'll take her. I've always played fair with you, chief. I'm playing fair now. . . . Oh, don't look so shocked! You locked the girl in. You made it clear that she was *kapu* to you, that you'd always be impotent with her. That's a hell of a thing to lay on any woman, even if it was a lie to protect her."

"My God," said Gunnar Thorkild softly. "I'd never thought of that."

"Then think of it now, chief," said Ellen Ching. "Time's running out. Look at us! Compare the life we have now with the life we had when we first came. Then we had order and drive and enthusiasm for what we were doing. Now we're crawling about, living shabby and unhappy, like sick folk in a laza-rette. It has to stop."

"How do we stop it?" asked Thorkild.

She turned away from him, stepped into the pool and began washing herself under the cascade. She beckoned him to join her. As he sluiced his body in the cool water she stretched out a hand and drew him to her. There was an odd, compassionate note in her voice.

"Chief, you walk about like a blind man. You listen like a deaf man who hears the sounds but not the words. We're going downhill. We've got to stop and begin climbing up again. We won't do it until you—yes, you!—make us bury our dead and start living again with whole hearts. That means you've got to start living with us. You wonder why I'm handing you to Jenny, whom I could very easily keep for myself. That's the reason. If this tribe goes down, I'll go down with it. If it goes up . . ." She drew him closer and laid her hands on his breast. "If it goes up, then there's still a place for Ellen Ching because the odd ones are as necessary as the normal ones. There's always a place where they can turn and be welcomed—be happy too in their own way. What about it, chief?"

Thorkild took her face in his hands and kissed her lightly on the lips.

"You're right, Ellen. I know it. It's the moment I need, the ritual moment, that makes sense to everyone. That's what I'm waiting for."

"Don't wait too long, chief. If you miss it, it may never come back. Ritual is a strange thing. Do it right, and you make the big hopeful moment that people remember and repeat all their lives. Do it wrong, and the people laugh first and hate you afterwards for mak-ing them feel ridiculous."

"You're a wise woman, Ellen," said Thorkild.

"Too wise for my own good," said Ellen Ching. "And I'm not easy to seduce. So get the hell out of here and make things right with a woman who really needs you!"

It was a strange, haunted Jenny who sat with him on the beach that night. The dumpling girl from Sunset Beach had gone away, long since. In her place was a woman, quiet and withdrawn, who listened in silence to his proposal and then told him gravely:

"I know why you ask me. . . . It's appropriate. I'm the last one left because they've arranged it that way. I don't mind. I've always been in love with you. I still am—although even that's changed. I've passed through a lot of hands. I've used up a lot of myself. I don't really know what's left of me. Whatever there is, though, I want to keep . . . because once that's gone, I'm nobody. I'm scared, Gunnar. Now there are two ghosts between us—Adam and Sally."

"This time, Jenny, they're friendly ghosts. They'd want us to be peaceful together."

"Is that enough? Just to be peaceful?"

"No, it's the beginning."

"You told me once you'd be impotent with me."

"I know. . . ."

"Now?"

"Not anymore. The *kapu* is lifted."

"As easily as that?"

"No, Jenny, not easily. A woman I loved I sent out to die with your husband. I exposed a boy to an experience for which he was unready, to influences I could not control. I have guilts to carry—and in a way I suppose that's my bride-price. I want you now. I need you desperately. The others need us too—to make a new magic for them."

"That's the point," said Jenny quietly. "That's the

price I'll have to pay. I'll never be sure whether you're marrying me for myself or for them. No, please. . . . !" She closed his lips with her fingertips. "Don't say anything. Just make it easy for me. Show me how to be happy. . . !"

"I'll try, girl," said Gunnar Thorkild with grave tenderness. "God help me, I'll try!"

Towards the end of the third month, Yoko Nagamuna's baby was born. A tiny black-haired girl-child. Simon Cohen was there; and when they laid the child in his arms he wept over it and kissed it and laid it back at her breast and sat with Yoko until she lapsed into an exhausted sleep. Barbara Kamakau smiled and told Molly Kaapu afterwards that—give her time with her Franz—she would make a man-child to cover that one and a dozen others. Three weeks later, Martha Gilman came to term; and that was a long, screaming battle which finally produced a son whom she held up to Hernan Castillo and demanded that he be named Peter Mark and made a Christian with Willy and Eva as his godparents. Hernan Castillo gave her the gift he had carved to celebrate the event: man, woman and child, all seated in the cup of a *pikake* flower.

A man and a woman made a new beginning. A new beginning demanded a feast and a feast was made at which Molly Kaapu, garlanded with flowers, held the two infants in her arms and pronounced them promised and betrothed and ready to wed as soon as they knew what to do with themselves and each other.

Simon Cohen announced that he had found a song for the occasion. Yoko stood with him and Barbara and Franz Harsanyi and they intoned together the old happy chant of the returning lovers:

"I have waited a long time.
I have tossed flowers into the sea.
I have seen the waves take them.
I have sent my heart to follow them.
Now my love comes back,
My high-born love,
Riding on the waves,
Wearing my flowers in her hair
And on her breast."

When the cheering and the clapping had subsided Gunnar Thorkild rose in his place and commanded silence. He looked grey and lonely, like the sentinel rock at the entrance to the channel. He did not orate like a high chief; he spoke softly and simply:

"My friends, this is a glad day because we have welcomed children into our land. They are the more precious to us because they take the place of those who are lost to us and are our promise of the future. Now we are back at the beginning of things. On this small island we have experienced the full cycle of human existence. We began with death, which we thought was unendurable. Today we have two new lives which promise that we will endure as a new people. I would like you to think on that . . . the newness of things. We are not any longer the same people who sailed here in the *Frigate Bird*. All of us are changed. All of us are scarred in some fashion. All of us have learned that, without each other, without love and companionship and support, we are lost and helpless like leaves blown in the trade wind. I, too, am changed. I, who was so arrogant a man, have found myself humbled before you. I failed you in so many ways. I have blood on my hands, guilts on my conscience which I can never purge out. Like you, I have needed and I have found at last a woman to support me." He paused and took the lei from his own neck and laid it over Jenny's head. Then he went on. "This is my woman. This is the wife of your chief. She will bear my son, the great-grandson of Kaloni the Navigator, on whom, one day, the *mana* will descend. . . . Last night I went up to the high place to commune with my grandfather and with Carl Magnusson and all the great ones of the past. They gave me only this hard word: the navigator has no choice but to sail on until he makes the landfall, or the sea swallows him, because it was so determined at the foundation of all things. What more can I say to you who have trusted me? I have brought you thus far, I shall try to hold you safe hereafter. . . . God help us all! . . ."

He stepped down from the dais and left them without another word. They watched him as he walked slowly down to the beach. They urged Jenny to follow him but she refused. They saw him stand by the water's edge, arms outflung in supplication, a giant figure, black against the rising moon.

POSTSCRIPT

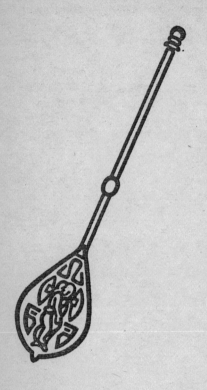

EXTRACT FROM REPORT NO. 375/AC from the Administrative Agent Iles Tubuai to the Administrator of Colonies, Papeete:

". . . On the fifteenth of this month, after three days of high wind and heavy seas, villagers on this island reported an outrigger canoe washed up on the beach. The canoe was of a type not normally seen in the region. The toolmarks and lashings were not of local workmanship. Extensive inquiries confirm that no inhabitants of either the Iles Tubuai or the Iles Australes have been reported missing at sea.

"Normally, I should have disposed of the matter at this point. However, it may have reference to another curious report, as yet unconfirmed, that a youth, said to be European, has been found wandering distraught and exhausted on the Ile Raivavae and claiming that he is descended from the Polynesian sea god, Kanaloa.

"This story, which came from native sources, is curious in other particulars. The boy is said to speak fluently in local dialect, and to be able to recite long passages of ancient chants and legends. He carries an old carved paddle which he claims was a gift from a long-dead island navigator. For the rest, it seems that he has been able to render no rational account of who he is or where he came from. I leave today, by lugger, to investigate. I shall communicate further in due course. . . ."

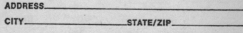